GUARDIANS OF HADES SERIES

Ares
Valen
Esher

Find out more at: www.felicityheaton.co.uk

CHAPTER 1

Rain hammered the pavement around him, scoured the walls of the towering buildings that hemmed him in and stole the clouds from view with their bright neon signs, and saturated the two daemons gathering their wits around fifty feet from him in the narrow Tokyo alley. It mingled with the black blood that turned the air rank and coppery, a stench he wanted to erase from this world.

And he would.

Esher moved forwards, through the heavy droplets that began to gather and condense, responding to the hunger mounting inside him—a desire to eradicate the foul creatures stumbling onto their feet now.

At the far end of the narrow street beyond them, a mortal male tucked beneath a clear convenience store umbrella paused and glanced their way.

Big mistake.

The darkness was swift to rise, to pound in Esher's blood like a tide that battered him, powerful waves that rolled over him and washed all the light away.

On a black snarl, he pressed the toe of his right boot into the wet pavement and launched forwards, little more than a blur as he closed the distance between him and his prey.

The male daemon swiftly turned his way and stepped in front of his comrade— a female. Protecting her? Valen had reported the daemons in Rome had done something similar.

As if the creatures were capable of feeling anything tender or sweet.

They were as devoid of softer emotions as he was.

But still the male reached behind him and shoved her in the hip, forcing her to stumble out of the firing line just as Esher threw his right hand forwards. The rain that had been gathering around him exploded towards the male, whipping into a spiralling spear as it zoomed away from Esher. It hit the male with the force of a tidal wave, sending him flying through the air. The wretched daemon hit the pavement near the far end of the alley and rolled to a halt next to the mortal.

Esher growled and spat on the pavement, the gnawing hunger growing stronger as he stared at the wretched human.

It would pay in blood for daring to remain near him, for daring to gaze upon him.

It would pay in its own blood.

His lips stretched into a cold grin, the lower one stinging as the cut on it pulled, filling his mouth with the metallic tang of his own blood.

He twitched as memories surged, wrapped around him and felt as if they were pulling him down into them with claws that shredded his insides—tore his heart to pieces.

Blood.

So much red.

He had never seen so much of it, had emptied his stomach more than once when they had been butchering the male in front of him, spilling crimson and flesh on the hay and dirt. Their sick laughter had prodded at him, ripping at his strength and dragging him down. He had been weak. Stripped of his powers. Left vulnerable. He had been an easy target for their fear, their rage. They had beaten him. Tore more of his strength from him. He had been weaker. Wounded. Bound and broken.

But fucking gods, he had shown them the error of their ways when his power had returned.

Just as he would show this human.

Esher reached his left hand out and focused on the mortal male. It took only a brief thought. One moment the male was standing, the next he was prone on the floor, blood leaking from his eyes, nose, mouth and ears. Weak. Humans were weak. Pathetic. Unworthy of the protection of the gods.

Thunder rolled overhead, golden lightning striking a split-second later, snapping at the buildings that loomed over him and tearing a fearful gasp from the daemons.

A warning from the king of gods.

His uncle could go fuck himself.

The mortals deserved death.

He wasn't on this plane to protect them. He was here to protect one realm—the Underworld. His home.

This entire world could burn and he wouldn't give a shit as long as his home was safe.

The male daemon picked himself up, pausing to look at the dead human, his dark eyes wide and a flicker of fear emerging in them as he turned them on Esher.

And the female.

The blonde staggered onto her feet, clutching her stomach, her limbs visibly trembling beneath her long black raincoat that matched the one the male wore. They had come prepared for the turn in the weather. It was almost a shame they hadn't come prepared to win. It had been a long time since he had fought a worthy adversary.

Keras's words rang in his ears.

An adversary was coming for him, one of the group bent on destroying the gates to the Underworld that he and his brothers protected, all in an effort to merge the worlds and claim dominion over both.

Esher just hoped they were worthy.

He wanted a good fight, one that would test him to his limit.

Fire tore through his right arm and he grunted and snapped back to the alley. The blonde bitch leaped away from him, her silver knife stained crimson.

With his blood.

It rolled down his forearm to his wrist beneath the sleeve of his long black coat and he raised his hand before him and watched it drip to the ground to dissipate in the water beneath his leather boots.

Water that began to vibrate, tiny droplets of it bouncing higher and higher into the air as he stared at the blood flowing along the side of his hand to bead at the tip of his little finger and fall.

Typical of inferior creatures to use weapons in a battle.

He had never understood why some of his brothers relied on them too, one or two of them even favouring mortal-made guns, when they were gods and wielded powers strong enough to defeat any adversary they might face.

Personally, he never used weapons.

His powers were more than enough.

Without even taking his eyes off the blood, he flicked his left hand towards the female as she launched at him again, her blade flashing in the neon lights and a battle cry on her lips.

It turned to a scream.

She dropped from the air, landing in a shaking heap on the wet pavement, her convulsions growing more and more violent as he slowly turned his gaze on her. Hatred seethed inside him as he looked at her, as he commanded every molecule of her vile blood to dance to his song. He despised using his power over water to end his prey in such a way, because it was just too easy, but she had brought it upon herself.

"No!" the male barked and sprinted towards her.

He sank to his knees at her side and grabbed her arm, pulling her onto her back.

Too late.

Black blood rolled from her eyes and her mouth, streamed from her nose and her ears.

Esher closed his right hand into a fist.

Her body lurched upwards as her heart exploded.

"Bastard." The male daemon shoved to his feet.

Esher slowly smiled. Crooked a bloodstained finger.

Flames licked over his left side and he grunted as he clutched it through his coat and grey-blue shirt. Waves of heat rolled through him, each stronger than the last. He gritted his teeth as his vision wobbled, shadows dancing across the alley before him, swirling around the corpses and drifting towards him.

No.

He wasn't sick now. He was safe. Healed. The intense burning in his side mocked him, screamed that he wasn't healed, was far from it. The wraith's blade had done more damage than anyone had suspected, and more than Ares's female could mend. He could feel it. It had been weeks since the attack, and his body could heal even the most vicious of injuries in less than a day. He should have healed by now, but the pain lingered, came in sharp bursts from time to time to remind him that he had let his guard down and paid the ultimate price.

Or he would have, if a mortal hadn't saved him.

He chuckled through his gritted teeth at that.

"You won't be laughing in a minute." The male voice came from behind him and Esher heard other words, in another male's deep voice.

Give your sister my regards.

3

Fiery agony streaked across his side, just as it had that night in that heart-stopping moment before everything had gone black, but this time the flames licked at his right side, just below his ribs.

He grunted as the pain combined with the lingering effect of the wraith's blade, stripping more of his strength from him. The shadows scattered as he growled and focused on the male behind him now, not the one who had been there on that rooftop almost two months ago.

Esher raised his right arm and slammed his elbow into the male's cheek, and grunted in time with him as the daemon was knocked sideways and his blade scraped over bone before sucking free of Esher's flesh. Heat spread down Esher's side, and he clamped his left hand down over the wound, spun on his heel and grabbed the male by his throat.

He kicked hard, shoving the male into the concrete wall of one of the buildings with enough force to break bone. The male screamed as several of them shattered and choked on blood that burst from his lips, coating them. Water streamed over his face as the rain fell harder, so thick and fast that it created a wall around them, shutting out the world.

Esher reined in his hunger, breathing hard as he wrestled with the need to butcher the male and then turn his sights on anyone else in the vicinity. He focused on each breath, his hand shaking against the daemon's throat with a need to reach into the breast pocket of his grey-blue shirt and pull out the noise-cancelling earbuds. He needed the quiet, the solitude. He needed to let the strings wash over him and sweep the world away.

He could have it, but first he had to ease back on the daemon's throat and do what he had promised to do.

"Who sent you?" Information.

He and his brothers had all agreed to get information out of any daemon that dared attempt to reach their gate, but Esher had forgotten all about it when the female daemon had clawed and bitten him when he had caught them near it, drawing blood and pissing him off.

Toying with the bitch had become priority one, shortly followed by killing her.

Getting information hadn't even ranked.

It was a miracle he wasn't bursting the male daemon like the pustule he was and was instead attempting to get something out of him.

Although, it seemed he had failed to rein his temper in quickly enough.

The male sagged in his grip, his weight tugging Esher's arm down and sending a fresh wave of pain rolling up it from the cut on his forearm.

Esher huffed and discarded the dead male.

The rain eased enough that he could see the female.

His brothers wouldn't be pleased that he had killed them both, but they would understand when he told them he had done his best. He wasn't the only brother with a habit of forgetting to get information. So far, Daimon was in the lead. His younger brother had killed almost fifty percent of the daemons who had attempted to get through the Hong Kong gate, only remembering after they were frozen popsicles or shattered into meaty pieces that he was meant to beat information out of them before killing them.

Esher drew his hand away from his right side and frowned at the blood coating his palm. It caught the light of the narrow signs that jutted out from each building, running their entire height to mark what was on each floor, and reflected white, red and yellow back at him.

The wound would heal rapidly, not like the wraith wound, but he would have to conserve his strength until it had knitted back together, which meant he couldn't teleport home. Stepping, as he and his brothers called it, would drain him, and it was only just gone one in the morning, meaning there were still another four or five hours of darkness in which another daemon could attempt to find the gate.

Or a Hellspawn, one of the accepted species in his father's eyes and one allowed to enter the Underworld via the gates, could call on him to open it.

So, he would have to do the unthinkable.

Public transport.

He ground his molars and reached into the breast pocket of his shirt, tugged the tiny headphones out and jammed them into his ears. Instantly, the soothing melody of Bach filled him, swamping the song of the rain and the grating noise of Tokyo.

Esher took a few deep breaths, giving the beautiful classical piece time to do its work, and then trudged forwards, past the two dead daemons. He didn't look at the dead mortal as he passed the male, kept moving onwards on auto-pilot, slowly constructing a wall of calm inside himself, a barrier that would shut the world out and allow him to venture down into the train station and tolerate the presence of the mortals as they surrounded him.

Crowded him.

As the strings rose, he spotted the airplane-wing canopy that stretched above the central entrance of Tokyo station, extending from the glass skyscraper to its right. Clouds swirled around the top of the towering structure, glowing yellow from the city lights. The rain continued to pour, soothing Esher as much as the music, but as he approached the entrance and the number of mortals rose, hurrying to catch the last trains, his grip on calm began to weaken.

He could do this.

He balled his right hand into a fist, and grimaced as the cut across his forearm stung as his muscles flexed beneath it, a flash of fire that tested him. He breathed deep, letting the flare of irritation fade without affecting his mood.

He was calm. In control.

Calm. Control.

Esher breathed through it, steeled himself and moved forwards, avoiding the busier paths into the building.

It was only a short trip. Barely fifteen minutes. He could do this.

A mortal female passed close to him and he tensed, his breath seizing in his throat as he leaned to avoid her even though she was more than ten feet away.

Breathe.

Calm. Control.

Keras would fucking kill him if he lost his shit and caused a bloodbath. His oldest brother had lectured him more than once about playing nice around the weak little mortals. By the gods, he tried. He could almost tolerate them now. He had even managed to speak with some when he was feeling strong, able to cope with breathing the same air as them.

But he wasn't feeling strong.

The coppery odour of blood clouded his senses, tugging at his memories, and it was hard to keep them shut out, to hold the wall of calm in place.

He shoved the bloodied fingers of his right hand through the longer lengths of his black hair, pushing the damp strands out of his face, and scrubbed at the shorter sides.

He could do this.

He took another step towards the building, a pressing sense of urgency building inside him and driving him to move as he picked up the warning over the public-address system. It was last train time.

Now or never.

He froze as a male passed him, flicking a glance his way that turned into a double-take before he pivoted on his heel and hurried away from the station.

Esher touched his face, drew his hand away and looked at his fingers. Black smeared their pads. Daemon blood.

He huffed, grabbed the handkerchief he always kept in the back pocket of his dark blue jeans and wiped the blood away, scrubbing his neck and face, and then his hand to clear it of both daemon and his own blood.

It took barely a second for the blood to roll back down to his fingers. He buttoned his coat to hide the crimson stain on his shirt, tugged the sleeve back and wrapped the handkerchief around his forearm, covering the wound there. It would have to do.

The last of the mortals ran into the building ahead of him.

Esher strode towards it, his left hand closing over his right side again as the wound below his ribs burned. He pressed hard against it, stopping the flow of blood down his side, and trudged forwards, moving as quickly as he could manage.

The lights inside the station stung his eyes and he lowered his head, letting the hand-length ribbons of his black hair fall forwards over his brow to shield them. He kept his head bent as he hurried past the closed shops towards the Yamanote Line. It would stop at Yoyogi Park and he could walk from there. The streets in that neighbourhood would be quiet.

Unlike the immense room around him.

Someone almost ran into him as they rushed towards the ticket barriers, and he bared his teeth at their back. Keras would have to forgive him if someone bumped him, because he wasn't sure he had the strength to stop himself from hurting them.

It was leaking from him as he passed his bloodied right hand over the card reader on the barrier, using his abilities to force it to open for him. It swung open and he passed through, scanned the area ahead of him and spotted the sign for the line. It was further than he remembered. He was going to have to use a little bit of power to make it to the train.

Not stepping. Just running.

6

He clutched his side and sprinted, passing the mortals with ease, and reached the platform just as the last train pulled in. He boarded at the first door, and moved down through the carriages until he found one that was quiet.

The seats near the next car were empty, so he slumped into them, arranging himself in a way that put off the mortals who were eyeing the spot beside him. He looked at his bloodied hand, felt a few mortals glancing there too, and then moving away. He was tempted to wipe it on his jacket, but since it was acting as a nice deterrent, he kept it on show. Another barrier to keep the mortals at bay.

He couldn't believe he had been reduced to using public transport. He eyed a few of the humans, issuing glares to the braver ones who looked as if they might chance it and sit beside him on the three-seater bench. Wretched creatures. The wall of calm cracked a little, and he drew in a deep breath. Mistake. His right ribs protested, a sharp pain echoing along them from the wound, worsening his mood and adding a few more cracks to the wall.

He closed his eyes as the train pulled away, meaning to shut out the crowded carriage so he could claw back the calm.

Not meaning to fall asleep.

He woke with a jolt as the train rounded a bend, and his black eyebrows pinched in a frown as he swept his blue gaze around the carriage. It was almost empty.

"Fuck," he muttered and peered out of the window, trying to see where he was as he silently berated himself for succumbing to sleep around so many humans. They weren't to be trusted. Fuck knew how many of them might have taken the opportunity to kill him if they had known what he was.

Building after building whizzed past outside, none of them standing out to him. The damned city looked the same no matter where he went in it. He rubbed his tired eyes and squinted at the display screen above the doors. Broken. Just his luck.

Had he missed his stop?

He looked at the two people in his carriage, assessing them, and then squeezed his hand over his side as he leaned forwards and looked to his left, into the next one. Five people in that one, none of them a threat.

He leaned back into the padded seat.

A shriek rose from his left.

Esher edged forwards again and glared into the next carriage. A petite raven-haired female with bunches and a fringe that cut a straight line above her eyebrows swatted at a male with her black backpack. Her thick-soled patent leather shoes skidded on the floor of the car as she swung again, causing her short black dress to rise up and reveal the tops of her stripy black and white stockings.

A little Lolita with a vicious streak.

Or a terrified little Lolita.

He canted his head, trying to figure out which one it was, and growing increasingly annoyed and disgusted with everyone in her carriage as they all pretended not to notice her plight.

"Chikan!" *Pervert.*

A public transport one in particular.

The male grabbed her again, snapping his hand tight around her delicate wrist. Still no one moved to help her.

Why the fuck was he forced to protect a people who cared nothing about their own kind? No Hellspawn or god would tolerate this female's cries.

She battered the male again, but the bastard pulled her towards him, undeterred.

Esher growled and shoved to his feet, not pausing to consider what he was about to do.

He was going to save a human for the first time in his life.

CHAPTER 2

Aiko swung with all her might, striking her assailant in the face this time. His breath left him in a rush, foul with the stench of alcohol and cigarettes. He swayed with the strike, but remained upright, and slurred something obscene at her. She tugged her arm, trying to twist free of his grip, her heart hammering against her chest, but he tightened his grip, squeezing her bones.

She gritted her teeth against the pain.

The only other man in the carriage looked in the opposite direction as she fought with the salaryman. Chikushō. *Damn it.*

The door beyond the male slid open and she froze as a handsome foreigner stepped through, his tall frame eating up the space. Black hair grazed his cheek, shorn short all around the sides but left long on top, swept forward so it almost obscured one of his eyes.

Those ethereal blue eyes locked on her.

She shivered, cold sweeping through her at the emptiness they contained, no trace of feeling.

The salaryman tried to pull her towards him again.

The newcomer strode towards her, his eyes turning stormy as he shifted them to the person manhandling her and closed the distance between them.

In the blink of an eye, his right hand closed around the man's throat and he was off her, slammed against the train door by the foreigner who stood at least eight inches taller than him. The man leaned in close to the drunk, looked as if he wanted to say something as the salaryman began babbling in fear, and then eased back.

She thought he might release the man.

He pulled him away from the door, and slammed him back against it with enough force that the man passed out and the entire carriage jolted. The foreigner huffed as he released the man and watched him slump to the floor, and wiped his hand on his coat, as if the man had some sort of disease that he didn't want to get.

When he turned towards her, those stormy blue eyes lowering to meet hers, she bent forwards and dropped her head.

"Thank you," she said in English, hopeful that he would understand and would hear the true measure of her gratitude in her voice. It shook as she bowed several times, unable to stop herself as her adrenaline waned and all the fear it had been holding at bay swept over her.

He responded in perfect Japanese. "Don't ride alone so late at night, or at least use the women-only carriage."

She wanted to tell him that the women-only carriage wasn't available on the last trains, but held her tongue, not wanting to appear ungrateful for his help. She nodded, rubbed the tears from her face with the back of her hand and sniffed as she straightened.

The man looked her over, his eyes revealing nothing to her. They settled on her hands as she clutched her backpack, and she tried to stop them from trembling, but no matter what she did, they kept shaking.

"Are you alright?" he said in Japanese again, and she swore there was a flicker of concern in those words even if it didn't show in his eyes.

She nodded again. "Fine."

The train eased to a halt and the doors slid open, and relief crashed over her when she saw it was her stop. She stepped off the train, glaring at the sleeping salaryman as she passed, tempted to level a kick at him. When she looked back to thank the stranger again, he was stood on the platform beside her, his eyes dark as he stared at the man, looking as if he wanted to do more than just kick him.

He huffed as he turned away, his motions stiff, as if he had to fight himself to do it, and muttered, "Fuck."

Aiko followed his gaze to the station sign.

The way he sighed had her eyes roaming back to him. He was at least seven inches taller than her, and probably would have been closer to ten above her five-six height if she hadn't been wearing her shoes. A black cotton coat that reached the ankles of his worn leather boots hugged his slender frame, tight to his chest but flared from his waist. The split down the front revealed blue jeans tucked into the tops of his army boots.

He shifted back a step, placing more distance between them, and looked away from her, back in the direction the train had come. "Guess I'm walking."

She had studied English in school, and took classes at her university, so she knew enough to understand him and the implications of his words—he had missed his stop.

"I could call... you... a cab." She managed, with only a few pauses to think of the right words.

While she studied English, she didn't get to practice it much. Her parents didn't know it, and she only got to speak it with her classmates, and a lot of the time they only wanted to speak Japanese and were just learning English so they could put it on their résumé.

He shook his head but didn't look at her.

She thought about going ahead and calling him a taxi anyway, her eyes drifting back down the height of him as she considered it. Her gaze stopped on his hand.

Blood covered the side of it.

"You're hurt," she said in English and pointed to his hand.

He looked at it as if it was nothing and wasn't bothering him at all.

Had he done it when helping her?

"Chikushō," she muttered to herself and thoughts of hailing him a cab were replaced by ones about returning the favour by helping him. It was risky, but she owed him, and she couldn't let him go without tending to the wound. She just hoped he knew enough Japanese to understand her. She pointed to his hand again. "My parents run a small clinic below our house. I can help with that."

He regarded her with cold assessing eyes, and she had the feeling he was the one who didn't trust her.

As if she could hurt him.

He was far more powerful than she was, and had proven it on the train. She wasn't a threat to him.

So why did he look as if she might be?

It was there in his eyes as she looked deeper into them, and she could feel it as she focused on him. Just a glimmer of a feeling, but it was there. Hazy, but clear enough that she could name the emotion.

Part of him feared her.

"I would like to help," she added softly, and he looked back down at his hand again, the black slashes of his eyebrows meeting hard above his darkening eyes.

When he lifted them back to her, they were colder than before, and she moved back a step as a feeling went through her, one that warned her away from him. He glanced over his shoulder again, and then back at the station sign.

Sugamo.

Which stop had he wanted?

"Why would you trust me?" His deep voice rolled over her, his accent almost perfect.

If she closed her eyes, she could easily fool herself into thinking she was talking to a Japanese man, not a foreigner.

Where had he learned her language? He spoke it as if he had been doing it every day of his life. Had he been born in Japan?

No, she could feel that he hadn't been born in this land, that he didn't really belong here. It was a sensation that he didn't fit or wasn't welcome, one that most people would put down to instinct, but that ran deeper in her.

In her blood.

She studied his face as she answered him. "Why wouldn't I?"

He frowned at her. "Because I could be trying to get into your tiny panties too."

She doubted he wanted to do such a thing, the emotions she had detected in him pointing towards a desire to get away from her as quickly as possible rather than get closer to her, yet his words sent a thrill through her, followed by a heat that had her pulse picking up pace.

"Come with me, or don't. I won't force you." She turned away, slipped her arms into her black satin coffin-shaped backpack and strode towards the exit.

When she didn't feel him following, she resisted the temptation to look back. She had offered him help, extended a hand to him. It was down to him to take it.

Aiko passed through the barriers and out onto the street. It was quiet, no cars moving along it, but she looked in both directions anyway before hurrying across to the other side.

"How far is the clinic?" His voice arrested her steps and she looked back at him where he stood in the entrance of the station, his left arm wrapped around him and the late-spring breeze stirring the damp lengths of his black hair.

"A mile." She pointed in the direction.

His face darkened. She presumed it wasn't the distance irritating him, but the fact she had intended to walk a mile through the maze of streets alone in the early hours of morning. She did it all the time, and she wasn't the only woman in Tokyo who had the same habit.

He looked as if he wanted to tell her to hail a cab for herself and then said something, but she didn't catch the words as she watched the emotions flitter across his handsome face, a kaleidoscope of them that moved so swiftly she couldn't take them all in. Fear was there though. For himself still, or for her? Did he worry about her walking alone at night? Something akin to anguish crossed his face more than once too, and that emotion was there in his eyes as he reluctantly crossed the road to her.

What internal war did he wage?

His question earlier had revealed more about himself than anything he had said or done so far.

He found it difficult to trust, so he couldn't understand how others could do it so easily.

She could trust him, because if he had wanted to get into her 'tiny panties' he probably would have done it when they had been standing on the platform of the station for ten minutes, not a soul in sight.

He had stopped the pervert on the train too, revealing a noble streak in his actions.

"You'll probably get yourself killed if I let you go home alone," he muttered in English, and she understood enough to get the meaning of his words.

He wasn't coming with her so she could look at his wound. He was walking her home because he wanted to protect her.

She led him through the narrow streets, their steps loud on the wet road. It had stopped raining at some point, and she was thankful because she had left her umbrella on the train. She glanced at the man and found him looking at the clouds, his gaze distant and his head tipped back.

His black hair grazed his temple, and she drank her fill of him, still finding it hard to believe she was walking with him to her home. Her grandmother would be proud of her. That feeling beat in her heart. She had taught Aiko to give aid to those who needed it, especially if they were from another place.

This man certainly was.

His blue eyes took on a troubled edge, and he slid them towards her, angling his head slightly in her direction so he could see her. She smiled and looked away, not wanting to upset him. When his gaze left her again, she snuck another glance at him.

He was handsome, with fine black eyebrows and long inky lashes that framed his deep blue eyes, and a straight nose and softly curved lips that were a shade or two darker than his skin in the low light. Sculpted cheekbones were accented by long sideburns that reached the lobes of his ears, and the sharp angle of his jaw. There was a coldness to his face though, the lack of lines around his eyes and mouth telling her that he rarely smiled or laughed. Why?

When he frowned at her again, she looked away and kept her eyes off him this time, not wanting to upset him.

His gaze moved away from her, but then came back to rest on her, and she kept hers fixed ahead of her, pretending not to notice the way he studied her.

Because instinct warned he would react harshly if she made it clear she was aware of him staring.

As they turned a corner onto her street and passed a small park, she swore he wanted to move closer to her, but he tensed and distanced himself instead, and his eyes left her. She looked at him, keeping her head forwards so he wouldn't notice. His eyes scanned over the low buildings that lined the street, most of the windows dark.

Aiko wanted to know his thoughts as he became absorbed in looking at everything but her, but held her tongue instead, not wanting to appear rude.

She hadn't met many foreigners, and had certainly never met anyone like him.

When she crossed the road, he followed, and when she stopped in front of one of the square modern buildings, he halted with her. As she pulled her backpack off, he stepped backwards and looked up the height of the two-storey building.

"Smaller than I thought."

She slid the key into the lock on the glass door and twisted it. "It's only a clinic. We have a few beds, but mostly father treats local people and prescribes medicine."

She pushed the door open and walked into the dark room, years of living in the cramped building allowing her to move through the pitch-black space without hitting anything. When she reached the door to the office, she reached inside and flicked on the light. She turned to tell the man to come in.

He stood right behind her, his eyes stormy again as he looked around, his shoulders tensed as he scanned the darkness, as if he was expecting trouble.

"Father normally leaves this light on, but I prefer to turn it off when my parents are away." She set her backpack down on the chair by the desk, and pointed to the gurney. "Have a seat."

The man eyed it with suspicion, but moved past her and arranged himself on the padded bench. Aiko didn't fail to notice the way his lips twisted as he sat, or the way his left arm tightened on his ribs.

"Is it just your hand that's hurt?" She edged closer to him.

His eyes darkened a full shade, but around his pupils they seemed to grow brighter, turning cerulean. Not the lights.

She changed course, heading towards the white cupboards instead of him, giving him a moment to forget her question. He was hurt, but he didn't want her seeing it.

Because he didn't trust her.

Maybe it had been a mistake to insist on helping him.

Aiko paused with her fingers on the metal handle of the top drawer. It didn't feel like a mistake though. Helping him felt like the right thing to do. She had said she would take care of his hand, and that was what she would do. She owed him that much. She wouldn't press him to let her see his other injury, or ask him how it happened, because now she felt sure it hadn't happened on the train.

He had been injured before saving her.

Yet he had still stepped in to help her.

"My parents are away visiting family." She opened the drawer as she rambled, filling the tense silence and giving him a clear sign that she wasn't going to press him for answers. "I was going to go, but university is too busy right now."

She found the bandages and opened a fresh roll, and grabbed the scissors and tape too. She placed them on the black seat beside him and found the cotton wool and saline solution, and a tray to place all the dirty items in when she was done with them.

When she pulled a pair of disposable gloves from the box and tugged them on, he frowned at her.

"You seem used to this." He nodded towards the items next to him when she looked at him.

Aiko shrugged and removed her short black jacket, draping it over the back of the chair, and rolled up the sleeves of her dress. "I grew up in a clinic, and I'm studying medicine at university. Can you take your coat off for me?"

He released his ribs and tugged the right sleeve of his coat up his forearm, making it clear he wasn't going to be removing the garment. Because he didn't want her to see the wound he was trying to hide.

She pushed the need to see it and tend to it to the back of her mind and focused on the one he would let her see and treat.

When she took a step towards him, he tensed and she flicked her eyes up to meet his. His were brighter, a sunny summer sky that deep inside she knew was a bad sign and not a good one. She kept still, watching the war rage in his eyes as his irises grew darker around the edges. She had never seen eyes like his, but then she had never met a man like him.

When his eyes settled, and he released the breath he had been holding, she risked moving. He didn't tense again as she approached him, keeping her eyes off him to give him time to calm himself.

His voice was gravelly when he spoke. "Is university the reason you were out so late?"

He was trying to fill the silence now, to take his mind off what she was doing, and she went along with it, wanting him to be as comfortable as possible. She soaked some of the cotton wool in the saline solution on one side of the tray, and then slowly turned towards him.

As she reached for the makeshift bandage he had wrapped around the wound, she answered him so he would have something to focus on other than what her hands were doing. "I had work tonight, and afterwards I met my friends in Shibuya. I meant to be home earlier than this, but it's so easy to lose track of time."

She drew the white handkerchief away from his arm and her eyebrows briefly knit as she looked down and spotted a tattoo peeking out of the blood on his wrist, just above a thin black bracelet that sat flush against his skin.

He noticed where she was looking and tensed, and she swore he was waiting for her to mention it as she turned and placed the soiled cloth on the tray.

It had surprised her, but she wasn't one to hold with the traditional view of tattoos. She doubted he was yakuza.

Aiko focused on her work, carefully wiping the blood on his arm and hand away with the saline solution until she could see the wound—a three-inch-long gash that ran at a diagonal across his forearm a few inches above his wrist.

And his tattoo.

A beautiful dark blue trident on the inside of his wrist.

"You shouldn't be out so late at night," he muttered as she dabbed the gash with the solution, making sure it was completely cleaned.

Clearly, he shouldn't be out so late at night either. It meant bad things for both of them, but at least she hadn't ended up with what looked like a knife wound. He must have been in a fight. Under the bright light of the inspection lamp, she had spotted more cuts on his neck, and a few on his face. Plus there was the one he didn't want her to know about.

How deep was that wound?

She risked a glance at his right side as she turned to toss the used cotton wool on the tray and reached for the bandages. His black coat was wet from the rain, making it impossible for her to judge how much blood he had lost. She frowned as she spotted a single tear in it, barely an inch long.

A stab wound.

He needed treatment, and she wanted to give it to him, but she kept her tongue in check and didn't mention it.

The wound on his arm must have been from the same fight, and it was already sealed and healing. The one he was hiding might be healing just as rapidly. Which only made the feeling she had grow stronger. He hadn't come with her for treatment. He had come with her to ensure she reached her home safely.

"This looks good." She carefully wrapped the bandages around his arm. "It should heal nicely. Hold this."

He placed his fingers on the end of the bandage where hers had been. She picked up the scissors and cut the ribbon of cream material, and then grabbed the tape and snipped off two long pieces.

She placed one just below his fingers, brushing them.

He snatched his hand away as if she had burned him.

Aiko pretended not to notice that too, or his sharp intake of breath and the way his eyes drilled into her, and that feeling rose again, warning her to move away from him. She refused and placed the second piece of tape, and smoothed them both down carefully.

Her fingers slowed as she looked at his arm.

Silvery scars spiralled around his forearm, from halfway down to his wrist.

She reached out to touch one.

He shoved the sleeve of his coat down, stealing them from view, and she jumped, her entire body tensing as she quickly drew her hand to her chest.

Words warred on her lips and in her heart, an apology battling a desire to question him, to know what sort of life he led to have such deep scars, to end up wounded and act as if it was nothing.

"Thanks," he muttered, the word hollow and devoid of the emotion that normally accompanied it.

"Would you like some tea?"

He was off the gurney before she could even finish that question, his long black coat swirling around his legs as he strode from the office.

"I should go." He was in the doorway of the clinic by the time she left the office, his figure nothing more than a silhouette in the light coming in from the street. He looked back at her. "But thank you."

He was gone.

Aiko stared at the doorway for a heartbeat and then hurried forwards, but there was no sign of him in the street. It was as if he had simply disappeared.

It wouldn't surprise her if he had.

His words rang in her head, his deep voice a soothing sound as she replayed them, focusing on the last three.

A thank you that had been genuine.

He had reluctantly thanked her for tending to his wound, but then she had offered him tea and he had thanked her from the heart?

Or was that thank you for something else?

She closed her eyes and relived that moment, and the way he had looked at her. The way his blue eyes had glowed in the slim light.

It struck her that he hadn't been thanking her for the offer of tea.

He had been thanking her for not breaking his trust.

For not hurting him.

Aiko tipped her head back and watched the patchy clouds racing across the inky sky, revealing hints of stars between them.

Strange man.

If she could call him a man.

CHAPTER 3

Esher stood near the outside wall of the main room of the mansion, the tatami mats warm beneath his bare feet, the slight roughness of them soothing as he listened to his oldest brother, Keras, drone on about the latest intel they had managed to gather on daemon movements.

He picked at the bandage around his right arm as his brothers began to file their reports, and Marek made dry comments as he noted them all down on his laptop from his perch in the cream armchair that stood to Esher's right and completed the rough semi-circle of seating around the TV in the corner beside him.

Keras sat on the couch opposite Esher, their youngest brother Calistos shifting to his left to give him room. They were a contrast, Keras's black hair the darkness to Calistos's blond light. Where Keras was neat and orderly, his hair kept short and immaculate, and his tailored black dress-shirt and slacks pressed, and even his black socks perfect, Cal looked like the tempest he was, his fair hair pulled back into a messy ponytail, and a worn khaki t-shirt that had more than one hole in it hugging his chest and faded black fatigues encasing the long legs he stretched in front of him, resting his feet on the coffee table.

Cal's pale blue eyes flicked towards the TV to Esher's right, and he could almost see his brother itching to grab one of the controllers and fire up the console to knock out a few rounds of one of the first-person-shooters in his collection.

Cal hated them treating him like a kid because he was the youngest, but he acted every second of the one hundred and seven year age gap between them. Fuck, it was better than being seventy years Esher's junior and acting twice his age like Daimon though. More than once, Daimon had remarked that he felt like the older brother to Esher and not the other way around.

Daimon was just lucky that he loved him most out of his six brothers, otherwise he might have been inclined to take him up on those fighting words, like their older brother Ares did whenever Daimon threw barbs at him.

Fire and ice.

Esher didn't miss the days of them brawling in the Underworld. He'd had quite enough of coming close to being flambéed or frozen.

Daimon scrubbed a black-gloved hand over his frosty-white hair, his blue eyes cautious as he gave his report to Marek.

"Speed up," Valen muttered from the couch nearest Esher. He toyed with a knife, flipping it end over end, his impatience showing. "This is taking too long."

His blue eyes fixed Keras with a glare when their oldest brother looked at him and sighed.

"You'd complain too if you had a woman waiting for you." Valen flashed a grin at Keras, who only sighed again and rolled his green eyes.

"It's bad enough I have to hear complaints from him." Keras jerked his chin towards Ares where he sat beside Valen.

The brunet had a death grip on his knees, his knuckles white as his fingertips pressed into his black jeans and his warm brown eyes flickering with amber sparks. Tension radiated from him, his broad muscled shoulders tensed beneath his black t-shirt, and Esher knew the source of it.

Megan.

His older brother wanted to return to his female.

Just as Valen wanted to return to Eva.

Esher had denied them entrance the last time his brothers had tried to bring them to the mansion. With the wound the wraith had given him still healing, he couldn't stand having the mortals present in his home. Ares had understood and complied immediately, taking Megan back to his apartment in New York to wait for him.

Valen had kicked up a fuss.

When Esher had threatened to butcher the human assassin, spelling out the exact reason he didn't want her near him, and Keras had been forced to restrain him, his brother had backed down and taken her away.

And refused to attend the meeting.

Esher wasn't sure he should be grateful for his attendance this time.

It had taken him five minutes to start complaining. He brought up the female at every opportunity, making it clear she had been working with him to protect the gate. As if that would curry any favour with Esher.

It only made him want to kill her even more.

Mortals had no place being near the gates, so close to his home.

Valen pushed his fingers through the overlong top of his blond hair, brushing it down over the right side of his face, so it almost concealed it from Esher's view. While Esher's haircut was similar, with short sides and back, and the long lengths on top swept forwards, the hair on the sides of Valen's head had been crudely cut, and it was longer on top, reaching his jaw.

He folded his arms across his chest, causing his biceps to tighten against the sleeves of his black t-shirt, and grumbled to himself about Eva.

Mortals had no place in this house.

Esher teased another thread free of the bandage around his right arm as he stared through the opening between the wood-framed white paper panels across the room to his left.

Sunlight played across the garden and the wing of the Edo period mansion beyond it, where more paper panels closed off the rooms from the covered wooden walkway that ran around the three sides of the horseshoe-shaped building. It reflected off the ribbed grey tiled roof that swept downwards and chased over the manicured bushes that dotted the small courtyard garden.

A few pebbles of the gravel beneath them were out of place, and one was resting on a stepping stone.

One of his brothers had been walking out there.

His brows drew down as he charted a series of footprints, his fingers fraying the end of the bandage. He would have to go out with the rake when his brothers were gone. The topiary had a few pine needles out of place too, and perhaps he could enjoy the cherry trees blooming in the larger garden beyond the pond while he fed the koi and soaked up the silence.

"Esher?" Daimon's voice cut into the peaceful image building in his head, shattering it, and he looked at his younger brother, his frown sticking. "You alright?"

He nodded, and looked around at his other brothers. They were all staring at him as if he had two heads.

Or was about to rampage through Tokyo.

"Someone walked on the gravel." Esher drew down a deep breath to calm himself, reining in the urges they had all spotted in his eyes, and probably in the favour mark on his wrist too judging by the way Daimon was looking at it.

Esher looked down, but the trident above his black bracelet that matched the ones his brothers wore on their wrists was a steady pale blue, not giving his feelings away.

He followed Daimon's gaze again and realised his brother wasn't looking at his wrist. He was looking at the bandage around his arm. A bandage Esher had been playing with.

He still couldn't believe he had gone with the human, or that he hadn't wanted to kill her when she had been tending to the wound.

Or that he couldn't get his mind off her.

It had been three days since they had met, and he kept thinking about her, kept replaying small moments of his time with her. Only eighty percent of the time, an urge to harm her rose inside him.

The other nineteen percent?

He wasn't sure how he felt then.

And the remaining one percent was reserved for a thought that had left him cold and confused.

He wanted to see her again.

He had ruthlessly shoved that desire out of his head and his heart, banishing it. It wasn't going to happen. She was human. Untrustworthy. Dangerous. A wretch.

So why did he despise himself whenever he thought of her like that?

Why did he feel as if he was the one who couldn't be trusted, the one who was dangerous, a wretched beast?

"Esher?" Ares this time.

Esher's gaze snapped down to him.

"You sure you're alright, man?" Ares looked him over, not at all bothered by the glare he levelled at him. "You seem a little more tense than usual."

"Daemons attacked the gate. I... was injured and a mortal might have..." He couldn't finish that sentence.

Keras sighed. "You killed someone."

It wasn't what he had meant to say. He had been teetering on the brink of bringing up the female, a desire to understand the conflict she caused in him almost convincing him to share her with his brothers, but then the thought of telling them anything about her had slammed his mouth shut.

He didn't want to share her with anyone.

He shrugged. "He saw the daemons and me fighting."

A reasonable excuse.

"You could have wiped his memory," Marek volunteered, his tone distant as he typed on the keyboard of the silver laptop, his brown eyes on the screen.

No, he couldn't have. Wiping memories was a talent they all possessed, but to do it he would have had to touch the human.

Which meant the male would have met the same end.

Touching humans was a definite no.

"You forget who you're talking to?" Calistos offered with a grin in his voice, and Marek looked up from his computer, regarded Esher with a look that said he might have but he knew now what a mistake the suggestion had been, and went back to his work.

He had touched the pervert on the train, and he had wanted to kill him too. He still wasn't sure how he had managed to rein in that desire and claw back enough control to stop himself.

What about the mortal female?

Had he touched her?

She had touched him.

Ninety-nine percent of the time he hadn't found it repulsive, or grounds to make her blood explode.

The remaining one percent?

He recalled her fingers had brushed his, and an electric jolt had lit him up inside, like Valen had just pumped fifty thousand volts into him for a laugh, only it hadn't been unpleasant.

He shook her out of his head and focused back on the room, because Daimon was intently staring at the bandage now and looking as if he was going to mention it. *Again.*

Daimon mentioned it whenever he visited.

Esher had refused to answer every question or suggestion.

"Daemons attacked my gate that night too," Daimon offered in a slow, measured way that made it clear to Esher that he was still debating mentioning the bandage again, pressing him for answers he didn't want to give.

"How many nights ago?" Valen looked from Daimon to him, his blue eyes bright with curiosity.

"Three." And Esher had gone over it from every angle. "It just felt like a regular attempt on the gate."

But now Daimon had mentioned an attack in Hong Kong at the same time.

Keras exhaled a curse, which was never a good sign. "Shit… Paris and London were hit that night too. I went straight from Paris to help Cal in London."

Marek finally looked up from his laptop. "Seville had a couple of visitors. Nothing I couldn't handle though. I hardly broke a sweat."

Everyone looked at Ares. His second-eldest brother was a wall of tensed muscle as he sat on the couch with fire in his eyes, the air around him shimmering like a heat haze as his face darkened.

"Five hit the gate," he growled, the flames in his irises burning brighter, and then said what was on everyone's mind, "It was a coordinated attempt. They're testing us."

"They must have hit the Tokyo and Hong Kong gates at the same time, to keep us both busy." Daimon curled his fingers into fists, causing his black leather gloves to creak as frost glittered on them, a sign that Ares wasn't the only one losing his temper as he considered the implications.

"Paris and London were hit in the early hours of morning. It would have been dark still in Rome, New York and Seville." Keras leaned forwards and rested his elbows on his knees, his black shirt blending into his equally dark slacks, and his fine jet eyebrows dipped low above emerald eyes that glowed a shade brighter than normal.

Really not a good sign. It wasn't like their fearless leader to let anything get to him.

A coordinated attack by daemons wasn't a threat. Daemons were weak. They could handle them.

It certainly wasn't a threat to Keras.

His brother could have stepped to every gate and dealt with all the daemons at each one in the blink of an eye.

Marek lifted his head again, his warm brown eyes reflecting his concern as he studied their brother. Daimon exchanged a look with Cal, and Cal casually leaned back into the couch, splaying his arms along the top of it, where Keras couldn't see him, and shrugged, his expression shifting to show he wasn't sure what was up with Keras.

Valen moved, crossing his legs so his black fatigues stretched tight over his left knee, and slowly dipped his hand into his pocket and eased his phone out of it. Esher frowned as he rifled through the charms dangling from it, his actions slow and careful.

So Keras didn't notice.

Valen's thumb stopped on a familiar silver sword and shield, and he pressed it into his palm.

Calling for back up?

Keras wouldn't appreciate it.

Esher had half a mind to tell his younger brother not to meddle, but something was wrong, and the need to take care of his family had him holding his tongue and hoping she would answer.

All of them had noticed that Keras hadn't been the same since leaving the Underworld.

Since leaving *her*.

"You think testing us has something to do with whoever is behind sending the stronger daemons to attack us?" Valen slipped his phone back into his pocket.

Just the mention of their enemy was enough to have the raging tide that Esher had been fighting to hold back for the past few weeks rising again inside him, surging through his veins and flooding his mind with a dark need.

A hunger to hunt.

"Rein it in," Daimon said softly, a bare whisper that curled around him and pushed back against the tide. "We are all safe. Everything is good here. Remember?"

Esher nodded slowly.

But everything wasn't good.

His left side ached, cold with the memory of what the wraith had done to him and how close he had come to something worse than death.

And how their beloved little sister had suffered that same fate.

Give your sister my regards.

Valen had filled him in on his theory when Esher had regained consciousness days after the attack. *Days.* He was still healing from the wound too, and it had been weeks now. Would it always bother him? Would he always bear this reminder that he had almost lost his soul, and owed a human his life?

He had enough scars to deal with, enough pain to last an eternity without this adding to it.

He rubbed at his side, his lips compressing as he gritted his teeth and anger surged again, a need to lash out and fight, to hunt down the wraith who had done this to him and make him pay for it, and for Calindria's deathless state.

Valen had broken it to him as gently as possible, but the idea that Calindria's soul was missing, sucked from her by that fiend, and was still lost now, centuries later, had sent him into a rage so dark and consuming that Keras and Daimon had been forced to shut him in the cage.

Esher shuddered as he closed his eyes and gripped his side, holding himself. Gods, he despised the cage. He hated feeling trapped and helpless, stripped of his ability to teleport and forced to endure confinement.

For the sake of the fucking humans.

It was their fault he couldn't bear it.

They should be the ones to suffer when he lost his fight against his other self.

They should be the ones to suffer when the lunar perigee hit.

Not him.

But he was the one locked away, bound just when the pull of the moon made him strongest, unleashed all the fury he struggled to hold inside him every damned day, for the sake of a race who didn't deserve it.

"Esher!" Daimon's palms hovered close to his face, framing it as best he could without touching him.

Esher's cheeks chilled anyway, just being close to Daimon enough to sap his heat. It was a bane both Daimon and Ares had to bear. Their powers had manifested in the mortal world, their ice and fire making them dangerous to touch.

"I want to kill him," Esher growled and pushed away from his brother. He paced a few feet across the open space between the TV area and the dining area, and then pivoted on his heel to face his brothers again. "He deserves to die. I want him dead. I need him dead… he should suffer for what he did."

He shoved the flat of his palm against his chest and dug his fingertips into his dark grey shirt.

"I can't settle until he's paid for what he did… or until she comes."

"We all want to kill him, Brother, but we need information first, remember?" Ares's careful words as he stood and moved to face him had Esher's gaze flicking to Cal, a brief glance that he hoped their youngest brother didn't notice.

Cal didn't know that the wraith had been responsible for what had happened to Calindria, and his brothers were right to keep him in the dark. He couldn't know. Not yet. Not until they knew whether they could retrieve her soul or not.

It would send him over the edge.

Esher huffed and paced across the tatami mats to the opened panels opposite the entrance, and stared into the garden, trying to find peace there even when he knew he wouldn't.

There was only one path to peace for him now.

Hunt the wraith.

Once the wraith was dead, and whoever was due to come after him finally made her appearance, he would find peace.

He needed to get it over with, needed to send them screaming into a black eternity of suffering.

Into a hell of his own making.

He would put their damned souls in the vilest, most horrific place imaginable, condemning them to rot there forever.

Esher scrubbed his hand over his side, wrapped his arms around his stomach and toyed with the bandage on his forearm again as a feeling went through him, one that had been bothering him since he had come around after the wraith attack.

Cal wasn't the only person his brothers were keeping in the dark.

There was something they weren't telling him too, and it unsettled him, kept him on the edge and made it difficult to retain control. It pissed him off too, even when part of him knew that if they were keeping a secret from him, it was probably for a good reason.

He tried to listen to his brothers as they discussed everything Valen had learned from the two daemons who had attacked him—an incubus and his succubus sister. Ares mentioned the daemon who had attacked him, one who had stolen his power. Both events had brought the wraith out of hiding.

Maybe when the female due to come for him finally attacked, the wraith would make an appearance again.

Esher would be ready for him.

CHAPTER 4

Esher tuned his brothers out as he sank into the glorious vision building in his mind, one where he overcame the wraith and captured him, not for information as Keras would want, but for the sheer pleasure of revenge. He would bind and torture the wretch until he broke and confessed what he had done with Calindria's soul, and then he would send him screaming into the darkest pit in the Underworld, and would inform their father about what the wretch had done. Gods, Hades would see to it the bastard suffered eternally.

His lips twisted in a slow smile.

Fuck, he would beg his father to give him a front row seat for that show.

A dark voice whispered in his mind, seductive words that tempted him to listen to them, coaxed him into ignoring his brothers' wishes and obeying the gnawing hunger inside him—the need to hunt. He wavered as the city beyond the garden flickered to the *otherworld*, the future of Earth should he and his brothers fail to stop the calamity the Moirai had foreseen—a calamity their new enemy intended to bring about by doing something to the gates.

A calamity part of Esher wanted to see.

The darker part.

The part that had been born centuries ago, and had whispered to him ever since, rising to steal control at times when he wasn't strong enough to hold it at bay.

A beast he fought to keep locked inside him.

A monster he had failed to contain more than once.

It had been hard enough to fight it when the only threat to his family had been the daemons and the humans, but it was growing impossible now that he knew the wraith had been responsible for Calindria's end. His war with it was constant, and he wasn't sure he could win.

He needed to avenge his sister.

His eyes narrowed on the flames that spiralled high into the black sky beyond the pristine white wall of the mansion grounds, sparks dancing like golden fireflies as the wind caught them, looking as if they were rising on the screams of the mortals whose flesh burned and the shrieks of the creatures who hunted and preyed on them.

A shudder wracked him, a shiver of pleasure that rolled through him as their screams surrounded him, creating a symphony that tugged at the darkness in him, made him yearn to make this future real so he could bask in the glory of it.

"Esher." The male voice intruded, shaking the vision of beauty before him.

He snarled, launched his left hand out and wrapped it around the offender's neck, squeezing it hard.

The male growled and countered him, and icy cold gripped his throat, burned like fire as it swept over him beneath his clothes.

"Get a fucking grip," Daimon snarled and shoved hard, sending him staggering backwards onto the raised wooden walkway that enclosed three sides of the smaller courtyard garden and shaking Esher's grip on him.

His back slammed into one of the thick square pillars that supported the overhanging roof.

His breath exploded from him as the timber cracked.

The sound of dropping water had his head snapping to his right in time to catch a glimpse of brightly coloured koi suspended in the air for a moment before they dropped back into the pond.

"Fuck," Esher muttered and got a grip on himself, pushing out the damned voice that still taunted him, told him to take pleasure in the destruction he wrought, not be ashamed of it, tempted him with thoughts of heading beyond the protective walls of the mansion to the city and unleashing the fury he had bottled inside him on the weak creatures who inhabited it.

It would be glorious.

"No." He grasped the sides of his head and squeezed until it hurt. "*No!*"

He didn't really want that. He was just tired and weak from the wraith's attack, worn down and vulnerable. Yes, vulnerable. He was too susceptible right now, not strong enough to shut out the damned voice and the things it wanted him to do.

"Listen to me, Esher," Daimon whispered, and he focused on his brother, using the sound of his voice to shut out the darker one just as they had practiced. "You're all good. Everything is fine. Everyone is fine."

But they weren't.

He saw that as he lifted his head and spotted the unmistakable trace of red beneath his brother's nose where Daimon hadn't quite managed to wipe all the blood away to hide it from him, and the dark bruises emerging around his throat just above the collar of his navy turtle neck.

"I'm sorry," Esher murmured, pain closing his throat as he considered what he had done.

He had hurt the ones he loved.

The ones he had vowed to protect.

The only ones who mattered.

"I'm fine." Daimon managed a smile and rubbed at his throat. "No harm done."

A lie.

He noticed the way Daimon's fingers trembled as he neatened his spiked white hair, acting casual when he was shaken.

Esher averted his gaze, but the pain and guilt lingered as he looked at the pond and the koi that were flapping around on the gravel surrounding it. He stepped off the walkway, crossing the pebbles without feeling them biting into the soles of his feet, and stooped to carefully pick up the fish and place them gently back into the pond.

He breathed easier as he counted them all, checking each one in turn, and saw none of them had been hurt.

His brothers' voices filled the silence behind him as he watched the fish, their words distant and lost on him, and he sensed them departing one by one.

Until only Daimon remained.

Had he harmed any more of his brothers? Gods, he hoped he hadn't.

It was getting harder to control himself.

His rage should have been directed solely at the daemons and the humans, not at his family. His family were the only ones who mattered. The Underworld was the only place that mattered too.

This world could burn for all he cared.

But if it burned, then the Underworld burned with it.

He watched a black and white koi he was particularly fond of, one he'd had for decades, swim past to join the group waiting near the walkway where it jutted out over the pond to his right, by his quarters.

An ache started behind his breast, one that was familiar to him.

He wanted to return to the Underworld.

He couldn't handle things here anymore. Today was proof of that. He wasn't strong enough to hold back the darker part of himself that viewed all the mortals as a threat to him and his family, and his world.

Just thinking about hunting them, watching them suffer, had been enough to have him slipping.

Hurting the ones he loved.

"You alright?" Daimon eased into a crouch beside him, his long black coat pooling around his feet on the pale gravel.

"Sorry." He kept his eyes on the fish, shame eating at him as he thought about what he had done.

Daimon had given as good as he had got. Esher's throat was sore, and it stung a little to breathe and speak, but the pain didn't make him feel better about what he had done.

"The moon is just fucking with you. It's almost full." Daimon ghosted a hand over his shoulder.

Esher wished he would touch him, because he needed to feel it, needed someone to hold him together right now because he felt as if he was falling apart.

He focused on the moon, picturing it in an attempt to soothe himself. It was distant from him, on the other side of the planet. He wanted to see it. Needed to see it. He needed the calming influence it had on him.

He forced himself to remain where he was though, because stepping that distance would drain some of his strength, and he had to remain strong in case the attack came tonight.

He rested his elbows on his knees as he remained crouched on the gravel at the edge of the pond, his eyes on the fish as they all slowly grouped before him, clearly having decided he was going to feed them from this spot instead.

They were beautiful as they glided around, the pattern of their colours constantly shifting.

His left fingers drifted across to his right arm as the sight of them soothed him, calming the turbulent waters in his soul.

The sensation of calm grew stronger still.

"Any injury you had would be healed by now." Daimon's careful words, softly spoken, floated through his mind and he looked down to find he was playing with the bandage again. His brother's pale blue eyes lifted from his arm to rest on his face. "Why are you so reluctant to discard it? Did a daemon get you? Are you infected somehow?"

Esher opened his mouth, but the words caught in his throat.

He stepped rather than answering him, appearing briefly at the front porch of the mansion to grab his long black coat and jam his feet into his leather boots, and then teleporting again.

The guilt over hurting his brother mingled with new shame as he landed on top of the covered footbridge that spanned the gap between two large buildings, allowing humans to come and go between them above the busy road that cut a path straight ahead of him and intersected with an equally as crowded road just two hundred metres from him in the heart of the Shibuya district.

Why couldn't he just tell his brother what had happened?

He was closest to Daimon, and they had shared everything in the past, leaving nothing unsaid between them. So why did he want to keep the female a secret?

Esher looked back in the direction of the mansion and sighed as the breeze blew the longer lengths of his black hair back from his face. He wasn't sure what was wrong with him, and he had no reason to keep secrets from Daimon. If he kept on like this, he would only cause his brother more worry, and he didn't want that. The next time Daimon asked him, he would tell him.

The female was nothing to him anyway, just another human in a world filled with them. He couldn't trust her. She was dangerous. A wretch.

If she knew what he was, she would react in the way humans always did, their fear of whatever was stronger than they were driving them to attack and kill it.

She would.

He looked down at the swarm of humans below him as they crossed the juncture between the four roads, hurrying from the station to his right or towards it.

If they knew what he was, they wouldn't understand. They wouldn't even try to. They would hurt him.

They would harm his family.

The black urge to hurt them first rose inside him, but he pulled the earbuds from his shirt pocket, stuffed them into his ears, and flicked through the classical music on his iPod until he found a soothing piece.

As soon as the piano and strings filled his ears, the volume loud enough to shut out the incessant noise of the mortal world, the tension drained from him and his shoulders relaxed.

Evening light, beautiful and rich amber, washed over the side of the high building in front of him on the other side of the crossing, turning the huge television screen mounted on it dull, and caught on the towering ones to his right. He stood at the edge of the roof of the bridge, soaking up the music, letting it calm him as he watched the mortals, and debated heading down.

He was testing himself again, just as he had been that night when he had stood in this same spot. That night, the moon had been full, pulling at him and weakening his resistance to the darker side of himself. That night, Valen had brought a mortal female, the assassin Eva, to the mansion, wanting to protect her from their uncle and their enemies.

That night, his guard had dropped, and the wraith had attacked him, plunging a tainted blade into his side.

And that night, a mortal had saved his soul.

Megan.

Ares's female had the power to heal, but it was a power that drained her when she used it on a god like him and his brothers, pushing her close to death.

She had risked it to save him.

Fuck, he still didn't know how to process that.

It haunted him.

He owed his life to a mortal.

Daimon wanted him to talk about it, and so did his other brothers, but he needed time.

Space.

Esher looked down at the mortals, the warm spring breeze toying with his long coat, making it flap around his boots. To think he owed one of them his life.

His left hand covered the sleeve of his black coat over the bandage on his right forearm as a feeling went through him, a need that had haunted him from the moment he had stepped away from that small clinic in the northern suburb of Tokyo.

An urge to return there.

He crushed it.

She meant nothing, was nothing. He was just confused, conflicted by what Megan had done for him, that was the only reason he had lowered his guard around another of her kind.

Esher closed his eyes and focused on the music, shutting the world around him out. He would go to Lion, one of his favourite cafés in Tokyo, and one that was a sanctuary for him. He would sit there as he always did, in a quiet corner, listening to the classical music they played and finding peace in that place his brothers had agreed was his, one where Daimon rarely dared to bother him and one where he could think.

A strange tingling swept through him.

Not a daemon. Their presence made his gut swirl with a sickening sensation and it was still light out. They would be in hiding for another few hours yet.

This was *different*.

He tilted his head to his right and opened his eyes, locking them on the source of it.

She shifted foot to foot far below him, her back to the statue of Hachiko, a faithful dog, where people often met, facing the exit of the train station. Her obsidian long hair had been twirled into twin buns at the back of her head, and a pink and black chequered bag bumped the front of her thighs as she anxiously swayed side to side, trying to see through the crowd.

There was a pause, and then she lifted her arm as she tiptoed. Waving to someone.

Esher almost growled as he sought the human she was signalling, but it died on his lips as he spotted a female waving back at her. The reaction had him taking a step back, that confusion rising again as he struggled to understand why the thought of her potentially meeting a male had pushed him close to stepping down and dealing with them before they could reach her.

Her friend eased through the crowd, and when they embraced, his mortal's violet fluffy jumper rode up to flash a strip of pale toned skin.

He growled now, and eyed all the males in the vicinity, ensuring none of them had noticed.

Satisfied that they hadn't, he looked back at her, and frowned.

She was gone.

Dammit.

Esher stepped before he had even considered doing it, appearing near the trees that encased the statue on one side, his eyes scouring the busy square for her.

He found her near the crossing, speaking with two females now, both of them with hair that barely reached their jaws and dark make-up around their eyes and a smear of red on their lips. They smiled and laughed, but all he felt was disgust and a need to wipe them from the face of the Earth.

His female however…

She was as cute as he recalled, although today she wore more conservative clothing of black jeans and thick-soled purple shoes with her violet jumper, and her bag was plain in comparison to the satin coffin-shaped one that had the winged cat toy dangling from the zipper.

Cute?

He stilled right down to his breathing as that word came back to slap him.

No, she wasn't cute.

She was…

The darker part of himself volunteered the word vile.

Beautiful.

Beautiful despite the fact she wore only light make-up, or possibly even none. Beautiful despite the fact she was human.

As beautiful and as full of life a butterfly as she moved with her comrades, flitting in front of them one moment with a smile on her face, and beside them in the next, her mouth parted on a laugh that filled her whole face with joy.

Esher trailed after her, ignoring the feeble humans as he pushed through the crowd, struggling to keep up with her and keep his distance at the same time.

Fuck, he felt like a damned stalker as he followed her down the narrow cobbled pedestrian street that branched off at a diagonal to the left of his favourite Starbucks, unable to take his eyes off her even when he knew he should walk away right now and forget about her.

He couldn't.

He swore she laughed every time she spoke, and every time her friends said something, oblivious to the way she drew the attention of the people around her, the males in particular. Esher made a mental note to kill them later, once he had drunk his fill of the fascinating little human.

He had never noticed that humans could be like her, buzzing with goodness.

Kindness.

He rebelled against that word, his mind hurling a thousand images that contradicted it and reminded him that humans were incapable of kindness. They were vicious, untrustworthy. Dangerous.

They would kill him if he revealed what he was to them.

Just as their ancestors had tried.

He slowed to a halt, his gaze still following her as his body locked up tight, the pain thrumming in his heart bleeding over into his muscles and making them clamp down on his bones as a need to lash out grew inside him.

He couldn't trust her.

She was weak, but a threat.

Dangerous to him.

But for the first time, he felt as if the danger he was in wasn't physical.

It was emotional.

She was weak, but gods, she could crush him.

He was aware of that as he watched her twirl and smile, her eyes bright with her laughter, and he felt a pull towards her, one that rivalled that of the moon.

He couldn't trust her.

She was mortal, and all mortals wanted to do was hurt him. If he trusted her, in time she would prove herself just like the others. She would wound him, try to break him, and gods, she might just succeed where others had failed and end up destroying him.

The crowd closed in around him, and his muscles cranked tighter, his heart pounding faster as his tension rose, the need to lash out growing fiercer with each passing second, until he teetered on the brink of showing her and all the other mortals that they were in the presence of something not of their world.

A god.

Paint the streets crimson.

Tear the world down.

Kill them all.

Before they can kill me.

Esher staggered back a step, shoving away from that voice that rose from the pit inside him, refusing to succumb to it, because if he lost control, if he allowed the other side of himself to emerge, he would hurt her too.

He wouldn't care that he knew her, or that she was gentle and for all he knew, would probably never hurt him. He would kill her just as easily as he killed the others.

He broke away from her and started walking, his pace increasing as he shoved through the crowd and struggled to focus on his destination, one far from her.

In the split-second between locking in a destination and teleporting, her eyes landed on him.

He felt it as a hot caress, one that had his blood boiling with need that demanded he stay and sate it.

A need that shook him.

It wasn't born of a desire to destroy or to shed blood.

It was born of a desire to touch, to risk everything in order to feel something.

A feeling that crystallised inside him as he landed on a rooftop a short distance from the café and made everything he had been going through the past few days make a dreadful sort of sense.

He needed *her*.

But he couldn't have her.

Because he couldn't trust himself. He was dangerous. A beast.

A monster who would crush such a delicate butterfly.

CHAPTER 5

Aiko slowed to a halt as awareness washed through her, a sensation that she was being watched. She turned on the busy shopping street in Shibuya and looked around.

"What's wrong?" Kumiko moved closer to her, and Aiko sensed her concern as the distance between them narrowed.

Megumi didn't seem at all bothered as she watched a man a little older than her walking past, heading towards the crossing and the station.

Aiko knew *he* was here. She could feel him. She moved to the side of the street, gripped the pole of a lamp and tiptoed, trying to see above the heads of the crowd. She scanned them, a sense of desperation growing inside her as she failed to find him.

He was here.

She was sure of it.

She swept her eyes back over the crowd, might have caught a glimpse of his wild black hair and the grey-blue scarf he had been wearing the night they had met.

The night he had saved her.

She had been thinking about him ever since, struggling to focus on her studies and her part-time job. Even her friends had noticed her spacing out and had started teasing her about it.

"Seriously, what's wrong?" Kumiko tugged her arm, pulling her down from the lamp post.

Aiko forced her gaze away from the other end of the street and shook her head. "I just thought I saw someone I knew."

Megumi giggled. "A man?"

"No." Aiko waved her hand in front of her face and tasted the lie on her tongue.

There was no way she was going to talk to Kumiko or Megumi about men. They were friends, but they weren't that close. They were in the same class at the University of Tokyo, and had grouped up during the week they had started there, but their backgrounds were very different and sometimes she felt it keenly.

Kumiko and Megumi came from rich families and had grown up together in a prestigious area of Tokyo, and she had grown up in a run-down suburb in a family that had often struggled to make ends meet. They were learning medicine because their families had decided upon it, neither of them really interested in having a profession at all, happy to live off their families' money.

Aiko was studying medicine so she could help out at her family's clinic.

They couldn't have come from more polar worlds. They couldn't have been more different in personality either.

Megumi made that abundantly clear as she grabbed her and Kumiko, and pulled them towards the next street. "Come on. I want to go this way."

Aiko didn't want to go that way, but she didn't say anything as Megumi dragged her along and Kumiko joined in, smiling from ear to ear as she talked about how she was going to get the host boys that always loitered on that street to flirt with her. They were men who made a living by being paid to drink with women in the host club, entertaining them for an evening, as if they were the woman's boyfriend. She had heard rumours that some of the men even took things further.

Both Megumi and Kumiko were open with relationships, and had told Aiko about several of the ones they had indulged in after joining university, many of them with older men, but most of them with men in other classes. When Aiko had found the courage to ask how long they had been sleeping with men, Megumi had confessed she had slept with a partner of her father's when she was fourteen, and Kumiko had given herself to the son of a wealthy neighbour at a party when she had been sixteen.

No, they couldn't have been more different.

But Aiko still loved spending time with them, even when she had no experience of many of the things they talked about—grand parties, lavish lifestyles and expensive holidays, and men.

She looked back the way they had come.

How had he gotten the scars on his arms?

They had looked as if he had been bound and had struggled. She had seen similar wounds on someone almost a decade ago, when she had been in high school and helping her father out over the summer. The woman had been brought to her family's clinic for rehabilitation after police had rescued her from a man who had kept her tied up and had done terrible things to her.

Had he been tied up like that, held captive against his will?

Aiko was so lost in thoughts of him that she didn't notice the host boys flirting with her until one was so close to her that his breath washed across her face and the heat of his body brushed hers.

Her heart slammed against her ribs.

Prickles swept over her skin and panic surged in her veins.

She shoved him in the chest, pushing him away from her as flashes of the train came back to her and she relived the terrifying feel of the man's hand locked around her wrist, his grip so tight she hadn't been able to break free, and how powerless she had been as she had struggled, the other passengers watching her and doing nothing to help her.

The host boy stumbled and fell into one of his companions, who caught him.

Megumi bowed as she muttered to the men, "We're sorry."

Kumiko shot her a worried look.

Aiko turned on her heel and hurried away from the men, her throat tight and breath wheezing as it tried to push through it. Her heart thundered, blood rushing as her legs shook and her hands trembled. She was safe. She wasn't back there.

A flash of the dark-haired man towering over her, his blue eyes tranquil and locked on her, filled her mind and her heart steadied at last, the adrenaline flowing from her as she slowed to a stop at a junction on the street.

She breathed a little easier as she focused on him. He had saved her. Nothing bad had happened to her. He had made sure of that. He had stopped the pervert, and he had walked her home, and for a brief moment, she had felt connected to him.

In a way she had never felt connected to anyone before.

"What happened?" Kumiko stopped beside her, a little out of breath, and Aiko waited until Megumi had caught up with them before she let the memory of the man slip from her mind and looked at her friends.

"I'm sorry," she whispered. "The other night, after we went out for dinner, a man on the train home... he... someone stopped him but he tried to..."

"Oh, Aiko." Megumi pulled her into a tight hug, one that squeezed the air from her lungs again. "I never would have suggested we go near the boys if I had known."

She nodded, closed her eyes and held her friend. "I know. I should have said something. I just thought I was over it."

But she wasn't, and she hated it. She hated being weak and letting things like that frighten her.

She released Megumi and plastered a smile on her face, when all she really wanted to do was give up and let someone see what she was really feeling. Only she didn't want it to be her friends. She wanted to show *him*.

She wanted him to see that whatever pain he held inside him, he wasn't alone. She hurt sometimes too.

Sometimes, she hated this world, but she picked herself up, held her head high and kept marching forwards, bravely embracing whatever came next and not letting fear hold her back.

"I could use a parfait," she muttered, and when Kumiko laughed, it was infectious. She smiled too, feeling it this time, because there was nothing in this world a good amount of ice cream, fruit, whipped cream and toppings couldn't fix.

It was something they had all agreed on shortly after meeting.

Megumi looped her arm around Aiko's left one. "Come on. It's been a while since we went to Nishimura Fruits Parlour."

It had probably been no more than a week, but their strawberry parfaits were by far her and her friends' favourites in the city. They had once joked about forming a weekly Nishimura Study Club, that they had decided would honestly involve some study and not just gossiping and eating parfait until they were sick.

Kumiko led the way back towards the main crossing, a bounce in her step now, and Aiko tried not to think about what had happened to her on the train, or the man who had saved her, but as she passed the spot where she felt sure she had seen him, she glanced that way and a feeling struck her.

She hadn't been afraid of him.

He had hurt the man who had tried to assault her, and had looked as if he had wanted to kill him and had barely restrained himself. He had a tattoo, scars and had been injured in a fight. He was probably dangerous.

Yet, she didn't fear him.

In fact, she ached to see him again.

Was it because he was different to the men around her?

She tilted her head back as it started to rain, and Megumi broke away from her together with Kumiko, both of them rushing for the parfait parlour nearby. The streets were quick to clear, and umbrellas popped up above those who had been more prepared for the unpredictable spring weather.

Aiko didn't run. She didn't put up an umbrella.

She let the drops hit her face, warm against her skin.

Let them linger rather than wiping them away, enjoying the feel of them, finding them comforting and soothing.

Because they made her feel connected to him again.

A single thought formed in her mind, a question her heart answered in the affirmative.

Was this his doing?

CHAPTER 6

Esher reached the narrow cobbled street that was barely wide enough for a car and paused outside the unusual grey façade of Lion, with its almost European arched entrance topped with blue Japanese roof tiles and two sets of windows flanking a large pill-shaped one on the upper floor.

Above him, the thick mass of electrical wires that chased along the street gave off a faint hum in his sensitive hearing as rain poured down, steadily growing heavier, soaking through his coat to his shirt and jeans.

The street was mercifully empty, the weather chasing everyone away.

Part of him felt bad about the rain, which was strange, and unsettling. He never felt bad when his mood affected the weather and brought rain or a storm.

So why did he feel bad this time?

He pushed the door to the café open and headed straight upstairs, to his favourite corner where the classical music played softly over the huge arrangement of wooden speakers visible on the balconied upper level sounded the best. He slid into the booth and breathed out a sigh as he sank into crimson velvet cushions.

The interior of the café was dark, the walls painted black and the furniture resembling ebony wood, and worn in places, but it felt like a sanctuary to him, the low lighting and the darkness of it allowing him to relax and enjoy the music as it kept the eyes of the locals away from him.

The female staff brought him his usual glass of water, setting it down as she bowed. He waited for her to rattle off the menu and walk away before he removed his earbuds.

A different classical piece washed over him, and he closed his eyes, tipped his head back and savoured it.

Her day was probably ruined because of him.

It hit him hard, coming at him out of nowhere, and he frowned as he opened his eyes and stared at the water, and felt the rain outside as it struck the roofs across the city, and poured down on the people coming and going in the streets.

That was why he felt bad.

She was probably getting rained on, and her day out with her friends wrecked, and it was all his fault.

He hadn't been able to keep a lid on his mood, and it had bled over, messing with the weather and spoiling what had looked as if it might be a beautiful sunset.

Esher shifted his focus to the glass in front of him on the dark wooden table and his breathing, narrowing the world down to that one small amount of water. It trembled, the surface rippling as it began to take on the full force of his mood, his anger over the mortals, and his darkest desires. When the rain outside slowed, the water in the glass began to drip upwards, beads breaking from its surface to hang in the air above it.

He toyed with them, moving them in time with the music, letting them distract him as they danced and played with each other.

The rain stopped, and everything seemed to still, outside him and inside him.

The music softly played, and the few mortals in the café were silent in their enjoyment of it, a contrast to the bustling world outside where they were normally noisy and intrusive, and he needed the music to shut them out.

But not her.

He hadn't wanted to shut her out when he had been with her, and he had welcomed her presence when he had been watching her with her friends, as she had laughed and smiled, so carefree.

He still couldn't believe he had followed her, studied her like that. She had never stopped smiling.

It had come close to affecting him at one point, before his mood had gone south and a thought had hit him.

Would she smile so much if she knew the real world and the future that awaited it if he and his brothers failed?

He wanted her to keep on smiling.

He wanted to keep her world from colliding with his to make that happen.

Daimon appeared in the booth opposite him, looked down and arched a white eyebrow at the glass and then lifted his icy blue eyes to his. "Your water is raining."

Esher looked down at it, watching the miniature storm he had created in the glass. Better it rained in there than outside, on her.

"I told you not to bother me here." Esher let the storm build, until the water turned choppy.

Daimon touched his gloved fingers to the outside of the glass, a brief caress but enough to affect the water. Tiny icebergs formed, and some of the rain became snow. Esher tossed him an unimpressed look.

"Our conversation wasn't finished." Daimon leaned back, rubbed his white hair and waved his hand, signalling the waitress. She bustled over, and his brother shifted to Japanese. "I'll have what he's having."

She bowed and walked away, returning a moment later with a tall glass of water.

"Cheers." Daimon nodded to her, and then turned to him and mock-scowled. "No making my water rain, alright?"

Esher ignored him, closing his eyes and trying to shut him out by focusing on the music, because he could feel the clouds building again outside, and he wanted to hold the rain at bay.

"Where did you go?" His brother just wouldn't shut up, would he?

He clamped his jaw tight, the muscles tensing in it as he gave up trying to control his mood. It was impossible when Daimon was poking his buttons, doing it on purpose to make him talk. His brother wasn't going to give up until he told him something.

It didn't have to be the truth.

He stared at the tall wooden speakers suspended on the wall above the ground floor and his thoughts returned to the female. He should stay away from her, should let her live her life in peace, but gods, he just couldn't bring himself to do it. Whenever he tried to push her out of his head forever, whenever he came close to shutting himself off from her, he ended up thinking about how much he wanted to see her again, and there was a part of him that didn't care if that placed her in danger.

He feared it was the same part that wanted to kill all the humans, and that by giving in to it, he might only be luring her to her doom, tricked by his own other self.

"I just needed some space. I didn't want to hurt you again." It was part truth. He really didn't want to harm his brothers, especially Daimon.

Unless they were sparring.

Then Daimon got what he deserved.

"Because of the wraith… or Megan?" Those words were carefully weighed, and Esher looked at him again.

He didn't like thinking about what she had done for him, because he didn't like owing his life to her, a mortal, not even when she was becoming part of their family now. Just as Eva was.

"Both," he murmured, and Daimon sighed, but he continued before his brother could speak. "The wraith's blade… don't tell anyone, because I don't need them fussing like I'm some special fucking snowflake… *swear it.*"

Daimon crossed his heart, his expression deadly serious, which was as much of a promise as Esher would get out of him.

"I'm still healing," Esher blurted.

His brother's white eyebrows dipped low, the corners of his lips turning downwards as his eyes brightened, his anger shining in them. "What do you mean? You should be healed by now."

He tried to reach across the table, and Esher swatted his hand away before he could grab his shirt and lift it to see the wound.

"It looks like a scar, but sometimes I feel it. It hurts, and I'm weaker than normal." Esher caught hold of his grey shirt when Daimon looked as if he might make another attempt to see and tugged it up enough to flash the scar at him.

Some of the worry in his brother's eyes faded, but a hell of a lot remained, and it was there in his voice too as he leaned towards him, pushing the glass of water aside. It instantly froze, and frost flowers grew outwards from Daimon's hands as he pressed them into the table top.

"Megan healed you though." Daimon's eyes darted between his, as if he could see in them whether or not she had.

"She stopped the toxin on the blade from killing me, and the wound healed, but what if some of it remained? What if I'm still purging it now, and that's the reason I took so long to come around?" It made too much sense to Esher to be anything else. He wasn't dying and didn't feel as if his soul was in jeopardy, but he wasn't quite right yet either. He ran his finger around the rim of his glass, making the water chase it. "I feel stronger every day."

"So you are purging it?" Daimon sounded relieved, but uncertain at the same time.

Esher nodded, because everything pointed towards that being the case, but it was taking a long time, and he was getting pretty damn sick of feeling weak, and could damn well live without the attacks that left him feeling as if he was going to collapse again. The memories the sudden flaring of the wound provoked were as much responsible for that temporary weakness as the toxin was though. It was a psychological reflex.

Like the one he had whenever he thought about humans.

Or the times he saw his brothers in danger.

His twisted fucking mind used it as a chance to bombard him with memories of events that tore at him, as powerful now as they had been when he had lived them.

"Come back to the mansion," Daimon said, cutting into his thoughts before they could lead him down a dark path.

He nodded in agreement, but only because he could see Daimon needed him safe now that he knew the toxin was still weakening him. His brother wanted him protected by the powerful wards that shielded the mansion, locking everyone but him and his brothers out of it.

Not because he feared the wraith would come for him again while he was weakened, but because he feared the female daemon their enemies had spoken of would.

It wouldn't surprise him if Daimon insisted on taking gate duty in Tokyo until he was healed and forced him to remain in the mansion at all times. He would go crazy if his brother did, which was another odd thing. Normally, he hated being out in the city, avoided it as much as he could.

But as they teleported back to the mansion, all Esher could think about was how he wanted to walk the streets.

Because he wanted to see her again.

When they landed on the porch of the mansion, the shoe rack was almost full, and he glared at Daimon.

His younger brother shrugged. "Don't kill me. It was Cal's idea."

Esher glared at the thick wooden door to his left, and the noise coming from inside the building, and the rain started again.

"Fucking hell," Ares grumbled from what sounded like outside, possibly in the courtyard. "It just stopped!"

Daimon pushed the door open to reveal Cal setting the long, low wooden dining table, and Valen arranging cushions around it with the help of Marek, and Keras pacing. Beyond them, through the open doors to the garden, Ares paused where he crouched on the gravel, and Esher canted his head at his older brother.

Tidying?

That wasn't like Ares. Normally, he lived in an apartment that looked as if Cal had swept through it in a mood, clothes and food cartons strewn everywhere.

But here he was, smoothing down the gravel so every damned piece was back in its rightful place.

Esher dialled his mood back, even when he wanted to demand to know what his brothers were all doing in the mansion just so he could watch them splutter excuses about everything from a family night to a meeting, to more flimsy ones like they had wanted to see his gorgeous face.

He appreciated the fuck out of one thing about this gathering.

Ares fixing the gravel.

The rest of it meant nothing, irritated him a little if he was honest, because it was obvious his brothers were only here to keep him occupied and protected. If they just happened to be in Tokyo on a night the gate was attacked, they also just happened to be on hand to fight either at his side or in his place.

He didn't need bodyguards.

Although he reluctantly admitted to himself that he would have behaved the same way if it had been one of his brothers in his situation.

But Ares fixing the mess in the garden—that was priceless. Gold. Smoothed the edges off his mood enough that he decided to stop the weather from raining all over his eternally-grumpy older brother.

Ares glanced up, his overlong tawny hair clinging in damp waves to his neck and cheeks where it had come free from the band he tied it back with, and then looked back inside at him. "Appreciated."

He nodded, showing his brother he felt the same way, and stripped off his coat, and went into the kitchen on the far left of the long room, beyond the dining table.

Daimon followed and parked himself against the cupboards behind him, hindering more than helping as they went to work on making dinner. He listened to Daimon drone on about the new building they were throwing up in Hong Kong, and how there wouldn't be any sky left soon, as he chopped vegetables. His brother liked to complain, but Esher knew he loved the view of the modern neon-lit skyscrapers from his villa on the side of Victoria Peak.

He pushed the vegetables aside, ignoring the fact that Daimon had managed to chop a single onion in the time it had taken him to chop countless vegetables, and focused on preparing the meat. Lots of meat. His brothers ate like pigs when he fed them. Probably because most of them didn't know how to cook, and relied on eating out or ordering in.

Cal's voice rose above the din in the other room, Keras's deep one joining it as he challenged him to a round, and Marek joked that he would pay to see Keras beat their youngest brother at his own game. Not likely to happen. Keras was awful at video games.

Where were Valen and Ares?

A soft female voice broke through the male ones, and Esher frowned, leaned back and glared into the room to his left.

At a slim mortal dressed in skin-tight black jeans and a halter-top, the hem of it lifting as she pushed a bright blue streak in her short black hair out of her cerulean eyes.

Eva.

Before he could ask what she was doing there, he spotted Megan beside her, the slender brunette's dark eyes bright as they talked while she tied her shoulder-length chestnut hair up.

Ares curled a protective arm around her waist, his all-black clothing a contrast to her jewel green t-shirt and blue jeans. Next to Eva, Valen grinned, the scar that ran down the left side of his jaw and neck pulling tight.

Both females were flushed, cheeks bright pink, and freshly showered by the looks of things. At least they had taken their shoes off this time.

He stilled as Megan gestured, waving her arms in a dramatic fashion.

Scowled.

Bruises littered her arms.

Had someone hurt her?

The thought that someone might have drew a startling reaction from him. He wanted to hunt them down and hurt them back.

Megan was family now.

His family.

Anyone fucked with her, they fucked with him too.

Even if she was mortal.

Eva spoke, arresting his attention, her Italian accent thickly lacing her words. "It was a good session. I think next time we should use some dummy weapons."

Eva was teaching Megan to fight?

Sensible, he supposed.

Mortals were weak, no match for a god or even a daemon.

The little female he had met hadn't even been able to fend off a human male. A powerful need filled him as that thought flowed through him, one that struck him silent and froze him in place halfway through drawing the knife down the chopping board to push the meat into the pot.

His mother's words swam in his mind, her voice whispering at him to forgive, and to learn to love the mortals again.

His own ones followed, a denial that had been nothing more than a growl at the time—that he would never forgive them and he would never love a mortal.

But he wanted to protect her.

His fascinating little butterfly.

CHAPTER 7

The day had turned hot at some point, and even with the panels opened to allow air to flow into his room, Esher hadn't been able to slip back to sleep after waking from a nightmare. Agitated from trying, he had left his room, grabbed a bite to eat and a glass of water, and had tried to focus on small tasks to keep his mind occupied. Trimming the topiary. Feeding the fish. Enjoying the cherry blossoms.

None of it had held his focus for long.

His mind had kept drifting, and it had always returned to one subject.

Her.

She had slipped into his usual nightmare, inserting herself into the scene, but not where he had expected her to be. Rather than being one of his tormenters, with the other humans, she had been the one bound before him.

They had tortured her to weaken him.

Gods.

Esher ran a shaky hand over his black hair and drew in a deep breath to calm his turbulent emotions as he walked, afraid that if they got the better of him Daimon would feel it and would realise he had left the safety of the mansion grounds.

He needed to walk.

He needed space.

He had been cooped up in the mansion for days now, and he was feeling stronger, more than able to take care of himself if anyone dared to attack him. Besides, it was daylight. Not even a strong daemon could withstand this much sunshine. They would be insane to try.

Strings harmonised with a brass section in his ears as he paused at a crossing and waited for the lights to change in his favour. Ahead of him, on the other side of the road, the park was busy, mortals soaking up the sunshine as they walked alone or with friends, and occupied the benches.

And seemingly every inch of the broad path beneath the trees.

Fucking Sundays.

Normally if he came for a walk in Yoyogi Park, he had it mostly to himself, with only a smattering of humans, a low enough number that it rarely bothered him.

But on a Sunday, it felt as if every person in Tokyo was trying to squeeze into the open spaces to enjoy the small pocket of nature.

He couldn't blame them, but that didn't mean he had to accept their presence.

The red light flicked to green on the other side of the street, and he edged away from the mortals as he crossed, giving himself at least three metres space. Better. Now he just had to survive the heaving park and find a quiet spot to make his own.

The solitude of the garden at the mansion was starting to look appealing again, but he needed this. He needed to see the modern buildings that crammed into every street around the park, and hear the noise of the trains as they constantly rumbled into the station, and the revving of car engines as they pulled away from the traffic lights. He needed it because it was miles away from how the world had been all those centuries ago, a contrast that reminded him that he wasn't there now. The world was different now.

His kind could move undetected through the streets, and even if a mortal witnessed something out of the ordinary, they normally kept it to themselves, believing themselves overworked, or even fucking blessed to have seen something they believed was supernatural.

It was a far cry from the days when just being different had been enough to raise an army or a mob against you.

Witches still had a bad rap though. Some of them for a good reason. He had met a few in his eight hundred plus years, and quite a number of them had deserved the reputation they had gained among mortals. The rest of them were alright, as long as you didn't cross them.

Even gods could be cursed.

He strolled down to the entrance of the park and looked up as he moved into the shade of the towering trees that stretched from either side of the dirt path to tangle together high above it. The air was instantly cooler, the perpetual shade keeping the heat of day at bay, and he breathed a little easier as it washed over him while the music danced in his ears and sunlight sparkled through the small gaps in the green canopy above.

Esher tugged at the collar of the grey t-shirt he wore beneath his dark blue linen shirt, wafting air down his chest, enjoying the coolness of it as it bathed his skin.

A human suddenly closed the distance between them, leaping into his path, and his hand twitched, a heartbeat away from backhanding them away from him when he froze, the awareness that blasted through him halting him in his tracks.

He lowered his blue gaze to the petite female standing before him, a vision in a black ruffled skirt, violet stockings, platform pink patent shoes, and a tank with a diamante skull on the front. Her bunches swayed as she canted her head and said something he didn't hear over the music pounding in his ears.

When she continued to speak, her enticing glossy lips shifting in a symphony in time with the rising strings, he gathered his wits enough to pull on the cord in front of his chest, tugging the buds from his ears.

"Sorry," he said in Japanese, and a pink hue climbed her cheeks. "Music was on."

"It's you again." Her smile hit him hard, reaching her dark chocolate eyes, and she rocked on her heels, her hands locked behind her back.

For a split-second, he considered leaving, and that was strange.

Because when faced with a human trying to interact with him without him prompting it, he always ignored them and moved on as quickly as possible, evading them.

But something about her, his little butterfly, soothed him and made him want to stay.

Calmed him more than being alone.

"How is your arm?" Her English words were stilted, lacking confidence that she seemed to exude when speaking her native tongue, and she nodded towards his arm when he just stared at her.

Esher looked down at it. He had finally taken the bandage off two days ago, had meant to discard it in the bin, but in the end had placed it in a box that stood on his chest of drawers in his room. Which was strange too. He had no reason to want to keep the used bandage, yet he couldn't bring himself to part with it.

"It's fine now, but thank you." He stuck to Japanese for her, wanting her to be comfortable so she would speak more with him.

Also strange.

Feminine giggling had her looking to her right and widening her eyes in a way that screamed 'shut up' at the pair of females sitting beneath the tree on a bench. The two females from the day she had been walking in Shibuya. Her friends?

They were dressed like her now, Gothic Lolitas enjoying a day off in the park. It was common on a Sunday in Yoyogi Park, the proximity of the Harajuku shopping street bringing them into the area.

"Wait." She held her hand up between them, and then hurried to her friends, grabbed a black satin bag with a crimson frill around the zipper and a collection of figures dangling from the strap, and a green drink in a clear plastic cup, and bounced back to him.

She sipped on the matcha iced smoothie as she walked away from him, her ruffled black skirt bouncing with each step, flashing a lot of leg. When she paused and looked back at him, a little frown wrinkling her nose, he followed, assuming it was what she wanted.

"I'm glad your arm is better. I was worried." She hit him with another high-beam smile as he caught up with her.

Had she really been worried about him?

She looked the type to worry about strangers, and she was studying medicine. She was gentle, and good, he could see it in her as she kept glancing at his arm whenever she had the chance, checking the wound that was barely a scar peeking out from beneath the rolled-up sleeve of his navy shirt, needing to see for herself that he was better.

He gazed at his boots as he carefully rolled up the lead of his earbuds and put them in his breast pocket. Her feet were tiny compared with his, her step light despite the thick two-inch platform soles of her shoes. With them on, she fell short of his shoulder. How small would she be against him without them?

"What's your name?"

When he looked up at her face, she covered her mouth, a blush staining her cheeks, and her obvious embarrassment over asking such a question outright, something out of place for a Japanese female, almost teased a smile from him.

"Esher." He had no qualms about her knowing it, mostly because she would offer hers in exchange.

"Esher. Esh-er... *Esh*-errr." She frowned as she tried to wrap her mouth around it, her chocolate eyes on the path in front of her. Those warm eyes lifted to him again, and another smile curved her lips. "I'm... you would say it... Aiko Matsumoto."

"It's a pleasure to meet you, Aiko." And it was. Strange.

She giggled. "How long have you been in Japan to know the language so well, but not learn the customs?"

"A long time," he countered, "but you didn't strike me as the sort to want to be given an honorific or go with tradition. I can call you Matsumoto-chan if you preferred? Or maybe Ai-chan?"

She laughed, the sound more entrancing than even the most beautiful classical piece, and shook her head as she waved her hand in front of her face. "No. Aiko is fine."

With that, she broke away from him, her eyes darting everywhere as she sipped her drink through the straw, taking in all the nature that surrounded her.

Its beauty was lost on him as he watched her, his little butterfly more stunning and fascinating than a few ancient trees.

She pirouetted to face him and walked backwards in front of him. "Are you alone in Tokyo?"

Esher shook his head, frowned when his hair fell down over his left eye and obscured her, and pushed it back, threading his fingers through the black lengths as he watched her. A flicker of sorrow crossed her features, but it disappeared when he spoke.

"I live with one of my younger brothers." Technically true, although Daimon was spending more and more time in Hong Kong recently.

Was she relieved because he didn't live with a female?

"What do you do? It's unusual for foreigners to live in Japan. Do you teach?" She moved back to beside him again.

Teaching was a common profession for foreigners, but the only teaching he did was to daemons and constantly trying to make them learn the lesson that he wasn't going to let them near the gate to the Underworld.

Still, he didn't want to be thought of as a teacher. It reminded him too much of long, boring lessons in the Underworld, listening to various tutors drone on about history and such, and it was leagues from what he really did.

"I work in defence." Also technically true.

Her eyes widened. "Like the military?"

He shrugged as they rounded a bend in the path, an enormous torii gate coming into view. "Something like that."

Aiko passed beneath the imposing wooden structure of two columns supporting a curved beam, with another beam intersecting them below it. Apparently, some believed it was lucky to walk through the gate that marked an entrance to a Shinto shrine.

Maybe if you were human.

Esher walked around the thick left column, feeling the power in the gate as he avoided it.

He never had gotten along with the local gods.

Even walking the sacred grounds on the other side of the gate as he was now was often enough to cause a mild sense of discomfort, as if someone was giving him the evil eye.

Aiko moved back to walk beside him, on his right this time, and her eyes fell to his arm. "You have so many scars."

Her words were soft, not meant to hurt, but they carved his heart open and he fell silent as he struggled against the surge of memories that collided with fragments of his nightmare. He battled them, trying to hold them at bay, but the nightmare had left him weak against them, allowing them to easily push at him, rousing his other side, the one that whispered to him and had him eyeing all the mortals passing by, a desire to punish them rising inside him. His gaze drifted over Aiko and back again. The need to leave warred with a desire to stay near her, to protect her from the cruel humans who wanted to hurt her, and him.

When they neared the grand shrine, she moved away from him, and he reached for her, his heart lunging into his throat. His hand stopped just short of her bare arm as she paused and looked his way, her eyes falling to it and then rising to his face.

"I just need to go inside. Come too," she said softly, warm light in the midst of the darkness raging inside him.

Esher shook his head and let his hand fall to his side, and she stared at him a moment, concern filling her eyes before she rallied, blinking and then smiling again.

"Will you wait?" She moved a step closer to him, and it struck him that she didn't want to part from him either, and gods, that was the strangest thing yet.

He nodded, still struggling with the tide of memories and unable to find his voice as they raged inside him, a violent sea he was trying to tame—for her sake.

She moved away from him, stopping at the rectangular stone trough of water beneath an elegant open-sided wooden structure topped with a sweeping copper roof that had gone almost turquoise over the centuries. She purified herself, and then walked towards the main gate of the shrine, an imposing wooden building that stood twice as tall as the walls around it, topped with the same sweeping copper roof, and he took a step towards the shrine, wanting to follow her.

An invisible barrier repelled him, and he bared his teeth at the shrine and the gods who forbid him to enter it.

He had tried to get them to manifest and explain themselves so they could understand each other, but the bastards refused to speak with him, merely repelled him whenever he tried to enter a shrine.

Unable to follow her, he drifted away instead, towards the shade of the trees where no humans ventured, and put his earbuds back in to block out the noise so he could focus on calming himself.

No matter how loud he made the music, the gnawing feeling persisted, thoughts of Aiko at the mercy of the humans filling his mind, tormenting him with images of her from his nightmare—bound and bleeding.

Close to death.

He closed his eyes, wanting to shut out the world, sure it was the presence of all the humans pushing him deeper into his memories.

It only worsened things.

Instead of seeing only flashes of images from his nightmare, he replayed the whole damned thing, felt himself bound and fighting against the ropes that bit into his arms, felt his throat burn as he screamed at them to stop and begged the bastards for mercy they refused to give.

The whispers grew louder, becoming chanting that goaded him into showing them no mercy in return.

They were ants, and he would crush them for what they had done to him.

Warm, soft fingers brushed his right hand, caressed the inside of his wrist where his favour mark stood pronounced on his skin, and chased the dark memories away, allowing light to filter back in and breath to fill his lungs again.

He slowly opened his eyes and looked down into Aiko's, and didn't stop her when she lifted her hands and carefully removed the noise-cancelling headphones from his ears. He stood mute, staring at her, shaken to his core and weak to his bones.

She smiled gently. "You moved, and your smile is gone. You're serious again."

Had he smiled for her? He might have. More than once, he had wanted to do it, and maybe he had, but he couldn't remember now. Everything was clouded again, just like the sky. Heavy black ones were rolling in, and he could feel the rain coming. It was partly his fault. His mood had taken a nosedive, speeding the weather that had already been building in the distance.

Strangely, he didn't want it to rain, was sure this time he wouldn't find any comfort in it, because it would separate him from Aiko.

But he couldn't contain his pain to stop it.

"I need to get out of here," he husked, his eyes darting over all the humans as they stared at him.

She nodded. "We can visit the teahouse by the pond. Hardly anyone goes there."

Sounded like heaven to him.

He followed her as the clouds reached them, blocking out the sun, and the wind picked up. They backtracked towards the torii gate, and she stopped a short distance from it, a frown marring her face as she stared at a sign and then at him.

"It's closed." She sounded as disappointed as he felt.

Esher didn't hesitate. He grabbed her waist with both hands, eliciting a squeak from her, and lifted her over the gate, doing his damnedest not to look at her panties.

They were pink.

She dropped to the leaf-litter on the other side, landing in a crouch, and moved aside. He vaulted the gate.

"I've never broken a law before." She looked more excited than upset about the fact she was breaking into the garden, and he didn't have the heart to mention that she was hardly going to get arrested for being in the garden when it was closed. Reprimanded maybe, like a slap on the wrist. This was Z grade breaking the law.

If she wanted to see A grade, he could show her.

She crept along the narrow path through the thick trees like a damned ninja, and he strolled past her, the need to reach the teahouse and the quiet driving him. If a human was around and spotted them, he would deal with them.

And for once, he didn't mean by killing them.

He would wipe their memory.

The elegant single storey wooden building came into view around a bend in the path, nestled with its back against the trees, and wood-framed glass panels protecting the walkway beneath the flared roof, and the paper panels of the interior.

It faced a sloping garden of grass and manicured bushes that resembled large smooth boulders in the dimming light, and beyond that a broad lake surrounded by trees.

The agony clawing at him began to fade as he looked at it, breathing easier as he sensed only Aiko nearby, and smelled the water and the coming rain.

The skies opened.

Esher grabbed her slender wrist and ran with her, trying not to pull her along as he raced towards the teahouse and used what little control he had over his powers and the weather to ensure not a drop of rain hit them.

When they reached the slight overhang above the exterior glass panels of the teahouse, she tucked closer to him, breathing hard. He released her, used his telekinesis to unlock the doors and pushed them back to allow her entrance. She stooped on the high stone step to remove her shoes, and then stepped inside.

Rain poured off the roof in torrents, cascading like a waterfall behind him as he removed his boots and followed her inside.

"I didn't get wet." She looked down at her clothes, over her bare arms, and then at him. Her expression shifted, going from one of surprise to something else, but if she noticed anything in his eyes, she kept it to herself.

She pushed aside one of the paper panels and stepped into the main, open room of the small building, her purple stockings a contrast to the creamy yellow of the traditional straw tatami mats. He trailed after her, catching her just as she moved to the front of the building and pushed more panels open to reveal the garden.

Aiko eased onto her knees in the middle of the open panels, her back to him, eyes on the outside world. The grass looked greener in the rain, and the surface of the lake had gone dark grey as it rippled with the heavy downpour.

It was beautiful.

She looked over her shoulder at him, her long black hair brushing her bare shoulders.

She was beautiful.

He moved towards her, drawn to her, unable to stop himself from closing the distance between them and easing onto his backside beside her.

Her dark eyes moved back to the world beyond the glass. "I like the rain... the melody it makes. It soothes me and seems to carry my troubles away."

When she glanced at him, he smiled at her, wanting to show her that he felt the same way.

She blushed and looked away again.

How old was she? Megan had mentioned something about being in her thirties, but Aiko appeared younger than her. Mid-twenties if he had to hazard a guess. She had barely seen this world, probably knew very little of its darker side other than what she had seen on the television or in movies.

Fuck, he wanted to keep it that way.

He wanted her to always be this pure, this full of life and hope, and happiness. He wanted to shield her from the darker things, to keep the light inside her shining.

Her blush deepened. Because he was staring at her?

Because they were alone?

That had a hint of colour rising onto his cheeks too. He wasn't sure he had ever been alone with a mortal, and he couldn't remember being alone with a female like this before either. He hadn't considered that when she had offered to take him to the teahouse, or when he had broken in with her.

He had just wanted to escape, to find peace, but he hadn't wanted to part from her.

"Do you feel better now?" Her gaze bravely came back to him. He nodded, and relief flitted across her face, and he wanted to say something, but could only stare into her eyes as she looked deep into his, and murmured, "You have eyes like the ocean."

He averted them, and she leaned towards him. His breath seized in his lungs as she moved closer to him, her soft floral scent teasing his senses, and her body heat brushed against him. He froze when her hand neared his right arm, his body coiling tight as he waited for her to touch the scars and mention them again, a spike of fear driving through him as he willed her not to do it, because he was finally on even ground again and he didn't want the memories to surface once more.

Rather than touching his scars, her fingers stroked a line over the trident mark on his inside wrist.

"The gods watch over you," she whispered, and he looked down at the favour mark, given to him at his birth by Poseidon, his uncle.

When she looked up at him, her face so close to his, he forgot what he had wanted to say.

He swallowed hard and stared at her, battling an urge that felt more powerful than any he had experienced before.

Not an urge to hurt her.

Far from it.

This urge had nerves sweeping through him, a fierce flood of them that left him shaking as he stared at her, his heart thumping against his ribs. She blinked slowly, shuttering her warm brown eyes, stealing them from view for a heartbeat before they locked with his again. Her pupils dilated, devouring her rich earthy irises, echoing the need that surged inside him.

He raised his hands, focused to stop the damned things from trembling, and swallowed to wet his parched throat as he edged them towards her, and finally, carefully, placed his palms against her cheeks.

Touching her.

Gods, she was warm, soft beneath his callused palms. His little butterfly, beautiful and delicate, trembling in his hands.

He meant to leave it at that, to release her and not risk anything else, but she shifted on her knees, placed her hands against the mats to support herself and brought her lips up to his.

Fire and lightning crashed through him as they brushed his, the sweetness of her lip gloss coating his, filling his mouth with the taste of strawberries, and hunger surged through him, a need to taste more of her, to completely devour her.

On a low growl, he slid his hand around the back of her neck and pulled her to him, his mouth claiming hers.

He tried to hold back his strength, the raging tide of his desire, the maelstrom of his need, but it was impossible as sensations collided and detonated inside him. He kissed her deeply, fucking clumsily if he had to admit it, his hand shaking against her nape as he stiltedly swept his lips across hers, and she blissfully responded, her own actions as jerky as his, as if desire was overcoming her too, stealing control.

Sweet gods.

The rain lashed down, striking the roof so hard that it shook the wooden structure, the weather turning more violent as a new need surged through him.

He wanted to touch her.

Intimately.

A growl tore up his throat, a need to go through with that driving him to obey, and he barely leashed it, holding it back as he broke away from her lips, shock rippling through him.

He couldn't believe he wanted to do such a thing, or the ferocity of his hunger to be inside her.

A mortal.

Esher stared at her, breathing hard, fighting to restrain himself and tamp down that need. She looked at him, lips swollen and red from his brutal kiss, her pale skin darkened beneath his palm by the pressure of his grip. He had been rough with her, but she hadn't pushed him away, and she still looked at him as if she wanted to kiss him again, as if what he had given her wasn't enough for her either.

Fuck, she was beautiful as she looked at him like that, something soft and almost affectionate in her desire-hazed eyes, her shy smile luring him in together with the way she was hiding nothing from him. Her warmth and honesty, her openness, drew him towards her, and he wanted to drown in her.

That scared him.

What the fuck was he doing?

It was dangerous for her to be around him, but he couldn't let her go. He needed her. He couldn't have her though. All it would take was the moon's sway to get to him, or his memories to overwhelm him. It would take only a momentary slip in control and he would hurt her. His powers had always been strong and as unpredictable as the ocean, and since what had happened to Calindria, he had been more than dangerous.

Aiko was strong, he could see that, but it was a strength of spirit, not of body. She was delicate, and he wanted to protect her because of it. He wanted her to always smile.

He released her and eased back, the hardest fucking thing he had ever done, and looked at the world outside. The rain was so heavy that he couldn't see anything beyond the glass. His fault.

As much as it killed him to stop, he needed to find some calm again, some sliver of control.

Because he didn't want to hurt her.

Gods help him, he didn't want to fuck up and be the one to kill that smile of hers.

CHAPTER 8

Aiko watched the rain, fascinated by it as it began to ease again, growing lighter the longer Esher was silent beside her. She could feel his struggle, that he needed time. Time she would give to him.

As the garden began to appear through the haze of the rain again, she wished her nerves would ease like the weather, and fade away. She couldn't believe she was sitting in the teahouse with Esher, that they had broken into this place. She knew she should feel bad, or it should feel wrong, but being around Esher only ever felt right.

Her lips still tingled from his kiss, her body alive with sensation as he sat beside her, his hands planted behind him to support him and his long legs stretched before him, the black denim wrinkled around his ankles where it had been jammed into his boots. His eyes remained locked on the world beyond the glass, and while he was close to her, she felt as if he was miles away.

She wanted him to come back to her, wanted to kiss him again, and feel his hands on her.

She glanced across at him.

He was on edge though. She could feel it in him. Something was troubling him. The same thing that had been troubling him when she had left the shrine and found he had moved away from it?

The moment she had stepped over the threshold of the shrine, she had sensed the gods' unease, and something that had felt like anger to her, and part of her had felt certain that it had been directed at Esher.

Because he was a foreign spirit in their land?

An intruder?

She moved onto her backside and drew her knees up to her chest as she studied his noble profile, focusing on him and trying to understand the sensation that swirled in her chest as she watched him. He didn't feel like a threat, but she could sense the darkness in him, just as she could feel the power of the tides surging through him.

He was one with nature, very in tune with it, and it awed her.

Her grandmother had been a shrine maiden in a small village high in the mountains, and she had always amused Aiko with stories of how she had danced with the gods and seen the spirits. Aiko had thought they were only tales, but after her grandmother had passed, and she had visited the shrine to pay her respects, she had felt the presence there and had been able to see a faint shimmering in the air that moved as if it was something crossing the space before her.

Over the years that had followed, her ability had developed, growing stronger, and now she could clearly sense spirits and had even seen one or two manifest themselves for her. It was the reason she visited the shrines as often as she could, so she could pay her respects to them.

Esher was different though.

He was flesh and blood. He lived and breathed, and even smiled at times. He was stronger too.

Was he more of a god than a spirit?

And if he was a god, was he benevolent or destructive?

His head tilted towards her, his gaze coming to meet hers, and in it, she saw a tempest building.

Or was he both?

She was tempted to peer deeper into his feelings, but she had learned not to abuse her powers. Her grandmother had always warned her that people were private creatures, and that she should treat them with respect. She hadn't heeded that warning until she had pried into the private feelings of some girls who had befriended her in high school, and had discovered they were only pretending to be her friend. Now, she read people the old-fashioned way, and Esher's body language told her enough about his feelings.

He was struggling with himself.

"I should go," he muttered as the weather turned worse again, the rain so heavy it was almost deafening as it struck the teahouse roof.

She wanted to ask him to stay, but there was something about his eyes that made her hold her tongue. They were haunted, shadowed, and she could feel fear in him. Unease. She could feel something else in him too, that what he wanted and what he said were two conflicting things, the complete opposites to each other.

He didn't want to go.

His pupils dilated, gobbling up the stormy blue, and his breath came faster as he stared at her, his chest heaving against his navy shirt and grey t-shirt.

The source of his unease hit her, and she knew how to soothe it.

She moved back onto her knees, coming to face him, and didn't hesitate as she framed his face with her hands and kissed him.

He was quick to respond, his trembling hands instantly claiming her hips and tugging her against his hard chest. She shook too, nerves getting the better of her as she thought about what she was doing, combined with the desire that flared inside her, startling in its intensity.

She drowned in it as he fell backwards, taking her with him, and she landed on his chest, his hip pressing against hers. She moaned as he rolled with her so she was on her back beneath him, his right knee wedged between her thighs and his left arm locked beneath her head like a pillow, caging her against him.

His kiss softened, his breath shaking against her lips as he skimmed his right hand down her arm, his touch surprisingly light, sending shivers of fire chasing over her skin. When his hand closed over her left breast, she arched into his touch and couldn't hold back.

"Don't stop this time." Those words leaving her lips in a breathless rush, both a plea and a demand in them, shocked her and her cheeks burned.

She could feel he was going to pull back and look at her, so she grabbed him around the back of his neck, his short black hair tickling her fingers, and pulled him down to her and kissed him.

His tongue plunged between her lips and she opened for him, couldn't breathe as he palmed her breast and sent wave after wave of hot tingles rushing through her, lighting her up inside. She moaned and he joined her, his left hand clutching her shoulder as he kissed her, his heart pounding as quickly as hers. He squeezed her breast again, and then hastily released it, and she wanted to chastise him but he stole her voice as he tugged her tank down to reveal her pink bra and brushed his thumb over the curve of her breast.

He groaned as he pulled away and looked at what he was doing, and she shivered as his hips surged forwards and his hardness pressed against her right thigh. Her heart skipped a beat as she gazed up at him, a little dazed, finding it difficult to believe she was doing this, letting him touch her like this, and that she wanted more.

His hand shifted so his palm sat over her heart, and she squeezed her eyes shut, her brow furrowing as his fingers slipped beneath the satin of her bra and brushed her nipple, sending a thousand volts shooting down to the apex of her thighs.

His mouth seized hers again, swallowing her next moan, and she trembled and arched into his touch, lost in the sizzling sensations as they whipped through her, an assault she wasn't sure she could withstand.

He angled his head and kissed her deeper still, his touch growing rougher as he shifted his hand over her stomach. When she realised where he was heading, when she felt his trembling worsen, his nerves rising, she couldn't hold back the moan that bubbled up her throat.

Couldn't stop herself from letting her left knee fall aside, revealing the apex of her thighs for him.

His low groan as his hand sank beneath the frills of her skirt to brush her satin panties had another shiver tripping through her, the burn of desire growing fiercer as she kissed him harder, unable to hold herself back anymore. He moaned as she surrendered to her need and plundered his mouth with her tongue.

He bucked against her thigh, rubbing himself along it, stirring her desire to dizzying new heights, filling her mind with a delectable vision of them entwined. She bit down on her lower lip as he slipped his fingers beneath the elastic of her underwear, her breath coming faster as he eased back and his gaze scalded her face. She struggled to open her eyes as his fingers drifted lower and his first caress sent her hips shooting upwards and a white-hot blast of heat through her. When she managed to get them open, they locked with his.

A storm raged in them, the blue of his irises swirling with the tempest, speaking to her of his need, of how this was affecting him as deeply as it was her. She let it sweep her along as she gave in to him, to the need that broke over her like a wave and carried her away. She rocked against his hand as he fondled her, finger teasing her pert bead, intense sparks of fire skittering through her in response to each one. With every stroke and press, the storm in his eyes built and the rain grew heavier, deafening now as she surged towards release.

She trembled as she gripped his shoulders, lost in his eyes as he sank his hand lower and eased a finger into her. Her need spiralled higher as she imagined him inside her like that, stretching and filling her, moving inside her. She needed that. Needed him.

She bit her tongue to stop herself from asking it of him though, aware that his fear hadn't gone anywhere, lingered even now as he lowered his gaze from her face to his hand where it touched her. He looked as if he was having a difficult time believing they were doing this. She was. She had never been intimate with anyone, had never felt the desire to do it, but she couldn't control herself around him.

He drove her wild, had her gripping his shoulders so tightly she feared she might hurt him as she reached a crescendo.

He stroked her deeper, rubbing the pads of his fingers over her flesh as he withdrew, and she shattered.

His gaze leaped to her face as she broke apart, a cry leaving her lips, so loud she feared someone might hear over the noise of the rain, and she was sure that he growled as he lowered his head and pressed his brow to her cheek, and his cock to her hip. It kicked and throbbed in time with each quiver of her body around his fingers, in time with each wave of bliss that rolled through her and crashed over her, stealing the breath she had managed to catch each time.

Awareness grew inside her as she lay with him, coming down from her high, and it birthed a need so powerful she couldn't deny it.

He needed release too.

She wanted to be the one to give it to him.

CHAPTER 9

Esher shifted onto his knees when Aiko moved, reaching for his jeans. "You don't have—"

He lost the ability to speak as she unbuttoned his fly and gritted his teeth as her small hand found his aching shaft. He hissed and tipped his head back, the heat and softness of her too much for him to bear. He couldn't stop himself from rocking against her, and as she stroked him, gaining confidence, he began to forget about his need to stop her.

Almost started to enjoy it.

Until a dark snarl burst from his lips, torn from him by a black urge to get her damned hand off him before she could harm him. He took hold of her wrist and pushed her back as he leaned away from her so she couldn't touch him again, controlling her in the only way he could without hurting her.

Without leaving.

He had to leave.

Her dark eyes fell to his hips, to the hard outline of his cock in his black trunks, and then lifted to his side. The desire that had been in them faded, replaced with concern, and a frown wrinkled her nose.

She reached out with her free hand and he shook as she edged it towards the scar above his left hip, visible now that he had leaned back, his shirt and t-shirt riding up his stomach to reveal it.

"Esher," she whispered softly, and he felt her worry. "I thought your wound was on the other side."

Her eyes darted to his, and he realised that for all his attempts to keep the stab wound from her the night they had met, she had been aware of it. But she hadn't mentioned it. She had been aware of something else too—that he hadn't wanted her to know.

He hadn't wanted her to be aware of just how vulnerable, how weakened he had been.

Easy to attack.

He stared at her. She hadn't attacked him though. She had tended to him, had taken care of him, had been gentle and kind. She wasn't a threat. She wasn't. Not even now, when he felt more vulnerable than ever. She didn't want to hurt him.

He sucked down a deep breath, released her hand and told himself again that she didn't want to hurt him, that her concern was genuine and she wasn't out to take advantage of his vulnerability. She wasn't like the others.

His gentle little butterfly.

He looked away from her, unable to look at her when he did this, exposed a vulnerability for the first time in forever, because he feared his other side would use it to seize control, to whisper poisonous things about her that he knew were untrue, but that would be his undoing.

56

Esher carefully lifted the right side of his shirt and t-shirt, revealing the faint mark where the blade had plunged into his side just below his ribs.

She frowned at it, and then lowered her gaze to his left side, to a wound that was still dark pink and healing. "Were you hurt again?"

He shook his head. "It happened before we met."

She lifted her eyes to his. "But the other wounds healed."

"I… it's healing… but I don't want to think about it." Because whenever he thought about it, it filled his head with doubts, gave rise to fear that felt as if it was choking him.

He looked at Aiko and realised he didn't want to think about anything right now.

He just wanted to feel.

He just wanted her.

He wanted to continue this madness they had started, wanted her to drive him out of his mind so he didn't think about what she was, because he couldn't think about it. If he did, he would end up hurting her.

Gods, it was the first time he actually wanted to be driven out of his mind.

Only he didn't want to be driven right into his other one.

He wanted that part of him silenced, gone, locked away so it wasn't a danger to her.

It had been when he had been touching her, lost in her, and it had been when she had touched him, before he had foolishly thought about what she was and what he was doing with her.

Fuck thinking.

It was overrated.

Feeling was better.

He took hold of her hand, shook only a little as he guided it towards his tight shaft, and gripped the waist of his trunks with his other hand. He needed her hand on him again, needed to feel it on his flesh this time. Now that he had started down this path, he didn't want to go back, didn't want to stop. It had been centuries, too long, since anyone had touched him, his experiences of it so few that he could no longer remember what it had felt like.

But Aiko's touch had been bliss.

He wanted more of it.

He wanted to forget everything else existed. There was only her in this world, and this moment.

He lifted the waist of his trunks, freed his cock, and moaned as he felt her gaze on him and looked at her. Her dark eyes were round, pupils blown with desire that ricocheted through him too, had him hot and needy, his shaft growing harder at just the thought of her touching him.

The rain grew heavier, the scent of earth filling the strained air in the teahouse.

Before he could make her touch him, her hand moved forwards, taking his with her.

He groaned and rolled his hips as her fingers skimmed down the length of his cock, from blunt tip to his balls, an exploratory touch that almost had him bursting.

She shuffled closer, the scent of her perfume mingling with the heady aroma of her release, filling his lungs and pushing all rational thought to the back of his mind.

"Gods," he muttered beneath his breath as she took him in her hand, encircling his cock with her fingers, her skin hot against his.

He released her and leaned back, couldn't stop himself as she moved her hand on him, up and down, her touch light but devastating. He alternated between closing his eyes and staring at her, torn between a desire to do both as she gained confidence again.

Her eyes remained rooted on his shaft, dark with need he could feel building inside her again, and he wanted to know her thoughts, needed to see if they matched the images coming to life in his mind, a vision of making love with her.

She brushed her thumb over the exposed crown, sending heat rolling down the length of his shaft to his balls, and he groaned. Bliss. Divine.

Her nerves rose, and he mustered enough brain cells to ask what was wrong, but before he could utter the words, she leaned over him and placed her free hand on his thigh. Her breath washed over the head of his cock, followed by a tentative flick of her tongue, and her hair brushed his stomach.

Gods.

He moaned as she tongued the crown, as she wrapped her lips around him and took him into her mouth, his hips bucking up to drive him into her wet heat. Some more noble part of him said to stop her, but fuck, he didn't want her to stop. He wanted to stay right where he was, wanted to feel her mouth on him like this forever.

Pure pleasure rocked him as she explored him with her mouth, taking him deeper. She was hot and wet, like molten fire scalding him, and he tried to hold back. It became impossible when she circled the base of his cock with her hand and began moving on him, sliding her hand up and down in time with her mouth, making sure every inch of him felt the bliss of her caress.

A moan rolled up his throat, and the urge to thrust deeper blasted through him, so powerful he lost himself to it, had his hand tangled in her pigtails before he was aware of what he was doing. He gripped her as she bobbed on him, pushing her back down whenever she retreated. She moaned, the muffled sound sending a wave of heat through him, a hit of pleasure that rivalled the feel of her mouth on his cock.

Outside, the rain fell harder, growing heavier in time with the pleasure surging inside him, rising swiftly to crash over him.

He grunted, each exhale a broken sound as his body rocked, writhed of its own will, searching for release.

When it finally broke over him, his entire body quaked from the force of it, his hand tightening in her hair as he held her in place and jetted into her mouth, a strangled shout lodged in his throat.

As the haze of pleasure dissipated, and he grew aware of the world again, embarrassment swept in to crash over him as fiercely as his climax had.

He released Aiko and hastily covered himself as she sat back, her cheeks pink, flushed with the pleasure he could feel in her.

"Sorry for doing that," he muttered, feeling like a monumental dick in the aftermath of it, when it had felt so damned good at the time.

"Don't be." Her cheeks looked as if they wanted to grow a shade or two darker as she shyly added, "I liked it."

His did.

Damn them.

Esher buttoned his jeans, and stared at her, reeling and trying to take in what had just happened, marvelling at her as she fixed her appearance and kept glancing at him, little looks that stirred something inside him, in the region of his chest, and had a single thought flowing around his mind.

He didn't want to hurt her.

He would sooner harm himself than hurt her.

Her face finally flushed darker, and she awkwardly smoothed one of the ruffles of her black skirt.

"Sorry," he murmured and dragged his eyes away from her, aware that his staring was the reason she felt embarrassed and nothing else. Not what they had done. Gods, that had felt as natural as breathing. "I haven't... this is... I haven't been with anyone like this in a long time. I'm not sure what to do... but I feel as if I should do something."

Except feel like a royal idiot.

Fuck, could he sound any more like one?

"The rain stopped." She managed a smile as she pointed towards the glass front of the building.

Esher looked there, his eyebrows rising high on his forehead as he uttered, "Oh, would you look at that?"

He cringed. What the hell was wrong with him? Acting all 'what a surprise' and 'how odd' when he had been aware the rain had stopped dead the second he had climaxed.

He had a feeling she was aware of it too.

There was something he hadn't been aware of though. He frowned at the sliver of sky he could see between the bottom of the roof and the trees across the lake. It was clearing now, revealing darker blue that signalled evening was approaching.

"It's getting late," he said and her eyes landed on him again, and when he looked across at her, a feeling struck him, a need that mastered him. He didn't want to take her home, didn't want to part from her yet. He needed her still. So he put it all out there, risked what felt like everything in that moment. "Are you hungry?"

She seemed to consider it for a moment before nodding. "There's a nice restaurant near here."

"I live close by." The words left him in a knee-jerk way, bursting from his lips as the thought of sitting in a crowded restaurant sent darkness surging through him.

He didn't want to let it come over him, not because he might hurt her, because he realised now that was impossible, but because he didn't want her to see that side of him.

He didn't want to frighten her away.

He realised he might have been a little too forward when she just stared at him. After what had happened to her on the train, she had every right to find it hard to trust another male. His first thought was to tell her that she could trust him, but could she really?

While he didn't want to hurt her, couldn't hurt her, he couldn't say the same of his other side. If it took control, he wasn't sure what he would do to her.

"Forget it… I'll walk you home." It was the more sensible course of action, especially when he considered that it would be dark soon, and the gate might need defending or a Hellspawn might want him to open it.

Or worse.

His brothers might show up at the mansion, popping in right in front of her to scare the shit out of her.

The thought of them doing such a thing had his darker side surging to the fore, but it wasn't his other self this time. It was the darkness born of his father's blood, a dangerous brand of possessiveness that was almost intoxicating, had him feeling a little hazy and vicious as he stared at Aiko, a need to wrap his arms around her and keep her all to himself beating in his veins.

He would kill anyone who tried to take her from him.

Including his brothers.

That thought left him cold, threw a bucket of icy water over the dark desire to possess her, and shook its grip on him, giving him back control.

He would never harm his family.

"Esher?" Aiko's soft voice pierced the dark veil of his thoughts and he blinked and looked at her, found her kneeling closer to him, the press of her hand light against his cheek. "I would love to have dinner with you."

He stared at her, fighting to take in her words and make himself comprehend what she was telling him. She wasn't talking about going to a restaurant. She was talking about dinner at his place.

She was trusting him with her safety, trusting that he wouldn't hurt her, and gods, he would do his best to live up to that trust.

He would show her that she had been right to place her faith in him.

He grinned at her.

"I'm a great cook."

CHAPTER 10

The sky had cleared by the time Esher stopped in front of a small gatehouse in the middle of a long white wall topped with traditional grey ribbed tiles and scrubbed a hand around his neck, rubbing at the short hair at the back of his head.

Aiko looked around at the street, including back the way they had come, towards the distant park, and then returned her gaze to him. Had he changed his mind and no longer wanted her to see the place he called home? It had to be close, because they had been walking a while, far longer than she had expected based on what he had told her.

Did he live in one of the box-shaped two storey houses that were set a way back from the white wall, giving the traditional building space and respect that it deserved? The houses around it were worn and basic, but he didn't need to be ashamed if he lived in one. They were as simple as her family's home, and what most of the population of Japan lived in now.

For an agonising moment, she thought he might insist on taking her home instead.

But then he heaved a sigh that stretched his dark shirt tight across his chest, let his hand fall from his neck and turned not towards the dull grey houses that were jammed close together, but towards the imposing wooden gate opposite them.

She could only stare as he pushed the heavy gate open and looked back at her, something that resembled nerves or possibly fear in his eyes.

If he thought she was going to say something negative about the fact he lived in a traditional house, or judge him for having such an expensive home, then he was mistaken.

But, *damn*, it was impressive as she stepped through the gate he held for her and came face to face with a sweeping mansion fit for an emperor. White panelled walls supported the width of the grey tiled roof, and dark aged wood enclosed the elegant entrance of the house in the centre of the building. The grounds between her and the door had been lovingly manicured, with topiary spotted around the gravel that bordered the entire front of the mansion and continued around the sides to her left and right, and beautiful cherry trees and maples on the grassy areas in each corner.

On either side of the path in front of her, ancient stone lanterns stood proud, almost as tall as she was, and to the left of the house, a covered walkway linked it to another smaller building.

Esher shifted foot to foot beside her, and she felt his unease ripple through her.

She wasn't sure she had ever seen a home so beautiful, so perfect. She had stayed with her family at inns that had looked similar, but this place felt different. More serene. Quieter.

Soothing.

Esher drew his hand over his face, glanced at her, and then closed the gate and led the way towards the house. He kicked his boots off at the entrance, one at a time, and set them on the rack. It was strange to see him do such a thing, and her earlier comment about how he hadn't learned the traditions of her land came back to haunt her. He knew them, and he respected them.

She joined him on the porch, removing one shoe and placing her foot on the wooden deck before stooping to remove her other one. When she handed them to him, he set them down next to his and stared at them, a glimmer of conflict in his eyes that disappeared when he blinked.

He opened the door for her.

Aiko followed him inside and stopped dead as the size of it hit her.

It was enormous.

The room spanned almost the entire length of the house, with a long polished traditional wooden dining table occupying most of the mats to her left, and a strangely out of place and modern group of couches and armchairs set up to her right, facing a huge flat-screen TV.

Esher kept moving forwards and she peered into the room beyond the dining table. A kitchen. Walls had been built around it, separating it from a wooden walkway that led to the smaller building she had seen outside. That walkway branched to the right too, past paper-panelled rooms that were closed off.

When light flooded the room, she looked at Esher and her breath left her in a rush.

He stood on a covered walkway beyond the panels he had opened, staring out into a garden that had her re-evaluating her use of the words serene and beautiful for the exterior garden she had passed through to reach the house.

This was beautiful.

She moved forwards, her feet carrying her towards the elegant formal garden enclosed by the three sides of the house, filled with pale gravel and perfectly positioned topiary, and mossy boulders. It turned to grass near a broad rippling pond that flowed beneath the wing of the house to her right, and a traditional red wooden bridge crossed it at a narrow point, leading her eye to the huge cherry trees in full bloom on the other side, where the garden undulated in a more informal series of hills and valleys.

Esher looked over his shoulder at her as she reached him.

She could feel him waiting to hear her opinion and whether she liked it.

"It's stunning," she breathed, a little lost in traversing it with her eyes, fascinated by finding things she had missed at first glance, hidden paths and lanterns, and a seemingly ever-changing vista as the sun moved, sinking lower. "How did you come to live here?"

He shrugged, but it was stiff. "Father bought it and it's been in the family ever since."

He didn't want her to ask more, but she wanted to know, couldn't see such an impressive house without needing to know more about it and the man who lived in it.

"You live here with only your brother?" She hoped he didn't find that question too intrusive.

When he almost smiled, she relaxed a little. "I do, but I have other brothers."

He turned away, heading back into the house, and as much as she didn't want to leave the garden, could spend forever looking at it and never grow tired, she wanted to know more about Esher.

She found him in the kitchen, rifling through a large modern refrigerator.

"How many brothers do you have?"

His voice came from the other side of the silver door. "Two older, and four younger."

Six brothers.

She couldn't imagine what it was like to have such a large family, but she felt a little envious as she tried.

"Are they all like you?" She moved to the other side of the kitchen so she could see him and rested against one of the wooden cabinets.

He poked his head out of the refrigerator, his handsome face etched in thoughtful lines, and frowned as he closed the door and set some vegetables down on the work surface. "We're all quite different really. Like fire and ice. Some more so than others."

He hadn't quite understood her question, but she didn't correct him as he set to work. She had meant were they all spirits, or possibly gods?

But he answered that question in a way, revealing one thing to her.

They were all elementals.

She took up a knife, and a chopping block, and moved to stand beside him at the cramped workspace. He didn't stop her when she took the carrots from him and started peeling them. He just stared.

When he had been staring at her for so long she started to feel self-conscious, she paused and glanced up at him.

"Sorry... I just always do the cooking. The only time I get help, it's under duress. My brothers are lazy." He picked up an onion and peeled it. "They prefer to sit in the other room waiting for me to prepare the meal."

He didn't seem bothered by that.

She leaned back, looked through to the other room, and then went back to chopping carrots. "I'd rather help."

She had the feeling that pleased him as he started cutting up the onion and followed it with a few potatoes, and then some beef. When she was done with her carrots, she set them aside and looked around at the small kitchen. Three rice cookers sat side by side on the counter opposite. Big appetites?

She supposed seven men would eat a lot of food.

While Esher finished up with the ingredients, she hunted through the cupboards for the rice and got it on for him.

"I was going to do that," he said as he took a large pot from one of the bottom cupboards and set it on the stove, and the note in his deep voice told her that this time he wasn't happy.

Because he wanted to impress her with his cooking?

She hadn't missed the pride that had shone in his eyes when he had announced that he was a competent cook.

"I can't find the sauce packet." She closed the final cupboard and looked over her shoulder at him.

He stared at her, blue eyes wide, a flicker of confusion in them. "Sauce packet?"

"For the curry." She presumed they were cooking curry rice anyway.

He chuckled and shook his head. "*Sauce packet.*"

Aiko could only watch as he opened a cupboard above the stove and pulled out an armful of different glass jars and metal pots, and proceeded to open them, measuring different herbs and spices out onto a plate.

So maybe he was a better cook than her, because she always used store bought sauce for her curry. In fact, she had never cooked it from scratch before and was sure she had never known anyone who did either.

When the curry was bubbling on the stove, and smelling mouth-wateringly delicious, she took some plates and bowls and set the table for him, picking the end nearest the door, where she had a view into the garden. It was growing close to sunset now, and the garden was even more breathtaking as the light turned golden and warm.

She hadn't realised she had paused to soak it in until Esher appeared in front of her, a pot of curry in his hands. She smiled at him, helped him arrange the heavy pot on a stand, and filled a glass with water for him as he went back into the kitchen, returning with the rice.

He chose the seat that had its back to the garden, and she knew he had done it on purpose, giving her the view.

"Thank you." She took the plate he offered to her, and the tempting smell of curry filled her nostrils, making her stomach grumble.

He filled his own plate, and set it down, and as she gathered a spoonful of both rice and curry, he stared at her, waiting again.

She popped it into her mouth, and her eyes widened as her taste buds lit up.

She covered her mouth. "Oishii!"

Delicious.

Esher smiled, the sight of it almost as delicious as his cooking. "You look like an anime character."

She shook her head. "I'm being serious. You're a good cook."

He averted his gaze and muttered, "I've had a lot of time to practice."

Aiko studied him as he fell silent again, enjoying her food and the time with him. She wasn't sure how long spirits or gods lived, whether they were truly immortal or only lived longer lives than humans. He looked no more than eight years her senior, but he could be thousands of years old.

Her mother had married her father and there was a fifteen-year age difference between them, and her grandmother had been almost twenty years younger than her grandfather.

She wouldn't care if there was an eight-year or eight-thousand-year age gap between her and Esher.

She felt connected to him. Deeply.

He glanced at her as he ate, and she had the feeling he wanted to speak but was struggling to settle on a topic.

"You'll have to share the recipe with me." She pushed her empty plate aside and smiled for him, hoping it would soothe him and help him find his voice.

"You can fight me for it." The twinkle in his clear blue eyes said he wasn't being serious, and it was strange to see this side of him when he had only ever been deadly serious around her.

His expression shifted as that thought drifted through her mind, turning awkward again, that conflict reigniting in his eyes as he grabbed the plates, rose to his feet in one fluid motion and walked into the kitchen.

Why did he find it so hard to be relaxed around her?

Why did he find it so difficult to trust someone?

She could feel trust was the source of his conflict, stirred feelings in him that he didn't like, or wasn't sure how to cope with them. Was it because he was a spirit or god, and she was human, and he wasn't used to talking with her kind?

She had encountered spirits at a shrine in the mountains once, and they had turned vicious when she had tried to communicate with them, chasing her from the sacred grounds. They had manifested enough to throw barbs at her, callous words that had cut her because they had been the first spirits she had encountered that had been violent towards her and a foolish part of her had started to believe all spirits were kind and gentle and enjoyed sharing their world with humans.

Aiko's gaze tracked Esher as he walked back to the table, and as he cleared the other dishes, following him back and forth between the kitchen.

He was troubled again.

She switched her focus to the garden and the outside world when he disappeared into the kitchen for the final time, and she wasn't surprised to see clouds threading the horizon. It was going to rain again if she didn't do something, and as much as she enjoyed the rain, she couldn't find it soothing or peaceful when she knew it stemmed from his turmoil.

When he stopped by the table again, she looked up at him and smiled as she found a subject he could talk with her about, one that was bound to take his mind off his troubles.

"Will you show me around? The house is beautiful, but I would love to see the grounds too." She was the one who waited this time, a little anxious to hear his answer, heart filled with hope that he would consent to it and wasn't about to mention taking her home.

She didn't want to go home.

Not yet.

Home was quiet, cold, and here she felt warm.

With Esher.

He tunnelled his fingers through his wild black hair, shoving the long lengths away from his eyes, and looked between her and the garden. His chest heaved with a deep sigh, and her hope faltered, cold already settling into her bones again as her fear that he was going to take her home caught hold of her.

When he finally spoke, heat washed that cold away. "Alright."

She pushed onto her feet and joined him when he jerked his chin towards the other end of the room.

"You've already seen the kitchen." He led her across the tatami mats to the couches that surrounded the wooden coffee table and television. "My brothers voted for this. I was against it at first, but now I think I spend half my time here, watching the news and documentaries."

Shows about real life, not fantasy. He preferred to experience the world in this way?

Or perhaps he merely wanted to know more about the one outside of Tokyo.

She wasn't sure whether he was bound by anything. Many spirits and gods were, forced to remain in one location, starved of information about the outside world. She had told a few about current events, and sometimes talked to herself when she visited shrines, just in case any spirits and gods in the vicinity were interested.

She pointed to a long, low side cupboard set against the far wall, beyond the cream furniture. "You have movies too."

It was stacked full of DVDs, and games too.

He hiked his shoulders. "I watch them sometimes. Mostly when my brothers are visiting."

"And you watch anime." When he looked at her, she added, "You said I was like an anime character, so I guessed you watched it."

He ran his blue eyes over her, quickly at first, but they slowed as he took her in, making her feel self-conscious again as he lingered on her ruffled black skirt and then her legs.

"You look like one," he muttered, voice low and rough, and heat flared in his eyes, banked but burning, igniting her own desire as she stood and let him look at her, didn't hide from him as she normally would from a man.

She liked the feel of his eyes on her, the way he looked at her as if he wanted to devour her, or possess her.

As if she was special.

Precious.

"You look like a J-rock star." She held back her smile when he frowned at her. "Your hair, the way you tuck the bottoms of your jeans into your boots, even the scarf you like to wear."

He scowled now, but there was no real anger behind it.

"I like it." She twirled away from him, felt his gaze boring into her as she headed towards the corridor, and found him staring at her, that heat breaking through in his eyes, as she spun to face him again.

Heat that said he liked the way she dressed too.

"What's this way?" She had never been so forward in someone's home before, knew it was rude to take the lead rather than wait to be shown, but she felt relaxed in the ancient house with him.

At home.

He trailed after her, fire still burning in his eyes. They were brighter now, the blue turning tropical as he hit the wooden walkway with her.

He gestured to the rooms to his right and her left as she walked backwards in front of him. "Each of my brothers has a room here. I should probably keep you out of them. Both wings are just our bedrooms."

She spun away from him and pointed to the far end of the wing. "And yours is above the pond."

He stopped walking.

His voice was a low growl. "How did you know?"

Aiko looked over her shoulder at him.

Surprise danced in his eyes, but a ripple of darkness marred it, turned his handsome face too serious for her liking and had a warning arrowing through her that told her to say something to soothe him.

She turned and took a step back towards him. "It was a guess."

Sort of.

She had figured that a water god would like to sleep close to his element.

His irises darkened, turning inky as his black eyebrows dipped low above them. "A *guess*?"

She didn't like the bite in his tone, or the way it sounded like an accusation.

She nodded and forced herself to take a step towards him rather than away. He wasn't a danger to her.

The way he eyed her said he might be, his expression savage and irises dark as he studied her, as if he was trying to see through her to the truth and wasn't going to be happy if he discovered it was as dire as he was imagining.

"It was just a guess." She spoke softly, held her hands up between them and edged towards him.

His eyes turned stormy and clouds rapidly multiplied overhead.

The scent of rain laced the thick air.

"You weren't spying on me?" he snarled, and she might have laughed and thought he was teasing if he hadn't looked so serious.

She shook her head. "No. I saw the way you looked at the lake at the teahouse, and the way you were looking at the pond after you had opened the doors when we arrived here… and I thought you would like the room that was set over the water."

The truth.

As much as she would tell him, because she wasn't sure how he would react if she mentioned that she could tell he wasn't human like her. His accusation rang warning bells in her mind that said he would react badly right now. He thought she had been spying on him.

Because he was finding it hard to trust her.

He was looking for a reason not to and telling him that she knew he was different to her was a sure-fire way of making him believe he couldn't trust her, that she was out to harm him or do something terrible to him. He would think everything they had been through, everything they had shared, had been a lie to manipulate him into letting her get closer to him. He wouldn't understand that she didn't care he was a god or a spirit, or whatever he was.

He wouldn't understand that she just enjoyed his company and felt a connection to him.

Felt attracted to him.

"I need to do something. Look around the garden." His voice darkened in time with his handsome face as he took a hard step towards her. "Do *not* venture too far or open any of the rooms."

She nodded, and he pivoted on his heel and stalked away from her, heading back towards the main room of the house. She remained rooted to the walkway, her pulse pounding as she tried to let his change in demeanour roll off her back and not let it cut her.

Maybe she had been right about him, and he was both benevolent and violent.

He moved past the open doors in the centre of the building, his head bent, gaze locked on the smartphone in his right hand.

He was calling someone?

About her?

She hadn't done anything wrong, but she had the feeling he thought she had, that he honestly believed she had been spying on him for some nefarious reason or was out to hurt him.

When he disappeared down the corridor that led to the other, smaller building, and didn't reappear, she blew out her breath and looked around her at the beautiful mansion. His snarled words echoed in her head, warning her not to open any of the rooms.

Or venture too far.

He wanted to know where she was at all times.

Didn't he trust her?

After what they had shared, that stung.

But what hurt her most of all was the feeling that she had been a fool, stupid for believing what they had shared had meant something to him, crazy for thinking it was going to become something.

And an idiot for trusting him.

He wasn't a man.

But he certainly acted just like one.

CHAPTER 11

Esher had lost track of Aiko at some point during his tense texted conversation with Marek that had resulted in his brother telling him at least a dozen times that a daemon couldn't breach the wards that protected the mansion.

Unsatisfied with that answer, Esher had asked whether one of them could bring a daemon into the grounds.

As far as Marek knew, they would have to mark a daemon with a specific set of counter-wards in order to bring them past the walls.

And as far as Esher knew, Aiko didn't have any such wards on her, and since only he and his brothers, and his father, knew which wards had been used in protecting the mansion, a daemon couldn't mark themselves with the counter-wards anyway.

It should have set his mind at ease, but now he couldn't find her.

And worse, Marek had mentioned telling their brothers and sending some back up because he was sounding jumpy.

Esher had sent a two-word response to that.

Fuck off.

He had then focused his power to reach his brother halfway around the world in a remote area near Seville and made it rain just on his villa. Marek had got the message loud and clear, and had sent a text back saying he wouldn't tell a soul, but only if Esher stopped bringing a biblical flood down on his home.

Esher had flipped the switch on it and had gone in search of Aiko, expecting to find her where he had left her.

Only she hadn't been there.

Something had flipped inside him on seeing that.

Something that had birthed a fierce, almost desperate need to find her, to know that she was still near to him, that she hadn't walked out of the mansion grounds.

Away from him.

Gods.

Fucking gods, he needed to find her.

Her fucking shoes had been gone from the front porch, a sight that had stabbed him in the gut and left him bleeding worse than any blade.

But she couldn't be gone.

Could she?

His own words haunted him, an accusation that sounded like a royal dick move now that he was looking back at it, but at the time the dark side of himself had been at the helm, had bellowed at him that she knew which room was his because she had been sent to harm him.

She was the daemon due to attack him.

He felt like a fucking idiot for latching on to that and running with it.

She wasn't a daemon.

If she had been one, she would have made his gut swirl and he would have smelled it on her, the unmistakable coppery stench of a daemon giving her away.

She was just a human.

One who had trusted him, had taken a leap today that had been as monumental as the one he had taken too.

Only he had ruined it by taking another leap afterwards, this one a massive leap to a conclusion that left him feeling guilty as hell.

He stormed over the red wooden bridge that curved above the pond, and followed the path on the other side, his boots loud on the gravel. She had to be in the garden. That was the reason her shoes were missing. She couldn't have left him. He didn't want her to be gone.

But fuck, he could understand if she was. He had to deal with his special brand of crazy on a daily basis and found it annoying enough. She had done nothing to deserve being hit with it.

His throat tightened, lungs squeezing as his heart laboured and the need to find her grew more desperate with each passing second, every minute that trickled past and left him empty handed.

Alone.

Beyond the wall, the sky burned in shades of pink and orange, fingers of clouds caressing the sunset and blazing gold.

It was beautiful, but he felt nothing as he looked at it, frantic with a need to find Aiko.

He chuckled mirthlessly at that.

When had he become so desperate to be with a human?

He despised them, wanted to destroy them, to make them suffer as they deserved.

Had he made Aiko suffer?

He stopped, eyes fixed on the setting sun as that question chilled him to his marrow.

Had he?

He pushed trembling fingers through his hair, tugging it back from his face, and gritted his teeth as the answer assaulted him, an onslaught of feelings that left him shaking. Weak.

He had.

He had and it killed him.

And if she had left him, then fuck he deserved it, because he didn't deserve her. He didn't deserve her light, her smiles, her laughter or her sweet company. He deserved this coldness, this loneliness devouring his soul as he watched a sunset that could have been magical with her beside him, but instead felt colourless and dead to him.

And, gods, he didn't understand any of it. Not the way she had trusted him, or how she had given a piece of herself to him, or the fact he wanted to spend time with her, craved her company as fiercely as he craved war with her kind.

He still despised humans. Still wanted them to suffer.

He would never forgive them, or trust them. He would never learn to love them again.

But he would make an exception for her.

He just hoped she would make an exception for him too.

He focused on the road outside her family's clinic, bringing it into his mind so he could teleport there to find her.

Movement on the very edge of his vision had him letting go of the power building inside him and a wave of emotion crashing over him that was so powerful it moved him, had him trembling with relief and a thousand other feelings, ones he didn't want to understand because he feared where this was leading him.

"Aiko," he breathed, deep voice rough, scraping low over gravel.

She turned her head towards him but didn't move from her perch on the smooth grey boulder beneath the huge blooming tree, looking like some sort of fairy as she sat with her knees tucked up to her chest, enfolded in her arms, and cherry blossoms spiralling down around her like snow to land on her bare skin and lace her hair.

Her dark eyes drifted away from him, down to her knees, and it was a gut-punch that he deserved.

"I'm sorry," he murmured and followed the twisting path to her, sank to his knees on the grass beside the boulder, and looked up at her.

She refused to look at him, and his frustration got the better of him, had him rising on his knees to frame her face with his hands and make her look at him.

"Was I wrong to trust you?" she whispered, each word cleaving his chest open a little more.

He slowly shook his head. "No... but I was wrong not to trust you. I have... I've been burned before. It makes it hard for me to..."

Explain for one thing.

He never talked about what had happened to him, not even to his brothers, or his parents. He had bottled it up inside him, his burden to bear.

But now there was a piece of him that wanted to share that burden, all in the hope it would lift some of the weight from his shoulders, and it shook him that he wanted to do it with her, a human.

She awed him by lifting her hands and placing them over his on her face, her touch gentle and soft, so far from what he deserved after how he had treated her.

"I thought you had gone." He couldn't hold back those words and couldn't hide the pain that thought had caused him as she gazed down into his eyes.

She canted her head, and moved her right hand to his cheek, her beautiful face soft with understanding and a touch of concern. "I found this tree... and it was so beautiful in the sunset that I wanted to enjoy it. The blossoms are so fleeting."

Like human life.

He felt the gravity of that as he looked at her.

They were weak. Breakable. Vulnerable. The slightest thing killed them. Images of her caught up in all the ways she could die, everything from something as simple as an accident to a disease, rampaged through his mind, provoking his darker, more possessive nature, rousing it until he was restless with a need to hold her, to shield her from the world and keep her safe from it.

Safe with him.

"Esher," she said softly, her fingers brushing his cheek, playing on the crest of his cheekbone and down to the hollow, and then to his jaw, her eyes locked on his, holding him immobile as the warmth and comfort they held crashed over him. "The sunset is so beautiful."

Don't spoil it.

He felt those words in hers, as clearly as he could feel the clouds building above him, born of a desperate need to control something which he knew he had no command over. He was a god, but not a god-king. Only Zeus had power over life and death.

And his father.

The ground trembled, a warning from his father that he knew the course of his thoughts.

Beneath his knees, flowers bloomed, blue Himalayan poppies sprouting up around him.

His mother.

He got her message loud and clear—ignore his father.

It also made him realise something. She was aware of Aiko, of the change in his temperament the little human had caused. Both of his parents were.

Which meant Hades had to be aware that he was at the mercy of the blood he had given him, and that now that his need of Aiko had been roused, he would move all the realms to keep her at his side.

He breathed through his pain, pushed out the terrible thoughts clouding his mind, and focused on his little butterfly as she shifted on the rock to face him, setting her feet down on either side of his knees.

Poppies bloomed around them too, tried to entwine with her shoelaces and creep up her leg, but she didn't notice.

"You never finished our tour." Aiko's gentle voice drew him back to her, helped the clouds scatter and let light flood back into his heart.

He pushed onto his feet, hesitated only a moment before taking hold of her hand, and led her towards the nearest wing of the house, away from his room. She was silent as she walked beside him on the narrow path that wound between mossy boulders, blooming azaleas, and under trees.

The one she had been admiring was one of the wards, a tree that had been in that spot since before Hades had built the mansion. His father had constructed the walls around two more trees of similar age, using their strong connection to the earth to strengthen the wards he had then placed on them.

Aiko's gaze leaped to him as he led her across a series of stepping stones set into the gravel that surrounded the house. When she stopped near the broad stone step beside the raised wooden walkway, he stooped and removed her shoes for her, helping her up onto the step. She waited as he removed his boots, and he placed them down at the corner of the walkway, near the courtyard.

She went to walk that way.

He caught her wrist and tugged her in the opposite direction. "You've seen the courtyard."

Her eyes grew a little wider.

"There's more?" Understanding dawned in her gaze. "The smaller building. I saw it from outside, and I wondered what it was for."

He hadn't intended to take her there, but the thought of leading her to that place, of stripping her bare and bathing with her in the huge stone pool had him wondering whether she would consent to such a thing.

There was still a little sunset left.

She led the way again, and he wondered if he would always follow her, trailing behind her so he could watch her, could see every fascinated glance she gave to the world, every smile that reached her eyes and lit up her face.

When she rounded the corner, she stopped so abruptly he almost collided with her.

The walkway continued down this side of the wing, joining with the wooden open structure at the far end and the white wall opposite to enclose one of his favourite spaces in the house.

"You have a zen garden." Her chocolate eyes leaped to his, the surprise in them matching that in her voice, and he wanted to smile at her.

Her gaze traced the swirling lines of gravel that swept around cragged rocks and always made him think of tides, flowing endlessly, unstoppable.

Beautiful.

He did smile when she shot him an incredulous look.

"Who looks after it?"

"Me. Who else?" He caught hold of her wrist again and risked a look back at her as he led her towards the bathhouse. "You wanted to know what was in the smaller building?"

She leaned to one side and glanced past him, towards it, a flicker of nerves emerging in her eyes as they landed on the building, with its thick wooden columns that supported the tiled roof, allowing the front to remain open to the elements.

Together with the huge bath.

It poked out from beneath the cover, half in and half out of it, so someone could laze in it and see the whole of the sky if they wanted it.

Steam curled from the surface of the water, kept at a perfect temperature by the thermal spring below the house that they drew it from, rich with minerals that made a good soak absolute heaven.

When they reached the bath, Aiko crouched and brushed her hand through the water.

"You must have been in plenty of hot springs before." He stilled when she looked up at him, the pretty blush on her cheeks telling him that she might have, but she had never been in any of the mixed ones.

He wasn't sure when he had implied they were going to bathe together, but now it was in his head, it was all he could think about. His eyes leaped between hers, a need to see what she was thinking tugging at him, making him restless.

Did she want to bathe with him?

Did he want to bathe with her?

Really want it?

It wasn't the thought of being naked around her that had his nerves rising. It was the fact that if he stripped off, she would see the extent of his scars. He wasn't sure how he would react if she pressed him about them. She had mentioned them before, and thinking about how he had gotten them had stirred his darker nature, and he had come close to ruining the moment.

He wanted to press her to promise not to ask, but it would only make her more curious, more liable to stare at them.

"I could just take you home." He could also just cut his wrists and let himself bleed out right now. Taking her home would have the same effect.

He felt sure he might die without her.

She shyly shook her head, stealing a little piece of his black heart.

"I'm not going to try anything. We'll keep our underwear on." He sounded like a damned virgin again, all jittery and awkward.

She nodded again, but remained where she was, staring at the water, and he wasn't sure whether she wanted to bathe with him or bolt for the hills.

Either way, she clearly needed a moment to overcome her nerves, and so did he, so he took himself off to the washing area and stripped off his shirt and t-shirt, and then his jeans and socks. When her eyes landed on him, burning into him, following his every move, it was damned hard to focus on washing himself with the soap and water.

She finally moved, taking measured steps towards him that screamed of nerves, but each one was more confident than the last, as if she was defeating her fear, and by the time she reached him, she looked as courageous as she had in the moment before she had kissed him.

Gods, he wanted to kiss her again.

He handed her the water scoop and cloth and made a fast exit instead, his nerves getting the better of him. Her gaze scalded his back, making his muscles tense in response as he waited for her to say something about the scars.

She turned away instead.

He released the breath he had been holding, stepped down into the hot water, and held back the groan as he sank into it, the heat of it instantly melting his tension away. It was hard to keep his focus off her as she moved around behind him, hard to shut out the images of her stripping off, and the ones of her washing herself as water sloshed around.

Esher grabbed one of the white cloths from the side of the tub, soaked it and placed it over his face as he groaned, his cock as hard as stone in his trunks and demanding attention.

Her attention.

This had been a bad idea.

Made all the worse by the images popping into his head, visions of his brothers appearing while Aiko was half naked in the water with him.

He growled under his breath, pushed the cloth up onto his hair and glanced over his shoulder to make sure she wasn't paying any attention to him, and held his hand out. His mobile phone shot into it, his powers proving themselves more than handy once again, and he fired off a group message to his brothers.

In a bad mood. Steer clear of Tokyo. I need a quiet night in.

Hopefully that wouldn't raise too many questions, or concerns, as it wasn't the first or thousandth time he had sent a similar message, but for good measure, he made it rain in every city his brothers protected as he tossed his phone on the deck beside him.

The sky above Tokyo remained beautifully clear though.

He started when Aiko's foot appeared close to him, a delicate thing that was a work of art.

One he found himself scanning for even a sign of a ward.

Fucking arsehole.

She wasn't a daemon. She wasn't out to hurt him. She trusted him, and he could trust her.

She dipped into the water, so it washed over her shoulders and made the ends of her black hair wet, and then sighed as she drifted away from him on her back, her pink satin panties and bra a shade darker than before.

"This is heaven." She loosed another low sigh of satisfaction.

It certainly was.

He couldn't take his eyes off her as she floated on the water. It was a struggle to keep his thoughts off the fact she was in his element, water he had command over, and it was all over her, in private places he wanted to explore.

He gritted his teeth and kicked that urge out of his head. He was not about to turn a perfectly nice bath into a scene out of some hentai anime involving a man manipulating water to be intimate with a woman. Not his scene.

Still, he was a little jealous that the water was getting to enjoy her more than he was, so he coaxed it a touch, just enough to make her float in his direction. She frowned when she turned and started drifting towards him, and rolled onto her front, wrecking his attempt to casually get her closer to him.

He offered her a scrap of cloth.

She shook her head. "I never get dizzy from hot springs."

Not a bad thing, because if she got all faint and woozy, he would probably lose his shit when worrying about her.

She smiled at him, another high-beam one meant to devastate, and he frowned and reached for her, wanting her closer.

She placed her hand in his and the moment her fingers closed over his palm, he gripped her and pulled her towards him. She shrieked, water spraying everywhere as she surged towards him, and giggled as her free hand planted against his bare chest to stop her from slamming into him.

Her laughter died as her eyes met his.

"You're missing the sunset," he husked.

She moved a little closer, her palm shifting to the spot over his heart, and her eyes fell to his mouth.

"I'll catch the next one," she murmured. "I like this view better."

And then her lips were on his.

CHAPTER 12

Esher flipped the last pancake out onto the plate, put it on the tray with the glass of juice and the maple syrup, and switched off the stove. Breakfast was served.

Although it was almost evening now.

Gods, he grinned at that.

After a long, lazy make-out session in the bath that had stopped at kissing, which had been more than enough for him because he couldn't get enough of kissing her, he had spent the whole night talking to Aiko, telling her small things about himself and listening to her talk about her family, and her studies, and then just lazing with her on the walkway in front of the entrance to the courtyard garden, watching the moon as it rose.

Savouring the fuck out of the moment.

He still wasn't sure how it had happened, how he had gone from wanting every mortal on the face of the Earth dead at his feet, to needing one of them with a ferocity that shook him and left him feeling off balance.

When the sun had broken the horizon and he had realised Aiko had fallen asleep resting against him, he had scooped her up and carried her into his room, set her down on his bedding and covered her.

Had even tucked her in.

Part of him had been tempted to stay with her, watching over her, breathing her in as he stole every second with her. In the end, he had convinced himself to go and let her rest, not wanting to disturb her.

Now the sun was close to setting again, she was bound to wake soon, and he wanted to surprise her with breakfast.

He lifted the tray and carried it through the main room, towards the walkway to his left that would bring him to his room, and Aiko.

The thought of seeing her smile at him when she woke to find him waiting with breakfast made the corners of his lips curve into a semblance of a smile.

It dropped off his face at the same time as the tray dropped from his hands when he spotted someone standing on the walkway outside his room, reaching for the panel to slide it open.

As the plate and glass smashed on impact, he launched himself at the male, closing his hand around his throat as a black need to protect Aiko blasted through him.

He hauled Daimon off his feet, twisted and came damned close to throwing him across the garden and starting a fight.

But his fucking hand froze up, ice covering it, sticking it to his brother's inky roll-neck sweater.

"I told you about doing that," Daimon growled, his eyes glowing almost white in the fading light, and Esher noticed the hand his brother had locked around his wrist.

He marched Daimon towards the main room of the house, because if he couldn't throw the bastard for coming close to intruding on Aiko, he could at least make sure his brother kept his distance from her. "And I told you all about wearing shoes in the house."

His hand burned, the cold searing him as viciously as any fire could have, but he didn't release his brother until he was as far from Aiko as possible. He set Daimon down on the mat near the front door and grimaced as he moved his fingers, cracking the ice covering them.

Daimon let him go, making the whole process easier, but no less painful. "You alright?"

"You startled me. You did get the text I sent?" He checked his hand over as warmth returned to it, relieved to find no permanent damage.

His element allowed him to withstand Daimon's ice a little, enough that he didn't get frostbite as easily as most of his brothers if Daimon touched him, but handling Daimon for an extended period of time was dangerous and liable to end with him losing his hand. He didn't want to have to grow a new one.

Everyone left that sort of shit to Valen, who had tested the extent of their regenerative abilities once. It had been disgusting watching his hand grow back.

He glanced towards the corridor that led to his room, at the broken glass and china scattered across the wooden walkway, and the ruined breakfast, and wanted to beat his brother to a bloody pulp for it.

"I did." Daimon rubbed at his throat, bent and tugged off his boots, setting them down at the door on a black mat Esher had been forced to add when his brothers had all started forgetting they were meant to take their damned boots off. "But something is moving. It hit New York and swept through Seville. We think it's coming this way."

"Fuck." He scrubbed a hand over his mouth, feeling sick to his stomach as his mind leaped forwards and filled in the blanks. "You think it might be…"

Esher really didn't want to think about the fact a strong daemon was due to attack him. He had forgotten all about it, had lost himself in Aiko, and it had been bliss, but letting himself get caught up in her and forgetting his duties, forgetting the enemy that was heading his way, was something he couldn't let happen again. He had a duty, and he was damned well going to fulfil it.

He crossed the room to the kitchen, grabbed a glass, filled it with water and practically inhaled it, needing it to calm his nerves as thoughts of the daemon coming his way brought memories of the wraith on their heels, shaking him. He was stronger now and he wouldn't let the bastard get the jump on him again, or the bitch who was targeting him.

He wouldn't.

He lowered the glass and stared at it. "You ever wish we could drink something stronger?"

Daimon's silver-white eyebrows knitted hard above now ice-blue eyes. "It's best we don't. The whole thing with Valen made it clear that it's too dangerous."

"What thing?" Valen appeared, thankfully not in his usual flash of lightning, because the house was made of wood and Aiko was sleeping, and if either of those two things came to harm or were upset in any way, he might just douse his brother.

"Your booze habit," Esher bit out with a cold smile and Valen toed off his boots before he could say anything.

His brother's face darkened, the scar tissue down the left side of his jaw and neck pulling tight as he flashed teeth at Esher. "Piss off. One drink."

Valen flipped him off, as if to emphasise the single drink with a single digit.

"And you destroyed a nightclub." Daimon eased past him, careful not to touch him. While Esher and Ares could withstand a little of Daimon's ice because of their element, Valen would be in danger of hypothermia or worse.

Valen turned to track Daimon as he grinned and pushed his blond hair from his eyes. "You didn't see what happened before that."

Esher couldn't hide his interest as he followed his two brothers towards the couches. "What happened before?"

Valen sidled closer, his voice a low purr as he wriggled his fair eyebrows. "Black box dirty dancing, nasty and rated triple-x adult for my pleasure."

Daimon caught the intrigue that must have been written across Esher's face, because he scowled at Valen, and then at him.

It didn't stop Esher from saying, "So it was good for a while?"

Ares's hand slapped down on his shoulder as he appeared behind him, nearly crushing him with a combination of strength and searing heat that licked along his bones. "Little brother, I'll hand you your arse if you so much as sniff alcohol."

He frowned at the smouldering patch on his grey t-shirt when Ares released him and moved away. "It was just a question."

At least Ares had had the decency to take his footwear off before entering the house.

Keras and Cal appeared next, his oldest brother looking as if he had gone ten rounds with a gorgon. Waiting for their enemy to reappear was taking its toll on him too, but it wasn't like Keras to show it. Normally, his brother appeared immaculate no matter what, but his black shirt had creases and he looked as if he needed another twenty hours sleep before the dark circles beneath his eyes went away and the dullness left his green irises.

Marek shot Keras a concerned glance as he appeared. "Thanks for the help."

Keras shrugged it off, yawned and drew his hand down his face. "They were stronger than anticipated."

"What happened?" Esher hated being out of the loop. His brothers had been in danger, and he should have been helping them, not sitting idle in Tokyo.

Because he had sent a message warning his brothers away.

He had lied to them to keep them away so he could be alone with Aiko, and they had needed him but hadn't called on him, had all been involved in a fight against strong foes and had left him on the bench because he had asked them to give him some space.

The gods only knew how he would have been able to live with himself if they had been hurt.

"Is it the moon playing on you?" Keras said, a wealth of concern in his tired green eyes as he looked across the group to Esher.

Esher's heart felt as if someone had poured lead into it as he thought about that. "It's two days until a full moon, and it's closer than normal. Not a perigee, but close."

Everyone exchanged glances, ones that had the guilt churning in the pit of his stomach growing more turbulent as he considered what that meant.

He wouldn't be able to leave the mansion.

He would have to remain within the barrier set out around the grounds, and someone would have to protect Tokyo in his place. He had risked venturing out during a previous full moon and had ended up attacked by the wraith because he had been distracted, so drawn to the moon that he had let his guard slip.

When the moon was full and closer to the Earth, it became harder to control his darker urges, and for the sake of the humans, he had to remain inside the mansion grounds, shielded by the wards.

When the moon hit a perigee, well, he hated those days.

They required more than just a few wards to keep him contained.

"We can deal with the gate," Daimon offered, and Esher nodded, thankful for their help. "Even if something is coming this way, we'll find a way to keep the city safe."

Because they couldn't risk letting him out.

The female daemon coming after him wanted him alive for some reason, he knew that much, had heard Daimon and the others talking about it one night when he had surprised them by attending a meeting while he had still been recovering from the wraith attack.

"It'll be daylight in New York when it's dark here. I can handle it." Ares shot him a reassuring smile.

"We missed Cal's birthday." Valen this time, and Esher knew what was coming next. "We should go out, tonight… come on. It'll be fun and we need to blow off some steam."

"Didn't we just blow off steam?" Ares put in, his face set in his standard scowl.

Cal grinned, his blue eyes bright with it. "I'm game."

Keras sighed. "Must I remind everyone two gates were recently attacked by a powerful group of daemons? It's not the time for fooling around."

Marek hiked his wide shoulders. "There's no evidence to suggest the attacks are related to our true enemy. I've been monitoring gate and daemon activity, and a few of the larger, older factions of daemon are making plans, mobilising forces, because they know we're being targeted. They want in on the action."

"Or in through the gates," Ares grumbled, his expression blacker than Esher had seen it in a long time. He folded his arms across his chest, pulling his black t-shirt tight across his shoulders, and rubbed his thumb across his lower lip as his dark eyebrows dipped. "Daemons would view this as a great chance to break through the gates and enter the Underworld. We have our hands full waiting for whoever is behind the calamity and dealing with them whenever they appear."

That made a sickening sort of sense to Esher, and judging by the looks his other brothers exchanged, they felt the same way, and none of them were happy about it.

This wasn't something they had anticipated. It was hard enough being on guard all the time, waiting for their enemy to attack them, without adding in other daemon factions wanting to try their luck.

Fuck, he could just imagine how his father would react if a group of daemons were able to slip past them. He had banished them from the Underworld for a reason, a damned good one. The wretches didn't deserve to live in a place ruled by a king they had revolted against and attempted to overthrow.

"So we're not going out?" Cal looked disappointed, his eyes growing greyer as he frowned at them all and the tips of his blond ponytail beginning to lift and flutter as if stirred by a breeze.

Esher caught the look Keras gave him, one that silently screamed of how they couldn't risk letting him outside of the wards just in case the attacks had been arranged by the wraith and his cohorts.

"Go. I'll stay here. It's fine." He didn't want to go out anyway. His brothers had disturbed his plans, and any moment now, Aiko was going to wake up.

He wanted his brothers gone before that happened.

Gods, he could just imagine the questions that would happen after he handed every single one of them their arses for just being in her presence.

"I suppose I could take a break from research." Marek looked himself over, taking in his dirty dark linen trousers and torn shirt. "Although, I might have to change. I can take a shower and grab some clothes from my room here."

The thought of Marek showering when Aiko was in the house had Esher close to growling.

Ares pulled a face. "I take it we can't bring the ladies?"

"Boys night out." The dark edge to Cal's stormy blue eyes warned he was serious about that. "I want it to be like old times. Just us guys. Esher included. I'm not accepting a no from you."

Esher tensed when the thunder of tiny feet came from the corridor behind him and all of his brothers looked there, several of them shifting into a fighting stance as the air thickened, anticipation rolling through it.

Aiko squeaked as she skidded to a halt on the threshold of the room.

He was quick to back towards her, and even quicker to growl when she pressed against his back, hiding there, and he reached around behind him to touch her.

She was only wearing her underwear.

"I heard noises and when I saw the broken plate…" She burrowed deeper into his back as she spoke in rapid Japanese, and he glared at each of his brothers in turn, even as the words she didn't say melted his heart.

She had been worried and had wanted to protect him, had come running to his rescue.

"Are you alright?" he whispered in Japanese, weathering the curious looks and moving to shield her whenever one of his brothers dared to try to peek around him.

"I'm dying of embarrassment." She pressed her palms to his back. "Your brothers?"

"The very ones." As much as he loved them, he was considering killing all of them.

Valen and Calistos moved a step closer to him, and Daimon side-stepped, trying to get a better view.

Esher twisted and flashed teeth at all of them, the desire to snap and lash out at them growing stronger with each passing second. He could almost feel the trident on his wrist darkening, and his eyes turning stormy with it.

"Is she Hellspawn?" Daimon leaned to his right, and Esher backed off a step, towards the corridor, his other hand claiming Aiko's hip to keep her hidden behind him.

With her pressed this close to him, it would be difficult for his brothers to be able to sense what she was.

Gods, he hoped her grasp of English wasn't good enough to understand everything his brothers were saying. He didn't want them to frighten her with talk of things that were not of her world. Not yet. Not until they had grown closer, and he felt sure she wouldn't run away from him.

"A goddess?" Marek frowned, but thankfully didn't move. At least one of his brothers had the sense not to provoke him. "Is she the reason you were asking all those questions about the wards? She's definitely not a daemon."

Everyone looked at him. Esher cursed him for making the whole situation worse.

"That was meant to be a secret." Esher glared at him. "I hope you enjoy the rain you'll be getting in Seville for the next month."

Marek huffed, looked as if he wanted to argue as he crossed his arms across his chest, and then as if he was chewing on a wasp as he remained silent.

"Is she a Carrier like Megan?" Ares hadn't moved either, probably because he had been struck dumb. His older brother's face was a blank mask, and Esher had the feeling that he knew the answer to that question.

Knew what Aiko was but found it so incredible he couldn't comprehend it.

"A vampire?" Valen offered.

Marek glared at him. "She'd better not be."

"Kyūketsuki… chigau yo!" The Japanese words for 'vampire… you're wrong' were muffled against his back, Aiko's normally gentle voice holding a wealth of denial. She wriggled and poked her head under his left arm, and spoke in English. "I am a woman, not a demon."

His brothers instantly sobered, all of the amusement fleeing their faces as they stared at her, and Esher glared at them as the rain started outside, pouring hard on the roof as his temper got the better of him and a need to drive his brothers away before they started questioning her raged through him.

Aiko's softly spoken words froze him in place though.

"I'm not like Esher. I'm human."

His eyes slowly widened in time with his brothers' ones, and he needed to turn towards her and see her face when he asked her the question blazing in his heart, but he would expose her if he did, and then he would have to kill his brothers.

Because no one but him got to see her this naked.

"You know?" Those two words hung in the air for an excruciating moment before her voice broke the silence to answer him.

"Yes." She wrapped her arms around him from behind, settling her hands on his stomach, and gods, it was a relief. "You're a water spirit... or a god... a good one."

"How did you know?" Damn, he wanted to see her, needed to look into her eyes and see that she really did know that he was a god, not like her, and she had always known.

He needed to see that what he was wouldn't come between them.

She rested her cheek against his back, and spoke gently in Japanese, each word soothing him like a balm. "I knew the moment I met you, but I think I truly understood what you are when we were in the teahouse... when I saw the ocean in your eyes and felt the power of the sea surging through you."

He was glad none of his brothers could understand her language as well as he could.

Daimon grinned, and said in perfect Japanese, "Really? I bet you felt it surging into you too."

Aiko gasped. Esher growled, and the only thing stopping him from grabbing his brother and hurling him across the room was the fact he would expose Aiko by moving.

"Not a damned word." He shot his brother a glare, hoping Daimon would see in it all the painful ways he would make him suffer if he dared to tell any of his brothers what she had said.

"Leave them alone," Valen bit out, and when everyone turned surprised looks on him, he sighed. "Leave them alone or I'll rip off your heads and leave you to bleed to death in a gutter?"

Cal, Marek and Ares grinned at that, and even Esher had to admit he was more comfortable with this side of Valen, the violent and tempestuous one that tried to turn everything into a brawl and preferred to tell the world to go to Hell.

Aiko tugged him backwards, towards the corridor, using him as a shield. He went with her, because he didn't want his brothers seeing her either. When they reached it, her hands slipped from his stomach and he mourned the loss of her touch as she broke contact with him. As the distance between them grew, it pulled at him as fiercely as the moon, calling him to her.

"So we are definitely going out. All of us?" Cal wasn't going to let it go now that someone had suggested it. Not even the fact that Esher had a human in the house, an almost naked one at that, had distracted him from his mission to party.

Which was a relief in a way. Hopefully, his other brothers would just roll with it too.

Ares's earthy brown eyes locked on Esher, golden sparks lighting them up. "Let me get this straight. You lied to us last night so you could get a little some-some?"

"No." Esher definitely hadn't lied for that reason. "It wasn't like that... but... I'm sorry. You needed me and I wasn't there. You should have called. You know I would have fought. You all know that, right?"

He shifted his gaze to each of his brothers in turn, needing to see on their faces that they did know he could be relied on, that he was as much a part of this fight as they were, and nothing would change that.

"We do." Keras's deep voice was smooth, commanding, sounding much like their father. "But I wouldn't have called on you anyway. It's too dangerous. It was better you stayed within the wards."

Cal's face twisted in grim lines, his eyes glowing brighter as he bit out, "But we are still all going out tonight?"

Cal had always been one for a party, was happiest when he was lost in a crowd, or swept up in a fight, or risking his damned neck on his motorcycle. He drowned himself in sensation, and Esher could understand why he felt the need to do that.

To forget.

In a way, it was Cal's way of coping. Esher had his music as a calming influence. Cal blew off steam to control his pain, used adrenaline to crush it.

But now wasn't the time to go off half-cocked looking for a fight or getting caught up in dancing.

"Maybe we shouldn't," he put in, and Cal glared at him, but he weathered it and continued, "With everything that has happened."

Cal looked to Keras

Their oldest brother nodded. "We will go out, all of us, but only because we are all together. Esher will be safe."

As if he needed protecting. He schooled his features so his brothers didn't see how much that pissed him off. He didn't want to go out either. He wanted to stay in the house with Aiko. Keras's expression said it wasn't going to be an option though, and he had the feeling his brother's change of heart had something to do with Aiko.

Esher was damned if he was going out just so Keras could lecture him while their other brothers were occupied with partying or poke his nose into his business by demanding to know about her.

"Take her home."

Those three words, spoken with a regal and commanding air, had Esher baring his teeth at Keras and unsurprised to feel his canines were sharper than normal, his darker side roused by his brother's demand.

"You're not my boss," he snarled at Keras before he could think better of it and took a hard step towards him, the rain outside falling faster as the leash on his temper slipped.

He curled his fingers into fists at his side, no longer caring if his brothers saw just how dark his trident mark was now, because he was damned sure the blackness of his eyes was giving away just how pissed he was.

Ares muttered dryly, "I think I've heard those words before."

Valen punched him on the arm. "You growled them better, and then you went off in a manly hissy-fit."

Ares glared at Valen. "It was not a hissy-fit."

Esher tuned them out as he focused on Keras, concentrating his rage on his oldest brother. Keras coolly regarded him, his green eyes impassive, not giving anything away.

He hadn't understood at the time, but now he could see why Ares had wanted to punch his brother all the times Keras had stood there with that aloof air and demanded he let Megan go.

Like fuck he was letting Aiko go, and Keras's demand was an order to do just that.

"Be reasonable, Esher." Keras moved a calm step towards him, his face impassive, tone collected. "It's dangerous for her. *You're* dangerous for her."

That stung, the barb sinking deep into his heart, tearing into it.

"I'm not," Esher bit out, the conviction he felt making those words as hard and unyielding as steel. "I would never hurt her."

Keras remained still, steady, unflinching in front of him.

Cal, Valen and Marek exchanged looks that said they found it difficult to believe. Ares stood firm, a pillar of support that Esher badly needed.

But it was Daimon who spoke up, moving to stand beside him, in his corner as always. "You've known her a while now. She gave you the bandage."

He nodded.

"I haven't hurt her yet, and I won't hurt her." He slid a black look at Keras. "But I will hurt whoever tries to take her from me."

"Sounds like you." Valen nudged Ares, a grin tugging at his scar.

Ares huffed. "You're one to talk."

"Sounds more like our father," Marek added, and his other brothers all nodded in agreement, an air of 'thanks for that gene, Dad' about them.

All but Keras.

Keras still didn't move, didn't back down, just kept staring at Esher with that damned look in his eyes that said to do as he had ordered.

It wasn't going to happen.

He took a fierce step towards Keras, but Daimon blocked his path, and his gaze leaped to his brother's ice-blue one as he spoke, his voice soft and rolling over him like a gentle tide.

"How did you meet?"

That had Esher settling back on his heels as a need swept through him, a desire to finally speak to Daimon about her. "I was hurt after a daemon attack on the gate, and I took the train. I fell asleep, and woke after my stop. She was in the other carriage... a male... he was trying to hurt her... and I stopped him. I had to help her."

He looked between Daimon's eyes, expecting to find surprise in them, but there was only warmth and understanding.

He couldn't say the same about his other brothers, but he tuned out their comments and focused on Daimon in the way he always did when trying to ground himself. The rain fell harder, memories of that night, of seeing Aiko in danger, rousing his anger to startling heights that had a need to hunt down the human and destroy him blasting through him.

"So you helped her, and then she helped you." Daimon's smooth voice rolled over him again, easing that need. "You saw her again, before I came to find you in Shibuya. You were acting... different... and the weather was bloody awful. Why were you upset?"

"It... I... I felt a need to hurt her." Esher's voice dropped to a bare whisper as he confessed that.

"Did you really want to do it? Or did you feel you should want to do it because it's how you always feel about humans?"

Esher considered that, dropping his eyes to his feet as he struggled to find the answer. Had he really wanted to hurt her? No. Even then, he had known that hurting her would be hurting himself. But he had been scared, confused by the feelings she had awoken in him, a need so powerful it overwhelmed him. He had feared she might hurt him, so the dark side of himself, his other side, had wanted to lash out first.

He slowly shook his head.

"I never wanted to hurt her. I would never hurt her." He lifted his chin, stared into Daimon's eyes and then at his brothers. He could see the questions rising in them, and he knew they were born of concern for him, but he shook his head again and implored them. "Let it go. I'm having a hard enough time with this as it is. If it feels strange to you, imagine how it feels to me."

He could understand their desire to protect him, and to protect Aiko, but they didn't need to worry about him. He was going to be fine.

Aiko appeared at that moment, a crinkle between her fine dark eyebrows as she looked up at him, her eyes flooded with soft concern that said she could feel his conflict, and she wanted to soothe it.

Gods, he wanted to drown in her when she looked at him like that.

But his brothers also all looked at her, and fine went right out of the window. He stepped in front of her, ushering her behind him as they stared, a dark need to gouge out all of their eyes so they couldn't see her in her tiny ruffled black skirt, purple stockings and black skull tank surging through him.

Keras frowned at her, and Esher shot him a glare, but his older brother didn't take his eyes off her as she moved out from behind Esher to stand beside him again.

Keras was testing him, trying to draw out his darker side and get a reaction from him.

It wasn't going to happen.

He wouldn't frighten Aiko like that.

She pushed her skirt down, clearly uncomfortable with the scrutiny, and he considered letting loose on his brothers after all, because it was a guaranteed way to stop them all from staring at her.

She looked up at him and softly said, "It's getting late... and I have work waitressing tonight."

No. He turned his frown on her now. He had plans. Perfect plans. She couldn't go. Not yet.

She tilted her chin up, her face towards him, and smiled gently, a hint of sorrow in her dark eyes that he felt sure echoed in his own as he faced a long night without her. He had wanted to learn more about her, had intended to take another bath and watch the sunset with her this time, and he had been planning to add just the right amount of cloud to make it incredible.

As beautiful as she was.

"A waitress where?" He forced himself to put his plans on hold, because as much as he wanted to convince her to ditch work and spend the evening with him instead, he knew Calistos wasn't going to let a night on the town go now that Keras had given it the green light. His younger brother would insist he join them in the no-ladies night and he would end up parted from Aiko anyway.

"Vampire Café… but I'm not a vampire," she said, her English a little stilted as she looked at Marek. "Just a human."

Everyone still looked shocked when she mentioned that fact about herself, and Esher wanted to tell them to go, leave the house and not come back until they had come to terms with the fact there was one human in this godsforsaken world that he didn't want to kill.

"It's your birthday?" She shifted her soft gaze to Cal, who nodded, causing a rogue strand of his blond hair to fall down his cheek.

Cal brushed it back, smoothing it into his ponytail, and shot her a charming smile.

Aiko mercifully returned her gaze to Esher before he had to kill his brother for stealing her attention for too long and spoke in Japanese. "I could get you a booth. If you show up when we open, then it's normally quiet."

Esher translated for her when five of his brothers tossed him curious glances.

Aiko added in English, "We have delicious cocktails."

Everyone looked at Valen and said as one, "No alcohol!"

"Dinner and a club sounds good." Cal had practically disappeared into his room nearest the TV area when he hollered, "I call first dibs on the shower."

Aiko grabbed Esher's hand and pulled him away from everyone, tugging him along the walkway to his room. She didn't stop when they reached it. She led him around the corner, so they were alone above the pond and his brothers couldn't see them.

He groaned when she tiptoed and kissed him, her lips temptingly sweet and soft as they glided over his. He dipped, wrapped his arms around her and pulled her closer, kissing her deeper as he let everything else fall away, until there was only her.

"Wait," he murmured against her lips, peppering them with kisses as awareness grew inside him, a feeling that she meant this as a goodbye kiss before she went to work. "We can go together."

He thought she might refuse, but then she kissed him again, and whispered, "I like how protective you are."

Fuck, she didn't know how deep that protective streak she liked ran, just what lengths he would go to in order to make sure she was safe and unharmed, and would always have a reason to smile and laugh.

He would do anything for her. Whatever it took.

And as he kissed her, the reason behind that need hit him hard.

He was falling in love with her.

CHAPTER 13

Esher had thought the sight of Aiko in her usual clothing had made her impossible to resist. He had been mistaken. She had every single drop of his attention, had his heart pounding and fingers itching with a need to sweep her up into his arms, as she moved around the warmly-lit room, drifting past the black coffin laden with red candles on its top, leading another couple into one of the booths behind the swag of a red velvet curtain.

He had to dig his nails into the black wooden table in front of him as she bowed, coming close to flashing her panties at the rest of the room in her ridiculous uniform.

She looked like a fucking French maid.

And damn, it got his blood pumping.

He just wasn't sure whether it was with a need to fight, or make love with her, or possibly both.

She straightened, her hands still tucked in front of her white apron that sat over the short black dress, and spoke with the newcomers, her smile bright as she recited the same thing she had said to everyone she had brought into the gothic room.

Esher raked his eyes over her for what felt like the millionth time, unable to stop himself, letting them glide from the little white frill that arched over her head on a band, down over her black dress that thankfully covered her chest and her upper arms too, all the way down to the white stockings that started just a few inches below the end of her skirt.

The tops of them had frills too, and gods, he kept imagining smoothing them down her shapely legs, kissing every inch of milky skin he exposed.

One of the other groups called her over, and he barely stopped himself from rising from the red velvet couch that curved around the table, his eyes tracking her through the sheer black curtain that draped across both sides of the booth, tied to the gaudy gold columns that looked as if they were meant to be supporting the roof.

The table of males all grinned and jostled as they spoke to her, and she *smiled* at them.

Esher growled.

He was going to kill them. He was going to kill every damned male in the room, and then he was going to cover her with his coat and take her far away from this place.

He couldn't bear it.

The sight of so many males paying attention to her when she was dressed in such a way, it was too much.

She bowed and giggled, doing only what was expected of her, but gods, it grated.

"So a mortal, huh?" Ares did his best to distract him, but Esher didn't rise to the bait, just kept tracking her around the room as she relayed the order to the backroom staff and then reappeared, seating another group in the busy room, this one at the table near the coffin.

He assessed all the males in the mixed group, none of which were a match for him.

"Anyone else?" Ares sounded pissed, and he felt his brother's gaze leave him. "Valen, be a dick or something."

Valen growled at Ares. "Why? You're being a big enough dick for both of us. Asking him about her being a human."

It was odd having Valen in his corner. It almost distracted him for a second. *Almost.*

But then a group wanted to photograph the resident male 'vampire', a human dressed in formal attire with fake fangs, and one Marek had spent most of the evening glaring at, and Esher saw red when the male picked Aiko as his 'victim'. *Again.*

As the male took hold of her from behind and pretended to bite her throat as she held her hands up in front of her, mock surprise on her face, Esher shoved to his feet.

His brothers were too fast for him though.

Before he could move, Ares had left the opposite side of the booth and had hemmed him in, and all he could do was shuffle further along the curved red sofa to accommodate him as his brothers all moved along one place, putting Valen near the other end now.

Daimon sat beside Valen, offering Esher an apologetic look that told him if he had been nearest to the edge and not Ares, he wouldn't have stopped him from stepping in.

"I need the toilet." Esher was tempted to shove Ares, but the chances of getting scalded were high, and the last thing he needed to do was cause his older brother's temper to spark.

The whole place would probably burn down.

Although, it would mean that Aiko couldn't work here anymore, and that damned male couldn't touch her again.

The vampire released her and went back to his station, serving other customers.

Keras gave Esher a doubtful look. "If you want her attention, you only have to ring."

His older brother reached across the cluttered table, picked up the tiny brass bell and shook it.

Aiko immediately came over, her warm eyes locking straight on Esher as she readied her note pad. "What do you want?"

Esher raked his gaze over her, hunger gnawing at him. What didn't he want? He wanted to devour her, over and over again.

"Water," he said instead, not wanting to make her blush in front of his brothers.

She didn't seem surprised by his request, just smiled and wrote it down, and then looked at his brothers. "The air spirit needs another drink."

Ares finished his fruity non-alcoholic cocktail at that moment.

Aiko took the glass as he pushed it away from him, and said in English, "Would you like another, Fire Spirit?"

"Bring us all the same again." Keras's green eyes were sharp as he eyed her, and Esher didn't like it.

He scowled at his brother where he sat in the middle of the table, Marek and Cal flanking him, and then pushed aside his irritation so he could enjoy the sight of Aiko again. She cleared some plates from the table with the help of another waitress, and then disappeared into the kitchen, smiling and giggling to her companion as she went.

She was so vibrant, so full of life.

His little butterfly.

"Can she read?" Keras.

Esher absently said, "I presume so. Japanese definitely, but she's studied English so maybe a little of that too."

Keras huffed. "No. *Read*."

He dragged his focus away from Aiko, settling it on Keras, and frowned as he thought about that.

"She must be able to." Because he hadn't told her what he was, and she had pinpointed Cal and Ares's powers without witnessing them.

Which meant she was a Carrier, a human with Hellspawn blood in their ancestry. Megan, Ares's female, was a Carrier too, possessing the talent to heal. Aiko could sense things in people, able to read the truth about them. The other form of Carrier could see the future in visions.

Keras plucked the damned bell from the table and rang again, and Esher's gut tightened, his mood taking a nosedive as he realised what his brother was going to do.

He had tested Megan, and he was going to test Aiko.

Ares gave Keras a black look, one that relayed he was as happy about their brother's plan as Esher was and he wanted to argue against it.

When Aiko arrived, all smiles and light, Keras stared at her, blocking him out, and said, "What am I thinking?"

Her face fell as she swallowed hard and glanced at Esher.

He tried to reach for Keras, wanting to punch the bastard for making her so nervous, but Cal caught his arm and held him back. A dangerous move on his little brother's part. Holding him back was like trying to hold back a tidal wave. You just didn't do it unless you wanted to get hurt.

"I don't... invade... people's heads like that. It is rude." She shook her head, and he could see she didn't want to do it, was afraid of what might happen if she did.

"Leave her alone," he growled, and she looked at him, her nerves fading a little as their eyes met. He gentled his tone. "You don't have to do this."

She looked back at Keras, and gods, he admired her when she stood a bit taller and squared her shoulders.

She took a deep breath and stared at Keras for so long Esher started to get twitchy again, restless with a need to stop her from looking at his brother.

A wrinkle formed between her eyebrows as she focused harder.

"Books?" she said, and then shook her head. "Not books. I'm meant… to read… your mind?"

"Keep going." Keras's voice was dark, challenging, and the need to punch his brother grew stronger, because he was pushing her, ordering her around as if she belonged to him, or was his to command.

Megan found it hard to heal them because they were gods, and it was obvious Aiko was struggling to read Keras. It was taking its toll on her.

She glanced at him, gave a tiny dip of her head to say she was fine, one that did nothing to ease the need to give his brother a makeover with his fists, and then looked back at Keras and focused again.

Her eyes turned glassy.

"Your thoughts… hazy." She swayed a little and reached out to grip the ebony table, leaned towards it and his brother as she peered deeper into his green eyes. "You are gods. I understand."

She went deeper still.

"What's in your pocket? You want something… in your—"

"Get out of my head," Keras snapped and shadows whipped towards her, but Valen had her out of their path in an instant, tugging her towards him as she flinched and closed her eyes, her hand flying to her forehead as if Keras had physically struck her.

Gods only knew what would have happened if his shadows had.

Ares was quick to move aside, levelling a hard look at Keras. Esher was out of the booth and beside her in a heartbeat, taking her from Valen and checking her over, leaving no inch of her uninspected as a need to see that she was unhurt raged through his blood.

"Are you alright?" He smoothed his thumb over her brow as he cupped her head, across the point she had touched when she had flinched, and relief beat through him when she nodded and opened her eyes, and lifted them to his, and he saw in them that she was. He turned his head towards his brother, clenched his jaw, and bit out, "Happy now?"

Keras lowered his eyes to the table and didn't respond. His hands gripped the black wood, so fiercely his knuckles were white, and Esher wanted to ask him what it was in his pocket that he desired and wanted to keep hidden from him and his brothers. What did he want to protect so much that he had been willing to harm a human to keep it secret?

Ares looked as if he wanted the answer to that question too.

If Keras dared to push Aiko around again, if he so much as looked at her funnily, then Esher was damned well going to find out.

He watched his older brother twisting the silver band he wore on his thumb around it, his eyes on it, a glimmer of something like pain in their emerald depths.

For now, Esher would let it go.

They were meant to be celebrating Cal's birthday, not getting into a fight.

He shifted his gaze back to Aiko. "You're sure you're alright?"

She nodded and he reluctantly released her when a few of the waitresses started looking his way and talking to each other. Aiko moved away, but he didn't miss the way she frowned at Keras before she went back to work.

Keras looked away again when Esher glared at him and slid back into the booth, on the edge of the red velvet seat this time, hemming Ares in against Cal.

"You serious about her? You seem serious. She seems a little young."

"Valen!" Ares snapped.

Valen shrugged, his shoulders casually rolling beneath his tight black t-shirt. "What? I'm just saying what you're all thinking. We all know Esher's history with humans is as black as Styx. What's the deal?"

Esher had thought they had agreed not to do this. He ignored them and continued to watch her. When she came with their drinks, he took his from her, and a thousand volts leaped along his bones when their fingers brushed. She stared at him, eyes wide deep dark pools that he fell into, forgetting the world for a heartbeat.

He leaned towards her, wanting to kiss her, and stopped himself at the last second, aware she was being watched again. She broke away, a blush staining her cheeks, and hugged the silver tray to her chest as she headed back towards the kitchen.

When she reached the other waitresses, they all burst into giggles.

"There's no doubt she likes you."

Esher turned a glare on Daimon. "I expected comments from them, but not from you."

Daimon just smiled, a teasing one that said he wasn't going to hear the end of this for a while.

"Are you serious about her?" Keras this time, and everyone looked at him again, seeming as surprised as he was to hear their older brother speak again so soon.

Esher looked back at Aiko and watched her as she talked with the other waitresses, all bright and beautiful. "She's different to everyone."

She made him see there was good in this world and gave him a reason to protect it.

When she took a tray of drinks and brought them to his table, setting them down in front of Valen, Daimon and Cal, he waited impatiently for her to be done. The second she lowered her tray, he caught her free hand, brought it to his lips and pressed a kiss to it.

She blushed again. "I'll be scolded."

But she didn't take her hand away. She lingered, showing him that she wanted his kiss, needed his hands on her, ached for the contact as fiercely as he did. He groaned and relinquished her hand, and watched her go, that restless need gnawing at him.

He wasn't sure how much longer he could go without holding her again, touching her again.

Kissing her again.

It was driving him crazy.

He felt his brothers watching him, but he couldn't take his eyes off Aiko, barely heard them as they spoke, lost in her and the need spiralling through him, one more ferocious than he had ever experienced before.

One that stemmed from the deepest place in his heart.

In his soul.

Ares's words broke through, quietly spoken and with a teasing note that said he was being only half-serious, but they struck Esher hard as he felt the gravity of them and knew them to be true.

"I think he's in love."

Daimon's muttered response echoed his thoughts.

"Gods help the world."

CHAPTER 14

Aiko pointed to the sign on the street marking the basement bar. It was one of her favourites in the Roppongi district. The skyscrapers towered above it, bright in the darkness, and the street was busy even at the late hour, people coming and going between the entertainment establishments in the area. A black taxi pulled up outside the club and two women clambered out of it, said something to the driver, and disappeared down the steps.

As Esher's brothers moved off ahead of them, blending into the night in their black clothing, looking like a group of deadly assassins as they prowled towards the steps that led down into the club, Esher slowed.

She slowed with him, a feeling growing within her with each step further his brothers moved from them, a heavy weight that pressed down on her and would only be lifted when they were alone.

When she could touch Esher again, could kiss him as she had been dying to all night.

She had caught the need that had flared in him from time to time throughout the night, an ache that had flared in her too, had made her burn whenever his eyes had followed her, or she had looked at him. It had blazed hotter than the sun when he had taken hold of her after Keras had made her read his dark mind, and again when he had kissed her hand.

She had never wanted to be alone with a man like this before, had never yearned with a need to run away and construct a wall around them both to isolate them from the world.

"I'm sorry about my brother," Esher said in Japanese as he lingered on the pavement near the steps, watching his brothers head inside, and she didn't stop him when he took hold of her hand. His was cool against it, but it warmed her, sending a pleasant hot wave rolling through her that had her stepping towards him.

Darkness reigned in his eyes, anger that she wanted to soothe.

"It was difficult, but… I did not mind doing it." Because she had the feeling it had been important.

She just wasn't sure why.

Before she could ask Esher, he tugged her towards the entrance of the club, leading her down the steps. He pushed the heavy door open and held it for her. Rather than moving through the crowd towards his brothers where they stood near the bar, gaining curious glances from many of the people in the club, Esher tugged her left.

Into the shadows.

Her heart leaped into her throat as he pulled her in front of him, beating frantically as he backed her into the corner and hemmed her in with his body, planting his hands either side of her head. He breathed hard, and she could feel his struggle. It echoed her own.

She caught hold of the sides of his dark grey shirt near his collar, tugged him towards her, and moaned when he dipped his head and captured her lips, his breath hissing from him as he kissed her.

Damn, she needed him.

It had been building inside her all night. She had been watching him too, putting up with her friends teasing, each second agony as she had counted the minutes until her shift would end and she could be with him again. More than once, she had wanted him to come to her, had wanted to sneak away with him into one of the empty booths and steal a kiss like this.

She opened for him, and he groaned and shuddered as his tongue tangled with hers. Her grip on his shirt tightened, and then she gave herself over to the need rising inside her, vanquishing her nerves. She released his shirt and pressed her palms against his chest, moaned as the feel of his hard muscles and his heart pounding frantically against her hands sent a warm shiver through her.

He pressed into her, kissing her harder, so hungrily that she got caught up in his fervour, forgot the world existed and they weren't alone. He shifted his hips closer, and she trembled as she felt his hardness against her belly.

Her hands shook as a need went through her, a wicked one that had her blushing.

One she had to obey.

It felt as if her very life depended on satisfying it.

She skimmed her left hand down his chest, feeling the tempting ridges of his stomach as he tensed, his breath hitching as he kissed her, driving her mad with a need for more. She trailed her fingers over the belt of his black jeans and hesitated for only a second before turning her hand and cupping his rigid length.

Esher groaned and whispered against her lips, "Touch me. I need you."

Aiko's cheeks blazed, awareness of everyone crashing back down around her, but it didn't stop her from doing it, because she needed to feel him too.

She rubbed her palm up and down his length as he kissed her, his moans quiet enough that no one would hear them over the thumping music, and the corner dark enough that she was sure no one could see what they were doing.

But damn, she wasn't sure she would care if someone did.

All that mattered was satisfying the need that had been steadily building inside her all night.

"Fuck, you're killing me," he uttered against her lips, kissed her again and then pressed his forehead against hers, his breathing as ragged as her own. "Put me out of my misery. I want to leave right now... go to that teahouse... make love with you."

She wanted that too, his words setting fire to a deeper need, one that had her leaning closer to him, trapping her hand between their bodies. She wanted him. All of him. It frightened her, but excited her more.

She tiptoed and kissed him, hard this time, unable to hold back any longer, needing to show him that he wasn't alone and she ached for him too, wanted to fulfil that vision he had painted of them together at the teahouse, making love beneath the moon.

Aiko froze and broke away from his lips, her gaze scanning the crowded room as a feeling arrowed through her.

"Why did you stop?" Esher dropped his head to her neck, devouring it with kisses. His hands clutched her hips, drawing her against him. "I still can't believe you know I'm a god and you want to be with me."

"I've been able to sense spirits for a long time now." She pressed her hands against his chest, pushing him back to stop him from distracting her, overloading her with sensation. The feeling grew clearer, her ability pinpointing his brothers and him, and something else. "That's why I can feel something is wrong. There are new spirits here. Bad spirits."

Esher immediately grabbed her and pulled her swiftly through the crowd.

His brothers jeered as they approached.

"Scatter, now!" His words seemed slowed in her ears as she spotted one of the spirits she had sensed at the entrance of the club.

The dark-haired male lifted his hand, his thumb coming down on something he held.

"Run!" Aiko shoved Esher hard, heart slamming against her ribs as adrenaline and fear surged through her.

A wave of heat and light rolled through the room, and Esher twisted her into his arms, pinning her against the bar and shielding her with his body. There was a deafening bang, the floor bucked hard, almost sending her to her knees, and then screams rang around her.

But the explosion didn't reach her and Esher, or his brothers.

She stared at Keras where he stood beyond Esher with both hands outstretched in front of him, at the flames and debris that hit an invisible barrier just inches from him.

At the blood that rolled down it like rain on a window.

Her stomach lurched, the sickening stench of burning flesh and other things assaulting her nose.

She pulled back to check Esher wasn't hurt.

Cold crimson eyes looked down at her.

And then he was gone.

Aiko sagged against the bar, heart frozen in her chest as Esher disappeared in a swirl of black smoke, only to reappear on the other side of Keras's barrier. He let out an inhuman snarl as he shoved the humans in his path aside, heading towards a second attacker. The fair-haired man fumbled with the detonator in his hand.

Before he could press the button, Esher had appeared behind him and had ripped the vest of explosives off him. The man frantically pressed the button as Esher held the vest up and glared at it, and then at him. A cruel smile twisted Esher's lips when it didn't detonate.

The man tried to run, and his feelings struck her. Fear. He hadn't been afraid to die when he had been on the verge of detonating himself, but now he was terrified.

Because Esher was going to kill him?

Some part of her thought she should stop him as she watched him capture the man by his throat and lift him from the floor, that she should be horrified by what he was doing as he stared at the man, his eyes blazing scarlet but as cold as ice, but the rest of her wanted him to do it.

She wanted the man to pay for what he had done, hurting countless innocent people, and what he had intended to do, killing those now struggling to escape, clawing their way towards the destroyed exit or away from Esher where he held the man aloft, staring at him.

Do it.

It was wrong of her, but she wanted him to do it.

Esher's eyes narrowed slowly.

The man began to flail, frantically kicking at Esher's legs and clawing at his arms, a wild thing in his grip. A grip that slowly tightened, until the man was choking. No, she realised as she watched blood trickle from the man's nose, appearing black to her, and from his eyes, and saw it began to creep from his ears.

It wasn't Esher's grip that was making him choke.

It was Esher's power.

She could feel it rising in him, and it was a dark and terrible tide, fuelled by anger that had his lips twisting in a satisfied sneer as he watched the man bleed.

The man convulsed, shaking violently in Esher's grip, but Esher remained unmoving, his arm steady and eyes locked on him, no trace of emotion in them as he watched the man bleed out. The man coughed up blood, thick streams of it that ran over his chin and formed a puddle below his feet where they dangled at least eight inches off the ground, splattering across the rubble and sending dust up into the air.

People continued to pull themselves away from him, desperate cries leaving their lips as they forced themselves to move, their fear pushing down on Aiko together with their pain, pulling her focus to them. They needed her help.

When she moved, Esher's gaze whipped to her.

His expression darkened.

The man threw his head back and blood burst from his lips, cascading down his face, and then he went still.

Esher dropped the body.

Turned crimson eyes on the people crawling away from him.

"Esher, don't!" Daimon called and was moving in an instant.

A cold feeling went through Aiko.

He was going to hurt the people next.

"Esher!" She took a step towards him instead of the people she had intended to help, and he looked at her again.

A flicker of blue shone in amidst the red of his irises.

Fire exploded in a wave behind him, knocking him forwards, and one of his brothers screamed his name.

A wall of ice and earth shot up behind him, creating a barrier, but not before the tip of the explosion caught Esher, the force of it hurling him to his knees on the rubble from the first blast.

Aiko was by his side in an instant, her heart in her mouth as she saw the torn up back of his shirt, a slick patch on the back of his head, and lacerations on his neck.

"Esher." She fluttered her hands over him, panic claiming hold of her, and then her mind emptied and her heart steadied, and something clicked into place inside her.

She instinctively followed her training, checking him from head to toe for wounds, and any sign of broken bones, no sound reaching her ears other than her own ragged strained breathing. When she saw only superficial wounds, she risked taking hold of his shoulders.

He responded instantly.

In the blink of an eye, she was tucked against his chest, his body shielding hers again and his grip so tight she found it hard to breathe.

He shook against her, hands trembling where they gripped the nape of her neck and her waist, pinning her to him.

"Need to protect my little butterfly," he whispered. "Keep it together and protect my little butterfly."

She realised that was her.

She wrapped her arms around him as best she could, holding him. "I'm fine. I can't sense any more of the bad spirits."

He refused to release her, kept her crushed against his chest. Safe.

His shaking worsened, and she caught his emotions as they grew stronger— rage, fear, and a darkness that frightened her a little, but she could also feel that he needed her, and that need was genuine.

Daimon stopped beside them, and she looked up his long black-denim-clad legs, over his dark roll-neck sweater, to his face. He crouched beside Esher, his pale blue eyes on him, concern flooding them.

"Everyone is safe," Daimon murmured, his words an odd contrast to the sobs and moans of the people around them, people who were injured. Dying. He didn't seem to notice as he focused on Esher. "Everyone is safe. The daemons are gone. You dealt with them. The threat is over. Everyone is safe. Focus on my voice, Esher. Focus on me now."

When Esher only held her closer and loosed another inhuman growl, Daimon glanced at his brothers, his expression revealing fear.

Why?

"Tycho," Daimon whispered and held his hand out, slowly, as if he was approaching a dangerous animal and feared getting his hand bitten off if he startled it. He kept his voice low, a soothing murmur. "Tycho. Focus on the word, Esher. Focus on me. Tycho."

Every time Daimon said that strange word, Esher's grip on her loosened a little, and she could breathe again. His trembling began to subside.

"Everything is okay now. Everyone is fine. Everyone is safe. See?" Daimon hovered his hand an inch from Esher's shoulder. "Look."

Esher drew back, but he didn't look at his brother.

He looked at her.

Aiko lifted her dirty hands and framed his face, keeping his eyes on her. They were blue again now, blue but so inky they were almost black, and only spots of crimson remained. Whatever that crimson meant, it was bad, and she wanted to know why it happened, and what to do to bring Esher back.

As Daimon had.

Beyond him, Ares appeared in a swirl of black smoke that clung to him and the pretty brunette woman in his arms.

"What happened?" She sounded American. Her warm brown eyes rose to Ares when she noticed the body of the creature Daimon had referred to as a daemon. "That looks like a nasty way to go."

"Better than exploding." Ares nodded to the spots where the other two daemons had detonated themselves, one close to where they had appeared and the other beyond the crumbling wall of dirt and melting ice.

Aiko wasn't sure the daemon Esher had killed had experienced a death that had been better than the other two. It had been drawn out, excruciating. Esher had made sure he had suffered.

Because he had felt a need to protect his brothers.

Her.

She looked back at him, at the way he was watching her closely, his dark eyebrows furrowed with the concern that flickered in his eyes, and knew she was the reason he had lost control.

When the woman started helping the injured, Aiko tried to get free of Esher's grip so she could help.

He immediately dragged her against him, his grip so fierce it hurt.

"I can help too," she said, but he showed no sign of releasing her. Her eyes darted between his. "I have to help, Esher. Let me help them."

"Let her help." Daimon weathered the glare Esher turned on him. "Everyone is safe now. Everyone is okay."

Esher drew down a deep, shuddering breath, and closed his eyes as he nodded.

But he still didn't release her.

Aiko brushed her thumbs across his cheeks, smearing the ash and blood. "I'm safe, Esher. No one will hurt me… and I am not afraid, because I know you will protect me."

He sucked down another deep breath, leaned forwards and pressed his forehead against her neck, and she stroked her palms over his back, and frowned as she felt the blood on her hands. His blood.

She needed to tend to him too.

But there were people in far more need of her than he was.

She looked at the people, at the ones who had already died, and those struggling to stem the flow of blood from their wounds, or desperately trying to help others.

"Please, Esher?" Because she couldn't sit idle any longer. She had to help them.

He inhaled hard, exhaled in another shuddering sigh, and finally released her.

She stood, her legs like jelly beneath her, body shaking as the adrenaline dump waned and she was left facing the cold reality of what had happened. The lights in the large room flickered on and off, and smoke curled from several places, making the air thick and hot, and difficult to breathe. She pushed herself to move, told herself that there were no more daemons left, that there was only Esher and his brothers, and the injured.

She had to help them.

She picked her way over the rubble to the woman Ares guarded and her eyes widened when she realised the brunette didn't have a medical kit.

She was healing the injured by holding her hands above them. The wounds beneath her touch knitted back together and Aiko could only stare in amazement. She didn't have such an incredible gift, but she could do her part.

"Let me help," Aiko said in English, and the woman looked up.

She nodded. "There should be a med kit. Grab it and patch up as many of the people with less life-threatening injuries."

"We need to get motoring or the authorities will arrive." Ares's deep voice became a growl when the woman winced, leaned forwards, and shook her head. He stooped and touched her back. "Megan, you're overdoing it."

She shot him a frown. "I'm fine. Stop fussing."

"I'll help." Aiko hurried across the room, feeling Esher's eyes tracking her, and searched behind the bar for the med kit. There were two. She took both and tended to a wound on the bartender's throat first, and then one on the leg of a woman.

She moved from person to person, her heart growing heavier as she did her best to help as many of the people as she could, their blood and dirt from the blast coating her hands and her clothes as she worked quickly.

So many of them were dead though.

She stopped near a woman, one of the group she had seen exiting the taxi when they had arrived, and checked for a pulse. When she felt nothing, she sank back on her knees and stared at the woman, cold blooming inside her as her eyes burned, and hot tears spilled onto her cheeks.

"Can you help over here?" Megan called.

Aiko brushed her tears away, pushed onto her feet and forced herself to move, but she couldn't stop herself from looking at every body she passed, and the tears returned, streaming down her cheeks no matter how hard she tried to stop them.

When she reached Megan and sank to her knees, she felt Esher's eyes on her.

She looked across at him as she applied pressure to a leg wound on a man while Megan worked to heal another on his side where a pipe had pierced him.

Worry danced in his blue eyes, his expression relaying his need to come to her and comfort her, but he kept his distance and all the light in his eyes turned dark when he glanced at the man she was helping.

"Esher." Keras regained his attention.

"It wasn't me who sensed the daemons. It was Aiko." When Esher said that, Keras looked at her.

He beckoned her with a wave of his hand, but he could wait, because she was needed where she was. She ignored him and kept pressure on the wound, still amazed at the way Megan was healing the man.

When Megan had closed the wound on his side, she smiled shakily. "Thanks."

Megan reached for the man's leg as he moaned, and Ares palmed her shoulders.

"You're doing great, Sweetheart," he murmured. "A couple more and we're done."

She nodded, blew out her breath and focused.

Aiko rose to her feet and brushed her tangled black hair from her face as she went to Esher. The moment she was within reach, he slipped his arm around her waist and pulled her to him, nuzzling her neck and holding her tightly. She sank against him, tired and aching, wanting to leave the carnage and try to put it all out of her mind even when she knew it would haunt her for weeks.

"How many daemons did you sense?" Keras said.

"Four." She wasn't really certain. Just as she found it hard to distinguish how many of Esher's brothers were near her when they were grouped together, becoming a mass of signatures to her, she had found it hard to count the number of daemons.

He frowned. "Four?"

She nodded. "Or three... it's hard to say."

"There's a big difference between three and four." Keras swiped a hand over his short black hair, his green gaze dark and handsome face etched in pensive lines as he stared down at her. "Three died. If there were four, then one survived."

She focused on the feeling she'd had when she had been making out with Esher in the shadows. At first, it had felt like one bad spirit, but then she remembered it breaking apart, and that was when she had alerted Esher.

Because there had been three of them.

"Three." She was sure of it now.

Above them, sirens rang out, muffled through the layers of concrete.

"Time to leave." Keras looked at his brothers. "Marek and I will finish up here. It won't take long to make the survivors believe there was a gas leak that caused the explosions."

They could do that?

Aiko looked at the room, and she supposed it wasn't that much of a leap. It was wrecked, the floor torn up in a way that made it appear as if a gas main had burst.

The lightning and air spirit disappeared, leaving shimmering black smoke behind. Ares dragged Megan onto her feet, ignoring her protest as she tried to reach another person to help them, and disappeared with her.

"Daimon, go with Esher. Make sure he is alright." Keras looked to the white-haired one, and the man nodded.

Because Esher was injured?

Or because he had lost control?

Keras slapped a hand down on Esher's shoulder. "Everyone is fine."

Esher nodded, but didn't look convinced.

"But the people." Aiko tried to pull towards them as a few of them moaned, and one cried out for help. It could take hours for the authorities to break through the rubble closing the entrance and reach them. They might die if she didn't help them.

Esher turned cold eyes on them, his tone empty. "We've done all we can."

He pulled her against him and the world spun around her, fading to black. Colours emerged, streaking through the darkness, and her head kept on spinning as Esher's house appeared around her.

He kept hold of her as Daimon appeared.

The first thing Daimon said was, "Everyone is fine."

Esher dragged a hand over his messy black hair and nodded, and she felt cold as he released her, breaking contact and moving away, drifting towards the bathhouse. She watched him go, her insides tied in knots as she tried to decide whether to go after him and help him, or question his brother.

When he disappeared from view, questioning won out, because she needed some answers.

She turned on Daimon. "People were dead. They were hurt. Not everyone was fine."

Daimon looked over his shoulder towards the bathroom as the water started running.

"To Esher they were." He sighed and returned his ice-blue gaze to her. "Everyone who mattered was fine. His brothers were fine... and so were you."

"What about the people?" She didn't understand. Esher had always been so nice around her, caring and gentle, but tonight he had been different. She had seen the way he had looked at the injured people after he had killed the daemon. He had wanted to hurt them.

She frowned as something dawned on her, and she wasn't sure how she hadn't noticed it before.

Esher hated being in a crowd. He seemed happiest when they were alone, somewhere peaceful, away from people. She had thought it was just because he wanted to be alone with her, but now she could see it for what it really was.

He didn't like people.

He didn't trust them.

Why?

She looked to Daimon for the answer.

He was quiet for a long time, tensed and still, a statue in black in front of her, the soft long spikes of his white hair dirty and stained with crimson in places, and ash streaking across his pale skin. "You've seen his scars? The ones on his back... on his wrists?"

She nodded. There were so many of them. Long silvery lines on his back, and thicker rings of scars on his arms. He looked as if he had fought a thousand battles that had been worse than the one tonight, and the one she had patched him up after on the night they had met.

"Ever wonder where he got them?" Daimon glanced towards the corridor to the bathroom and lowered his voice. "If you need answers, you could start by asking him... because not even I know the full story. Tonight, you were okay, and so were we, but it might be different next time, and you need to know what you're getting yourself into."

He disappeared, leaving ribbons of black smoke behind, before she could ask him what that meant, giving her no choice but to ask Esher instead.

She hesitated, a touch of fear trickling through her. Esher hadn't liked it when she had looked at his scars. How would he react if she asked about them?

She had wanted to more than once, needed to know the story behind them, because she felt sure knowing was vital if she was going to move closer to him, as close as she wanted to be.

She pulled down a steadying breath.

She didn't want to hurt him, but she needed to know.

She needed to know what had happened to him to make him so unfeeling towards humans, because gods were meant to protect them, not despise them.

Aiko kicked off her shoes, and bravely strode forwards, following the trail of ashy boot prints that led to the bathhouse.

She found Esher to the left, where a series of shower stalls were set into a stone wall. He stood beneath the spray, his head bent as he leaned with his hands against the white tiles, the water cascading over his black hair, down the tensed muscles of his bare back and over the contours of his bottom.

He didn't seem to notice her as she stripped down to her underwear, or as she stepped into the cubicle behind him.

He kept standing there, with his head under the water, letting it run over him as if it would carry everything that was bothering him away.

Aiko touched his back, feathering her fingers along the most vicious of the scars, one that started in a thick circle below his left ribs and darted up towards his right shoulder, growing thinner as it went.

He didn't tense as expected or turn to rail at her and make her stop.

"How did you get these?" she whispered, voice trembling as badly as her fingers.

He let out a long sigh. "What did Daimon tell you?"

"Nothing." She stroked a smaller, thinner scar that arced over his spine. "He told me to ask you."

He stood silent as she explored him, charted more scars and then her eyes drifted to the ones around his arms, the ones she had wanted to know about from the moment she had met him. She wanted to reach for him, to caress them and ask him about them in particular, but he started to tremble as his hands tensed against the tiles, fingers pressing in as if he needed to grip them to keep himself upright.

To stop himself from falling.

Her heart ached for him, chest growing tight as she felt his struggle, his immense pain.

He slowly turned his head towards her, and that ache deepened as his blue eyes met hers. They were as deep as the ocean, as blue as the sky, but there was a threat of a storm in them, and a touch of crimson.

He shifted towards her, claimed her cheeks with his palms, and stared down into her eyes. Water rolled down the long black lengths of his hair, but when it dripped, it hung in the air, suspended between them as he shook.

"I'm glad you're okay," he croaked, and tears filled his eyes, tearing at her. "But I'm not… and I haven't been for a long time."

CHAPTER 15

He shouldn't do this. It was dangerous. Not for her, but for him. He shouldn't trust her. She was human.

But she was Aiko.

And she needed to know.

For the first time in his life, Esher needed to tell someone about his past, needed to lower that barrier and let someone step through it. It was vital. That feeling rang deep in his bones, vibrated in his soul, sang in his heart. Telling Aiko, revealing the darker part of himself, was vital, and it had to be now, before things went any further between them.

Because if she found out later, when he was so lost in her, so in love with her that he couldn't live without her, and she left him.

It didn't bear thinking about.

The whole world would know his wrath.

Esher stared down into her warm brown eyes, aware that his still held a hint of crimson and that she had caught a glimpse of that side of himself he fought to keep under control. It had been but a shadow of his other self, provoked by the thought of her in danger, born of a need to protect her, but she had witnessed it.

She had watched him kill that daemon, drawing out his death and making him suffer, giving the wretch what he had deserved.

There had been no condemnation in her eyes though, no trace of horror or disgust as he had made the daemon bleed.

He wasn't fool enough to believe that meant she wouldn't run when she knew the truth about him though.

He broke away from her, needing some space and room to breathe, to gather his thoughts so he could figure out where to start. The beginning sounded good, but that came with its own perils.

Like revealing his age to her.

She knew he was a god, had probably had contact with other creatures she believed were spirits, and she had never shied away from him because of it. She didn't seem to care that there was a possibility he was thousands of years older than her. He clung to that as he sank onto his backside on one of the stools and dragged his left hand down his face, his nerves threatening to get out of control. He drew down a deep breath, and then another, and focused on each one to calm himself.

Aiko crossed the short span of floor to him, but rather than stop in front of him, she filled one of the scoops with water, and wetted a cloth, and moved around behind him. He kept still as she dabbed at his back with the damp cloth, absorbed her gentle touch and the care behind it as she worked to clean him. The wounds stung, but the pain was lost on him as he focused on her and on his past.

"I never used to be like this," he murmured, and cleared his throat when his voice sounded raw, fragile.

He didn't want to remember, but it was necessary. Aiko would keep him calm. He wouldn't hurt her. He stared at the showers, watching the water running as she carefully cleaned his back, tending to his wounds. The droplets danced, and he played with them, needing to keep his mind occupied as he let it all spill out.

He kept part of his focus on Aiko though, monitoring her because he needed to know if anything he told her frightened her, or pushed her away. He needed to feel her every reaction to what he was going to tell her.

"Six centuries ago, my father, Hades, sent me on a mission to the mortal realm to meet a demigod and bring him to the Underworld through one of the gates." Esher stared blankly as the water danced in front of him, and Aiko remained calm behind him, not at all affected by the fact he had just admitted to being older than six hundred years. "At the time, neither myself nor my brothers could pass through the gates with our powers, because it was safer that no god had power in the mortal realm as they carried in the Underworld."

"The Underworld is like Hell?" She peered over his shoulder, and he glanced at her. The scarlet was emerging in his eyes again, but she didn't seem bothered by it. She was wholly concerned with him, her rich brown eyes echoing her worry.

He nodded, but then shrugged. "Not Hell like you think it. It's a beautiful place. Every soul goes there, good or bad, and they all live in different realms, some nicer than others."

She seemed relieved to hear that, and went back to washing his shoulders, working her way down to his arms.

He tensed when she reached his left wrist and the scars that ringed it, and she knelt and looked up at him, her hand lingering on his forearm.

Esher swallowed hard, fought for breath, for his voice, and the will to hold back the tide of pain beginning to surge inside him, one that felt as if it was ripping his every molecule apart.

He lifted his eyes to hers and tried to lose himself in them, but the pain grew fiercer. "I was friends with the demigod. I had known him for more than a century, and he worked for my father, so we often spent time together. He wanted to stay a little longer in the mortal realm, and I was young and foolish enough to agree. I didn't think anything could go wrong."

"But it did," she gently prompted as his throat closed and he nodded tightly as memories of that night assaulted him, flickering over the present to brand him with a vision of bloodshed.

"We were attacked near a village, when we were heading to the gate. Humans had seen my friend use powers, only telekinesis... but it had been foolish of him. Humans fear that which they don't understand, and that which is stronger than they are." He spat those words before he could stop himself, anger curling through his veins, heating his blood, and waited for Aiko to look at him differently, but she remained placid and calm, her eyes filled with understanding and not disgust. He looked away from her, back to the water as it drummed on the tray of the shower, focusing on affecting it to stop his mood from affecting the weather.

Because he was liable to cause a storm that could easily wipe out half of Tokyo.

"With my powers bound, I wasn't strong enough to fight a mob. There were at least forty of them, armed with farm tools and some with swords. My friend, he tried to fight, and they hurt him, and I couldn't do anything." His throat closed again, so he cleared it, wanting to hide the depth of his pain from Aiko even when she could sense it in him. Gods, he wanted to look strong in her eyes, not weak, not like this. He didn't want her to think that he was weak. He gripped his bare knees. "When I came around, we were bound, and the humans were angry, vicious as they called us daemons, said we were devils and had to die."

"Esher," Aiko started, but he shook his head, telling her not to speak yet.

He needed to get it all out, as quickly as possible now, because the storm was building inside him, threatening to tear him apart.

"They kept yelling it as they tortured him, held my head up and made me watch as they attacked him with pitchforks and daggers, made him bleed and then left him in agony, slumped against the post they had bound him to opposite me." He gritted his teeth and growled. "I tried to get free. I tried... but I wasn't strong enough. Gods, I thought I would die there."

He looked at her, meant only to glance at her but lingered when the pain in her eyes, the worry wrapped around him, telling him that she cared for him, that she hated that he had suffered like that.

It had been agony. Not having his powers when he had grown used to them, when they had always been there when he had needed them. He had been weak without them, practically mortal, and gods, he had hated it. He wasn't like them. He wasn't human. He was a god.

But he had been a powerless one.

"It went on for weeks..." His voice hitched, and he released his knees, and curled his fingers into tight fists. "I kept trying to get free, but whenever I tried, they turned their wrath on me, cut and stabbed me, made me bleed. I tried to use my powers, but nothing happened. I couldn't stop them."

"How did you hold on?" Aiko's soft voice offered comfort even as it cut him.

He looked down into her eyes. "I thought of my family... and that they would come for me... they would find me... and that I had to survive so I could protect them and keep them all safe from harm, from suffering as I had. I had faith in them, and it kept me going, kept me hanging by a thread as the wretched humans murdered my friend... as my own life slipped away, my body battered... mind destroyed... fractured."

Fractured.

Split in two.

The male he had once been, and the monster he had become.

A monster who awakened whenever his family were in danger, because he had focused on them in that black time, using them to keep his will to live going, enduring the pain and torture so he could be with those he loved again, vowing over and over again that he would survive so he could protect them.

"But they found you?" Aiko rose on her knees and gently cupped his cheeks, keeping his eyes on her.

He was sure they were all crimson now, no trace of blue left in them, because he could feel his other side, feel it writhing and whispering to him, telling him to repay the humans in kind and make them bleed, make them suffer, make their loved ones howl in agony.

"Father was distraught," he murmured, trying to shut down the pain that blazed in his heart before it raged out of control. He couldn't hurt Aiko. He wouldn't risk it. He was stronger than that darker part of himself. He wouldn't lose control. Not while she was holding him like this anyway, her palms soft against his face, keeping him grounded and with her. "He couldn't find me since my powers were bound and I was practically mortal, so he asked the oracles and then begged Helios to aid him, just as he had aided Demeter in her search for Persephone."

"Helios found you?"

He nodded. "Father was preparing to leave the Underworld to free me when the lunar perigee hit."

Her brow crinkled.

"When our moon is closest to Earth… it affects me because of my power. Water. The perigee caused a surge in my powers, enough that they broke whatever restraint the gate had placed on me." He looked away from her, not sure he wanted to see her face when he admitted what he had done. "I destroyed everyone at the village… daubed their blood on my face and went on a rampage across the land, devastating everything with storms. Father found me as the moon waned, and it took all of his strength to subdue me and convince me to return to the Underworld."

Because he had wanted to continue his rampage until there wasn't a single mortal left in the world.

He sucked down a slow, deep breath, and closed his eyes, and then forced them open again, because he needed to see her reaction to what he was about to say.

"When the perigee hits, I'm a danger to everyone. My brothers lock me away. When the moon is full, I'm dangerous, and I have to remain within the mansion grounds. If I see my family in danger… those I love… then I'm dangerous." He paused when her eyes widened slightly, and he saw she knew the part of him that he had wanted to hide from her a little longer—the part that was falling in love with her. "I'm dangerous, Aiko. I'm fractured. There's… a side of me… I never want you to see."

"But I saw it—"

"No," he cut her off. "You haven't seen it, and you never will, not if I have a say in it… but I don't… I… sometimes I can't hold it back."

He grabbed her arms, and she tensed and gasped.

"There's a side of me, and sometimes I can't stop it… and if I ever change around you… run. As fast as you can, as far as you can. Just run and don't look back… because I don't want to hurt you, and I'm afraid I might."

She paled, but then rallied, brushed her thumbs across his cheeks and calmly held his gaze as she nodded.

Relief poured through him.

"Do you hate humans?" she murmured.

"Yes… no… not all of the time." He pinched the bridge of his nose. "Sometimes. A lot of the time. I can't forgive them."

"I understand." She truly did, he could read that in her eyes, feel it in her as she continued to hold his face, her touch offering comfort. She cared for people, strangers, cried over them when they were hurt, and wanted to help them all.

He had witnessed that tonight. She had love inside her, love so deep that she had enough for everyone. He only had enough for a few, wasn't sure anyone else deserved his compassion or a single shred of affection from him.

She had wept for the dead, had hurt herself by struggling to help them, causing herself emotional pain, but she had done it anyway. She had looked so fragile, so small as she had moved from person to person, battling on, helping as many as she could. She had been so brave. Her strength had amazed him. He would have left them to die, but she had done all she could for them, and would have done more if he hadn't forced her to leave with him.

She was stronger than he had thought.

His beautiful butterfly.

He cupped the nape of her neck, drew her to him as he frowned, and pressed his forehead against hers, a maelstrom of emotions ripping at him, everything from love to rage, from light to darkest black.

Gods, he prayed that if she ever witnessed his other side, she would understand, and wouldn't fear him.

Wouldn't leave him.

Because he wasn't sure he could live without her.

She was light in his dark existence, gave him warmth when he was cold, soothed him when he raged and gave him strength when he was weak.

"I never realised humans could be like you," he husked, holding her to him, needing to feel her pressed against him. "You give me strength, Aiko... faith, and some belief that I am doing the right thing by protecting the gates between our worlds, and the humans."

She smiled softly, tipped her chin up and swept her lips across his, and he tugged her to him and seized her mouth, needed her kiss more than air, more than anything. She didn't fight him. She melted in his arms, even though he was rough with her, was sure he was hurting her. When he had tasted his fill, he convinced himself to release her, and gods, it was a struggle.

She rewarded it by rising onto her feet, taking hold of his hand and bringing him onto his. She led him to the pool, and he stepped down into it, sank under the hot water and let it wash over him, his closeness to his element smoothing the edges off his mood even as it stung the cuts on his body and the back of his head.

He floated in the pool, anxiously listening to Aiko as she washed herself, waiting for her to join him as he studied the faint stars that were giving way to morning as the sun edged towards breaking the horizon.

Tokyo would be safe for tonight, the daemons not strong enough to withstand the sunlight.

He breathed a sigh of relief.

The sound of water rippling had him moving onto his knees and he froze as Aiko stepped down into the pool.

Naked.

He swallowed hard at the sight of her petite curves bared to him, and she looked down, a blush scalding her cheeks that had nothing to do with the temperature of the water as she sank into it, using it to cover herself.

His heart pounded, the thought that she trusted him after everything he had told her, was willing to take this next step with him enough to have a shot of adrenaline bursting through his veins.

He wasn't sure where to look.

He wanted to stare at her, drink his fill of her and make her stand so he could see her clearly, but he didn't want her to feel awkward, embarrassed by being naked around him for the first time.

He settled for kicking off and drifting to her side of the pool, and resting beside her on the raised stone that acted like a seat. She glanced across at him, a shimmer of heat in her dark eyes, need that called to him and stoked his own.

It had been a long time, a very long time, since he had been with someone, and then he had only taken things all the way a few times. After what had happened to him six hundred years ago, he had avoided intimacy, partly because he found it hard to trust himself and partly because he feared letting anyone into his heart, afraid of adding another to the small list of those he cared deeply about and was liable to lose control over if they were injured.

But Aiko was already beyond the barrier, held close to his heart, far closer than anyone.

And he would never hurt her.

"Esher?" she whispered, her eyes shifting to the zen garden and then the sky. "What's Tycho?"

He frowned. Daimon must have used it around her, but he didn't remember it. Had he been that far gone?

Perhaps she had seen more than a glimpse of his other side after all.

"It's the opposite of a trigger word. It calms me, helps draw me back and give me control again." He sank back against the smooth stone of the bath, leaning his head on the walkway behind him, and stared at the fading stars. "I need you to remember it. It's important, Aiko. If you ever fear me, if I look like I'm... say it to me."

He had never thought he would be handing out a safe word to anyone outside of his family, let alone giving it to a human to use on him, but he needed her to have it. He needed her to have some power over him, because he needed to boost his faith that he wouldn't hurt her.

"What does it mean?" She moved in the water, and when her arm brushed his, he realised she had been shuffling closer.

Her thigh pressed against his and he couldn't stop himself from lowering his gaze to her legs, and that enticing patch of dark at their apex.

His mouth dried out.

His cock stirred.

He took one of the squares of white cloth from the side behind him and placed it over his groin. It hid nothing from her, only ended up making her look down to see what he was doing, and the pink hue that washed over her cheeks and the flicker of hunger that filled her eyes was enough to have him remembering the way her mouth had felt on his cock, which had it growing as hard as stone.

"Tycho?" He forced the word out, his voice tight, and tried to focus on anything other than the visions of him dragging her onto his lap and seating himself inside her, a fantasy that built in his head as he struggled to talk. "It's the brightest crater on the moon."

He looked for it but couldn't see the damned thing now that he needed something to get her eyes off his aching length.

He caught her cheek instead, his hand dripping water all down her, and brought her face up so her eyes met his. The water rolled down her chest, to the swell of her breasts, and he struggled not to look at them, painfully aware he could see her nipples clearly just below the surface.

"Father gave the word to me, because he wanted me to see and remember that even in the darkest times, light can still shine through." Relief went through him when that had her focus settling firmly on his face and his words, not his body. "Tycho is that light to me, because I have such a strong connection to the moon, and I've spent centuries reinforcing my bond with it, and that crater, making the power the word has over me stronger. It still only works when I'm partly conscious, when the other me isn't fully in control."

Which was the reason Daimon apparently hadn't bothered to spring it on him when the wraith had injured him.

Esher couldn't remember much about it, because his other side had been firmly in control. He only knew he had lashed out at his brothers and threatened their females.

Gods, if he had wanted to hurt them, could he honestly say he wouldn't hurt Aiko if his other side seized control?

He shook that thought away, because contemplating it would only allow fear to take root and shake his faith that he would never hurt her.

"Tycho?" she murmured the word, and he instantly felt calmer, the way she said it more soothing to him than when Daimon uttered it. "I will use it if I have to."

But she didn't want to.

"It doesn't hurt me." He needed her to know that. "It just... calms me."

She half-smiled and moved onto her knees beside him, so her breasts crested out of the water and he had a damned hard time not looking at them.

"Tycho." She leaned towards him, pressed her right hand to his chest and scalded him, branding him with her touch as she brought her mouth close to his.

"That is *not* going to calm me. Just inflame me." He snaked his arm around her waist and hauled her onto his lap as his other hand seized the back of her neck, tangling in her wet black hair.

He meant to kiss her, but as he looked at her, all clean now, the dirt of the blast scrubbed from her pale skin, he froze and another need overcame him.

He crushed her against him, trembling with the force of it as he held her, clutching her nape and squeezing her tightly.

She was fine.

Rather than trying to break free of him, she leaned into him, wrapped her arms around his neck and held him.

Just held him.

It hit him that she needed comfort too, that he wasn't the only one who had been rattled tonight and she was struggling to cope with the things she had seen—things she had probably never witnessed before.

Minutes ticked past and neither of them moved. He absorbed the comfort she gave him, memorised the way she held him and how he could feel her love in that embrace, how much she cared about him. How much she wanted to help him.

How much she wanted to be with him.

Finally, as the sun broke the horizon, he convinced his grip on her to ease. She drew back, her brown eyes warm and bright, a mixture of love and passion shining in them as she gazed into his, the negative emotions he had felt in her gone now, erased by him holding her, giving her the comfort she needed.

He lowered his eyes to her lips, his pulse picking up pace as he stared at their soft curves and felt her body beneath his hands, pressed against him.

He could feel her nerves as she trembled slightly in his embrace, could sense her desire as her breath came in shorter, sharper bursts, and her hands settled against his shoulders, and need built in her dark gaze.

Need he was going to satisfy for both of them.

CHAPTER 16

Her kiss seared him as fiercely as her touch as he claimed her mouth, trying to keep it tender and gentle, but finding it impossible as she leaned into the kiss and her tongue brushed his lips. Her moan was his undoing, unravelling the ties that bound his passion, so it flooded through him, washing away all of his restraint.

Esher gathered her closer, crushing her to his chest, needing to feel every inch of her pressed against him. Water rippled around them as he skimmed his hands down her sides, claimed her waist and moved her. As her knees parted, allowing his thighs to press between them, and her backside settled on his knees, her kiss grew tense.

He could feel the nerves in her.

Was he rushing her?

He didn't want to rush her, wanted everything to happen at a pace that she set. He would wait forever if she asked it of him.

And when she finally gave herself to him, he would be gentle, tender, everything that she deserved. He would hold back his own need, the searing passion that consumed him, and be careful with her.

He would never hurt her.

It echoed in his head, a soft chant that filled the silence that stretched between the sound of water lapping at their bodies, her delicate moans, and his own ragged breathing.

When Aiko shuffled closer, her knees coming to press against his hips, he groaned and resisted pulling her closer still, until she brushed his heavy shaft. It throbbed, so hard that it hurt, so sensitive that each time the hot water swept over the crown, he had to grit his teeth.

As if sensing his need for relief, Aiko lowered her hand, running her fingers over his chest in a maddening way that only made him even more sensitive, had sparks skittering over his flesh and pebbled his nipples. He groaned and tipped his head back as she brushed the head of his cock, damn near wept as she stroked and teased it, sending waves of heat rolling down it, tingles that swept through him and had him verging on begging her for more.

"Aiko," he breathed, swallowed hard and managed to open his eyes and lift his head and look at her.

Her brown eyes were dark, pupils dilated in a way that called to him, but it was her beaded nipples that stole his focus. He wrapped his arms around her, hauled her up onto her knees and latched onto her right one, her moan music to his ears as her hands instantly came down on his shoulders. She gripped him hard as he suckled and teased her with sweeps of his tongue, tasting the water on her.

Her small hands shifted to his hair, tangled in it as she clung to him, clutching him to her.

The need to turn up the heat, to tear another passion-drenched sigh from her, had him dropping his left hand and snaking it around her bottom. She tensed and then melted into him, her moan loud in the early morning air, as he found her core and stroked along it towards her bead. It tightened as he brushed it, and gods, he answered her moan with one of his own as she arched her back, raising her bottom, allowing him easier access.

He shook with the need, the hunger building inside him as he explored her with his fingers, stroked them up and down, back and forth between her nub and her entrance, his heart pounding each time he neared it. A desire to press into her had him lingering a little longer each time, judging her reaction as he suckled her nipple.

She moaned again as he tugged it a little harder, rolled it in his teeth, and he found the courage he had been missing.

He pressed the tip of his finger into her damp core.

Gods, it was hot, deliciously warm and wet, tight around his digit as he sank as deep as his first knuckle.

She bucked and moaned, gripped his hair so tightly he feared she might pull some out as he withdrew, lowered his hand to her nub and teased it again, his cock fit to burst as a need to be inside her crashed over him. He needed to feel her around him, tight and wet. Needed to fill her and make love with her, and make her belong to him.

He needed to mark her as his female.

Needed to make her want only him, forever.

That need consumed him, a dark desire that was powerful, overwhelming him and driving out all other thought, until only that primal urge to claim her remained.

He sank his finger back into her, lifted his head and swallowed her moan in a kiss. He angled his head, pushed past her lips and tangled his tongue with hers, feasting on her moans as she clung to him, her body trembling with each gentle press of his finger and each withdraw.

Esher couldn't stop himself from adding a second finger and probing her a little deeper, as deep as he could go in the position she was in. It was hard at first, but as he kissed her, touched her, she grew wetter, allowing him to easily slide his fingers in and out.

And then she started writhing her hips and seized command of the kiss, her tongue invading his mouth as she drove him back against the side of the bath.

Her need flooded him.

Mingled with his own and made it impossible to deny.

On a low growl, he withdrew from her, grabbed her backside in both hands and pulled her to him. She moaned and rocked against his cock as she made contact, sliding up and down it, filling the air with the sound of water splashing as she frantically rode his length.

He lifted her, not breaking the kiss, and angled his hips so he could reach his cock. He shuddered as he pushed the head through her folds, groaned in time with her as he inched into her tight sheath.

Tensed with her when he hit a barrier.

"Aiko," he whispered, clutching her hips, torn between continuing and stopping.

Stopping won.

112

Because he didn't deserve this.

She finally opened her eyes and looked at him, the hunger he could feel in her still shining in them. No flicker of shame lit her features. No embarrassed little blush.

There was only the barest hint of anger directed at him.

"Don't stop," she murmured and wriggled, and gods, he had to bite down on his tongue to stop himself from doing as she wanted, focusing on the pain rather than the pleasure she unwittingly caused by rotating her hips around the head of his cock.

She was making this hard on him.

"I want this." Her low soft voice curled around him, banished the doubts that were creeping in at the edges of his mind to darken it with thoughts that she would regret what they were doing if he took her virginity, that she would hate him for it, because he was a monster. Her eyes met his, no trace of hate in them, no sign that she would come to despise him either, or that she thought him unworthy. "I want this with you, Esher."

He wasn't sure how to respond to that.

It was too much for him.

The darker part hissed that this was a trick, that the human meant to lure him to his doom with her body, pull him into her snare so she could hurt him.

Esher shut out the damned voice, because his heart screamed that Aiko wasn't like that. There wasn't a bad bone in her body, and he loved her for it. He loved her for being the one human on this wretched plane who looked at him as if it would kill her to hurt him, as if she would sooner hurt herself than another.

As if she loved him.

The thought that she was untouched, an innocent, had the darker side born of his heritage rising to the fore, flooding him with a need to make her belong to him, because she would be his and his alone, and that it was further proof that she was meant to be his.

Light to his darkness.

Innocence to his wickedness.

But perhaps not too innocent.

Because she took the decision out of his hands, pressing her body down on his, a look of sheer concentration on her face as she inched him deeper inside her. He groaned and gave up the fight, struggled to focus so he could make it feel good for her, even when he knew it had to hurt. She was tight, small compared with him.

It didn't stop her.

When she flinched, he gathered her to him, stopping her, and kissed her, distracting her with it as he held her with one hand and teased her nipple with his other one. She was tense for a moment, and then she moaned, and he felt her relaxing, loosening around him as desire built again. He kept kissing and teasing her, dropped his hand to fondle her bundle of nerves, drinking her moans as they grew louder.

His own joined them as she moved again, sinking onto him, and he gritted his teeth when she took a sharp breath and pushed down hard, and the tip of his shaft struck as deep as she could take him.

He kept kissing her, aware of her pain, and rubbed his thumb across her pert bead, stroking it to ease her and replace the pain with pleasure.

Gods, he wanted to move, wanted to lift her off him and sink back into her, but somehow he found the strength to stay where he was, still as a statue.

Inside her.

That sank in, and he drew back and looked at her, found no trace of pain in her eyes, only desire and excitement, and affection. He couldn't breathe as he thought about the fact they were one. He was inside her, and she was his now.

His forever if he had his way.

His little butterfly.

He only hoped she didn't fly away from him.

He lifted his hand and cupped her cheek, held her gaze as she leaned into his touch, and felt the weight of that thought press down on him, a fear that wasn't welcome but one he couldn't shut out. She tilted her head, pressed a kiss to his palm that lingered, and then did the one thing guaranteed to make him forget his fears.

She moved.

Her hands clutched his biceps and she rocked her hips, nothing more than a swirl at first, but then she grew bolder, and gods, he could only watch her as she bloomed before his eyes.

He sank against the side of the bath as she began to rock on him, small strokes that barely pulled him an inch out of her, and then two, and three, and sweet fucking gods, he wasn't sure he could take it. His breathing turned as ragged as hers as she began to ride him in earnest, making the water lap against his chest as she rose off him almost all the way and then sank back down again.

She needed to go higher.

He wanted her to feel heaven in his arms, bliss in this moment.

Esher caught her hips and she leaned towards him and captured his lips as he started to move her on him, so she almost pulled free of his cock on each stroke. She gasped and shivered, moaned louder as he drove back into her, long slow thrusts that had her breath and his coming quicker.

Her arms looped around his neck and she kissed him harder, and he felt the need rising inside her as she began to move again, fighting his control. He pumped his hips each time she sank down on him, driving his cock into her, quickening their tempo as his own need built towards a crescendo.

She groaned as he slid lower on the seat, the angle allowing her body to brush his as she came down, and he tore another from her as he sank his hand beneath the water and stroked his thumb across her nub, teasing her in time with his deep strokes of his cock.

A soft, startled cry left her lips as she arched backwards, her hands clutching his shoulders, and breasts thrusting into the air.

Gods, she was beautiful as she came undone, her body quivering violently around his length, each jerk and flex of it pushing him closer to the edge.

He deepened his thrusts, drank his fill of her as her heat scalded him and she moaned with each plunge of his cock into her, each stroke that drew out her climax and added to it. She leaned back, the angle making her tighter still, and release surged through him.

He tipped his head back, his entire body quaking with the force of it as he loosed a hoarse shout, his fingers pressing into her soft flesh and pinning her on his cock as it throbbed, pulsing so hard every inch of him kicked with it.

He fought for air as he held her there, every muscle tensed as heat and a thousand stars exploded inside him, and the world drifted away.

Aiko sank against his chest, her heart thundering in time with his as she trembled.

Gods.

He wrapped his arms around her and held her to him, clutched her as she murmured something and settled on him, their bodies still intimately entwined.

Time drifted past, the sun rising to bathe the world in gold hues, and when he looked down at Aiko to mention they should leave the bath, he froze.

She was sleeping.

He carefully scooped her up into his arms, trying not to wake her, and stepped out of the tub. He stared at her as he carried her towards his room, watching over her as she slept.

Protecting her.

He lifted his head and looked off to his left, to Tokyo where it flickered between the present and the future that would happen if he and his brothers failed, a city broken and blazing against the blackened sky, filled with the terrified shrieks of humans and the wretched snarls of daemons.

His gaze drifted back down to Aiko.

She was dangerous. He knew that. She was a weakness now, one his enemy might exploit to get to him, as they had with Eva for Valen.

Valen would have turned to their side for her, just as his brother had said, Esher believed that.

He gazed down at Aiko.

What would he do for her?

He would destroy the world.

CHAPTER 17

Aiko slowed as she placed her clothes back in her backpack, drawing out the process because she didn't want to leave yet, even when she knew it was necessary.

When she felt Esher's gaze on her, she paused and looked over her shoulder at him, finding him stood in the doorway of his room, the pretty courtyard garden and the other wing of the house a beautiful backdrop for the god who was stealing her heart.

Or might have already stolen it.

That heart felt heavy as she looked at him, catching her feelings echoed in his sombre blue eyes. He didn't want her to leave either, even when he knew it was necessary.

The original plan had been to part from him yesterday, but when he had taken her home, he had held her so tightly, had been so reluctant to let her go, and when he had finally released her, it had been to tell her to get some things because he wanted her to stay another night.

He was pushing himself. The fight that had happened with his white-haired brother, Daimon, when he had returned to the mansion with her in tow was testament to that. He had been vicious, darker than she had ever seen him as he had warred with his brother, arguing against Daimon's orders to take her home.

Daimon had eventually given in when Esher had promised to message Marek should he take a turn for the worse and the moon affected him, allowing the rugged earth god to take her home in his stead.

Things had been strained for a while after Daimon had left, but Esher had settled as they had walked the grounds, and watched television, and when she had cooked dinner for him for a change.

When the moon had risen, and she had seen only a sliver of it was missing, she had felt the gravity of what Esher had done.

This afternoon, after spending another day with him alone in the house, savouring every second of it, she had asked him to take her home.

Because she had grown aware that he didn't intend to do it, that he wanted to keep her with him even when the full moon rose tonight.

He had told her about the way the moon affected him, and she could see that it was already playing on him, had shortened his temper and caused him to fight with his brother, and had him restless. All day, he hadn't been able to keep still. He had spent most of it in the garden with her, walking the snaking paths with her, taking in the cherry blossoms, or walking without her whenever she grew tired and needed to take a break above the pond on the walkway outside his room.

His restlessness had grown throughout the day, becoming pacing accompanied by glances at her that spoke of worry. Fear. He was afraid of hurting her. Feared that other side of him might emerge when the moon rose and he found himself in the presence of a human.

So she was taking the decision out of his hands.

"You don't have to go," he husked, the pain in it tearing at her, weakening her resolve.

"I do. It's only for a couple of days." She smiled at him.

She had discovered that he liked it when she smiled, and she was determined to keep on smiling for him, even when she hurt inside.

Damn, she was going to miss him.

"My parents are due home today, and I don't want them worrying when I'm not there."

His expression darkened.

"But *I* need you here," he bit out, and a flicker of regret crossed his face and he looked away from her, fixing his stormy blue eyes on the pond to his left. "Sorry."

She shook her head, crossed the room to him and took hold of his hand. He looked down at it, and then up into her eyes.

"You did nothing wrong." She pressed her fingers to the palm of his hand and brushed her thumb over his knuckles.

He huffed and shoved his fingers through the longer lengths of his black hair, pulling them back from his face as it twisted in agony. "I shouted at you."

He had hardly shouted. She had seen him shout. His words to her had barely been raised, only a small snap in them as his emotions had gotten the better of him, nothing to apologise for.

Before she could say anything, she was pressed against his chest, his arms steel bands around her as he pressed his nose against her hair and exhaled hard.

"Gods, I'm going to miss you."

Aiko smiled at that, wriggled her hands free and wrapped her arms around his waist. She held him, offering him all the comfort she could.

"I'm going to miss you too. You can text me. Call me. Whenever you want." She stroked his back through his light grey t-shirt.

He pushed her back, gripping her shoulders and holding her at arm's length. "You mean that?"

She smiled again. "Of course. Here, give me your details."

She pulled her white phone from her backpack, and he fished his out of the pocket of his blue jeans. He held it out to her, and she transferred their details, and a little something else she knew he might need. When she was done, he took it from her and stared at the screen.

At the picture of her.

It was a year old now, and her hair had been shorter, but the way his eyes lit up said he didn't care.

He looked at her, and then back down at his phone, and then at hers, and she frowned as he fumbled with his, pressing the screen. What was he doing?

It became apparent when he scooped her up in his free arm as if she weighed nothing, holding her off the floor at his side, and reached his arm out in front of him. She smiled for the camera and leaned her cheek against his shoulder as he snapped the picture, and when he grumbled something and went to take another, she pressed a kiss to his cheek.

He froze, leaned into the kiss and then reluctantly set her down.

She pulled his arm towards her so she could see the picture. This time, she wouldn't have been able to contain her smile if she had tried.

Esher was blushing in it, his blue eyes wide as she kissed his cheek.

Before he could protest, she transferred it to her phone.

"It's an awful picture." He tried to get her phone from her, but she evaded him, giggling as he came close to catching her.

"It's mine now. I'm keeping it." She dodged him again, edited the picture with some text and graphics, and added it to his name in her contacts.

This time, when he reached for her phone, he did it in earnest and she wasn't quick enough to get away from him. He had her phone in his hand before she could blink.

But he was the one who blinked at her as he looked at the picture.

"Watashi no kareshi?" He lifted his eyes to her, that hint of a blush on his cheeks again, tempered by the fire blazing in his eyes that told her he liked it, and that if she didn't leave soon, it was going to be even harder to leave because she would be swept up in him again, in the need that overcame her whenever he looked at her that way.

As if he would die without her.

She nodded. "Would you prefer 'my lover'?"

He growled, swept her up into his arms and kissed her. "Boyfriend is just fine with me."

She kissed him back, and it was hard to force herself to stop and make him put her down. Mostly because he kept growling at her whenever she tried, the inhuman sound leaving his lips no longer frightening her.

When he finally set her down, the sun was lower.

"I don't want you to go." He smoothed his hands over her hair, down her cheeks, and framed her face, his blue eyes tearing at her resolve again as she drowned in them and the pain they held.

"Two nights. We can talk all through them." Although that did depend on whether he was grounded enough to talk to her.

Daimon had caught her alone at one point yesterday and warned her that even when it wasn't a perigee, Esher could be a little different during a full moon.

She refused to let that scare her.

Esher let out a long sigh, slipped his hand into hers and led her towards the main room of the house. When he reached it, he paused and looked as if he wanted to say something. He didn't. He walked with her to the door of the house, jammed his feet into his army boots and waited for her to put on her shoes, and then took her hand again.

"Ready?" He pulled her close to him.

No. She wasn't. But she nodded, even as that ache in her heart grew.

He sighed again, wrapped her in his arms and she closed her eyes as the world whirled around her. When it settled again, he continued to hold her, and she couldn't let him go either. She clutched his t-shirt in both fists, fighting tears that felt foolish and stupid, part of her wanting to hold them back so he didn't see them, so she didn't make this harder on him.

She convinced herself to release him, took hold of his hand and walked across the small play park where he had landed with her, towards her family's clinic.

The door opened, and she flinched as her mother bustled out, dressed in a blouse and pencil skirt that made her look more like she had just returned from a day at the office rather than a vacation.

"Aiko!" Her mother called, all smiles as she waved her hand.

That smile dropped off her face when she noticed Esher.

Aiko felt his gaze land on her and she knew what he expected. He thought she would let go of his hand, be ashamed of him because he was a foreigner, or something like that.

She held it tighter, showing him that she wasn't going to let him go. She loved her parents, but their opinion wouldn't sway her. Whether they liked him or not, her feelings for him wouldn't change.

She would always love him.

"This is Esher, my boyfriend." A smile tugged at her lips as he immediately bowed.

Her mother eyed him, and spoke in Japanese, clearly believing a foreigner wouldn't understand her. "Where is he from? Where did you meet him? He looks dangerous."

Everyone looked dangerous to her mother. The postman looked dangerous. The high school boys and then the college boys that Aiko had known through her friends had looked dangerous. Even the local children playing in the park looked dangerous.

"I'm not a danger to your daughter." Esher's response in perfect Japanese had her mother's eyes widening in horror.

"Does he teach?" She looked to Aiko, as if Esher was incapable of answering for himself.

"No. He's lived in Japan a long time, Mother. If you have questions, you can ask him." Aiko wasn't surprised when her mother gave her a look that said she wouldn't. She sighed and turned to Esher. "This is my mother, Fumi Matsumoto."

He bowed again. "A pleasure to meet you. Aiko has spoken much of the work you and her father do here."

She hadn't, but he scored points for trying to get into her mother's good book.

"Anata," Fumi called over her shoulder, a term of endearment for Aiko's father, and she wanted to cringe.

Her gaze strayed to the sky as she waited for her father to appear, awareness that evening was falling growing stronger as the sun sank lower, painting the blue with swaths of pink and gold.

Esher needed to go, but she knew that he wouldn't, not when her parents wanted to question him and see what sort of man had stolen their daughter's heart.

Not even when it was becoming increasingly dangerous for him to be outside the mansion grounds and the wards that protected it.

"What's the fuss?" Her father halted behind her mother, and when his eyes lifted to land on Esher, he blinked. Looked at Aiko for an explanation.

"Esher, this is Hirotami Matsumoto, my father." She waited for him to bow before turning to her father. "Father, this is Esher, my boyfriend."

He didn't seem pleased to hear that.

"We can argue about this later. Esher needs to go now." She ignored the way Esher scowled at her, because they had all the time in the world after the moon was no longer full for him to win over her stubborn parents.

It was probably going to take at least another four or five full moons, or even more, before they accepted that she was in love with a foreigner.

She didn't even want to think about how long it would take for them to accept she was in love with a god.

She could only thank those gods that her mother hadn't inherited her mother's gift as Aiko had and wasn't aware that Esher wasn't human.

When neither of her parents showed any sign of moving, Aiko turned away and tugged on Esher's hand. He refused to move, and she looked back over her shoulder at him, a sigh leaving her as she found him staring down her parents with a look in his stormy blue eyes that said he was ready to do battle.

She pulled on his hand again, and he glanced her way this time.

She smiled for him and said in English, "After the full moon."

He looked as if he didn't want to accept that, but then he turned with her and followed her back towards the park. She stopped near the gate, under the shade of the trees, and wrapped her arms around him, not caring that her parents were still watching. She needed to hold him, and hold on to him a little longer.

He sighed and wrapped her up in his arms, held her so tight she wanted to cry, and buried his face in her neck. He didn't resist her when she twisted her head towards him, was swift to capture her lips and kiss her, his desperation matching hers as they clung to each other.

When he eventually released her, it was to pull back and reach into his jeans pocket.

"I made something for you." He pulled his hand out, held it between them with his palm facing downwards, and opened his fingers.

A small, round ginger cat dropped from the black string looped over his middle finger.

It had tiny white wings.

"I remember the one you had on your backpack that night, and I noticed you didn't have any charms on your phone, so I made one for you. Do you like it?" He sounded as if his life depended on her liking it, a hint of nerves in his deep voice as he looked at her.

"I love it." She took it from him, pausing for a heartbeat when her fingers touched it and she felt the power in it.

She settled it in her palm and stared down at it. It was cute, but no ordinary charm. The sensation she got from it was similar to what she felt when she neared the ancient cherry trees in Esher's garden, and some of the lanterns and boulders, and one of the maples.

He scrubbed his hand around the back of his neck. "I might have put a little magic in it."

Aiko attached it to her phone and gripped it as she lifted her eyes to his. "What sort of magic?"

"Protection." He reached out, took hold of her hand and uncurled her fingers, revealing the cat. "They're gods, you know? Every one of them. This one will protect you."

They were?

She wasn't sure she would ever look at a cat in the same way again.

Esher's gaze drifted away from her, and she frowned as it turned distant.

"Esher?" She touched his hand, and her black eyebrows pinched together as she saw the trident on the inside of his right wrist, just above one of his matching black bracelets, was dark.

"I better go," he muttered, as distant as his gaze, and then shook his head and looked down at her. "I'll see you in a few days?"

He didn't sound sure, so she nodded, tiptoed and kissed him one last time, a slow one that held all the love she had in her heart for him.

He pressed his forehead against hers, growled as frustration rolled off him, and then kissed her again.

"Be safe," he whispered against her lips, and then he was gone, leaving only wisps of black smoke behind.

She looked around, glad that no one was watching them, and couldn't hold back the sigh that rolled up her throat as her heart grew heavier. It was only two nights. She could survive that long without him, and it didn't do to depend on a man too much. She was strong, independent, and able to take care of herself.

But she still grinned like an idiot when her phone vibrated.

She opened it and smiled at the screen and the message there.

Miss you already.

She fired one back as she turned on her heel and walked towards her home.

"Miss you too. Be safe. I'll be waiting."

CHAPTER 18

Ares glared and stoked his mood, keeping it at a rolling boil as he sat on the dark red couch in the cream living room of his apartment, twisted at an angle and hunched over towards Megan where she sat beside him, her knees touching his and his hand in hers.

At her mercy.

He set his jaw, refusing to let his mood even out like it wanted to as she focused on what she was doing to him.

"Remind me again why I'm doing this?" he growled low, showing her just what he thought about what she was doing to him.

Her soulful brown eyes left her work to meet his, shining with amusement over what she was doing, and a lot of warmth and love.

Gods, he loved her.

Maybe that was the reason he was putting himself through this.

He would do anything for her, a trait that had earned his brothers calling him everything from sentimental prick to lovesick idiot. He didn't care. The only thing that mattered was Megan looking at him like this, her eyes bright and smile quick to come as she pushed her rich brown shoulder-length hair behind her ear and went back to work.

He raked his eyes over her, down her fitted teal jumper to the dark blue jeans that hugged her lean legs, to her pink-tipped toes. Like candy. He wanted to kneel before her and suck on them.

"You lost a bet, remember?" Her words had him forgetting worshipping her and going back to glaring at her.

He grumbled at that little reminder. It had been a stupid bet, and he hadn't imagined this would be the forfeit for losing it.

"I'm being nice to you, and you only have to wear it for a week." She moved, angling her body away from him as she reloaded her weapon, and he scowled at his nails as she turned back to him and painted another one with a second coat of black lacquer. "I could have chosen pink."

He dropped his eyes to her toes and shuddered.

He supposed she could have, but he still wasn't amused by his plight. A week. His beautiful vixen knew how to torture him.

She was good at painting nails though, hadn't got a speck on his skin yet.

He cocked his head to his right.

And the black did look pretty good on him.

A swirling sensation went through him.

"Wait!" She swatted his hand when he grabbed the brush from her, clumsily put it into the fiddly pot, and stood.

"Time to go, Sweetheart." He held his hand out, his holster whipping into it as he pulled Megan against him, and pictured Central Park and the gate there.

"Fucking daemons," Megan snapped as she clung to him, her words echoing in the brief flicker of darkness as he connected with the Underworld and bounced back out again, landing on the dewy grass in the middle of the dark park.

His thoughts exactly, but he was pissed at the disturbance and the fact a daemon was daring to near the gate, and she was pissed about his nails.

He focused on them as he released her and tossed his guns to her, releasing just enough control over his power to allow his heat to dry them. It was second nature to control it around Megan now, but it still slipped beyond his grasp from time to time. He'd had to buy her a lot of new clothes since she had moved in.

Megan slipped her arms into the black leather holster and drew one of the silver guns, checked it was loaded like a damn expert and eyed the darkness.

It was quiet, too quiet.

"You sure you sensed—" She cut off with a squeak as he pushed her behind him and slammed his fist into the daemon that had suddenly appeared behind her, sending the male sprawling out on the grass.

The male crab-crawled backwards, trying to gain some space.

Ares stalked towards him and cracked his knuckles.

"You be careful of that polish!"

He wasn't sure whether Megan aimed that order at him, or at the daemon. The male popped to his feet, turned tail and ran. Ares huffed. He hated it when they ran.

Why attack his damned gate and then run?

Daemons needed to learn to have a little backbone and follow through with a plan when faced with him. It would make it quicker to deal with them.

He took a step forwards, intending to chase the male, and frowned as he slowly turned his head to his left.

Another daemon sauntered across the grass towards him, a female with blonde hair tied in a mass of waves at the back of her head, a dark gold metal bikini that was all swirls and spikes, and eyes that glowed gold in the dim light from the streetlamps.

A valkyrie?

Wings erupted from her back as she launched at him, hitting him at the speed of a train, sending him flying through the air with her. Gunshots snapped through the still night, bullets whizzing past the valkyrie's half-leather half-feather wings as her clawed talons closed around his throat.

He growled and unleashed more of his power, and she hissed through sharp teeth and dropped him as she recoiled.

He stepped, disappearing and reappearing next to Megan, who didn't take her eyes off the winged bitch.

"What the fuck is that?" She fired again. Once. Twice. A third time as the valkyrie swooped.

The bitch shrieked as the bullet tore through her bare calf and went down, hitting the grass and skidding across it. Bullets wouldn't kill this one. They would only piss her off.

"Valkyrie." He risked a glance at Megan, taking his eyes off the female for only a split-second. She was gone when he looked back though, and he turned in a circle, keeping Megan in his line of sight so the female couldn't target her. "A daemon. One of the powerful sort. Think of them as a sort of mash-up between immortal angel, demon and a harpy. She's not a true harpy, just an off-shoot from that species, but she's just as dangerous. She'll have a charm, an enchantment that protects her. We'll need to break it."

Easier said than done.

The valkyrie proved that by swooping out of nowhere, grabbing him by the throat and lifting off with him again, taking him high into the night sky.

He growled and grabbed her arms, and unleashed more of his power, letting flames lick over his hands. The smell of scorched flesh filled his nostrils, and she screamed like a banshee, but didn't let go this time. Resilient bitch.

"Ares!" Megan called and he could feel her fear, her need to see he was alright. So he unleashed a little more of his power.

Might have gone supernova and lit up the whole fucking sky for her.

Flames licked over every inch of him, and over the valkyrie too. The second they touched the gold feathered tops of her wings, she released him.

He didn't release her.

He dug his nails into her flesh and growled as he sent all the flames covering him rushing down his arms and over her body.

She cried out and lashed out at him like a wild thing, slashing with her talons. Fire seared him, blazing along each slash, but he held on, stoked the flames and grinned as she unleashed another long ear-splitting shriek as her flesh charred beneath his hands.

"You picked the wrong brother to fuck with."

Her golden eyes snapped down to him, all the fires of the Underworld raging in them.

She got her feet against his stomach and kicked hard.

He didn't have a chance to teleport.

He hit the grass like a meteor, carving a groove in it and ending up in a crater in the dirt, earth showered all over him. Every inch of him burned, a combination of pain from the impact and the heat of his own flames.

Flames that he loved but that had consequences when he unleashed them like that.

Not even the best fire-retardant material could withstand them.

He grunted as he hauled his naked ass out of the crater just as Megan came stumbling to a halt near the pushed up dirt around its edges. He looked up at her as she stared down at his body.

"You doing a Superman sort of thing?" She held her hand out to him, but he didn't risk taking it, afraid that in his current state he might hurt her.

"Ha ha." He dragged himself out of the pit. "Superman came to Earth as a naked baby."

"That's what I'm seeing. A big, naked, baby. One who cried over getting his nails painted." She ignored him when he tried to stop her from taking hold of his hand, resisting his attempts to gently swat her away. "At least *they're* still in one piece."

Which was more than she could say for him.

He huffed and brushed the dirt off himself. "Any idea what part of her I need to break?"

He knew Megan had been searching the valkyrie for the charm while he had been fighting.

"I'll break her eyes if she sees you like this." Megan scowled at his lack of clothing. "Can you at least fall back to regroup in your apartment for like, five seconds, long enough to put some clothes on?"

He grinned down at her. "Sweetheart, I do believe you're jealous."

She turned that pretty glare on him. "Just don't let your better parts touch her."

"It's all yours, Baby." He stepped before she could roll her eyes and appeared in the air in front of the valkyrie, cutting off the blonde as she arrowed towards Megan.

He caught the female by her neck, twisted in the air and hurled her with all of his strength, sending her slamming into the dirt hard enough that she made her own crater.

He liked to give what he got. He was nice like that.

He dropped to his feet as she did some gardening, landing on the grass a few metres from Megan.

Light shone from behind him, a bright dazzling burst of violet followed by a multitude of colours as the gate awakened, the rings that hovered like a disc above the earth spinning in opposite directions as they expanded.

Valkyrie stared at it as if it was precious and she wanted it, needed it more than life in her breast.

Movement on the edges of his senses had him glancing towards Megan, a desire to pull her to him and shield her bursting to life inside him, but she moved too, raised her gun and pulled the trigger.

Nailed the other daemon between his eyes.

The male slumped and twitched on the ground like someone had pumped fifty thousand volts into him.

Megan put another two rounds in his skull. "That's for trying to ruin his nails."

Damn, she was going to be pissy with him if he had scuffed them.

Valkyrie staggered onto her feet and stumbled towards the gate, not seeming to notice he stood between her and it as her eyes remained locked on it. She reached a hand up, stretching towards it, and he felt a little cruel as he held it open, luring her to her doom.

Her skin began to heal as she took each laboured step, her eyes glowing brighter the closer she came to the gate.

"Her metal wrist band thingies." Megan never had been good with her words. When he slid her a sideways look, she pulled a face at him, as if she knew his thoughts. "Cuffs. Her cuffs."

"Vambraces," he corrected, mostly to provoke another glare, because sometimes her scowling at him stoked the fire in him in a good way.

Ares looked at the ones the valkyrie wore, gold in colour and covering her forearms from wrist to elbow. There were markings on them that weren't valkyrie. It was worth a shot.

He launched towards her.

Her eyes focused, but it wasn't him they snapped to, they shot to her left.

A patch of violet fog grew there, swirling outwards and growing rapidly, and a sensation of dread went through Ares. He changed course, heading towards Megan, and reached her just as a pale hand emerged from the portal and a disembodied voice spilled from it.

"You are needed elsewhere." The male hand gripped the valkyrie by her wrist and pulled her into the violet smoke as she opened her mouth to protest, and then the portal disappeared.

Ares didn't let his guard down. He scanned the park as the gate slowly shrank to his right, keeping Megan tucked close to him, his heart pounding and adrenaline surging through him as he waited.

Waited.

When nothing moved for close to ten minutes, he let out a long slow breath and loosened his grip on Megan.

"You think she's the one after your brother?" Megan moved forwards, just a step so she was level with him, but it was enough to have his heart lodging in his throat and a need to pull her back racing through him.

He swallowed and nodded, because it made sense to him in a way, but not in others.

"I need to speak with my brothers." He stepped with Megan, landing in their apartment above Central Park, and caught the phone she tossed at his back as he paced towards the bedroom, using his power to bend it around to his hand.

She had started playing keeper-of-the-phone when he had melted his last one during a fight. It eased him to know she had it too, that she could contact his brothers for help if he needed it, or if she needed it.

He fired off a message calling a meeting in ten minutes, and even that short span of time felt like an eternity as he washed off and dressed in a fresh pair of black jeans and a matching t-shirt, and found another pair of boots.

When he was ready, he held his hand out to Megan.

She placed hers into it, stepped into his embrace and kissed him as he teleported with her, soothing his temper and easing his fear.

She was safe.

But gods, he had been so afraid the wraith would target her.

It wouldn't take much for such a powerful daemon to kill her.

They landed in Seville, in warm morning sunshine on the broad paved deck outside a sprawling white villa with a ribbed terracotta roof that stood on a hill above sweeping plains that seemed to stretch forever around him. The air was thick with the scent of the nearby olive groves that lined the sides of the hill and dry earth, and the buzzing of busy insects.

Keras paced the length of the white wall of the villa, his pressed tailored black slacks and shirt out of place in such a remote, wild and desert-like place. His older brother worried his black hair, raking his hands over it again and again, not noticing him. He had been on edge since getting Aiko to read his mind, as if he feared the tiny human.

Or maybe he feared what she might tell them.

Whatever his brother was hiding, it would come out eventually, whether he liked it or not. Things had a way of happening like that. Keras couldn't control everything in the way he controlled himself, even if he liked to think he could.

Marek lounged on a wooden recliner in the dappled shade of one of the larger trees to the left of the villa, yawning as he stretched, his pale linen shirt and earthy brown trousers far more suitable clothing for the climate.

Cal sat in the recliner next to him, dressed in cargo shorts and a black tank that fitted to his athletic frame and revealed packed muscle, his bare feet on the padded seat and his eyes concealed behind sunglasses as he sipped icy fruit juice like he was on vacation.

Daimon appeared, looking worn down as he slumped into a chair on the covered area of patio to Ares's right, next to the wooden table. "Nothing up at the Tokyo gate yet."

That was good news at least.

"Did Aiko go home?" Keras finally stopped pacing.

Daimon nodded. "A day late, but she's home now. Esher isn't happy. He not-so-politely kicked me out when I went to see him."

Ares could understand that, but he had a feeling they would be disturbing him again soon enough, even when he didn't want to worry his brother when he had enough on his plate coping with the sway of the moon.

It was strange having a meeting without him. It wasn't the first time they had done it, and Esher never really said much during the meetings he did attend, but Ares still felt his absence. He felt for his brother too, stuck in the mansion, wrestling with himself because of the damned moon, and unable to be around his woman.

Gods, it was weird to think that.

Esher with a mortal?

Unthinkable. Insane.

But then love often picked the craziest of choices or made people do the craziest of things.

Valen became a case in point as he appeared, still tugging his black t-shirt on and smoothing it over his combat trousers.

His hair a neon shade of violet.

"What happened?" Daimon jerked his chin towards Valen when Valen looked at him, his eyes on his hair.

Valen rubbed a hand over the long lengths that swept over the top and hung down to his jaw on his right side and scrubbed it around the chopped sides and back. "Eva did it. Pretty cool, huh? She said it suited me."

He didn't look sure.

Everyone stared at him.

It was strange seeing Valen so happy, and so damned colourful. Ares shrugged. It did suit him though.

"You look like a pansy." He grinned at Valen.

Valen glared at him, and then it melted away as he looked down, and a slow smile curved his lips. "You're one to talk."

Ares hiked his broad shoulders again, raised his hand and admired his black nails. "I lost a bet and this is my forfeit, and I sort of like them."

Valen chuckled at that. Keras looked unimpressed, as if a change in hair colour and painting of nails was a sign the entire group was unravelling and going to lose against the daemons.

Keras never really had figured out how to live a little.

"So, what's this meeting about?" Valen looked to Keras, who pointed at Ares.

"New York just got hit, and we're not talking regular daemon this time. We're talking our enemy." He shifted foot to foot as everyone looked at him, a silence settling over them and all light draining from the air around him as they all turned serious. "A valkyrie. It's been a while since I fought one, and longer since I killed one."

"Longer, meaning you didn't kill this one." Keras's green eyes darkened a full shade. "What happened?"

"Our wraith showed up, dragged her kicking and screaming through a portal before I could break the enchantment that protected her. Said she was wanted elsewhere." Ares fielded a few scowls and some of his brothers muttered things.

But it was Daimon who spoke. "You think she's the one meant to go after Esher?"

He nodded, and then shook his head. "It's possible, but I don't know. Why would she be in New York playing with me if she was meant to go after Esher?"

"Because of the moon?" Calistos offered, and when Ares peered over Megan's head at him, his younger brother pushed his sunglasses up his forehead. "Esher is more dangerous right now."

"It wouldn't hold her back." Keras this time. "The female is meant to make Esher her pet, according to the wraith and the intel Eva gave us. That means the female is prepared to tackle his darker side, and somehow bring it to heel."

"Which means, fighting him when he's under the sway of the moon wouldn't bother her, because it would probably make it easier for her to achieve her goal." Marek sat up, placing his feet down on either side of the recliner, his earthy eyes dark with concern. "But right now he's protected."

"Maybe that's the reason she decided to play with your ugly arse?" Valen grinned at Ares when he glared at him. "She can't mess with Esher."

Which was a relief.

The wards around the mansion would keep him safe, as long as he stayed within them.

"Any more ideas on the nightclub attack in Tokyo?" He looked to Marek, who nodded.

"It was crude, and clearly unplanned. I've gone over everything, all of our accounts, and we've never been hit when we've all been together." Marek pushed to his feet and paced towards Keras. "The daemons must have realised we were all together and hastily took advantage of that."

"Which means it isn't our enemy, because they want us alive to open the gates." Valen looked between them all when no one agreed.

A cold feeling went through Ares, and he looked down at Megan.

"Not necessarily," Daimon said. "The enemy must know that we would be able to protect ourselves from such a pathetic attack, even without warning. We wouldn't have been killed if the explosion had reached us. Injured yes, but not killed. So if they were behind it, what were they doing?"

Ares stared at Megan, that cold feeling growing, forming ice around his heart. "They were trying to provoke a response."

"Esher," Keras bit out, a snarl edging his voice. "But they failed."

"Esher would have flipped his shit if one of us had been hurt." Cal looked to Keras. "Wouldn't he?"

Keras shook his head at the same time as Ares. "Not if we were hurt. He's proven he can hold it together when we're wounded."

"Aiko." Ares didn't take his eyes off Megan as ice chased over his skin and he felt the weight of everyone's gazes on him. "They're targeting Aiko."

"Aiko mentioned her father ran a clinic in the Sugamo district." Megan quickly took hold of his arm, and he stepped to that part of Tokyo.

He swept Megan up into his arms and ran as fast as he could around the streets, looking for any clinics, his heart thundering. He had to find her before their enemy did.

A bright light washed across him and he glanced down at Megan where he cradled her against his chest.

She flashed the phone screen at him, revealing a map marked with red dots. "Marek sent it."

There were only three clinics in the area.

He stepped to the first one and banged down the door. A kind looking gentlemen answered.

"Aiko?" he said, and the male shook his head.

Fuck.

He kicked off, running out of sight before teleporting to the next one, where he met the same end, which meant the last one had to be Aiko's house.

He landed outside of it, dropped Megan to her feet, and hastily pounded his fist against the glass door.

A middle-aged woman answered.

"Aiko?" he breathed, struggling for air as he panted.

The woman shook her head, and he thought he was shit out of luck and was going to have to kill Marek for missing a clinic.

"She went... with her... boyfriend. Foreigner." The woman didn't look happy about it either.

Had to be Esher.

He nodded to thank her, swept Megan back up into his arms and sprinted away from the clinic, waiting until he was out of sight before he stepped.

He landed in the mansion grounds, heart labouring from the exertion of using his power so much and the anger stirring in his veins.

He was going to kill Esher instead.

He couldn't believe his brother had been idiot enough to leave the mansion when the moon was full, not after what had happened last time. Or that he was willing to risk Aiko by keeping her around him when he was easily influenced by his power and his darker side.

He didn't bother to remove his boots, just shoved the door open and stormed inside, ready to give Esher a piece of his mind.

Only his brother looked miserable as he sat on the cream couch to Ares's right, staring at his phone.

That cold feeling returned.

Aiko wasn't here.

Ares hesitated, knowing it was a bad move, but he couldn't not tell Esher.

His brother lifted sombre eyes to land on him, the phone light making them eerily blue, but they quickly darkened, black emerging around the edges of his irises as he rose onto his feet.

"What are you doing here… with her…" Esher snarled, pinning black eyes on Megan.

Gods, he was really going to do this, wasn't he?

He couldn't not tell him. Esher would never forgive him.

"Aiko—" Ares cut himself off when Esher fell to his knees, his phone tumbling from his hand, his face going slack as he stared up at him. It killed him to hurt his brother, to push him like this knowing it would probably send him right over the edge, but Esher needed to know. "Aiko is missing. Someone looking like you showed up and took her."

Red emerged in Esher's eyes and he bared fangs at Ares.

"No!" He surged to his feet, and outside, the rain fell in a thick sheet that sluiced off the roof and hammered like a waterfall into the courtyard garden to Ares's left, disturbing the gravel as it pummelled it.

Shapeshifters were rare, a daemon more legend than real, but it was the only explanation Ares had. Someone wearing his brother's appearance had shown up, and Aiko had gone with them.

"She's in danger, Esher, you need to focus."

"No, no… *no!*" Esher's fingers dug into the pale yellow mats and Ares backed off a step as his nails transformed into short obsidian claws that scraped long grooves in the straw.

Daimon appeared. "What the fuck did you do?"

Ares flinched and gritted out, "They have Aiko. I had to tell him."

"*Fuck.*" Daimon instantly moved to Esher's side. "Ty—"

Esher didn't give Daimon a chance to use the word on him. He swept his right arm out, hitting Daimon in the chest with his forearm and sending him flying through the paper panels and into the courtyard.

Black swirled around Esher's bare arms.

Before Ares could stop him, he disappeared.

Outside, the rain fell so fast that the courtyard was already an inch deep in water, pooling around Daimon as he struggled onto his feet.

The scenery flickered to the otherworld, where the rain fell as streams of white-hot fire, devouring the buildings, a product of Esher's rage.

Gods help the world.

Because if Esher didn't find Aiko in time, if he couldn't save her, it was doomed.

His brother would see to that.

CHAPTER 19

Aiko sat up on her bed and set her phone aside, her focus shifting from the picture of her with Esher to her surroundings. She was sure that she had felt him. She looked outside at the moon where it rose above the taller buildings across the park, full but faded in the late afternoon sky, clearer now the sun was sinking lower. It wasn't possible.

Downstairs, the doorbell rang.

She pushed off the bed, her pulse picking up as she felt Esher again, and exited her small bedroom. Her father was already crossing the hall below when she reached the stairs, heading towards the clinic door.

It couldn't be him.

She glanced at her phone again, at the last message from him that had sounded strained to her, had made her want to go to him and risk it.

Maybe he had decided to be the one to risk it all instead.

If it was him, she would make him go back to the mansion and call one of his brothers, Daimon perhaps. He seemed to have the most influence over Esher.

She reached the bottom step and tucked her phone into her jeans pocket as she crossed through the clinic to her father where he stood at the door.

Sure enough, Esher stood on the step.

Her father gave her a look that conveyed how unimpressed he was with her boyfriend showing up and then sighed and walked away, leaving her alone with Esher.

"What are you doing here?" She moved to stand in the door.

The moment she was within reach, Esher grabbed her wrist and pulled her out into the street. Warmth curled around her, both from his touch and the fading heat of day.

"Wait." She twisted free of his grip, went back into the clinic and slipped her shoes on.

She barely had the laces tied before he grabbed her again, pulling her with him.

"What's wrong?" She looked up at the back of his head as he marched her towards the park, into the shadows beneath the trees. "Is the moon affecting you?"

"No." He snarled that word, and she tensed, but then he softened as he added, "Yes."

He rubbed his hand across his brow, causing his blue-grey shirt to tighten across his shoulders as he wiped beads of sweat away. Was he sick?

"You should be back at the mansion." She reached for her phone. "I should contact Daimon."

Esher hadn't been happy when Daimon had given her his details, but she was glad that she had ignored his outburst and had taken Daimon's number now.

"No." He turned sharply and reached for her phone, and she held it behind her and frowned at him.

"You need to go home." She could see it in his blue eyes as they glowed and feel it in the tightness of his grip on her. "I'll go with you."

That seemed to please him and his hand loosened around her wrist. She went with him as he started marching again, pulling her along at a rapid pace that she struggled to keep up with as he crossed the road to the shadows of the buildings, and from there towards the centre of the district.

Her eyes lifted to the back of his head again as something felt off to her. "Why aren't you teleporting me there?"

He glanced at her and a streak of light caught him, turning his skin golden and threading the longer lengths of his black hair with pale highlights. He flinched and sank deeper into the shadows, avoiding the light.

Or maybe her question.

For a moment, he looked as if he wouldn't answer, as if her question had caught him so off guard that he didn't have an answer to give her because he wasn't sure himself, but then he turned to face away from her again and spoke.

"The moon makes it difficult for me," he bit out, voice a low snarl of agony that she could feel in him.

She moved closer to him and he didn't back away this time, didn't flinch from her touch as she stroked his cheek. Her poor Esher. She hadn't realised the moon would have such a terrible effect on him. He looked sick.

He twisted away from her again and she looked down at his hand on her wrist as they hurried towards the main road, at the way he was holding it tightly, as if he feared her breaking free. She had to call Daimon. Something was wrong with Esher. He shouldn't be out in the city, not when the moon was clearly affecting him badly.

That sensation that something was off came again when he hailed a cab on the main road.

It wasn't like him.

He had always avoided people when she had been with him, had made it sound as if he couldn't bear being around them, but now he was willing to take a taxi somewhere and be in close proximity to a human other than her? The trains were still running, and at this time of day they could have half a carriage to themselves, all the space he needed.

It wasn't like the Esher she knew at all.

But then she didn't know what he was like when the moon affected him.

Maybe the need to reach his home quickly again had him bearing being around a single human, maybe it was better than being on a train where there would be more people.

She reached for her pocket again.

Esher grabbed her wrist, stopping her, and pushed her into the black taxi as it pulled up.

"Ginza station," he said as he slid into the back seat beside her and the door closed.

Aiko looked across at him. "You need to go home."

He ignored her, and that sensation grew stronger, churning in the pit of her stomach. Something was wrong. Esher wasn't taking her home, he was taking her somewhere that would be filled with humans at this hour, the popular shopping street a destination for locals and tourists alike.

It was dangerous for him to be around so many people.

The journey to the heart of the Ginza district was short, and Esher pulled her out of the cab before she could stop him and make the driver take them to the mansion instead.

"Come on." He tugged her with him, close to him, and looked around at the crowded street, his eyes darkening as he watched the people.

What was he looking for?

Why had he brought her here?

"Take me to your home, Esher." She tried again, but he only glared at her, his eyes narrowing and darkening further.

Something was very wrong.

She focused on him, trying to read his feelings so she could figure out what was wrong with him, but it was as if a wall stood between them and she couldn't penetrate it.

"Where are we going?" She didn't move when he started walking, was going to refuse to take another step until he answered her question.

"Keep moving," he growled and turned on her, and when she shook her head, his grip on her wrist tightened and he forced her, pulling her along the street and tugging at her arm whenever she stumbled.

Hurting her.

Aiko stared at his hand on her and focused on him, trying to read him, because something was more than wrong. Esher had shown her countless times, had told her to her face that he was terrified of hurting her, but now he was squeezing her wrist so hard it felt as if her bones might break.

It wasn't like him.

She reached for her phone, sensing the power of the protective charm through her jeans, and that feeling grew stronger. He was so desperate to keep her safe from harm that he had made a charm for her, and now he was pulling her through the crowd, not stopping to look at her whenever she stumbled and fell, just dragging her back onto her feet and forcing her to continue.

Maybe he needed her to calm him. There hadn't been any red in his eyes when he had looked at her, but maybe the power the moon exerted over him was pushing him too hard, had him on the verge of losing control, at a point where she could bring him back with the safe word he had given her and calm him.

Before he did something terrible.

She looked around her at all the people who were watching her being tugged along by him, at the people who were going to suffer if Esher lost control.

She had to protect them.

She opened her mouth, the word on the tip of her tongue, but then the sensation that something wasn't right struck her again and her heart whispered that this wasn't Esher. The Esher she loved would never hurt her, would never treat her like this. She focused again, but she still couldn't read him, and that left her cold.

"Clavius." The word left her lips, pushed up from her heart as it began to race, and fear trickled through her veins.

Esher stopped and looked over his shoulder at her, his black eyebrows knitted tightly above his dark blue eyes.

"Um... Stadius... Rheita... Copernicus..." It was hard to stop herself from trembling as she said each word, naming the craters she had come across when she had passed a few hours researching the moon to fill her time and make the wait to see Esher again less painful.

His frown hardened. "Why are you mentioning parts of the moon?"

A flicker of relief went through her. "You're hurting me, and so I thought to calm you by using the word you gave me... only I forgot which crater it is."

Her pulse doubled again, her nerves rising back up as she faced him, looked him in the eye and prayed that she was mistaken.

"Which crater is it again?" Her voice shook, and she swallowed hard. "Clavius, Rheita, Stadius or Copernicus."

Tycho. Please say Tycho.

She stood before him, knees weakening as she waited, hoping he would chuckle at her and say it was none of them, and fearing her test would reveal something terrifying.

His handsome face turned pensive.

"Clavius. I didn't hear you the first time." He smoothed his hand over her wrist as he loosened his grip. "I'm sorry. I'm calm now."

That cold in her veins turned to ice.

As she stared into his eyes, his words hollow in her ears, she felt a glimmer of something from him, the barest flicker of sensation but one that confirmed her worst fears.

This wasn't her Esher.

It was someone else.

She was in danger.

Her first instinct was to run, but she forced herself to nod and smile, and focused on her breathing, trying to get her heartbeat to level out so he wouldn't notice. Whoever he was. He looked like Esher, acted like him, must have been studying him, learning about him so he could mimic him.

Now Esher was locked away because of the moon, and this man had seen it as the perfect opportunity to grab her.

Because he wanted to use her to get to Esher.

That had her blood turning colder, but she held it together, maintaining her smile despite the fear building inside her. She needed to get away from him, or somehow contact her Esher.

"We should head home." She managed to keep her voice calm, hiding the way she shook inside, her heart threatening to race again as adrenaline rushed through her, and her instincts screamed at her to run.

Because this person before her was a daemon.

One of Esher's enemies.

She felt sure of it as she looked at him as he wiped a hand across his brow again, clearing the sweat. Esher had told her that daemons couldn't stand the sunlight, that it hurt them and weakened them. Now the fake-Esher sticking to all the shadows and choosing to ride in the taxi cab where the tinted windows would offer respite made a sickening sort of sense.

Fake-Esher was a daemon, dangerous to her, more powerful than she was but also weak right now, vulnerable in a way she might be able to exploit in order to escape.

"Let's go home." She placed her hand into his.

He looked down at it, and then up into her eyes. "No. I can't. The... gate needs me."

Was fake-Esher going to target the gate?

Esher's enemies wanted to destroy them to merge the Underworld with this one, creating a single realm. She couldn't let this person attack the gate. She had to do something.

She just wasn't sure what she could do.

Fake-Esher pulled her along, and she went with him, wracking her brain and trying to think of a plan, something that would stop him from attempting to reach the gate.

She kept her eyes on him and struggled to keep up so the people passing her by wouldn't think she needed their assistance, even when she wanted to scream for help. If someone tried to aid her, the daemon would kill them, she was sure of it.

She wouldn't place people in danger like that. She would find a way to escape him by herself, once they were away from the crowd.

He led her into one of the skyscrapers, and into an elevator, the look he gave those waiting for it too enough to have them all reconsidering and moving aside to take the next one instead.

Her nerves threatened to get the better of her as he pulled her close, slinging his arm around her shoulder, and her stomach turned as she played along, sliding her hand across his lower back above his black jeans.

She slipped her other hand into her pocket.

His eyes darted down to it, and he smiled as he turned towards her, took hold of her arm and pulled her hand out again. "I just want a moment alone with you. I've missed you. Once I've dealt with the gate, we can go home."

She relaxed and nodded, and he glared at her phone that poked out of her pocket, looking as if he was going to demand she hand it over.

"I won't call anyone, don't worry." She pushed it back into her pocket and held her smile in place. "I was only going to have it ready to take another picture. I love the last one we took together and thought maybe we could take one with the gate. I haven't seen it yet."

His eyebrows dipped low, but he nodded. "Sure."

The elevator pinged, and the doors opened, and she didn't resist fake-Esher as he pulled her along the corridor to a door at the far end. He pushed it open and ascended the steps, and she flinched as she hit the roof and wind buffeted her, blowing her hair in her face and whipping her cream blouse around her waist.

Fake-Esher was too intent on searching the roof to notice the wind that made the longer lengths of his black hair on top of his head dance around. His blue eyes scanned everything, irritation flaring in them when he turned on the spot and looked at the other side of the roof.

"Where's the gate?" she said, and his eyes leaped to her and then away, and he glared at the horizon where the sun still lingered above it.

"It will open soon." He looked confident about that as he stalked towards the centre of the roof.

Aiko looked out across the incredible panorama, taking in the city that stretched around her, pockets of taller buildings creating an undulating skyline. She spotted Sugamo just off to her right, and further to her right and closer to her was the sprawling green that surrounded the Imperial Palace. To her left, Tokyo Tower speared the sky, bright orange and almost glowing in the sunshine.

It would have been beautiful if she had been standing here with her Esher.

She glanced down over the edge of the roof, at the stomach-turning drop to the busy street below, and then followed fake-Esher when his eyes landed on her and she felt his impatience. As she neared the other end of the roof, the air began to hum with power. It vibrated through her, lit up her body and had her gravitating towards it.

Fake-Esher's gaze tracked her as she drifted forwards, towards the source of the power.

There was nothing there, just an expanse of grey roof, but at the same time there was something. She could feel it. Dark. Powerful. Like nothing she had ever felt before.

"I feel it, but I can't see it." She paced the area, and then lifted her head and pinned her gaze on fake-Esher. "Should I be able to see it?"

"Humans can't." He turned and scowled at the city, and the sun, and then moved closer to her. "But you'll be able to see it when it opens."

So he knew she wasn't wholly human, that she had a power of her own.

"You can get your phone out now." Fake-Esher's cold tone had her looking his way again, pulling her gaze away from the patch of roof where the air hummed strongest.

She pointed to it. "There's no gate. I wanted to take a picture of us with the gate, not with a roof."

His blue eyes narrowed and he took a hard step towards her. "I need you to get your phone out and message my brother. I'm not feeling so good."

No. He wanted her to message one of his brothers because he wanted word to reach Esher, because he knew Esher would come for her, and then the daemon would force him to open the gate.

She shook her head and backed off a step. "If you're not feeling well, we should just go."

His jaw tensed and he held his hand out to her. "Give me your phone."

"Use your own one," she countered.

He was quick to respond. "I forgot it."

He was even quicker to close the gap between them. She gasped as he appeared before her and turned to run, but he grabbed her arm in a bruising grip and yanked her to face him.

She shoved her hands against his chest. "You're hurting me."

He growled, twisted her arm, and she cried out as pain blazed up it. "Just give me the fucking phone."

Tears filled her eyes as her arm throbbed, the pain so intense it stole her breath, and she wanted to shake her head, but the look in his eyes warned her that he would hurt her worse if she didn't do as he wanted.

Her fingers shook as she reached her free hand into her pocket and fumbled with her phone. Before she could try to send a blind call for help to someone, fake-Esher grabbed her wrist and pulled her arm up, forcing her to pull her phone from her pocket.

He smiled coldly.

Reached for the phone.

Bellowed in agony as he went flying across the roof to land hard against an air-conditioning outlet.

Aiko looked down at the glowing ginger cat charm dangling from her phone.

Her phone vibrated, the small display on the cover revealing Daimon's name.

Fake-Esher lumbered onto his feet and shook his head, snarling dark words in a tongue she didn't know. Before she could open her phone and warn Daimon that a daemon had her and tell him not to let Esher know and to come for her, the daemon appeared before her again and knocked her hand, sending the phone tumbling across the flat grey roof.

Only when she looked up, her heart lodged in her throat, it wasn't fake-Esher standing before her.

It was a beautiful tall woman with long deep violet hair that shimmered black in the light and eyes like quicksilver, silvery pools that constantly shifted and changed, swirling as Aiko stared into them.

Her black-painted lips twisted in a cold smile.

Aiko gasped as the woman grabbed her by her throat, hauled her off her feet and marched her towards the edge of the roof. She frantically shook her head, her pulse rocketing as she looked down and the edge of the roof appeared below her feet, and then there was nothing but a terrifying drop to her death.

"Please." She grappled with the woman's arm, holding it tightly as fear swamped her and she tried to reach for the edge of the roof with her toes. The woman pulled her back, and she breathed a little easier as her feet touched the raised wall. "What do you want with me?"

"First, I want you to message that bastard of yours." The woman glared at the phone on the roof off to Aiko's left.

Aiko breathed through her fear, calming herself enough that she could focus again, and turned that focus on the woman. It was hard, but it wasn't as difficult as when she had tried to read Keras.

"And then what?" She had to keep the woman talking, keep her distracted, so she had time to go deeper, to penetrate the layers of fog that clouded her thoughts.

The woman's smile widened. "And then you become Esher's collar. With you in my possession, he will do anything I demand... even turn on his own brothers."

No.

Her focus faltered as cold swept through her.

She couldn't let that happen. Hurting his own brothers would kill him, but she was sure he would do it for her. He would bear the pain, because he loved her. She wasn't going to let this woman put him through that hell. She had to get away, somehow.

Aiko focused on the woman again and pushed harder this time, forcing herself to keep going even when her head ached and her nose stung as if she was going to get a nosebleed.

A hazy feeling came to her.

Fear.

Not her own.

The woman was afraid. Of Esher? His brothers?

She focused harder, and managed to penetrate the woman's mind, enough to catch a few words.

It wasn't Esher or his brothers the woman feared. It was another woman, someone powerful, someone who would kill her if she failed in her task. Esher was vital. A key. Key to what?

Them winning or something else?

"Get your phone and make the call." The woman pulled her towards her and Aiko shook her head.

"No." She wouldn't alert Esher to her plight, because he would fall right into the woman's hands, and she couldn't let that happen.

The moment her footing felt sure enough, she pushed forwards, barrelling into the woman. When she knocked the woman backwards, surprise rang through her. She had expected a daemon to be stronger, able to withstand her slight weight.

Maybe she wasn't strong.

Maybe the reason she hadn't held Aiko over the drop for longer than a few seconds was because she had been weakening and had feared dropping her.

Aiko kicked her hard in her shin, broke free of her grip and ran for her phone. If she could just get hold of it, she could use the power of the charm to repel the daemon.

The daemon snatched her wrist before she could reach it and twisted with her, spinning her back towards the edge of the roof.

She hit it, screamed as she toppled forwards and lost balance, tumbling over the edge.

The woman snagged her arm and Aiko screamed again as she slipped through the daemon's grip. The woman grunted and lurched forwards with her, her stomach hitting the raised edge of the roof, but she managed to keep her hand locked around her as it hit Aiko's wrist.

Aiko looked down, heart hammering and on the verge of stopping as the street below zoomed in and out.

"Give me your other hand!" The woman lowered her free one.

Aiko scrambled, trying to grab it, swinging wildly as the woman grunted with each attempt that pulled her closer to falling too.

Part of her said to pull the woman over the edge with her, that she could spare Esher if she sacrificed herself, because she was sure the fall would kill the daemon too.

Esher.

The thought of never seeing him again brought tears to her eyes.

She couldn't do it, not even to save him. She wasn't strong enough.

She redoubled her effort, desperately trying to get hold of the daemon's other hand as the woman stretched it towards her, her legs flailing beneath her.

Her phone vibrated again and the woman looked towards it, and Aiko was glad that she couldn't answer it and lure Esher to her, that the charm would protect it from the daemon.

She knew that it was him calling now, because rain came out of nowhere, hammering her and getting in her eyes as she fought to reach the daemon's other hand.

He knew she was in trouble.

He was coming for her.

If she could just hold on, just claw herself back up onto the roof, she could attack the woman again and maybe this time get the upper hand. She could reach her phone and make a run for it, telling Esher where she was so he could save her.

Her heart lodged in her throat as her wet arm slipped through the woman's grip.

She suddenly felt empty—no emotion, no sensation, nothing.

But one thought.

She didn't want to die.

CHAPTER 20

Marek stalked through the industrial neighbourhood, slipping between the shadows as he tracked his prey, dark hunger licking through him. Stars twinkled above him, the lights of the city centre dim this far from it. In the distance a car horn sounded, and his prey twitched, one of the males twisting towards the source of the noise.

Marek leaned deeper into the shadows, using his senses to track the vile creatures instead as he waited for the male to move on, following his comrades through the huge crumbling warehouses.

When he had picked up their trail and tracked them to this area in the outskirts of Madrid, he had expected them to head towards one of the grim high-rises. They had surprised him by breaking off the main road and heading over the tall fence that surrounded the industrial complex.

His fingers closed over the blade sheathed against his hip and he stroked the worn hilt, the leather smooth beneath his fingers from years of use.

He itched with the urge to break cover, to attack the group before it reached the warehouse, but held himself back, aware that a greater prize would be his if he had a little patience. They would lead him to the others, and he would attack them then, dealing with them before they could raise the alarm and scatter like rats.

When the small group moved on, he slipped from the shadows and along the side of one of the buildings, keeping close to it and using the boxes and dumpsters as cover.

He reached the next warehouse and paused, assessing the route ahead of him.

His smile was slow as the group banged on the door of the next warehouse along. It opened, revealing another of their kind, one who greeted them with jibes he didn't pay attention to as the hunger swirling inside him grew stronger, pushing him to attack now.

Soon.

He would drench his blade in blood soon enough.

Would scratch this itch that wouldn't leave him alone, had been irritating him for close to a week now, telling him that he had gone too long without a fix.

Gods, he needed it.

The group moved inside, and he almost groaned as he finally broke cover, awareness of what was to come, that his patience had paid off, sending a hot jolt of pleasure through him.

Now.

He stalked towards the corrugated steel building, his heart pumping harder with each step, muscles coiling tighter. He grinned as he pulled the curved blade from his black combat trousers and it flashed silver beneath the lights mounted on the sides of the warehouses.

His senses reported twenty of them. No, thirty. He did groan now, a low moan of pleasure as he quickened his pace, the hunger to get started overwhelming him now that he knew so many of them were in one location.

His for the killing.

His lips stretched into a broad grin, flashing his emerging fangs.

The bastards wouldn't know what had hit them.

It was going to be glorious.

Thirty of the rats against him, the odds in their favour because he would stick with his vow to use only his blade, *this* blade, against them.

Marek looked down at it, at the beauty of it as it curved from his palm, the metal nicked in places, worn from centuries of use.

Centuries of eliminating their kind.

He lifted his boot and slammed it against the door, sending it flying off its hinges. It smashed into one of the creatures and it went down with a groan, the scent of its blood swamping the air.

Sickening him.

Close to thirty pairs of eyes whipped his way.

Glowing red in the darkness.

Fucking vampires.

He launched into the middle of them, his blade gutting one before it even saw him coming, and as the creature hissed in pain and the silver devoured its insides, a cacophony rose around him.

Music to his ears.

He grinned as he lashed out again, blood spraying over him as he swiped the blade across a throat, and then twisted it deep in the chest of another vampire, and then plunged it behind him, stabbing one in the thigh as it tried to get the jump on him.

They swarmed him then, their shrieks and roars ringing in his ears, and he grunted as two big males hit him from behind, knocking him forwards. The sound of his shirt ripping filled his ears, and fire swept through him, blazing along the tracks of the vampires' claws. He didn't give them the satisfaction of hearing his pain as he shook them off, as he dispatched one of them and drove the other back. He made no sound as he blocked and parried, shoved his blade into the heart of another, and then cut a female's throat and kicked her away from him.

One latched onto his arm, sinking fangs deep into his flesh, stealing his blood to weaken him.

Marek kicked him in the knee, breaking it, and then brought his knife down into the back of his skull as he crumpled. He yanked it out, twisted to dislodge a second vampire before their fangs could pierce him, and swiped the silver blade across the chest of a male who appeared before him.

The male hissed and leaped backwards.

Marek launched after him, catching the flicker in his crimson eyes that said he was going to run.

Not on his watch.

He caught the bastard by his shirt and pulled him back, grinned as he shoved the blade deep into his side and the male jerked in his arms, his keening cry rising above the growls and hisses that surrounded him.

More claws slashed at him, and another vampire managed to sink her fangs in while he was distracted with shoving a male away. He grabbed her by her head and ripped her away from him, and when she tried to break free, snarling like a wild animal at him, he squeezed.

Hard.

Her skull gave under the pressure, and blood sprayed over his chest, coated his hand and splattered up his arm, hitting his skin through his shredded dark shirt.

He growled and shoved her corpse away from him, and turned, bringing his blade up as he spun on the spot to face his next opponent. The vampire leaped back to dodge, but didn't run. He roared, his eyes wild and wide, and lashed out.

With a blade.

Marek dodged backwards, but the blade caught him across his chest, carving a shallow line straight across his pectorals.

He glared at the vampire and made him acquainted with his own blade as he came around behind him, faster than the rat could track. He plunged his silver knife into the male's back and whipped it out again as he flailed and fell forwards, hissing as he tried to reach around to grab it.

Marek launched it at a vampire who was trying to run. It spun end over end through the air, a silver blur, and lodged in the female's thigh, sending her down. She shrieked and clawed at the blade, her agony palpable as the silver ate at her flesh.

He stalked towards her, pulled it out and stared down at her, feeling nothing as she desperately tried to claw away from him.

He strode after her, watching her suffer, watching that false hope spark to life in her eyes as the pain subsided and she neared the exit.

When she was within a metre of it, he stepped into her path.

She froze, looked up at him and shook her head, her eyes pleading him.

He had no mercy to give her.

He brought the blade down hard, deep into the back of her skull.

Pulled it out.

Wiped it off as he walked back towards the centre of the warehouse, his arms and back stinging from the claw marks and bites, and the only sound in the expansive building his own ragged breathing.

Gods, he felt good.

Alive.

Marek took in the beauty of the carnage he had wrought, the bodies fizzing as they decayed and the blood that covered everything glistening like a sea of rubies in the dim light coming in through the windows.

Satisfaction hummed in his veins.

The hunger sated at last.

With close to thirty kills, it would be at least another few weeks before the need to hunt rose again.

He sheathed his blade at his hip.

He had been a victim of it for centuries now, ever since he had made his vow to hunt and destroy every single one of their kind, despite the fact his father classified them as Hellspawn.

He needed to kill them.

Couldn't help himself.

They needed to pay for what they had done to him.

A slow clap shattered the silence.

He wheeled to face the intruder, his blade back in his hand and in front of him in an instant, his heart pounding faster as adrenaline surged again and the urge to fight returned, pushing out the pain.

He stilled when he spotted the lone female sitting on top of a group of crates, her slender legs folded and the silver filigree that decorated her thick black knee-high boots catching the light as she rocked her right leg forwards.

Her hands pressed into the crates on either side of her hips, her matching black vambraces covering them from wrist to elbow, and she leaned forwards, flashing cleavage in her silver and black chest-piece that he diligently kept his eyes off.

Together with the ridiculous scrap of leather she was apparently calling a skirt today.

"I thought for a moment there was going to be a war." The disappointed ring to her regal voice was exactly what he expected of her. "But it was merely a massacre. Do you feel better?"

She studied him, her pale jade eyes bright with interest, surrounded by black make-up that only made them seem even greener.

Her red-painted lips offered a teasing smile.

He huffed, cleaned his blade of every last speck of blood on the body of one of the vampires, and then sheathed it. "They got what they deserved."

She canted her head, surveying the carnage. "How many times a month do you feel the need to do this?"

Marek rolled his shoulders, because that was personal and he wasn't in the mood to share. No one was meant to know about his little habit.

"Vampire numbers must be getting low now." She uncrossed her legs and swung them back and forth, like a damned kid.

Not a several thousand year old goddess.

"I do have to keep going farther afield, but the vermin breed quickly, which is lucky for me." He stepped to his villa in the hills near Seville.

Wasn't surprised when she appeared behind him barely a second later.

He strode into his bedroom and stripped off his ruined shirt, dumping it in the trash, and quickly replaced it with a fresh black one, not because he gave a damn whether she saw him half-naked, but because someone else would if they found out about it.

And Marek liked breathing.

"Your aim is a little off again." He tossed his blade into the drawer of the oak bedside table, and walked back into the living room, pretending not to notice the way she scowled at him now, her beautiful face as dark as the world outside. "Surely you meant to land a few hundred miles north of here?"

She casually seated herself in his dark cream armchair in front of the fireplace and kicked her feet up onto his coffee table, and he would have complained but he was guilty of doing that more times than he could count in Ares's apartment. He could hardly tell her not to do it when it was another habit of his.

"No." Her voice was light despite her dark appearance, no trace of nerves or any negative emotion in it as she casually flicked her long black hair over her left shoulder and tucked it behind her ear, revealing the three beaded braids that blended so well into her hair he rarely noticed them in her visits.

He moved around to her right, because he liked keeping an eye on what she was up to, and the way she wore her hair, parted off centre with the left side sweeping across her forehead and partially over her eye on that side, often concealed her face if she turned to her right.

She gave him a dazzling smile. "I am exactly where I mean to be."

But not where she wanted to be.

He wasn't stupid. He could read between the lines. Especially when the writing there was written in neon marker.

"How is business?" He walked into the kitchen that joined onto the living room, his boots loud on the orange terracotta floor, and grabbed two bottles of water.

He offered one to her as he slumped onto the couch on her right.

She wrinkled her nose at it and waved her hand in a refusal, and a silver flask appeared in it. He cracked open his water as she flicked her thumb up, uncapping her flask, and he caught the scent of the drink it contained.

Ambrosia.

She had vowed she had given it up a decade ago, but clearly she was back on the sauce. Because of what was happening with him and his brothers, and the fact their enemy was finally making itself known?

She was worried about them.

Him.

"So the other day, we all went out and Keras ended up having to protect us from suicide bomber daemons, which is something new." He eyed her, and didn't miss the way she clammed up, suddenly fascinated with her flask, as if she had never seen it before.

When she remained silent for more than five minutes, he rose onto his feet.

"What do you want, Enyo? I'm a busy man." He set his water down and walked away from her, sure she would follow, because he could feel a need to speak brewing in her.

"I could see that." She trailed after him, out into the night, and drew down a deep breath. "The stars are beautiful here."

"You didn't come to stargaze." He turned, slouched onto the recliner and kicked his feet up, grimacing as his wounds stung. "Spit it out."

It didn't do to push a goddess, but he was tired and wanted a shower, and no damn way he could do that with her around.

"Something is brewing." She kept her eyes on the stars, her head tilted back and her profile to him. "Word on Olympus is that it is coming in hot. Ares can feel it."

Not Marek's brother, but the real god of war.

Her brother.

"Our enemy?" He sat up now, needing to know more.

She shrugged. "Ares is not sure, but I believe so. They are strong if Ares can feel them."

"Stronger than a daemon?" Because that would be bad.

There were plenty of creatures in the world who were stronger than daemons, including the beasts that protected the gates on the Underworld side, and other creatures of the Underworld, and Olympus.

Including Hellspawn and gods.

"He doesn't know." She lowered her gaze to him. "I will see if I can get more information from him. I just... wanted to warn you."

He nodded. "Thank you."

When she didn't leave, when she lingered and returned to looking at the stars, an awkward air growing around her, he waited for her to speak, because something was on her mind.

She remained silent again.

Typical of her.

She never had been very good at communicating her feelings.

But then, Keras sucked at it too.

"Are you just enjoying my company or was there another reason you came?" he prompted.

She squirmed, very unbecoming of a goddess and very unlike her, and then unfastened the black leather cuff around her left arm to reveal a silver bracelet. She held her arm up and the tiny shield and sword charm twinkled in the light coming from the villa.

"I received a message from Valen." Her words were low, cautious, edged with the smallest trace of fear. "Something happened."

Marek knew what she was talking about, because Valen had mentioned it to him too, and all of them were worried.

He sighed. "Valen wanted to face the enemy alone after Esher was almost killed and Keras lost his temper a little."

Her beautiful face softened, her pale eyes glittering with concern.

"Go to him, Enyo," he whispered, urging her softly, half of him hoping she would do it even when he knew she wouldn't. "Speak with him."

Her eyes closed, and she frowned as she lowered her head away from him, clearly pained by what he was asking. Her black hair fell over the left side of her face, and she turned her head to her right, hiding it from him.

"Keras needs you." He felt close to getting through to her, close enough that this time he wouldn't give up.

She was worried about Keras, and Keras needed her. If he could get the two idiots together, even if it killed him, it would be worth it.

She shook her head. "I cannot."

He wanted to ask her why not, but being so forward with her would only cause her to lash out at him. The last time she had lost her temper, he had come close to losing his arm.

He knew that parting had hurt her and it had hurt Keras too, even when both of them always insisted they were only friends. That was true, but it was utter bullshit too. They had been more than friends, were more than friends, but neither of them had made a move or said a word, and then Keras had been sent to the mortal world with him and their brothers.

Marek also knew what would happen if Keras lost control, and it wouldn't be pretty. Things had been a little rough when they had first arrived in the mortal realm, before their father had found a way to inhibit Keras's powers. They would be more than a little rough if Keras lost control and those powers manifested at their full strength. He wasn't sure the mortal world would survive it.

Keras was under too much strain, was pulled too tight by events and worry for his brothers, and it was only a matter of time before something snapped.

"Visit him." Marek knew he was pushing his luck when her eyes flicked open and she narrowed them on him. "Just speak with him. I'm sure you can give him the strength he needs."

"No!" The ground shook with the force of that word, jolting him and cracking the white wall of his villa, and a flash of regret followed by pain crossed her face. She disappeared, her whispered words lingering in the warm air. "It hurts too much."

He couldn't understand that. He had never loved anyone that deeply.

His heart called him on that lie.

He had loved someone that much, with all of himself, had given her every drop of him.

And in return?

She had betrayed him.

CHAPTER 21

Her scream was the first thing that hit him on landing on the rooftop, tearing his world asunder.

Esher launched forwards, shoving the female daemon aside and sending her flying as he hit the edge of the roof. His heart plummeted in time with Aiko.

"No!" He vaulted over the edge and stepped, reappeared in the air but not close enough.

He teleported again, desperate to reach her before she hit the pavement, and reappeared closer to her this time.

Her brown eyes held his, tears flowing from them as she sailed through the air, the wind whipping her hair upwards as her arms flailed towards him. Love shone in her eyes, love and fear that ripped at him, screamed at him to save her, to take that fear away for her.

He stepped again, wild as he roared and his fangs emerged, darkness swirling around him. He blasted out of it below her this time, the pavement coming at him fast, and twisted in the air.

Reached for her.

His boots hit the pavement, legs buckled as fire burned up his bones, his right tibia fracturing from the impact. He crumpled and growled as he reached for Aiko.

He caught her arm and kicked upwards, countering her movement to slow her descent and calling another teleport at the same time.

Shadows flickered over him but her weight pulled him out of the teleport as she slammed into him, her legs against his chest.

He hit the pavement, and she struck it a split-second later with such force that her mouth snapped open as her head flew upwards and blood burst from it. His lungs burned, the impact sending the air rushing from them, sending a wave of pain rolling through him that had him numb, but he sucked down a breath and roared.

"No." He gritted his teeth and shook his head as he struggled to sit up, forced himself to move and pulled her into his arms. Her blood instantly covered his hands, making it hard to keep hold of her. It drenched her pale blouse. He gently shook her. "Open your eyes, Aiko. Look at me. Please look at me."

When people crowded him, he snarled at them and flashed his fangs. Screams rose as shadows flickered around him, racing outwards across the wet pavement to snap at the humans, driving them away.

He rocked with Aiko, his eyes glued to her face, tears burning in them as he leaned over her and smoothed his right palm across her ashen cheek.

"Open your eyes, Aiko," he whispered. "Please?"

Rain hammered down, washing the blood from her skin, making it swirl across the pavement beneath her.

He tried to listen, finding it hard to hear over the thundering rush of his blood and that of the rain. His relief as he heard her heart beating was short lived, lasted only as long as it took him to realise it was slowing.

She was dying.

"No, no… no… you can't leave me." He brushed trembling fingers across her cheek and along the street, water exploded from the drain covers, gushing like geysers, sending a river swirling around her and him. "Look at me, Aiko."

Her eyelids fluttered.

His heart missed a beat.

He cupped her cheek. "Look at me."

Her eyelids lifted, revealing the dull brown of her irises and red where the white should have been in her beautiful eyes.

He wanted to scream at that, wanted to throw his head back and roar again, but he forced himself to hold it together, even as a need to tear down this world rose inside him.

It was cruel.

Vicious.

It had given him something beautiful, and now it was going to steal it away.

He couldn't bear it.

"I'll get you to Megan," he whispered, voice hoarse and tight. "Megan can fix this."

But he couldn't bring himself to move. Fear froze him in place, the thought of hurting her by moving her, of killing her by trying to teleport her to Megan in the mansion locking his muscles up tight and chilling the blood in his veins. He stared down at her, fighting to convince himself to move, to do something, because she was going to die if he didn't. Despair joined the fear as instinct whispered she was going to die anyway.

He couldn't save her.

The rain fell harder, pounding the pavement around him, and a torrent swept past him as he held her, gazed down at her and told himself to move, because if there was only the tiniest chance he could save her, it would be worth it.

But, gods, he couldn't bring himself to hurt her by moving her.

She tried to lift her hand, but it fell weakly into her lap as she coughed, and blood streamed from her lips. He gripped her hand and lifted it for her, pressed it to his cheek as tears streamed down it, an unstoppable flow that dripped onto her face, cutting through the fresh blood.

"Don't leave me." He shook his head, his insides tearing apart, his heart shattering into a thousand pieces. "I'm sorry. I should have come quicker. I should never have left you. Please don't leave me."

The corners of her lips wobbled and fresh tears came, hot and fast down his cheeks as he realised she wanted to smile for him.

This world was cruel. Vicious. It would see just how cruel and vicious he could be in return.

The ground shook, the rain coming faster, but it didn't touch her now. It curved above him, striking the pavement around them instead.

"I love... you," she murmured, and he leaned towards her so she didn't strain herself trying to speak with him. He pressed his forehead to hers and pulled her into his arms, clutching her tightly as he shook from the force of the pain building inside him. Pain that needed out. She managed to brush her fingers over his cheek, her touch light, killing him. "I'm not scared for me... I'm scared for you... I don't... want you... to be... alone... again... never."

She slumped in his arms.

His lower lip wobbled and his face crumpled, and he held her closer, tighter. "I love you too."

But she would never know.

She would never know how much he loved her, would always love her, because she was gone.

Stolen from him.

He threw his head back and roared, and every drop of rain exploded, bursting to form a haze that swamped the city before it began falling again, harder than ever, a torrent that turned the streets into raging rivers.

The ground shook beneath him as he stumbled onto his feet, lifting her into his arms, and looked down at her.

Sirens wailed, a tsunami warning.

Not the only one.

By now, they would be ringing along the coast of Japan, and around the world.

Because the only light in this dark world was gone.

He stepped with her, landing in the middle of the main room of the mansion, and stood there staring down at her as the television talked of flash floods across the globe and tidal waves hitting south-east Asia already, wiping out villages in their paths.

Ares and Megan rushed to him.

"Oh, Esher." Megan choked on a sob as she saw Aiko's lifeless body in his arms.

But he couldn't take his eyes off her.

"There's nothing we can do now." Ares reached for him.

Esher evaded him and backed off a step, because there was something he could do.

He wanted to destroy this world, wanted to see it all burn, bring it to a painful bloody end, hungered to obey the darker part of himself that said to unleash all of his agony on it, to return it a thousand-fold.

But Aiko wouldn't want that.

She would want him to go on without her, to protect this world for her.

But he couldn't do that either.

He couldn't live without her.

Even if she grew to hate him, he needed her, and that meant she had to live.

"Heal her body." He gently set Aiko down on the floor and growled when Megan didn't move. "Fucking heal her."

"Calm down." Ares stepped between him and Megan. "She's gone, Esher."

No. He wouldn't accept that. *Couldn't.* There was something he could do, and it meant a fight he probably wouldn't win, but he couldn't give up without trying.

"Heal her." He looked to Megan. "Please?"

She clearly had more heart than his brother, because she nodded, even though he could see she didn't understand what use it would be to heal Aiko's body now.

He turned to Ares. "Protect her."

Not Megan. Aiko. He needed his brother to protect Aiko while he was gone.

"What are you going to do?" Ares tossed him a worried look, one that had a hefty dose of wariness in it that said he knew what Esher was going to do but didn't want to believe it.

Esher pressed a kiss to Aiko's lips and smoothed her matted hair from her face. "Wait for me... just as you promised."

"Esher, where are you going?" Ares moved a step towards him, a measured one that warned his brother was trying to close the distance between them in a subtle way.

He knew where Esher was going.

And he wanted to stop him.

Hypocrite. If it was Ares in his shoes, and Megan in Aiko's place, his brother would be long gone already, risking everything for her.

Just as he was going to risk it for Aiko.

Esher shot to his feet, clenched his fists and regarded his brother with cold eyes, daring him to even think about leaving his place at Aiko's side while he was gone.

"I'm going home." He disappeared before Ares could try to stop him, landing in an elegant apartment in London that looked as if a tornado had hit it.

Clothes, magazines and food cartons were strewn everywhere, occupying almost all of the antique furniture in the high-ceilinged pale-grey-walled living room.

Cal turned away from the sash window to the left of the fireplace, no trace of surprise to see him in his eyes.

"I know what your favour mark can do." Esher stalked towards him, kicking clothes and books out of the way as he closed the distance between them, pain tearing up his right leg with each step.

Behind Cal, the weather took a turn for the worse, rain falling in a thick sheet that obscured the buildings across the street.

Cal closed his hand over the dark blue script that tracked up the inside of his right forearm. "You know what happens if you go back there."

He did, and he didn't care. He was prepared to fight his father on this, would fight the world if it brought Aiko back.

"I don't have time to deal with the gatekeepers on the other side of the Tokyo gate... *she* doesn't have time. I have to reach her now." Before his father assigned her soul to a realm and she was lost to him forever. "I'm sorry, Cal."

He stepped, appearing behind his brother, grabbed his arm and tore his fingers from it to reveal the words written in the language of the Underworld.

"Tell me how to make it work," he snarled.

Cal twisted free of his grip and shoved him in the chest, knocking him back against the window. "I will, but you need to calm the fuck down, because focusing is a fucking big part of it or you'll end up some place far from where you want to be."

Esher breathed through the need to grab his brother again, pushing out the fury and locking down the pain so he could focus.

He had one shot at this.

He had to appear in the right place.

Any other place and he would have to fight his way to the fortress. His father would know he was coming, would send legions to deal with him, and he didn't have the strength to fight them and his father. Teleporting once he was in the Underworld was out of the question too. He was tapped out now, body already on the verge of breaking. He needed what little power he had left to battle his father.

So he needed to appear at the palace if he was going to save Aiko.

Cal held his arm out. "Read the words, and when the portal appears, you need to step through it while thinking about where you want to be. You have to really picture it... *really* want it."

He wanted it enough.

Whether or not he could focus through the pain for long enough to appear in the Underworld rather than back at Aiko was another matter. She kept popping into his head, his heart screaming to return to her because he needed her. Cal's favour mark, a gift from Hermes, could transport him anywhere he wanted to go, wherever his heart desired, whether it was in this world, the Underworld or Olympus.

Esher just had to convince that heart that he wanted to go to the palace.

Not Tokyo.

He read the words, and as thunder peeled overhead and the floor shook, bright blue light burst from the letters on Cal's forearm and a portal formed beside him, shimmering like water in a multitude of colours.

Esher focused on the ancient fortress, because Aiko was there now, not in Tokyo. Her soul was there, waiting for him to come for her. He built a picture of the imposing black building that resembled a series of enormous Greek temples, each towering structure surrounded by fluted columns that were a single row supporting the roof along the sides, forming a walkway around the building, but were two rows deep at the front to support the weight of the triangular pediment. Columned enclosed corridors connected each temple. Beautiful gardens surrounded it, the colours a dazzling contrast against the dark stone.

He wanted to be there.

He stepped into the portal.

Blue light engulfed him, heat searing him as he was pulled from London, zipped through the air and caught flickers of places around him, and then a lot of black. It smelled of earth. The air grew thicker, and he grunted as his boots hit the ground again, his tibia protesting as his weight pressed down on it.

He lifted his head.

Relief rushed through him, sweeter than anything, as the central temple of the palace rose before him, flanked by two smaller ones that were set back slightly, the enclosed hallway that joined them making them appear to be one enormous temple. Black mountains rose behind it, taller than any on Earth, fractures in their faces glowing gold, illuminating the dull grey sky and the smoky clouds that swirled across it.

"Halt!" A sentry at the gate in the wall, a towering male dressed in black armour, moved towards him.

Esher didn't have time for this. He threw his hand towards the male and he grunted, gargled as he went down clutching his throat. The other two sentries met the same fate as they rushed from the gatehouse. He didn't spare them a glance as he limped forwards, his leg aching with each step.

The high square black doors of the fortress flew open with a flick of his wrist, hitting the walls with a thunderous boom, and he stalked through the cavernous building, heading past the two-storey high statue of his father in full regalia and bident in hand that stood in the centre, surrounded by flickering oil lamps and offerings. He picked up his pace as he rounded the statue, struggling to resist the temptation to run. He could manage it, but the pain would steal more of his strength, and he needed every drop of it if he was going to succeed.

He passed through the door at the other end of the temple, into a smaller building with corridors that branched off it, heading towards the other buildings in the complex, and exited it to cross the courtyard, where flowers bloomed and brought dazzling colour and life to the palace. He headed for the next building, a wide one that had a more modern flair, still fronted by columns, but only the central third of it had a pediment, the two thirds on either side of it kept flat so it almost resembled an old country estate in England.

Esher breathed slowly, gathering his strength as he moved as quickly as he could while also buying his body time to stop shaking. The pain wracking his heart made that difficult, had him trembling and on the verge of screaming whenever he thought about Aiko, saw her body laid out on the tatami mats, drenched in her own blood.

He curled his fingers into fists, his claws biting into his palms as he entered the main building and crossed it, heading straight for the high door opposite him. He shoved it open and took the steps downwards into a tunnel.

He winced with each step that took him down through the rock, his senses on high alert as he scoured the path ahead of him, and behind him. More sentries would come. He didn't have time. He had to reach the other end.

Had to reach the throne room.

He could feel his father waiting there.

The tunnel seemed endless, longer than he remembered, each step agony as he thought about Aiko, saw himself holding her, heard her last words to him, and the ones he had said to her.

Ones he would say to her again when she was back with him.

He reached the bottom of the tunnel and stepped out into the lower building of the palace that sat on the banks of one of the rivers, the opened sides to his left and right revealing the water where it flowed around a bend and enclosed the temple. Ten thick black fluted columns set two metres apart supported a lintel decorated with a frieze on either side of him, the statues atop each one glaring down at him, their backdrop the swirling sky and the imposing angry mountains that spewed lava. Those marble columns led his eye forwards to the wall at the far end.

Where a tall black throne constructed of bones stood empty, the trench of flames that ran along the bottom of the wall low and barely flickering.

"Father!" Esher threw his head back and bellowed.

Hades stepped out from a column to his right, his hands tucked behind his back beneath the thick crimson cloak that swirled around his ankles. The black armour that hugged his lean six-eight frame clinked as he walked, the pointed toes of his metal boots scraping on the black marble floor with each step.

His father regarded him with cold pale blue eyes and lowered his hands from behind his back, so his clawed gauntlets brushed the plates of armour that extended down in thick pointed tabs from his waist, covering his thighs.

He flexed those claws as he stepped up onto the dais and curled them over the arms of his throne as he sat down and tipped his chin up, causing the spikes of his black crown to blend with his short jet hair and the obsidian bones.

"You are not meant to be here," Hades drawled in the language of the Underworld, and gods, it hit Esher hard.

This was his father, a male he hadn't seen in centuries now, since he had banished Esher and his brothers from the Underworld and forced them to protect the gates.

Esher had hated him, had thought he wouldn't care if he never saw him again, but now he was home.

He was home.

He looked around the temple, and beyond it to the river, and the mountains. *Home.*

Away from the mortals, away from the pain, away from the daemons and their vile machinations.

Free of it all.

No, he wasn't free. He wasn't free of the pain. He wasn't home either. His home had been stolen from him.

"I need her back. It wasn't her time to die." He stumbled over a few of the words, unused to speaking his native language. "Give her back to me."

Red ringed the edges of his father's irises.

Anger flared hot inside Esher, rage condensing in his blood as that look ignited it.

Because he knew what his father was going to say.

But it didn't prepare him for the agony, the sheer fury that blasted through him when his father calmly sat on his throne, not a trace of emotion in his cold eyes as he opened his mouth and spoke a single word.

"No."

CHAPTER 22

No.

Such a small, simple word, but it cut Esher deeply, and the control he had over his rage snapped, the violence twisting with the darkness inside him as he gave himself over to the hunger rising swiftly within him. His claws lengthened, echoing his father's armour, and he felt his eyes change, the red emerging in them as he stared him down.

Around him, the river boiled, the surface churning in response to his rage, tipped with grey crests and beginning to foam.

Esher stepped towards Hades and roared as all the pain, the trauma of losing Aiko and the agony born of the thought he might never see her again, twisted tighter inside him, pushing him closer to the edge.

"Don't you dare deny me!"

His father remained relaxed, cold and calm in the face of Esher's fury, completely unaffected by it.

Esher threw his arms out at his sides and dragged them forwards, gathering the entire river and hurling it as a wall of black at his father, his heart slamming hard against his bruised ribs as he bellowed and his muscles strained, his entire body quaking as he put all of his strength into the attack.

The water dropped to the ground before it reached him, revealing Hades where he stood with one hand outstretched.

Esher snarled as the dark water rolled back into the riverbed, obeying his father.

He should have known he wouldn't be strong enough.

Calm swept through him in the wake of that thought, washing it away, and he stared at Hades, into the bastard's cold eyes and let it flow over him.

He was strong enough.

He had just forgotten how strong he really was, and it was his father's fault.

He reached for the black bracelet on his right wrist, and Hades reacted at last, his eyes narrowing on what he was doing, a warning ringing in them.

Esher didn't care.

He snapped the band and power flowed into him, surged through him and rocked him forwards, lighting him up like the strongest drug. He growled as strength poured into his muscles, his bones, his very soul. It had been too fucking long since he had felt the true depth of his power, had put up with it being limited in order to protect the mortal world, but no more.

His father *would* give Aiko back.

Even if he had to kill him to make it happen.

He snarled through his fangs and whipped his hands forwards again, sending two spiralling funnels of water at Hades.

His father deflected the first one with a wave of his hand, and grunted as the second hit him, sending him slamming into one of the black marble columns to the left of Esher. It fractured under the blow and Esher kept pummelling him with water, hurling thick streams of it at him until the column shattered, collapsing on top of Hades.

The water splashed to the ground as Esher severed control over it.

He breathed hard, staggered back a step as the exertion hit him and barely maintained his footing. He had forgotten the toll his power took on him, but he wouldn't let it hold him back.

His father would give Aiko back.

The broken column rolled towards him and Hades pushed onto his feet, his crimson eyes sliding to lock with his.

He mustered his strength and faced his father, growled and focused on the river, calling it to him. It rose as a wall around them, towering higher than the plateau above them on which the main palace stood. He raised his hand, felt the strength of it surging through him, power that he would bring down on his father's head, would condense into a prison that would force Hades to agree to his terms.

Or drown.

He dropped his hand.

The water crashed down.

Hit an invisible dome and slid harmlessly over it to land back in the riverbed.

He snarled at his father.

He needed to be stronger, hit harder. He needed to make his father give in. He needed Aiko back. Pain shot through him at that thought, bringing tears to his eyes as his heart fractured. He needed her. Gods, he needed her. His father had to see that. His father *would* see that.

He would make him see it.

That thought drummed in his head and his heart as he gathered his strength again, his body shaking from the exertion of commanding water that was under his father's control. Water that he would never be able to use to convince Hades to return her, because his father was stronger than he was and would always win.

He was being weak.

Water wasn't his strongest weapon.

He was allowing fear of truly harming his father to hold him back.

But if he was weak, if he allowed fear to restrain him, Aiko would be lost to him forever.

The only way to bring her back was to make his father submit.

Was to defeat him.

Esher narrowed his eyes on Hades, focused on his pain and the agony ripping him apart inside, and his need to see Aiko again, to have her back in his arms. He would do anything for her. Even this.

He had to defeat him.

His father's crimson eyes narrowed.

He had to do it. His father had left him no choice. He couldn't command the rivers, but he could command another liquid, one Hades had no power over.

He closed his eyes and focused through the rage burning inside him, let it stoke his strength and crush the part of him that whispered not to do it, that there was no going back if he did such an atrocious thing, that Aiko wouldn't want him to do this.

He had to do it.

He focused on his father.

On the blood in his veins.

And shut out the regret.

Because this was the only way to bring Aiko back.

He would destroy the world for her.

His world.

He flicked his eyes open. Narrowed them on his father. Focused his power.

Hades grimaced and lifted his hand, visibly struggling as Esher began to seize command of his blood. His father curled his clawed fingers as if grasping something.

Esher's throat closed.

His focus shattered as fire banded around his neck, burned him as he wheezed and fought for air, his windpipe blazing as it compressed.

He fell to his knees on the wet floor and clawed at the invisible hand on his throat, cutting his own flesh as he desperately tried to breathe. Tears burned his wide eyes as he choked, and panic replaced his fury, fear that he was the one who was going to die.

His father was going to kill him.

One thought rang in his mind as his father glared down at him and squeezed harder, cutting off his air supply entirely.

He would never see Aiko again.

Hades would make sure of that. He would banish his soul to a place far from hers to punish him.

"You dare attack me over this?" Hades boomed and squeezed harder still. "You act like a mortal."

He struggled to focus on his father as his vision dimmed, his heart labouring and body shaking as the need for air became dangerously real.

A slender pale hand settled on the black metal plates of his father's gauntlet and the hold on Esher weakened, allowing him to get a little air into his tight lungs.

"Not a mortal, my love, but he is much like his father." A voice as soft as a summer's breeze swirled around Esher, easing his panic and fear as he sucked down all the air he could get and his head began to clear again. "Did you not rail at Zeus and threaten all residing in Mount Olympus when Demeter demanded my return? I see much of the young god-king who claimed my heart in our son, and I love him all the more for it."

She was calm, soothing in the chaos, a force to be reckoned with as she worked her magic on Hades.

The pressure on Esher's throat lessened and air whooshed into his lungs through his burning throat, his skull splitting as he choked on it.

When the hold on his throat disappeared, he fell forwards, pressing both hands into the wet black floor and coughing, each one stirring the water beneath him. Tears joined the water, sparkling and mingling. He struggled to breathe, but for a different reason as fear of death swept away and pain swept back in, ripping at him, tearing him apart as he realised he had failed.

"What is wrong?" Persephone's soft voice reached out to him, but he took no comfort from it this time.

"Aiko is dead… the daemon killed her." He choked on the sob that wracked his entire body. "I need her back."

He stared at the floor, feeling weak and pathetic. He couldn't even beat his father for Aiko's sake. He shook his head, causing water to drip from the tangled ends of his black hair that hung in his field of vision, obscuring his parents and close to brushing the marble tiles. No, he couldn't give in. He wouldn't surrender. Not while there was still fight left in him.

Cold swirled through him.

With the moon still affecting him, and Aiko's death weighing heavily on him, it would be dangerous to unleash his full power.

He would lose control of himself and change.

But he had to do it.

He couldn't let her die.

He pushed himself up a little and reached his right hand across, shaking as he mustered the last of his strength. He clenched his teeth and breathed hard, shut out the weaker side of himself that said not to do it, and closed his fingers over the band around his left wrist.

Bare feet appeared close to his left hand where it pressed against the flagstones.

Jagged layers of sheer black fabric pooled around them to blend with the floor as she crouched.

Her fingers were warm, smelled of sunshine and flowers, lilies, as she pressed them to the underside of his chin and lifted them.

Esher obeyed, raising his head and his eyes to meet her glittering green ones through the threads of his hair. Sorrow shone in them, love that knew no bounds, no drop of darkness as she gazed down at him.

Aiko had looked at him like that.

Now she was gone.

"Everything will be alright," she murmured, her voice reaching him this time, soothing the edge off his temper, but it refused to fade. "Calm now."

He couldn't.

The tide of his need was too strong, pulling him under.

His fingers tensed against the remaining band.

"Your father will respond better to his son, not this. Tell him what is in your heart." She lowered her head, causing her wavy crimson hair to spill over her shoulders and the black layers of her dress, and lightly touched his left hand, and then his right one, and eased it away from the bracelet.

He clawed back control, piecing enough together that the rage boiling in his veins, the black need to fight to force his father to give Aiko back, receded, helped by her touch as she held his wrists, supporting him, using her link with nature to suppress his and ease the effect of the tide on him.

She smiled gently.

Esher drew down a shuddering breath as he eased back into a sitting position on his knees. He couldn't bring himself to look at his father or his mother when he saw the destruction he had wrought. More than one of the temple columns lay broken, and the right frieze was fractured, the statue that had been above the point where it had cracked now shattered on the ground.

He hated losing it, but he hadn't been able to stop himself.

He needed Aiko.

His father had to see that now.

But one look into his father's cold blue eyes said that he was wrong.

His father didn't care that he was hurting, that he needed her back, and that had the anger he had managed to calm rising back up again, engulfing him as the water in the river grew choppy and rose higher, becoming rolling waves that crashed over the small piece of flat land on which the temple stood.

"Esher," his mother whispered.

He refused to calm.

She was wrong. Hades wouldn't respond better to him if he spoke to him as his son. He had tried that, and then he had tried violence. Neither had worked.

Which left him only one recourse.

His heart ached at the thought, soul screamed not to do it, but if it meant Aiko lived again, that the world was warmed by her smiles and graced by her presence again, he would do it.

"Take my life instead and give it to her."

Those words fell hard in the silence.

A flicker of astonishment surfaced in his father's blue eyes. "After all you have suffered, you would sacrifice your life for the sake of this mortal?"

Esher sniffed back the tears that threatened to come as the thought he would never see her again after all rang in his mind, tormenting him, and nodded. "I don't want to live in a world without her."

Hades snorted. "Sentimental fool. The human world has affected you."

Esher pushed onto his feet, gritting his teeth as his entire body ached, and faced his father. "You were once a sentimental fool too."

Hades glanced at Persephone.

She took Esher's arm, gently supporting him, her green eyes filled with sympathy. "Your father cannot simply return the human's soul. You know this. Zeus does not permit such things, and neither does your father. Those who have died cannot be given back their life without some form of payment."

He slid his gaze towards her, the way his father scowled at her words making him pay close attention to them, because she was trying to tell him something.

He wracked his aching brain, mulling over her words, desperate to find the answer hidden in them.

When it hit him, his eyes widened.

"I'll do whatever it takes to regain Aiko's soul." He turned to his father, and Hades's face darkened, his eyes beginning to glow crimson again. "I'll stand any trial."

His father stepped down from the dais, that single step shaking the ground as his words rolled over Esher. "You must lead her soul from the Underworld, on foot, and never once look back at her until you have left the realm."

Esher's blood chilled, and he teetered on the brink of begging his father for a different trial, anything but that one, but set his jaw and held his tongue.

The challenge was almost impossible, and all had failed it.

It was his father's favourite trick, and he had been foolish enough to think that because he was his son, Hades wouldn't play such a horrible one on him.

"I won't fail," he bit out. "I will save Aiko."

Hades smiled.

Esher couldn't tell whether it was a cruel one because he thought Esher would fail or whether it was a satisfied one, because Esher was willing to prove his strength and that he deserved her soul by besting a challenge all else had failed.

"Turn then, and I shall release her soul." Hades held his left hand up. "She will follow your lead through the Underworld."

He did as instructed, his muscles tensing as he waited, sure he would feel it when Aiko was released to follow him. He breathed through his nerves, trying to settle them as he told himself that he could do this. His father had given him a chance to save her, and he wouldn't fail her.

Persephone rounded him and opened her right hand to reveal a new black bracelet. He lifted his right hand, and she gently took hold of his wrist as she slipped it on for him.

"Be strong, my son, my love, and do not look back. Only look forwards," she whispered, her voice so low he barely heard her, and touched his chest. "Aiko is in here, and up there, not behind you. Focus on that and your desire to save her."

She embraced him and pressed a kiss to his cheek, and he wrapped his arms around her, held her tightly as his fear and pain mingled together, threatening to overwhelm him already. He clung to her words, repeating them in his head.

"What are you doing?" Hades growled. "You had better not be telling him things that you shouldn't."

Persephone released him, all smiles and lightness as she looked beyond Esher to Hades. "I would not do such a thing."

Hades huffed.

Esher frowned at the corridor ahead of him that would take him up to the palace.

He could do this. Finding the route to the nearest gate would take time, but he could do it, could deny the temptation to see Aiko behind him. He wouldn't fail. Gods, he already wanted to turn.

He clenched his fists.

Marched forwards.

Doubts began to cloud his heart as he ascended the steps, his leg aching with each one. He wanted to look back, yearned to see Aiko, to see she was following him. He couldn't feel her. His father was playing a trick on him. She wasn't really there.

He needed to see she was there.

He went to turn his head.

A tiny flower glittering in the darkness on a step just ahead of him caught his eye.

He frowned as he spotted another one further up, and when he passed that one, there were two more. He followed them, up the tunnel, across the vestibule of the main palace, and along the path through the courtyard garden and the main temple. They faded whenever he reached them, wilting and turning to ash, leaving no evidence behind.

Esher looked ahead of him at the paths that branched off in all directions beyond the wall of the palace. If he took the wrong one, he would end up deeper into the Underworld, and further from the gates. He had to pick carefully.

He scanned them all.

His eyebrows dipped as he passed a boulder that separated two paths and his gaze drifted back to it.

A flower.

It was small, blue.

His colour.

He walked towards it.

A Himalayan poppy.

His mother was guiding him, risking his father's wrath to show him the path. She knew the ways around the Underworld, the ever-changing routes to the gates, her connection with nature guiding her towards it at all times.

He followed the flowers, not slowing and not stopping, crossing rivers and mountains, until his feet were sore in his boots and his leg stopped throbbing, the journey so long that the bone had healed.

He focused as his mother had told him, on the path ahead of him, because Aiko wasn't behind him, she was in his heart and up in the mortal realm. She was in his heart.

He pressed his palm to his chest, she was in his heart and she always would be.

It belonged to her.

He lost track of how long he had been walking, but he passed through several of the darker realms. Thankfully, none of the residents seemed interested in attacking him as they normally would those who came to the Underworld for such a thing as the soul of their loved one. He knew several who had attempted the trial had met a grisly end.

Were they avoiding him because of who is father was, or because they could sense his power and his foul mood?

The moon had waned again, releasing him from its influence, but the need to reach the gate grated on him, had his anger at a constant simmer in his veins, stoked by a desire to see Aiko again.

The path grew steeper and then dropped into a wide valley filled with towering black pinnacles.

In the centre of it, a colourful disc shimmered, the bands of glyphs lazily rotating in opposite directions.

He wasn't sure which gate it was, and he didn't give a fuck. It was a gate, and it would take him to Earth.

He was going to beat his father's vicious game.

The ground shook as a gargantuan biped beast with mottled grey skin stretched over muscles like mountains stomped around the corner, five-storeys tall with a head full of grey-blue horns, its silver eyes glowing as it patrolled the valley.

A gatekeeper.

He wasn't going to stick around to tangle with it.

He sprinted and skidded down the side of the mountain, hit a boulder and leaped off it, landing further down. He stumbled forwards as he reached the valley basin and the ground levelled out, and broke into a sprint.

The beast made a low grumbling noise and looked around.

Unleashed a roar as it spotted him.

Too late.

Esher hit the gate at a dead run. Colours swirled around him and then sunshine washed over him, blinding him, and he almost fell as he hit the edge of the gate that hovered above the grass. He dropped off it before any of the humans using the large park noticed him levitating, because he was fucked if he was going to get called in to pay penitence when he had to get Aiko's soul back to her body.

The moment his boots hit the grass, he turned, adrenaline rushing through him, excitement on its heels.

It died when he found nothing behind him.

"No."

He had done exactly what his father had wanted.

He growled, earning a look from a passing human, and glared at the gate as it shrank. It started to open again, responding to him as he commanded it, because he was going back to the Underworld to fight his father all over again and he wouldn't stop fighting until either he was dead or he had Aiko back in his arms.

The temperature dropped as the park grew dark, clouds rolling in to block out the sun as he focused on the gate and fighting his father.

Rain poured down, the humans running for cover as it soaked New York, and the gate expanded and then flashed as it halted, signalling it was ready for him to open it.

A small blue Himalayan poppy sprouted between him and the gate.

He stared at it, sure it was a sign, a message from his mother.

Her words rang in his head again.

Had she been trying to tell him something, just as his father had suspected?

He clenched his fists and recited her words as he touched his chest. "Aiko is in here, up here, not behind me."

He looked down at his fingers, focused on his heart.

A strange warm feeling tickled his chest, filled him with a familiar sensation, one he'd had before.

Whenever Aiko had smiled at him.

A chill swept over his back and down his arms.

His mother's words suddenly made sense.

A soul didn't have a form while it was awaiting his father's judgement, which meant it wasn't capable of following him of its own accord. In order to leave the Underworld, it needed a vessel.

His father hadn't placed her soul behind him, that was just a trick meant to tempt him into looking there so his father could keep her soul.

Hades had placed her soul inside him.

He was her vessel.

His father had mingled her soul with his so he wouldn't feel it, and because he hadn't looked back, it was still there, waiting for him to reunite it with its own vessel.

Aiko's body.

He stepped to Tokyo, landing in the mansion.

He growled when Aiko wasn't where he had left her, and Megan leaped off the sofa, her brown eyes enormous.

"You're back!" She scooted around the couches and pointed towards his room. "We moved her somewhere more comfortable."

Esher ran there, his boots striking the wooden walkway hard enough to shake the timbers of the house, Megan hot on his heels.

The panels that formed the door of his room were open, and he halted as his gaze landed on Aiko where she lay on top of his bed, her skin as white as the moon, lips drained of colour, and her little hands folded over her bloodstained blouse. Beside her on the mats, a single lamp glowed softly, and her white phone rested beneath it.

He lifted his gaze to his brother, wanting to know how it had come to be back in her possession when he had seen it on the roof near the gate.

Ares stopped pacing and looked across at him. "I never left her. Daimon retrieved it. He tried calling her as soon as we knew they were targeting her."

Esher nodded his thanks, fear that this wouldn't work robbing him of his voice as he lowered head again and stared down at Aiko.

He wasn't sure what he was meant to do now.

He took a step towards her, drawn to her as always.

The moment he neared her, tremendous pain tore through him, ripping a roar from his throat as his chest bowed forwards. Bright light burst from it, filling the room, and it felt as if someone was ripping a piece of him free, the agony of it so fierce his lungs seized.

When it faded, and he could breathe again, he sank to his knees, shaking violently as he struggled to remain conscious.

The light flickered and died.

And then a blue glow drifted in front of him.

He fought to focus on it, his vision hazy at first. As it cleared, another chill swept over him.

A delicate, iridescent blue butterfly fluttered around in front of him, dipping and dancing, shining so brightly it brought tears to his eyes.

Aiko.

His little butterfly.

This was his interpretation of her soul, and it was beautiful, like her.

He held his trembling hand out, his palm facing upwards, and the butterfly drifted down, fluttered higher, drifted lower still, and gave one more burst of its glowing wings before it finally descended and settled on his fingers.

He shuffled towards Aiko's body, his eyes on the butterfly, and carefully lowered his hand towards her when he was close enough. The butterfly flew away from his fingers, danced in the air as it drifted lower and lower, casting a blue glow over Aiko.

When it landed on her chest, it glowed bright white, the light of it filling the room.

And then it was gone.

Absorbed into her.

The light spread through Aiko, shining through her skin, spreading colour over it again.

She lurched off the bedding, mouth opening on a gasp as she sucked down air.

Esher was beside her in an instant, gathering her carefully into his arms and cradling her, terrified of hurting her. She struggled for air, each rasping breath killing him, but as the seconds trickled past, they began to come more easily, until she was breathing softly in his arms. Her skin slowly heated beneath his hands, soothing him, but not taking away his fear.

He wasn't sure what damage to expect.

The thick beard covering his brother's face warned he had been gone for a long time, longer than he had thought.

What if her soul being out of her body for so long had caused permanent harm to it, or to her mind?

He brushed his fingers across her brow, sweeping her fringe away from her eyebrows, and feathered them down her cheeks. He would help her through it. He would make her strong again, would bring back her smile and keep her safe. He would shake Olympus and the Underworld until every god and goddess vowed to help him with her and he made her whole again.

"Esher?" she murmured, and he shot Ares a look.

Ares took hold of Megan and disappeared, leaving him alone with Aiko.

"I'm here," he whispered, smoothing her black hair again, doing it to soothe himself as much as he did it to soothe her.

"I had a bad dream." She winced when she tried to move, and he held her still, afraid she still bore injuries even when Megan hadn't warned him that she did and he knew she would have if it had been the case.

"It's over now." He stroked her cheek, moved her so she lay with her head on the pillows and stretched out beside her, pressing the full length of his body against hers.

She groaned as she ignored his attempts to keep her on her back and rolled onto her side, pressing closer to him, and when her eyes fluttered open, their warmth hitting him hard, he didn't have the heart to make her lay on her back again.

He wrapped his arm around her, and she used it as her pillow, resting her soft cheek against it, her hair tickling his skin.

Understanding shone in her eyes as she gazed at him. "You saved me."

He only wished he had done it sooner, hadn't failed and put her through so much pain.

He smiled for her, not wanting her to see how much that hurt him, leaned towards her and pressed a kiss to her lips.

"I love you too," he murmured against them, unable to hold the words back any longer, needing her to know them and the feelings he held in his heart.

She broke down, each sob racking her body, more violent than the last, and he gathered her to him, letting her pour out her pain and feeling like a bastard as he realised he had reminded her of what had happened, had brought it all back to her. He pressed his lips to her forehead and kept them there, held her gently and weathered the pain each of her sobs caused as it tore at him, every one of them his fault.

Around them, blue poppies bloomed, until a sea of them filled his room and spread across the walkway, and through the garden. He floated on that sea with Aiko, holding her as her sobs finally began to subside, her shaking stopping. She let out one final cry and then swallowed hard, wriggled against him as she wiped away her tears, and lifted her bloodshot eyes to meet his.

He wiped the remains of her tears away, careful as he brushed his thumb across her cheeks.

"Do you hate me?" He wasn't sure he could bear it if she did, but he needed to know.

She knew what he had done, remembered it all, he could see it in her eyes.

She put him out of his misery.

Shaking her head.

Speaking words that washed his pain away.

"I love you."

He gathered her to him and kissed her forehead. "I won't fail you again."

It was his solemn vow.

He had a second chance with her and this time he wouldn't mess things up, he would keep her safe, just as he had promised.

He would protect her.

Always.

CHAPTER 23

It had been three days since Esher had brought her back, and gods, the anger hadn't gone anywhere. It simmered in his veins, leashed but still there, not satisfied by her return. He wouldn't be satisfied until the daemon who had killed her met the same fate, suffered at his hands and was torn apart by his power.

Relief that Aiko was back with him came and went, and sometimes he couldn't breathe until he saw her again, found and saw with his own eyes that she was safe.

Alive.

It had been easier until yesterday, because he had only needed to head the handful of strides to his room and check on her where she rested in his bed.

But yesterday, she had decided she was strong enough to leave his room, had asked him to walk with her, and had finally smiled for the first time since she had come back when he had practically smothered her, walking so close to her that they constantly brushed each other. He couldn't help himself. He couldn't bring himself to be more than an inch from her, needed to feel her and be aware that she was alive, safe, well.

Well.

He wasn't sure he could apply that word to her yet.

She was low in spirit, her smiles rare now, and her eyes holding pain sometimes before she noticed him and it drifted away. Her thoughts weighed her down, had her silent during mealtimes when he came to sit with her in his room, keeping her company.

The first day she had been back, she hadn't said more than a handful of words to him, hadn't smiled once, and he had started to fear she would never be the same again, would continue to grow distant from him until she receded so deeply into herself that she was lost to him.

When he had been called for punishment for speaking the language of the Underworld on Earth, and had gone to tell her where he was going, not wanting her to worry about his absence because Daimon had come to protect her in his stead, she had come alive.

She had shot to her feet and pleaded with him not to go, had come close to convincing him to do as she wished as she had shown him the depth of the love that she still held for him in her heart.

She hadn't been afraid because he wouldn't be around to protect her.

She had been afraid he would be vulnerable by leaving the mansion grounds, would come under attack.

He had vowed that he would be safe because he was stepping from the mansion straight to Olympus, but it had still taken time to calm her enough that he could bring himself to leave her.

Nemesis had demanded one hundred extra lashes for his tardiness.

Esher hadn't felt them, or the other one thousand. He had thought about Aiko constantly, desperate to return to her, worried about her.

When he had returned, he had managed to convince himself to wash first rather than head straight to her, had borne the pain of wearing a t-shirt over the fresh wounds, for her. He didn't want her to see them. She was suffering enough without witnessing what Nemesis had done to him as punishment for speaking his native tongue in order to go to the Underworld to bring back her soul.

She would blame his pain on herself, and she already had too much pain in her heart to bear.

He wanted to take some of that pain unto himself for her, tried to steal slivers of it whenever she was feeling bright enough to spend time with him.

He stared at the empty bed in his room, the white covers rumpled and pushed aside. Where had she gone?

He followed the stepping stones across the gravel, strode over the arched crimson wooden bridge that spanned the pond, and wove through the garden, following his heart.

It whispered where she was.

He rounded a bend between two stone lanterns and found her sitting on the large grey boulder, her bare feet dangling above the grass, her eyes locked on the cherry tree and her profile to him. His robe swamped her, the black cloth wrapped tightly around her tiny form, reaching her ankles.

Below her feet, blue poppies bloomed.

He looked at the tree, frowned as the blossoms that had been faded were bright with life again, almost glowing with it as they danced in the gentle warm breeze.

His mother.

She was watching over Aiko for him, trying to soothe her troubled soul with something Aiko found beautiful, giving her something bright in this world to draw her away from the darkness of her death.

Aiko looked across at him, and relief hit him hard when he saw her brown eyes were brighter today, and there was finally colour in her pale cheeks again, a dash of pink that darkened as he stared at her.

"I thought the tree was done blooming." She glanced back at it and her lips curled in a faint smile.

"It probably was." He looked at it, and then crossed the patch of grass to her, and she frowned at his bare feet.

He didn't need to look to see what was happening.

The way her eyes widened told him.

She lifted them to his, searching them for an explanation.

He stooped, plucked one of the poppies that were blooming around him, and tucked her black hair behind her ear, fixing the poppy there. It was her colour too.

"Mother," he said.

Aiko shimmied to her left. He took a seat in the space she offered, and the moment she pressed against him, he couldn't stop himself from lifting her onto his lap and wrapping his arms around her, keeping her angled in a way that allowed her to see the flowers and the cherry blossoms. Her black robe blended into his jeans and shirt.

"She's a goddess of nature… Persephone." He tucked Aiko a little closer to him and wanted to groan as she snuggled into his arms, the pleasure of feeling her in them a soothing balm to his battered heart.

"It makes sense." Aiko leaned back, settling her head on his shoulder, her temple pressing against his neck. "You and your brothers all control elements of nature."

That was true.

Persephone had power over more than just nature though, balanced Hades in his power over death.

Aiko was proof of that.

He had only realised it yesterday, when he had found her in the garden, in this spot, and had berated her for being out of bed so soon. She had countered that she felt strong enough to leave her bed.

She had looked tired though, worn down, pale, and he hadn't been convinced.

When he had tried to make her return to her room, seizing her hand, she had stood firm.

Unmoving.

He had looked at her then, really looked at her, and had seen the poppies blooming around her feet, and the glow that lit her eyes as she told him flat that she wanted to walk the garden.

She was stronger than before.

It wasn't only her soul's journey to the Underworld and back again that had affected her.

He had the feeling that while her soul had been there, his mother had found it.

Aware of his pain and his love for the mortal, and that he would come for her soul, but he would always worry something would happen to her again, because she was weak and vulnerable, Persephone had done what she could to ease his fears.

She had blessed Aiko's soul.

His mother had made her strong.

Strong enough to walk in his world, as immortal as he was.

It had soothed the worst of his fears, but had done nothing to crush the other ones, ones that weren't so easily vanquished and would always be a part of him, because he loved her. He would always worry about her, afraid of putting her in danger. Just as he always worried about his brothers.

"What are you thinking?" she murmured on a contented sigh and stroked her fingers along his arm, back and forth, calming him.

She was reading him again, picking up his turbulent emotions.

He pressed his cheek against her forehead. "I'm just worried about you."

She tilted her head towards him and back, pressed her lips to his chin. He turned and kissed her, smoothed his palm across her cheek and held her in place as he savoured her lips, her kiss made all the sweeter by the way it relaxed her, seemed to chase away her sombre thoughts too.

She stilled against his lips. "Your brothers are coming."

They were?

He frowned as he felt the first one appear, closely followed by another.

He had thought they had more time before the meeting.

Aiko slipped from his lap, and he caught her wrist. She looked down at it, and then up into his eyes.

"You don't have to be there." He held her hand.

It trembled slightly in his, betraying her nerves, but she nodded. "I'm ready. I want to be a part of the meeting."

She wasn't ready. She was pushing herself, for his sake, for the sake of his brothers, and their worlds. When he had told her Marek had called a meeting, she had asked to attend, had insisted when he had tried to deny her, telling her to wait in his room or in the garden.

"I have information." She twisted her hand in his, slipping her fingers over his palm and taking hold of his hand instead, and tugged on it. "I think I should be dressed though."

That had him moving, because he was damned if his brothers were going to see her in just his robe.

She didn't protest when he scooped her up into his arms and carried her like a princess through the garden. She looped her arms around his neck and rested her head on his shoulder.

"I'll cook curry rice later," he said to fill the pleasant silence. "We can eat at the table today."

"I'd like that." She wriggled closer, her sigh telling him just how much she liked the idea. "I'd like a bath too."

He stopped dead, heart slamming against his chest at the thought of bathing her. He crushed it a second later. She was strong enough to bathe herself.

"You can have a shower." He looked down at her, and she frowned at him.

"I want to float on the water." She almost pouted when he went to shake his head, and he sighed again, an exasperated one this time.

"The water is too hot. What if you faint?"

She hit him with another smile. Two so close together. He wasn't sure he could take it, his heart doing a flip at the sight of it and the thought she might be getting better after all, might pull through and expel the darkness that lingered in her soul, filling it with light again.

"You'll be there to save me." She meant the words lightly, teasingly, and damn temptingly, but they hit him hard.

Left him cold.

"I'm sorry," he croaked and held her closer, crushed her against him and clung to her, his fingers pressing into her ribs and her knee. His stomach churned, acid boiling in it as he saw her falling, failed to catch her in time and watched her die.

She pressed her cheek to his, and he wasn't sure if it was her tears or his that wetted his skin.

"Help me forget," she whispered, a desperate note to her voice. "I want to make new memories… happier memories. I want to fill my head with them so I can forget the bad ones."

Gods, he could do that for her.

They would make a million memories, ones so bright they filled her heart with light again, drove out the darkness and brought her nothing but happiness and a reason to smile, to laugh.

He nodded stiffly. "I could do with some of that myself."

Because every time he closed his eyes, whenever fatigue crept up on him and he fell asleep, he saw her falling.

Saw himself failing her.

Watched her die.

He felt Valen nearby, braced himself for a smart-ass comment, but when he looked at his brother, Valen averted his blue eyes and turned away, giving him some time alone with Aiko.

Didn't even mention the fact Esher was crying like a fucking baby.

He buried his face in Aiko's neck and held her, just stood there in the middle of the bridge and held her, not giving a shit if his brothers all saw him, or that he was making them wait. Aiko said she was ready to speak with them, but he wasn't. Keras was going to tear him a new one. Everyone was going to kick up a fuss. Or they were going to tread on egg shells around him, as if he would flip his switch if they said a word out of place.

He wasn't sure he could bear it.

He just wanted to be alone with Aiko.

She brushed her fingers through his hair, teasing the short back of it, and then the sides, and then the curve of his ear, and pressed kisses to his throat and cheek that pushed away the pain, had him focusing on her and the present, and that she was in his arms.

Warm. Safe. Alive.

Immortal.

He kissed her again and groaned as she met it with a passionate one, her lips fierce against his, filled with desperation that called at him, made him want to drown in her until they were both smiling again, light filling their souls and their pain forgotten.

"Your brothers are waiting," she murmured against his lips, her heart telling him that she didn't care, that she didn't want to end this moment yet.

"Let them wait." He kissed her again, held her closer and gave her what she needed—a reminder that she was alive, they both were, and nothing was going to change that.

Nothing was going to separate them again.

When she was breathless and panting, he eased back, slowing the kiss and bringing her back down.

She broke away from his lips, nuzzled his nose with her own, and whispered, "Thank you."

He didn't deserve that, so he didn't respond to it.

Instead, he pressed his forehead to hers, and growled, "Gods, I fucking love you."

She giggled.

Sweet ambrosia, it rushed through him like fire, lit him up and chased out the lingering cold.

"I love you too." She pressed her lips to his, but her kiss was brief, sweet, too damned chaste now she had him fired up. "So can I have that bath later?"

Who was he to deny her?

If she wanted to float on water, she would float on water. Whatever she wanted, she got.

He nodded. "I'll keep an eye on you."

But that was all he would do. As much as he wanted to give in to his need of her, ached to kiss her and touch her, and make love with her, he would hold back and just bathe with her. She wasn't ready for anything else yet. He felt sure of it, and he didn't want to push her.

He carried her into his room, set her down and closed the door panels, shutting the world out. She tortured him as she shed his robe, revealing her bare curves, and he averted his eyes, not sure he could bear it. He knew she wanted his eyes on her, that it made her feel alive, just as his kiss had, but he had a damned meeting to attend, and he was in danger of forgetting all about it.

If he looked at her while she dressed in the clothes Megan had brought for her, a faded pair of blue jeans she had to roll up at the ankles, a dark pink camisole that hugged her breasts, and a deep blue sweater, he might be tempted to strip them all back off her and make a better memory with her, one he hoped might put a smile on her face.

"Ready." She slipped her hand into his.

She wasn't.

He could feel her shaking, could sense her nerves.

He squeezed her hand and gazed down into her eyes. "If it gets too much, if you want a break, just say. Promise me you'll say."

She managed another smile. "I promise."

He huffed. "Let's do this then."

CHAPTER 24

Esher led Aiko from his room, keeping hold of her hand. He wasn't going to release it until the meeting was done, and they were alone again, and even then he was only going to let it go so he could wrap his arms around her.

She walked with her chin tipped up, her eyes bright and a confidence in her step that conveyed the courage she had found, one she had probably been gradually building up all day to get it to the point where she felt ready to speak about what had happened to her.

Gods, he was unravelling, falling apart, as she grew stronger, each day tearing at him as it restored her.

His own courage faltered as he neared the main room of the house and heard his brothers talking. When he walked in, they would all stop and stare, would bring up what he had done, might even lash out at him, or berate in him Keras's case, and he steeled himself, preparing for it.

He entered ahead of Aiko, ready to weather everything his brothers threw at him.

Valen laughed over something Cal had said, both of them lounging on the couch beside each other, no longer looking like each other as they used to.

When the fuck had Valen dyed his hair violet?

Megan giggled, her chocolate eyes bright with her amusement. "And then I told him he'd lost the bet and he had to pay up. He wasn't happy."

Ares, sitting on the armchair beneath her and playing cushion, a wall of black beneath her blue jeans and crimson t-shirt, jabbed his fingers into her ribs, eliciting a squeak from her as she wriggled. "I'll win next time."

Gods, it all felt so normal.

It hit Esher hard, shaking him, knocking him back on his heels as he absorbed the sight of his brothers gathered around the TV, joking and laughing with each other. Valen slung his arm around Eva, their choice of black combat clothing making them blend into each other, and pulled her to him.

She smiled at him, her short black hair swaying to flash the electric blue stripes in it as she leaned towards his brother, landing a hand on his chest. Her cerulean eyes were bright, her light voice laced with her thick Italian accent as she said, "Maybe we should paint your nails next."

Valen made a face.

Daimon laughed. "I think pink is his colour really."

That had Valen turning his scowl on Daimon.

Keras looked over the back of the couch at Esher and rose onto his feet. "Join us."

He eyed his brother and cautiously led Aiko around the couch. She settled on it beside Marek, and Esher went with her, placing himself between her and his brother, keeping an eye on Keras, still wary of his older brother, even as he moved away, long black-clad legs carrying him to the other side of Ares, near the TV.

Marek leaned forwards and looked across at Aiko. "You look well. How are you feeling?"

She lit up the room with another smile, but Esher could feel her strain, the darkness beginning to press back down on her as she did her best to deny it. "Better. Esher has been taking care of me."

"I'll bet," Valen sniggered, and Esher glared at him.

"Ignore the idiot," Ares put in and wrapped his arms around Megan's stomach. "We're all glad you're alright."

"Thank you." She brought her bare feet up onto the couch and clutched Esher's hand. "I know you took care of me."

Ares's rugged face and earthy eyes gained an uncomfortable edge as he shrugged. "Megan did most of the work."

Megan flinched and elbowed Ares in the ribs. He grunted and glared at the back of her head.

Aiko didn't seem too bothered by Ares's careless words, ones that might have reminded her of the mess she had been in, so Esher let his brother live another day.

"Marek, you called this meeting." Keras paced a few strides towards the other couch and then stopped himself, and Esher frowned as he caught the way his green eyes darkened, black swirling around their edges before he got the better of himself.

Marek had done something to anger Keras. What?

Esher looked at his other brothers, but no one seemed to know what had put a bee in Keras's bonnet.

And then Marek huffed, raked fingers through his short wavy brown hair, and spoke.

"I received a message from Olympus."

And Keras's mood made sense.

Enyo had visited Marek.

Keras paced again, his strides clipped, his eyes dark as he twisted the silver band on his right thumb around it with his fingers.

"Her brother can feel something coming. Something big. I asked for more information." When Marek said that, Keras's gaze whipped to him, and for a moment, Esher thought he would speak.

He went back to pacing, his emotions disappearing one by one, until his handsome face was a blank mask. "It's hardly information. We all know whatever is coming is building to a crescendo. It doesn't take an informant from Olympus to tell us that. We can see it in the otherworld."

Esher couldn't blame his brother for being angry with Enyo, or Marek. It was low of her to speak with Marek and not Keras. Heartless. She must have known Keras would be aware that she had visited Marek the moment he came into contact with his brother again.

Marek sat forwards. "I told her to get more information. She said she would do her best. I told her to speak with you—"

Keras turned on him with a snarl, flashing fangs, a shadow flitting across his face that had all the females in the room gasping, and then he disappeared.

"Fucking idiot," Valen muttered, fielded the glare Marek shot him and shot one right back. "Don't ever fucking tell him you tried to *force* her to speak with him. What kind of dumb shit move is that?"

Marek looked at his other brothers when everyone nodded in agreement.

"It's a bit of a dick move," Daimon said, rolling his shoulders when Marek frowned at him. "How would you feel if I told you I just tried to force someone to speak with you, someone you cared about? That she had to be *forced* to speak with you, and even then she didn't want to do it."

Ares shook his head. "He's going to be pissed for a while."

Cal flashed two thumbs up. "Great job. Now I get to deal with him. You guys really need to think about the consequences before you open your mouths. You don't have to live with him."

"Think we should continue without him?" Esher wasn't sure, because Keras had never flipped like that and left a meeting before.

Something was up with his brother, something more than just Enyo's visit to Marek upsetting him.

"Is this because I went home?" He looked at each of his brother's in turn, relieved when everyone shook their head.

"Nah." Ares pulled Megan closer to him. "He's been off for a few days and now I know why. He can sense her when she's in this world, you know?"

Marek's earthy eyes widened. "I didn't. Damn her. I told her to go away. I don't know why she always has to bother me."

Esher felt for him. He had done nothing to deserve Keras's wrath, but he was going to be feeling it for a while.

"Anything turn up in the research about the valkyrie?" Ares rubbed his palms over Megan's thighs and she clucked her tongue at him and slapped them to stop him from teasing her.

"Valkyrie?" Esher looked to him.

"I got hit by one in New York. Wraith showed up and said she was meant to be somewhere else. I figured he meant Tokyo, that she was the one after you, and then we figured out Aiko was being targeted that night at the club, not us, and I came here with Megan to protect her." Ares's brown eyes flickered with gold and red flakes as his mood darkened. "I'm sorry I wasn't quick enough."

He shook his head in time with Aiko.

"The one who took me… looked like Esher. Smelled like Esher. Felt like you." She looked at him, nerves in her eyes, coloured with regret. "I should have known, but I was worried you had come to see me and I went with you… with the daemon… so I could convince you to go home."

He smoothed his palm across her cheek and shook his head again, holding her gaze. "It wasn't your fault. I shouldn't have sent you home. I should have realised they would go after you and asked you to go with Daimon."

But the thought of her being around another of his brothers, alone with them, had tormented him so much he had refused to go through with it.

"When I realised it wasn't you, I tried reading them. They tried to make me contact you, and I refused when they told me they wanted… they wanted to use me as a collar to control you." She squeezed his hand so tight it actually hurt and tears lined her black lashes.

It would work too. He would do anything for her. Anything. All someone had to do was get their hands on her, and he would do whatever they wanted. But they didn't have her. He did, and he would protect her.

"They tried to make me and the phone repelled them." Her voice hitched. "And then it all happened so fast."

He pressed his palm to her face, drew her to him and rubbed her cheek with his, his heart aching as her pain went through him. "That's enough. You don't have to say anymore."

She nodded, and then shook her head, sniffed back her tears and drew back from him.

"The daemon, I read her thoughts." Her eyes searched his, and he stared into them, reeling from what she had said. "They were hazy… but she was afraid. She feared someone. Another woman. She believed the woman would kill her if she failed, because you were vital. A key."

To the gates? He exchanged a look with his brothers. As far as they knew, the daemons still believed the amulets he and his brothers wore when opening the gates were the keys to them, and what they needed to get their hands on.

But what if they knew the keys were in fact he and his brothers?

If his enemy caught Aiko, he would open the gate for them, and so much more. He would destroy the gatekeeper guarding the other side of it so they could enter the Underworld.

One look at Ares and Valen, and he knew his brothers felt the same—they would do whatever it took to protect their females.

So why were they targeting him in particular?

It had to be more than his ability to open the gate.

He looked at Aiko, and the reason hit him.

They knew all about him, enough for the shapeshifter to mimic him, which meant they knew his history, and how deeply he hated Hades for forcing him to live in this world filled with the humans he despised so much.

They wanted to play on that hatred, to bring it to the fore to unleash his other side, one they could control with promises of retribution, a side of himself that wanted to watch this world burn and rule the hellish remains of it.

Their plans had hit a bump when he had met Aiko.

Now, rather than using his other side to control him, they were going to try to use her.

With his power over one of the two dominant elements in the world, and his loathing of this realm, and anger towards his father, he was the perfect candidate for joining their ranks. He could let them in the gate, could destroy the damned thing with little more than a thought, and then this world with his next one.

He felt Aiko's steady gaze on him, her thumb stroking the length of his, and focused on her, using her presence beside him, that love he could feel in her, and her worry, to calm him.

He wouldn't be used as a pawn against his brothers in this war.

He wouldn't destroy his home.

He would destroy his enemy.

He would hunt down the one who had tried to take Aiko from him, the one who had hurt her, and he would butcher them.

Aiko lifted her hand and rested it against his cheek, drew his head around to face hers, and her eyes met his.

He fell into their dark chocolate depths, felt calm sweep over him again when he saw in them how much she needed him, how badly shaken she still was by everything that happened. It was a struggle, but he managed to tamp down the urge to hunt, to paint his face in the blood of the bitch who had killed her.

When he was level again, the hunger to hunt back to a faint gnawing in his heart, he nodded.

She turned back to the others. "The woman didn't want to kill me. She tried to stop me from falling."

That did nothing to improve his mood.

"She did though." His words were little more than a dark snarl. "Even if she didn't want to do it, it happened."

And gods, if she had remained in the grip of that daemon, she would have had a worse existence, would have suffered more. He knew that. He had lived it before. He had watched someone he cared about tortured and maimed, and eventually killed by wretches in some sick desire to torment him and make him suffer.

He didn't want to think about what the daemon would have done to Aiko if she hadn't fallen and changed their plans. He hated thinking about her dying, saw it too many times each day, knew it would haunt him for decades to come, but she was back now, and stronger because of it.

Safer because of it.

Her death tormented them both, but gods, maybe it was better than the pain she would have gone through if she had lived, pain that would have been both physical and emotional, a torture designed to keep him on a firm leash, desperate to do whatever they wanted in order to save her.

"We'll get her," Ares said, his voice as dark as Esher's had been, a promise in his fiery eyes as he looked at Esher. "She will pay. We'll make sure of that. Her, the wraith, and that fucking valkyrie."

Esher had forgotten about the valkyrie.

Dealing with the shapeshifter would prove tricky enough. Adding a valkyrie into the mix would make the coming fight dangerous for everyone involved. They were powerful, protected by charms stronger than the ones he and his brothers could make.

"But we just have to rip those cuffs of her and you can take her down, right?" Megan twisted at the waist to see Ares.

"Vambraces," he corrected, and nodded, and relief speared Esher's soul as he realised they already knew what to target on the valkyrie in order to weaken her.

"What about the other woman?" Eva said, and Ares shifted his gaze to her. She glanced at Esher, and then Marek. "Benares... the wraith said to him that he never understood why she favoured him so much."

"It might be the Valkyrie he was talking about," Marek offered.

Ares shook his head. "She didn't strike me as the boss. The wraith treated her in a way that made it clear he was senior to her, pulled her kicking and screaming through that portal of his."

"And we're thinking he's junior to the female he mentioned?" Cal leaned forwards to rest his elbows on his black-combats-clad knees. "So there's another female?"

Esher nodded at the same time as Ares, and felt just as happy about that judging by his brother's grim expression.

"One who wants to get her hands on the Underworld." Valen frowned at his knees, and then lifted troubled blue eyes to land on Ares. "When Benares died, he said she had promised they would rule this world... him and his sister, Jin. Not the Underworld. This one. Benares hadn't been interested in the gates either. He had wanted dominion over the mortal world."

"I doubt a valkyrie would want to rule the Underworld, and the wraith would be more interested in feeding on souls in this one," Ares growled, his face darkening. "Which I'm guessing means they've all been promised something if this succeeds and this female, the one they keep mentioning, gets what she wants—her hands on our home."

Everyone fell silent, the air thick with tension that pressed down on Esher as he mulled over everything and kept drawing the same conclusion.

"We need to capture the shapeshifter." Six of the hardest words he had ever had to say.

He didn't want to capture her. He wanted to kill her, after she had suffered.

It was necessary though, he could see it as he looked at his brothers. The wraith had killed Amaury before Ares and Daimon had been able to convince him to say anything, and Benares had died before he had revealed anything too. If they were going to stand a chance at stopping the calamity from happening, if they were going to have a shot at winning this war, they needed intel on their enemy.

That meant reining in his anger enough that he could capture the shapeshifter.

It was going to be hard.

Even now, he wanted to kill her, wanted to see her blood on his hands and paint it on his face as he went after the wraith and the valkyrie, and whoever was the mastermind behind everything.

"Capturing her alive isn't going to be a cakewalk." Valen eyed him. "We don't know whether her power can affect us like it affected Aiko."

It was going to be dangerous. He could already feel that, was already uneasy, on the edge. If the shapeshifter knew him the way he thought she did, and he was susceptible to her illusions, she would try to screw with his head.

Her physical appearance wasn't the only thing under her control.

She could cast illusions to manipulate her surroundings.

He screwed his eyes shut, not wanting to think about the things she might use against him.

He had to do this.

"You won't be alone," Daimon said, and Esher opened his eyes and met his ice-blue ones across the room. "I'll be with you."

"Me too," Ares growled.

"Count me in." Valen grinned.

"No." Esher shook his head, and they shot him daggers. He refused to back down. He didn't want them involved, didn't want them away from their females.

It was bad enough that he was contemplating putting his own little butterfly in the firing line.

They both shouted at him, Valen shooting onto his feet and Ares struggling as Megan kept him pinned, their words blurring in his ears.

"I need you to protect your females." When he said that, they both fell silent, their struggles ceasing, and grumbled a few choice things beneath their breaths.

Valen sank onto the couch, and Ares glared at Esher, both of them making it clear they were pissed at him for benching them.

"Marek, I need you to speak with—" Esher cut himself off when Keras reappeared, face a mask of calm now, no trace of black in his emerald eyes.

They were cold again, emotionless.

Empty.

"What did I miss?" he said, as if nothing had happened, and beside him, Aiko frowned and leaned forwards.

Trying to read his brother?

He squeezed her hand, telling her silently to leave him be. He appreciated her wanting to help him understand what was playing on his brother's mind, but Keras might hurt her if he realised she was probing his thoughts, and he didn't want to fight with his brothers today.

"Keras, I know it takes a lot out of you, but I need your shadows." Esher ignored the frown his older brother levelled on him. "I need you and Marek to work together."

Keras looked as if he wanted to glare at Marek, but he nodded, keeping his eyes away from him. Esher was pushing his luck pairing them, but hopefully it would help Keras get over his anger. Besides, Esher was damned if he was going to have Keras lay his hands on Aiko, and not only because his brother seemed too unpredictable right now. Marek was the better choice for teleporting her.

If Keras touched her, Esher would want to go after them and rearrange his face so it was a little less handsome.

"I'm staying here then." Ares tossed him a look that warned him not to argue. "I'll protect the gate if I have to, or the other gates. Megan will be safe in the mansion, within the wards, and we might need her to heal us."

"Me too. We'll take care of the gates while you deal with this bitch." Valen wrapped his arm around Eva's slender shoulders. "Eva can help."

Cal raised his hand, the tips of his blond ponytail fluttering as he sat forwards, on the edge of the couch, his voice holding a hint of a snarl that spoke of his temper. "What about me?"

He thought everyone had forgotten him, when Esher was counting on him.

"You're coming with me." Esher looked from him, to Daimon. "I'll need all of our powers combined."

Ares and Valen kicked off again.

"Daimon I get, but Cal?" Valen snapped and Cal grabbed him by his hair, dragged him into a headlock and rubbed it.

"I'm as powerful as the rest of you." Calistos grinned as he pressed his knuckles harder into Valen's skull.

"He's less destructive too, and far less likely to let his power control him." That earned Esher a glare, but he didn't take it back or apologise.

Valen and Ares were the two most likely to be seduced by their power and cause damage to the area, and he intended to have this battle in a very public arena.

Valen huffed. "But it's Cal... he's the baby."

He was Valen's junior by only eighty years, and just thirty-eight years younger than Daimon, the second youngest. He wasn't a baby, and Valen knew it, was saying it to ruffle his feathers, and it worked.

"I'm always on the fucking bench. It's about time I got off." A flash of regret crossed Calistos's face, and he opened his mouth to amend what he had said, but it was too late.

Valen grinned. "You a virgin still?"

"Fuck off." Cal didn't even move, but Valen went flying across the room, his ankles clipping the low dining table as he shot towards the kitchen.

He hit an invisible wall before he smashed into the kitchen one, striking it with so much force he grunted and his arms and legs flew forwards.

He didn't drop to the floor.

He struggled in thin air as he recovered, kicking and clawing, trying to punch his way out of Calistos's hold.

It wasn't going to happen.

Valen's eyes brightened and sparks chased between his fingers.

"Don't even think about it," Esher snarled and shot to his feet. He turned to Cal. "Put him down, or you're on the bench too."

"When did you get so chatty and bossy?" Cal huffed and dropped Valen, who landed on his feet and stormed towards the couch, on the warpath. "Text me the details."

Calistos disappeared, leaving Valen growling at the spot where he had been.

"Little shit." Valen stalked around the couch, snatched Eva's wrist and growled as he pulled her into his arms. "I need angry sex."

Her eyes darkened at that and she wrapped her arms around him as they disappeared.

Keras pulled a disgusted face and teleported, and Marek followed suit.

"You'll be okay?" Daimon said and Esher nodded. "Call if you need me."

He stepped, leaving swirls of black smoke in his wake.

Esher met Ares's gaze, nodded again to let him know he really was fine, and breathed a sigh of relief as his brother disappeared with Megan and he was finally alone with Aiko.

"Sorry," he muttered, and wondered if he would ever stop feeling the need to apologise for his brothers.

She smiled softly. "What did Calistos mean?"

He sighed and leaned back into the cream couch as he slipped his arm around her and pulled her against him, savouring the feel of her as she settled her hand on his chest and tucked her knees against his thigh.

"I used to be quiet, distant in a way… before you." He brushed the backs of his knuckles across her cheek, looked deep into her eyes and marvelled at how he had changed because of her, how she had drawn out the side of himself that had been locked away for longer than he could remember.

A side he had thought he would never see again.

She nestled close to him, her fingers playing across his chest, circling the buttons of his shirt and driving him mad with need. "What do you want me to do?"

He half-smiled at that, should have known she would see through him and would be aware that she had a part in his plan.

"How are you feeling?" he whispered and brushed his lips across her brow, pressed a kiss to it and breathed her in.

He didn't want to put her in danger again, and she wouldn't be, he would make sure of that.

"Strong… in body… not as tired as I thought I might be." She sounded confused by that, and he kept his theory about what his mother had done to her soul to himself, for now.

When she was stronger, when this was over, he would tell her.

"Strong enough to help me?" He angled his head so he could see her face.

She jerked away from him, sitting bolt upright, and nodded. "I want to help."

It was strange to see that flash of hunger in her eyes. Such gentle eyes. It unsettled him, because he knew the source of it. She wanted revenge. He wanted to refuse her, but he couldn't, not when that desire stemmed not only from her own suffering, but from a need to protect him. She didn't want him to suffer, wanted to make sure the daemon couldn't hurt him, or turn him against his brothers and everyone he loved.

And gods, he loved her for it.

"We're only going to make it known you're alive. I'll walk you home, and Marek and Keras will make sure you're safe. As soon as the daemon shows, they'll take you back to the mansion."

She nodded and her brow wrinkled as her eyes searched his. "Are you going to capture her?"

He could see she didn't want him to do that, that she was afraid of being in the same building as the daemon, and it made him want to kill the bitch and forget questioning her, but he couldn't.

They needed information.

But it wasn't going to be easy.

It was going to be dangerous, and there was a chance he might not be the victor, that she might prove too powerful for him, or might do something to make him snap.

He framed Aiko's face and stared into her eyes, grounding himself to push away from his fears, clawing back his strength and pulling up his courage, using the sight of her to vanquish all of his doubts, because winning was the only option. Losing didn't even factor in when winning meant seeing Aiko again.

"I'm going to try."

CHAPTER 25

Aiko caught the fear in Esher's blue eyes, a flare of it that he tried to conceal from her. It rang through her veins, as clear as her own feelings, together with something else. Need. He needed her as fiercely as she needed him. It had been building inside her since her return, a steady welling that had come on so gradually that she hadn't noticed it until today, when he had come to her, and it had felt as if she had seen him with clear eyes at last.

And he had been beautiful.

Breathtaking.

When he had come to her at the cherry tree, all of his feelings on show for her, none of them hidden, and the light had played over him, the peace she had been feeling had grown, completed by his presence, and it had dawned on her that she loved him. Truly loved him. It was deep, unconditional, infinite. A love she knew would never die. It would only ever grow stronger. Through every trial they faced, every setback and every victory. All of it would mould that love into a stronger form.

She had never realised love could be so powerful, so consuming, and so beautiful.

Fear of what was to come flowed in her veins too, colliding with everything that had happened to rouse a need in her, a deep and desperate desire to lose herself in a moment and forget the rest of the world existed. She wanted to narrow everything down to only them, and that feeling grew stronger as she stared into his eyes, saw it reflected in them. He needed it too, ached as she did with a desire to forget, to push tomorrow aside and focus on today, on the here and now.

She wanted to crush the darkness too, to let light back in and feel alive again, to forget what lay behind her and focus on the now, on the fact they were both alive.

He didn't resist as she captured his lips, or when she crawled onto his lap, settling herself astride his thighs, the position making her remember when they had made love in the bath. He lowered his hands from her back to her bottom, exhaled hard as he drew her against him and angled his head, kissing her deeper, sending the rest of the world and her worries drifting to the back of her mind.

A thrill chased through her, a surge of desire stirred by the way he pulled her closer still, pressed her against his hips and had that moment in the bath rushing back into her mind. The memory of him inside her, their bodies joined, had the heat of passion flaring hot in her veins, and she wrapped her arms around his neck and pushed her fingers through his hair, clutching him to her as she kissed him, tangled her tongue with his and lost herself.

He groaned and swept her up into his arms, tearing a squeak from her as he stood. She held him tighter, kept kissing him as he carried her, each step making her desire flare hotter, her blood run quicker, heart beat faster. An ache started low in her belly, flames licking outwards over her body from it, making her restless in his arms. He moaned again as she gripped the back of his head and raised herself in his arms so she could kiss him as deeply as she desired.

When he reached his room, he set her down, his mouth still fused with hers, his kiss turning wild and deliciously desperate as he skimmed his hands down her sides, up again and over her breasts.

She lifted her arms when he grabbed the hem of her navy jumper, tugged it up and broke the kiss for only as long as it took to get it over her head. He tossed it aside and groaned again as she fumbled with the buttons of his black shirt, some of them snagging in her haste to strip him, her need to have her hands on his bare flesh again.

He helped her, dealing with the last few buttons, and shirked the garment as he continued to kiss her, his breath coming faster now, rising to match the pace of hers. She moaned as she pressed her palms to his chest, frustrated as she met cotton, and slid them down, that heat blazing hotter as his muscles tensed, delighting her fingers as they traversed each powerful ridge. When she reached the hem, she dipped beneath it, and moaned all over again at the feel of his soft warm skin stretched tight over hard muscles.

He shuddered and stilled, breathing ragged against her lips as she explored him, charted every muscle and each scar, feeling them on his skin.

"Aiko," he groaned, the sound rough and low, strained as he trembled.

It was too much for him. She knew that, because it was too much for her too, had that need rising to startling heights where she felt as if she was losing control, would die all over again if she didn't kiss and lick every inch of his bare flesh and satisfy the need rolling through her.

She pushed his dark grey t-shirt up, exposing his stomach to her eyes, and trembled at the sight of him as he pulled it off, the action of raising his arms above his head making his muscles even more pronounced.

She leaned towards him and kissed the scar on his right side, and he froze with his arms in the air, tangled in his t-shirt, his breath rushing from him. She gently kissed across his stomach to the other side, brushed her fingers down the scar above his hip that was paler now, finally healing. She dipped her head and kissed it, willing it to no longer bother him, aware that it was a source of pain and conflict for him, that it had something to do with their enemy.

One had hurt him, and damn, she wanted to make them pay for that, a fierce need to protect him as he protected her rushing through her, setting fire to her temper.

He tipped his head back and moaned, shuddered as she licked the scar and travelled lower, towards his navel. She kissed around it and followed the fine trail of dark hair downwards to the waist of his black jeans.

For a moment, she feared he would stop her, would treat her as if she was too delicate for this, still weakened by what had happened to her when she was strong now, wanted this moment with him with all of her heart.

He remained immobile, hands trapped in his t-shirt, breath stilled in his lungs. Waiting.

She undid his fly, carefully slipped her hands around his hips, under his trunks and jeans, and eased them down, her eyes glued to him, drinking her fill as she revealed him and not wanting to miss a thing.

She moved to kneel before him as she pushed his jeans down his legs, as he stepped from them and finally discarded his t-shirt, and when he was naked, her eyes lifted, taking in every honed inch of him, some deep part of her purring in approval at the sight of him.

He moaned again when she leaned towards him, his breath hitching as his bright blue eyes followed her. He tensed, his entire body going rigid as she stroked her tongue over the head of his shaft, and his low groan went through her, had her stroking him again, hungry to hear that sound she had pulled from him again, wanting the thrill that had come with it.

She circled his cock with her right hand and wrapped her lips around the blunt crown, drank every groan that left his lips, each moan that stirred the heat inside her and had her growing restless.

When she moved her hand on him, his shot down to grip her wrist, and she looked up at him.

His eyes were dark as he shook his head, his pupils gobbling up the blue, revealing the depth of his desire to her.

He was still a moment, and then he pulled her up to him and kissed her hard, pressing his rigid length against her belly as he gathered her into his arms. She clutched his shoulders, swept up in the kiss, losing herself in it as she clung to him, her passion slipping beyond her control.

She needed him.

Now.

The urge was desperate, hit her so hard that she couldn't hold it back, clawed at his shoulders and kissed him harder, matching his fervour and groaning when it didn't satisfy the need rolling through her, one that only grew more frantic as he dropped his hand and cupped her through her jeans.

She rocked into his touch, moaning into his mouth, swept up in the moment and needing more, wanting more.

"Esher," she whispered, shocked by the sound of her own voice, so raspy and needy.

He growled and tackled her jeans, his movements jerky and rough, as if her desperation had flowed into him and was affecting him now, had him on the verge of losing control, frantic with a need to take things further, faster.

She could barely breathe as he pulled her dark pink camisole off, tossing it aside, and swooped on her breasts. He tugged her left nipple into his mouth and she gripped his shoulders again, his head, couldn't decide where to hold him as she rose on her toes and melted under the onslaught, her entire body singing and coming alive.

Giving her everything she needed.

He pushed her jeans down, growled again as he struggled to get them off her feet. She kicked at them, heart thundering, that desperate need mounting again as cool air washed over her body, each brush of it a blast of sensation that made her finally feel alive again.

It overloaded her, had her crying out as Esher stroked his hands over her sides, her breasts, and lower, delving one between her thighs. She tiptoed, threw her head back and moaned, holding nothing back as bliss swept through her, each caress of his fingers between her folds and his tongue over her breasts sending her out of her mind.

This was what she had been craving, needing. This bliss. This heaven.

Nothing else existed here.

There was only her and her beautiful Esher.

Lost in each other.

In their love.

He dropped to his knees, and she cried out as he pressed his mouth between her thighs. The first stroke of his tongue had her tensing, and the second had her grabbing his head, the onslaught of feeling almost too much to bear. She rocked against his face, shame forgotten as she spiralled higher, flew on wings he had made for her, each stroke of his tongue over her flesh sending a thousand volts rushing through her, cranking that feeling in her belly even tighter.

"Esher," she moaned, bit her lip and frowned as she desperately rode his tongue, the hard press of his fingers against her thighs sheer ecstasy.

He lifted her left knee, spreading her thighs, and she cried out again, not caring if anyone heard her as he licked her, flicking his tongue over her pert bead, sending electricity arcing along her every nerve.

Her entire body jerked as release slammed into her, crashed through her and had her breath lodging in her throat as she quivered, tingles and heat sweeping through her, the suddenness of her release stealing her voice as her mouth opened on a silent cry.

Esher lapped at her and moaned as he slowed his assault. Her legs trembled, her heart starting to race again as the haze of her climax began to fade and a new one built inside her, each gentle stroke of his tongue teasing her back towards the precipice.

She needed more from him this time.

He seemed to sense it, rose to his feet and kissed her, swept her into his arms and carried her the short distance to his bed.

She kissed him as he lay her down on it, moaned as he covered her with his body, and sighed as he eased into her, so slowly that she could feel every hard inch of him.

He pulled back, gazing down at her and stroking her hair and her face as he joined them, his blue eyes brighter than she had ever seen him, filled with love that touched her.

She savoured it just as he did, focused on their bodies fusing as one, the bliss of it even more powerful than it had been the first time they had made love.

His black hair hung forwards, brushing her forehead as he looked down at her, body still inside hers, all that love shining in his eyes but tainted with another emotion.

Fear.

Aiko framed his face with her palms, holding his gaze, trying to show him that he didn't need to be afraid. She was stronger now, wiser, and she wouldn't let his enemy hurt her again, and she believed in him, knew he would protect her and keep her safe. Nothing was going to happen to her.

"I love you." She brushed her thumbs across his cheeks.

His eyes darkened.

He swooped on her lips, kissed her so fiercely that she couldn't breathe as his pain flowed into her, swept through her and dredged up her own. She pushed back against it, refusing to let it overcome her and ruin this moment, and softened the kiss, coaxing Esher back from the brink, leading him. His kiss slowed until he was gentle again, each sweep of his lips across hers making her feel lighter inside, until she was floating in his arms.

She moaned as he moved, reminding her that he was inside her, joined with her, and his answering groan came out strained. The fear that coloured his emotions gradually drifted away with each long, slow thrust of his cock into her, each kiss she pressed to his lips.

When he pulled back again, she locked gazes with him, fell into his blue eyes and into the moment, feeling him do the same. He stared down at her, his emotions playing across his eyes as he rocked into her, slow and measured curls of his hips that had the darkness inside her receding, the light growing brighter again.

She held on to him, as fiercely as he clung to her, his fingers pressing hard into her shoulder as he wrapped his arm around her, tucking it beneath her. He lowered his other hand to her side, clutching it as he drove into her, and she breathed in time with him, each one leaving her as a soft moan as pleasure built inside her.

He groaned and lowered his head, pressed his brow to hers as he slid into her. "I love you."

He growled and gathered her closer, held her so tight it almost hurt, but all she felt was bliss as he clung to her, his love flowing through her, mingling with her own. She wrapped her arms around him.

Breathed against his lips.

"I love you too, Esher."

He moaned, captured her mouth and thrust harder, faster, tearing a sigh from her lips. The pressure built again, each plunge of his hips, each slide of his length into her cranking her tighter. His chest brushed hers, teasing her nipples, and his tongue caressed hers, his kiss deepening as he held her closer, his hand sliding lower to capture her hip.

She couldn't hold back the moan as he took her higher again, each brush of his body against hers sweet agony, each deep thrust of his cock sending waves of tingles over her belly.

Light filled her.

Warmth flowed through her.

Every breath, every movement, was bliss, pleasure like she had never experienced before, filling her with light and life, with emotion that felt as if it would soon become too much for her, and she would drown in it.

She cried into his mouth as she broke apart, a cascade of hot tingles racing through her, sweeping up and down her as she jerked against him, every quiver and throb of her body around his cock sending a fresh wave rolling through her.

Esher drove deeper, harder, faster, his breathing ragged as he pressed his forehead to hers and held her tighter.

He grunted and jerked to a hard halt inside her, pressed deep in her as his cock throbbed wildly, kicking and pulsing, his warmth flooding her, making new delicious waves of bliss sweep through her with each one.

She wrapped her arms around him as he sank against her, holding him close.

He tilted his head, captured her lips and kissed her softly.

She kissed him back, forming a vow in her head and sealing the promise with each brush of her lips across his.

She would never let him go.

He would never be alone again.

She would always be there for him.

Forever.

CHAPTER 26

Aiko tugged at the fluffy black jumper, the softness of the material comforting her as she fought to breathe normally. Beside her, Esher glanced down at her and squeezed her other hand, a silent reassurance that everything was going to be fine as they walked through Yoyogi Park.

She smiled up at him, battling another bout of nerves as the sky grew darker, night rolling in.

"You look pretty," he said, outwardly calm when she could feel he was nervous too, didn't like exposing her like this and placing her in danger.

Aiko looked down at herself, at the clothes he had bought for her today. The over-knee black socks, faded denim skirt, and fuzzy jumper were definitely more her style than the clothes she had borrowed from Megan, and when she had put them on, she had felt more like her old self.

But she had the feeling that she wasn't.

She felt stronger.

Reading Esher and his brothers was easier than ever now. She only had to think about tapping into their thoughts to be able to read them.

It was how she knew Esher believed his mother had done something to her soul.

Something he wanted to hide from her.

It had been born of a desire to protect her when she had been feeling unsteady, overcoming what had happened to her, so she could forgive him for keeping it from her.

But she could feel that she was different now. It was as if power flowed through her veins, filling her up, making her stronger than a normal human. Power she knew stemmed from Esher's world.

In her dreams, she saw flickers of a dark world, and then green and golden light that felt warm, like life itself, chasing back the coldness. There was a gentle touch, and soft words in a language she didn't know, but one she somehow understood.

After that, the cold came, sweeping in, and then she felt Esher's pain, his fury, and his darkness, but that darkness receded as a light slowly filled him.

And then she woke in his room, with him watching over her, fatigue and relief written in every line of his handsome face.

They were memories, and they grew clearer each time the dream came.

Aiko turned her head and studied his noble profile, tracing every line of it, memorising it and the way he made her feel—safe, secure, warmed from head to toe.

Happy.

He looked down at her, his steps slowed as their eyes met and he came to face her. She welcomed his kiss when he bent his head and pressed his lips to hers, melted into him when he wrapped his arms around her and held her, tucked her close to him so she could feel his heart pounding.

It betrayed his nerves, spoke of them to her and had her circling his neck with her arms, holding him in return to soothe him, to reassure him that she was fine and she wasn't afraid, because she knew he would keep his promise and he would protect her.

If it helped him defeat his enemy, and protect the world, she was happy to play bait for the daemon. Their public walk would show the daemon she was alive and would make her believe she had a second chance to use her as a collar for Esher. The daemon would make a move to secure her.

And she would fall right into their trap.

When he drew back, his hands falling to her waist, she smiled for him, showing him that she was going to be just fine. This was a hurdle they needed to overcome, something they had to do, so they could be together, and she wanted it over with now, so it no longer hung over their heads.

She wanted the daemon to pay for what she had done to her, and to Esher.

He pressed his forehead to hers, rubbed noses with her, and then started walking again, leading her along the broad path that flowed beneath the tall trees, heading towards the shrine. He had wanted their walk to be somewhere more public, somewhere he would have the water in the city pipes on hand, but she had convinced him to choose the park instead, not wanting innocents to be caught in the firing line, reminding him that the park had lakes he could draw on with his power.

She scanned the trees and the fields beyond them, just as she knew he was doing. Waiting. His hand was tense in hers now, clutching it tightly, and she could feel his nerves, the anxiousness eating away at him. It ate at her too.

She needed to speak to fill the dreadful silence and calm herself.

"Thank you for the clothes, and for getting my phone."

He glanced down at her, his eyes darkening as he raked them over her, the flare of desire in them pushing her fears to the back of her mind. "They suit you... but I didn't get your phone. You have to thank Daimon for that."

She hadn't realised that he had been the one to retrieve it for her. "I'll thank him later."

When this was over.

Esher tensed up again, and she smoothed her thumb along his, trying to calm him and using the connection between them to soothe herself too.

"I should thank him too." Esher looked down at her again out of the corner of his eye before he went back to scanning the park. "He tried calling you when they realised you were in danger."

She had suspected the first attempt to reach her had been his brother, but now she knew for certain she would be thanking him for it. "You tried to call too... I was afraid the daemon might be able to answer it, but the phone repelled her when she tried to take it from me."

He slowed again, grinding to a halt beside her, and she turned and looked back at him. His eyes were dark in the low light, but they glowed blue around his irises, giving away the feelings she could detect in him—the anger, the fury, the pain.

"She'll pay for what she did to you, Aiko. I swear it," he growled.

His power surged and she closed the gap between them and cupped his cheeks in her palms, hoping to help him control it as his face twisted, a scowl knitting his obsidian eyebrows as he stared down into her eyes, darkness shining in his, black needs that were easy to feel in him.

Someone had hurt her, had taken her from him, and provoked the side of himself that he feared, the one the enemy wanted to harness.

"Esher," she whispered, keeping her voice low and soft, coaxing him back to her. "I'm fine now. Remember that. I'm safe. Don't let her get to you. Remember that I'm safe."

She lowered her right hand to his chest, flattening it over the spot above his heart. It beat hard against her palm. Strong. The feel of it reassured her. He was powerful. He could handle the daemon. She was sure of it. He would come back to her.

His eyes dropped to her lips.

She tiptoed and seized his, couldn't stop herself as a need rushed through her, commanded her to kiss him and not let him go, to stay by his side where he needed her even when she knew he needed her away from him more, needed to know she was safe and protected, and the daemons couldn't reach her.

Couldn't hurt her again.

He tensed, going rigid beneath her hands.

A chill swept down her spine.

Familiar contempt laced with darkness and a hunger that shook her blasted through her, directed right at her, and every instinct she possessed screamed she was in danger.

She opened her mouth to scream at Esher to run, fear of him being hurt or worse forcing the word up her throat, making her desperate to tell him to forget fighting the daemon, to plead him not to go through with it because she was terrified of what might happen to him.

Before she could squeeze the word past her tight throat, masculine heat wrapped around her, his scent of earth evoking images of the green and the gold she had seen, the gentle voice and the soothing warmth, and darkness swallowed her.

It evaporated, revealing the main living room of the mansion, and Ares and Valen as they shot to their feet, concern washing across both of their faces.

Marek released her and she turned on him.

"Take me back. He needs me." She fisted his charcoal linen shirt, and for a moment, his rich brown eyes, flecked with gold and green, softened and she felt sure he might listen.

But then Keras appeared beside him, ribbons of shadows still clinging to him, fluttering around the arms of his black formal shirt and trousers, and over the soft spikes of his black hair.

His green eyes hardened. "We can't do that. Esher needs to know you're safe."

She knew that, but she still needed to go to him, even when she was sure she would only be a hindrance, and not a help. Her presence would push at him, provoking his darker side, and his need to protect her would split his focus between her and his enemy, placing him in danger.

Ares moved around the couch, a wall of muscle dressed in tight black clothing that matched Valen's, although his build was twice that of his purple-haired brother.

His dark brown eyes lit with sparks of gold as he looked at her. "Listen to Keras, Aiko. Esher needs to know you're here, and you're protected."

She forced herself to nod, and drew down a deep breath, holding it to calm herself so she kept her head. Losing it wouldn't help Esher. They were right about that. He needed to know that she was at the mansion, safe within the wards, with his brothers watching over her.

"How about we make some tea?" Megan said as she left Eva's side, her pretty face and brown eyes warmed by her sympathetic smile, and her rich orange t-shirt and blue jeans a contrast to Ares's black clothing as she passed him.

His eyes tracked her, a flare of fire heating them as he watched her walking towards Aiko.

Esher looked at her like that, as if she was his whole world, and that was the reason she was going to remain where she was, where he needed her to be, because she didn't want to see pain in his beautiful blue eyes again. She wanted them to always be warm and bright, filled with sunshine.

She glanced at the rain-swept courtyard and the garden beyond it as she turned with Megan, and damn, she needed to be out there, needed to run to Esher and help him. The thought that he was fighting now, in danger, pulled at her, had her aching to go to him even when she knew that she wasn't strong enough to do such a thing, that his brothers were right and it was best she remained here, waiting with them.

She wanted to tell them to go to him, to help him, because she couldn't. They could though. They were powerful. Strong. They could help him.

Keras stepped into her path and took hold of her shoulders, darkness reigning in his eyes, turning them almost black, leaving only a sliver of green around his pupils.

His voice was a low growl, one that said he knew her thoughts, offered comfort and reassurance, and buoyed her heart.

"I swear to you, I will not let anything happen to Esher."

She nodded and managed a smile to thank him, even as her heart began to grow heavy again, her thoughts weighing it down.

Fear that she would never see Esher again.

CHAPTER 27

Esher wanted to growl the moment Marek appeared and snatched Aiko from his grasp. He wanted to step and follow her home, to attack his brother for daring to lay a hand on her even when it had been the plan all along. Instead, he breathed through the twin needs and focused on the park ahead of him as he strode out of the cover of the trees and onto the dark swath of grass.

Into the open.

He raised his gaze to the moon, using its beauty to calm himself. It was barely a sliver now, would be a new moon soon.

A good time to do battle.

A new moon affected the tides as strongly as a full moon, and in turn affected him, drawing his power to the surface, making it well up inside him.

He reached out with his senses, aware that somewhere in the park, the daemon lurked, watching him, waiting for her moment to attack him now that Aiko was gone, her trump card stolen from her. Darkness welled in time with his power, coaxed him into hunting the bitch down and butchering her for what she had done to Aiko. The female would pay. He would see to that.

After she had talked.

He would break her, would squeeze every drop of information from her, and then he was going to kill her.

He *was* going to kill her.

Keras wouldn't care once she had served her purpose, was no longer useful to them. His brother would let him do as he pleased with her, despised daemons as much as the rest of them. Gods, he would probably want to lend a hand.

But this kill belonged to Esher.

He wouldn't share it with anyone.

Not even Daimon and Calistos where they waited in the wings, his white-haired brother hiding in a tree close to the torii gate across the field to Esher's right, and their blond tornado casually reclining against a lamp post to his left, near the entrance of the park.

Doing the complete opposite of what he was meant to be doing.

He glared at his brother, even though Cal wouldn't see it, and twitched his left hand.

Cal tipped his head back as the weather changed, more heavy mist than rain at first, but becoming a steady downpour as Esher focused on his power and the environment, allowing his anger and the burning need for violence to slip its leash enough to affect it.

His youngest brother kicked away from the lamp-post and disappeared as the wind picked up, gusting hard across the field and battering Esher. It whipped through the trees, shaking the branches, filling the still night air with ominous creaks and the steady swish of leaves brushing each other.

Daimon moved, Esher sensed it as he dropped from his perch and teleported, shifting into position.

Any moment now.

The swirling sensation in his gut grew stronger, warning that it was almost time, and the coppery scent of daemon hit him as the wind battered him.

It blasted through the trees opposite him, so fierce that branches flew into the field, together with something else.

The daemon.

Esher grinned and spread his feet shoulder-width apart, readying himself as he called on his power and darkness spread through his veins, whispering delicious words about revenge.

He launched his hand forwards, drawing on the lake of the teahouse, and a wall of water swept behind her, cutting off her escape. It turned to ice as Daimon joined him, becoming a glittering white barrier three storeys high that curved into a semicircle thanks to Cal's wind.

Now he just had to form the other side of her cage.

He caught a glimpse of a female with long inky violet hair and silver eyes that glowed as brightly as the moon, a black dress hugging her figure, and then she was gone.

Together with the park.

He turned left and right, his pulse rocketing as a different scene constructed itself around him, bright sunshine and endless green rolling hills replacing the darkness and the trees. A worn mud road snaked through the hills, leading his eye towards a distant village of stone buildings.

His stomach sank, fear curling through his veins and his throat closing as he stared at that familiar village.

His heart laboured, kicking hard against his chest, and his mind screamed at him to run, to flee.

Now.

They were coming.

Chants filled the air, had him spinning on his heel, desperately scouring the landscape for their source. When he turned back towards the village, a sea of humans blocked his path, barely a metre from him, torches and farm tools clutched in their hands, their dirty faces filled with fury as they shouted at him, jeered and waved their weapons.

Someone screamed.

His head snapped to his right, desperation flooding him as he tried to stop them from grabbing his companion. He lunged for the ones who held him, fear of what was going to happen spreading like poison through his veins, weakening him.

When he was already weak, without his power. Stripped of it. Left vulnerable.

He stilled, eyes widening in horror as the humans seized him and he saw his companion being dragged kicking and screaming towards the village.

Aiko.

Her fear rushed through him, roused the darker part of himself, and he snarled as he pushed at the people trying to contain him, lashed out and struck one of them hard enough to send them down. The male remained on the ground, blood pouring from his face.

Blood.

Esher gritted his teeth, mustered all of his strength, focused on the bastards who were hurting Aiko as they pulled her by her arms, some of them moving to grab her legs. She kicked at them, hit one but it wasn't enough to stop them.

He was.

He would stop them.

He growled and focused harder, willed their blood to do his bidding.

But it refused.

They remained unaffected as they carried her, hollering vile things about her, calling her a witch.

Burn the witch.

Cold swept through him, followed by fire that blazed so hot he couldn't contain it. He snarled and managed to get his arm free, punched someone as they tried to hold him back and kicked at another, desperation driving him. He needed to reach Aiko.

He needed to save her.

He couldn't fail her again.

Something slammed into him, and he frowned as the world around him wobbled, the scenery rippling like a flag in the wind, and he saw a flicker of a different place, a darker place.

The invisible force struck him again, knocking him right out of the world he had been in, landing him in a park.

"No!" He pushed against the weight on him, growling through his fangs as he tried to get it off him. "Aiko needs me."

He had to get back to her.

"It's a fucking lie." Cal seized his shoulders and rattled him, slamming him into the grass, breaking the scenery that had started to build around him again.

Esher stared up at his brother.

Cal breathed hard, sweat beading on his brow, running down his jaw.

No, it wasn't sweat rolling down to his chin.

It was tears.

The shapeshifter could cast illusions, just as they had feared, and she had shown Cal something terrible.

"Cal?" He grabbed his brother's arms. "Are you alright?"

Cal stared blankly at him. "Of course I am. Why wouldn't I be?"

"What did she show you?" He feared asking that, but he needed to know.

"Nothing." Cal pushed off him, frowned and stared at the grass. "Something. I... I was over there, where I was meant to be... and then I was... where?"

His brother's blue eyes turned stormy grey.

"I don't remember." Cal shoved away from him, gripped the sides of his head in trembling hands, burrowing his fingers into his blond hair and tugging strands loose from his ponytail, and gritted his teeth. "I don't fucking remember."

He never did.

Thank the gods for that.

For a moment, Esher had feared he would be able to remember the illusion he had seen, a messed up version of his past if Esher's had been anything to go by, and it was better Cal didn't remember the details of what had happened back then.

Esher wished he couldn't remember the things that had happened to him.

"Shitting, fuck, fuckety fuck." Daimon was sounding particularly eloquent as he sprinted over to them. "I saw you both go down. What the fuck happened?"

"I don't know." Cal stared at him, eyes wide, irises swirling like a tempest.

Daimon looked as if he wanted to embrace him, to hold him until the storm passed and he was calm again, and then shifted his ice-blue eyes to Esher.

"I saw my past, but Aiko was there... they took her." Gods, Esher didn't even want to think about what he had seen.

It was too much.

It roused the darkness in him, had brought him dangerously close to giving into it. If he had seen the rest of the illusion, he would have surrendered to it.

"We need to find a way to combat..." Daimon trailed off as the ground heaved and split open, and a huge black Grecian temple rose from it, earth and grass tumbling down the pitched roof as it pushed up. He leaned sideways towards Esher but didn't take his eyes off the familiar building. "You see that?"

Esher nodded.

Their home.

Cal stopped muttering to himself and stared at it, his mouth hanging open. "I don't like this."

Hades stepped out from between the towering fluted columns of the temple, dressed in his black armour, his eyes bright crimson and his bident gripped in his left hand. Persephone moved out from behind him, her red hair tumbling down around her pale shoulders.

"Wrong," Cal said exactly what he was thinking.

Rather than the black dress of mourning that their mother had been wearing since losing Calindria, she wore a bright green dress, the sheer layers cinched with gold at her waist.

"I'm getting sick of these." Daimon curled his gloved right hand into a fist and lifted it, and spears of ice shot up from the ground, impaling Persephone.

Her blood rolled down the white ice, stark against it.

Hades leaped out of the path of them all, dodging them with ease, closing in on Esher and his brothers.

Esher swept his hand across from right to left, hurling a wall of water that Hades ran straight into, one that transformed into clear ice a split-second later, trapping the male.

"You think one of them was her?" Daimon cautiously peered at the trapped Hades and the dead Persephone.

It was possible the daemon participated in her illusions, used them to mount an attack after weakening her enemies with their worst fears.

"Aiko mentioned she wasn't strong. It stands to reason that she would employ whatever tricks she had at her disposal to win a fight." Esher slowly slid his gaze towards his right and then his left as two more temples rose from the grass, and two more sets of his parents strode out of them.

Followed by another two, and then another two, until there were ten Hades staring him down, with ten Persephones beside him.

"Any guess which one might be her?" Cal turned his back to Esher as the illusions spread out, forming a ring around them.

Esher assessed them all, searching for any differences, and shook his head when he found none. "We just have to kill them all."

"It feels wrong killing our parents." Said the male who had driven an ice spear through their mother's heart without hesitation.

Esher was going to pick Daimon up on that later. Esher had hesitated, the false Persephone so lifelike that his heart had almost been fooled into believing it was her. Daimon had stuck a spear through her.

Although, he supposed the presence of Hades was a dead giveaway that these weren't their real parents. Hades was trapped in the Underworld, bound there and unable to leave.

Cal and Daimon broke away from him, each attacking a section of the group surrounding him. Daimon threw small spears of ice, each one only a metre long, and Cal directed them with his wind, making sure none of the illusions could evade them. They buried three in each one, working together as they had practiced a thousand times in the Underworld, easily taking down their foes.

Esher scanned the group again as more illusions appeared to join the others, replacing the fallen, keeping his brothers busy. There had to be a tell, a way of pinpointing which of the illusions was the shapeshifter.

"Esher!"

He turned as Aiko's voice rose above the din of the battle and frowned as he spotted her running towards him across the park, her eyes round and filled with fear. Behind her, a female with a mass of blonde waves tied at the back of her head, and a bikini made of golden swirls pursued her. Wings burst from her back as she kicked off, feathered on the top half and leathery below that, and she shot towards Aiko, closing in on her.

A valkyrie.

He reached for Aiko, the desperate need to save her rising inside him again as she threw a terrified glance over her shoulder and ran harder.

"Damn it. Cal!" Daimon's deep voice shattered the silence, and wind swept across the field, striking the valkyrie and sending her hurtling through the air, tumbling and struggling to right herself.

Daimon's gloved hand closed over Esher's wrist, ice burning his flesh through his long black coat, and pulled him back. "It's not her."

"It is." Those two words burst from his lips, filled with certainty even as his heart wavered, was no longer sure whether it was really Aiko before him.

He couldn't risk standing by and doing nothing. If it was really her, and she was hurt again, he would never be able to live with himself.

Bright light off to his right had him squinting and looking down.

Daimon tapped the send button on his phone. It was hardly the time to message someone.

The phone vibrated almost instantly, and his brother turned the screen towards him, revealing a picture of Aiko holding a clock that showed today's date and a time that almost matched Daimon's phone.

"It isn't her." His brother pocketed his phone, darkness washing across his face as he glared at the Aiko running towards them. "She wouldn't be here. She knows better. Remember that."

Esher tried to drum it into his head, but it was hard when Daimon launched himself at Aiko. His little butterfly. She shrieked and brought her arms up to cover her face, cried out and stumbled backwards as Daimon attacked her, pulling none of his punches. Rage curled through Esher's veins, a need to attack his brother building inside him even as he focused on the image Daimon had shown him.

Aiko wasn't here.

The bitch was just trying to weaken him and find a way to attack him without him putting up a fight.

Aiko was that weakness.

The valkyrie loosed a fierce shriek as she finally righted herself and swooped towards Cal. Cal blasted air at her, forcing her to sway side to side to dodge each attack. She kept plummeting towards him, her talons at the ready as she grinned, her golden eyes glowing in the darkness.

Esher lined up his attack and let it loose, sending a spiral of water at her so fast that she didn't have a chance to see it coming. It struck hard, pummelling her right side and slamming into her wing, bending it at an awkward angle and ripping a cry from her throat as she veered off course. Cal grinned and stepped, landing on her back and shoving his boot into the back of her head, sending her hurtling towards the ground as he leaped off her and dropped at least twenty metres to land in a crouch on the grass.

The valkyrie hit it hard, tumbled and twisted, and found her feet, skidding backwards with her right hand clawing the earth to slow her to a stop. The second she stopped, she kicked off.

Esher snarled and stepped, appeared and slammed into her side, knocking her back down. He seized her throat and growled as she lashed out at him with her talons, raking them over his black coat and leaving long tears in his sleeves. Her foot caught him in his gut and he grunted as the air pushed from his lungs, and tightened his grip on her, cutting off her air supply.

Fucking Keras would want to question her too.

Aiko screamed.

Esher's head snapped towards her.

The damned valkyrie pressed her feet into his chest and kicked hard, knocking him onto his arse and freeing herself. She was gone before he had flipped onto his feet, her wings beating the air hard as she made a break for it. Cal casually stepped past Esher and a smile curled his lips as she started to slow, and then hung in the air, her blonde hair streaming behind her in tangled waves as she battled the wind, making no progress.

"You got her?" Esher moved the moment Cal nodded and started towards the valkyrie.

He broke left, running towards Daimon where he fought Aiko, telling himself on repeat that it wasn't really her.

The park shattered again.

"No!" He slammed to a halt, his pulse kicking up a notch as the village rapidly constructed itself around him.

He didn't have time for this. Daimon and Cal needed him.

A distant scream reached his ears.

Cal.

His heart thumped against his chest and he turned, tried to see the park through the illusion as it continued to build.

She was fucking with his little brother again and she was going to pay for it.

He pushed off in the direction the scream had come from.

Or would have, but he couldn't move.

Esher looked down and swallowed hard at the sight of his wrists bound in front of him, the rope wound around them up to his elbows.

No. He shook his head, squeezed his eyes shut and ground his teeth, fighting the pain that surged inside him and the fear as it pressed down on him, both of them threatening to crush him.

It wasn't real.

Another scream, only this time it was feminine.

Aiko.

His eyes shot open, head whipping up and heart stopping as he saw her.

She struggled against her bonds, wriggling her shoulders as she grimaced, tears streaking her cheeks. Her brown eyes were wide, wild as she watched the males around her as they stacked wood against the platform on which she stood. She fought harder, kicked at the thick pole against her back, and frantically shook her head.

"I'm not a witch." Her bloodshot eyes tracked a male with a torch. "Please... I'm not a witch."

It wasn't real.

Esher clenched his fingers into fists and stared down at them, focused on them and his breathing, trying to shut out her cries for help and the fear that flooded him. Her fear. Darkness welled, pushed up from his heart, whispered things that were honey in his ears, had him stilling as they swept through him, chasing out the fear and the pain.

Kill them all.

The humans didn't deserve his protection. They deserved death.

He grunted as a stone struck his temple and leaned to his left, his skull aching from the fierce blow as warmth trickled down his cheek. Another followed it, cracking off his neck, and then another bit into his brow, between his eyes, and blood flowed down his nose.

The dark voice grew louder.

Kill them all.

The humans deserved to burn. They deserved his retribution. Not his protection. They were vile. Wretched. Unworthy.

He bowed his head as stones pummelled him, each one a shard that pierced his heart, made it bleed. He was weak. Stripped of his power. Unable to fend them off. Why? Because his father wanted to protect them. His father had sent him, his son, to the world of humans without his powers, vulnerable to their wrath.

His father had banished him too, had forced him to come to this world.

To protect them.

They didn't deserve his protection.

They deserved to die.

They feared him, so they beat him, tortured him and tried to kill him.

He would give them a reason to fear him.

He growled and pulled his arms apart, easily snapping the ropes that held him, and devoured the startled gasps and fearful murmurs of the humans as they backed away from him.

He pushed onto his feet, swayed a little as he gathered himself and got his bearings.

"Esher!" Aiko screamed.

His little butterfly.

He would butcher them all for hurting her.

His eyes snapped open and he grinned, baring fangs at the pathetic mortals quaking before him, and water swirled around his feet, gathering speed as the darkness poured through his veins.

He would make this world burn.

And the Underworld would follow it.

CHAPTER 28

Aiko wouldn't want this.

It was there in the back of his mind, an irritating buzz that refused to be silent as he cut through the humans, slashing throats with his claws and hurling spears of water that hit them so fast they punched holes straight through their chests or their skulls.

Esher didn't care.

The humans were getting what they deserved, and it was glorious. Beautiful. Gods, it was beautiful. He groaned, pleasure rolling through him as he caught a male by his throat and focused on him, only a split-second of his attention but enough to have blood pouring from his eyes and nose. He tossed the dead mortal aside and sought his next target, his scarlet eyes scanning the carnage.

A female ran, wailing as she tried to escape.

He stepped, landing in front of her so she slammed into him.

A growl curled up his throat.

"You dare touch me?" He lifted his hand and her scream cut short as water blasted upwards from the ground, impaling her, spraying as blood from her skull. "Impudent wretch."

He spat on her corpse and turned in a slow circle, hungry for another kill, his chest heaving as he breathed hard.

When he saw only the dead, he stooped, ran his hands through the blood coating the earth and smeared it down the side of his face.

A hunting he would go.

He grinned.

The path before him wavered and he frowned. He turned his head, and his scowl deepened as the village became transparent at the edges of his vision, allowing him to see something else beyond it.

Another plane.

One that his brother stepped through from, his wet white hair plastered to his brow and his blue eyes showing a flicker of fatigue, and wariness.

Fear.

"Esher." Daimon slowly raised his hands. "Listen to my voice, Esher."

No. He didn't want to calm down. He was hunting.

"It isn't real, Esher." Daimon edged towards him, and Esher's eyebrows dipped lower, a sensation that he might be telling the truth going through him when Cal stepped through the wall of a building beyond him, dragging a shrieking valkyrie by her broken wing behind him.

"Anyone know what her charm is?" Cal's words slowed as he looked around and arched a blond eyebrow. "What's with the change of scenery?"

"I think the daemon is weakening, allowing us to move between the illusions." Daimon didn't take his eyes off Esher. "You need to calm down now, because you're dangerously close to doing what she wants."

He blinked and looked between his brothers. What who wanted?

He was doing what *he* wanted.

He wanted to kill all the humans.

It was time they all paid for what they had done to him.

"Aiko needs you to pull your shit together, Esher. Don't do this to her. She needs you to be strong and not let the darkness pull you under." Daimon held his hands up, revealing a device that held an image in his right one.

A female.

He stared at her.

Aiko.

His little butterfly.

"They're going to burn her." Cold fear gripped him and he pivoted on his heel, his voice dying as he stared across the village.

Aiko was gone. So was the platform where she had been bound.

"It isn't real." Daimon moved another step closer to him, grunted and stilled, and looked down.

The scent of blood swirled around Esher.

Familiar blood.

Daimon touched his side, pulled his hand away and stared at it.

Crimson coated his glove.

"Son of a bitch," he muttered, and then threw his head back and roared as he swept his arms up into the air.

A thousand shards of clear ice shot up around them, forming a wall thirty metres tall.

Esher continued to stare at the blood.

The darkness that had been fading swept back in, stronger than before, pushing at his fragile control. Daimon was hurt. His brother was in pain. Wounded.

Not by humans.

But by a filthy, fucking daemon.

He snarled and scanned the village, but only his brothers stood with him within the wall of ice that cut through several of the buildings.

It wasn't real.

The illusion wavered in places, thinning around the edges of his vision as he scanned it again, but solid wherever his eyes landed. Daimon was right, and the shapeshifter was weakening, her strength drained by using her power to create the illusions, but she also had the upper hand, had managed to stab Daimon before any of them had sensed her.

Wind whipped past him, pushing him sideways towards his brothers as it built, forming a wall within the barrier of ice, one designed to keep the daemon contained and where Esher wanted her.

They were back on track with their plan at least.

He glanced at Daimon, at the wound he clutched as he growled obscenities.

When Daimon noticed him looking, his brother turned towards him and clapped a hand down on his shoulder, the touch brief but enough to reassure him, and leave a glittering patch of frost on the black material of his coat.

Valkyrie came around, shrieking like a banshee. She didn't have a chance to move. Cal was on her in a heartbeat, hands against her shoulders, pinning her to the ground.

"What was her charm again?" He looked up at Daimon and then Esher.

"Vambraces." Esher nodded towards the cuffs protecting her forearms.

She screamed and frantically wriggled, her gold eyes flashing fire as Cal shifted his weight, using his knees to trap her shoulders as he caught hold of her arms. He tore one vambrace off her and then the other, and she sagged, fear flooding her eyes as she stared up at him.

"I really want to kill you." Cal sounded as happy about Keras's capture-and-question plan as Esher felt. His brother leaned over her and ran a hand down his face, over three red streaks that cut over his jaw and down his neck. "I'll make you pay for this later."

Her eyes widened.

"For now, it's night night time." Cal smashed his fist into her face, and she slumped, body going lax beneath him.

His brother was a cheat when it came to fighting with his fists, used his control over the air to propel his punches so he hit with the force of a tornado.

Cal pushed off her and the moment he was clear of her, Esher directed some of the rain at her, focusing it there. Daimon used it, crafting a box of clear ice at least a metre thick on all sides, leaving the valkyrie stretched out on a floor made of it.

Esher drilled a single hole in it, because Keras would be annoyed if she died from asphyxiation.

Satisfied that she wasn't going anywhere, he turned his focus back on his surroundings. The village illusion held, but it was still thinner at the edges of his vision as he glanced around, revealing the park.

His senses sparked.

He turned on a pinhead and lashed out with a whip made of water, cracking it hard in the direction of the movement.

It hit nothing in the illusion.

But something screamed.

Something female.

The coppery and vile scent of daemon blood flooded his nostrils.

The village wavered and some of the buildings crumbled, the ground transforming into the grass of the park.

His gaze zipped to the far side of their icy arena as something moved there, and he kicked off, darkness swallowing him for a heartbeat as he stepped, teleporting into her path.

He froze as he landed and Aiko stood before him, her fluffy jumper soaked from the rain, and her short faded denim skirt saturated and sticking to her legs. She pushed her wet hair out of her face and gazed up at him.

"You're alright. I was so worried." She reached for him.

He watched her hand edging towards him, told himself to move, to smack it away and step, but he couldn't convince his body to obey him.

Her brown eyes warmed, showing her love, heating him through.

He shook his head, trying to clear it, because it wasn't her. It wasn't Aiko. It was just another illusion, one meant to weaken him and lure him away from her. Aiko was at the mansion, not here in the park. She was safe.

He shot his hand out and it went straight through her.

Her laughter rang through the park, gaining a strange echo, and then another, and he slowly looked around him, his eyes widening as a hundred Aikos looked at him, laughed at him.

One of them was the shapeshifter.

He scanned as many as he could, seeking the source of the blood he could scent in the air, sure he would find the wound on the Aiko that was the daemon in disguise.

Three of the Aikos threw themselves at him, and he grunted as they hit him, knocking him backwards.

"Which is the daemon?" Cal hollered as he fought six of them off, scattering them with a blast of wind, sending them toppling into the others.

"I have an idea." Daimon stepped and appeared beside Esher, ripped one of the clones off him and pushed her aside.

Esher closed his eyes and shoved the other two, unable to bring himself to fight them when he was looking at them, seeing Aiko before him.

"Make it rain harder." Daimon closed ranks with him, and Cal joined them, fending off the false Aikos as they tried to reach him and Daimon.

Esher nodded. That he could do. It took only a brief thought and it was lashing down, the rain a thick wall around them, soaking him and his brothers to the bone.

Daimon's eyes brightened, began to glow white in the darkness.

Frost swept over his gloves and up his arms, spreading and forming ice flowers as it branched outwards and thickened.

Esher gritted his teeth as he felt the pull on his power as Daimon focused his own on it, ripping command of the raindrops from him one by one.

"You... might... want to... shield... us." Daimon bit the wounds out, breathing hard between each one as his eyes blazed white.

Not good.

Esher pushed his focus to the rain, fighting to control it at the same time as Daimon forced his will upon it, and Cal grunted beside them, wavering on his feet as his own power came under their brother's influence.

Esher had barely managed to convince the rain to avoid hitting them, forming a dome over them that spread three metres in all directions, when it hit.

A polar vortex.

The temperature dropped so suddenly, it stole Esher's breath, had his teeth chattering as frost formed on his clothes and sent Cal to his knees as he shook, gripping himself and desperately rubbing his arms.

Esher struggled for air as it thinned, the effect of the vortex created by combining Cal's wind and Daimon's ice as he chilled the rain Esher had provided making the atmosphere within the boundaries of the vortex thinner than beyond the towering thick ice walls surrounding them.

The temperature plummeted further as Daimon growled, shards of ice forming on his shoulders and rising from his hair like a crown, his outstretched hand trembling as he struggled to control the vortex he had created.

Snow blanketed the ground, creeping towards them.

"Daimon, dial it back," Cal snapped, sounding weak now.

Esher shoved Daimon hard, shattering his focus, and the wind eased, the snow halting and the air grew thicker, easier to breathe.

It remained freezing within the sphere of the ice walls though, the temperature well below zero, closing in on minus fifty Celsius.

As the stormed cleared, and the temperature slowly rose, Esher's eyes gradually widened.

Daimon's plan had worked.

The illusion was gone, and in the centre of the icy arena, on a thick blanket of snow, the daemon sat clutching her knees, her breath fogging the air.

Esher had half a mind to kill her, would be easy given the freezing temperatures too. Any water he called now would become ice in an instant, and gods, he wanted to drive a spear of it right through her black heart.

But he had promised his brothers he would capture her.

So he trudged towards her through the knee-deep snow, savoured the way she lifted her head, revealing ashen skin that was almost blue and suited her black lipstick, and how she whimpered when he closed his hand around her throat and hauled her onto her feet.

How fear lit her eyes as he squeezed his fingers tighter.

Kill her.

It was tempting, beyond tempting, and he struggled against the urge as he stared at her, at the bitch who had killed his beloved Aiko, who had hurt his brother, and threatened his world.

"Esher," Daimon's voice cut into his dark thoughts. "We need to mark her with the counter-wards and take her to the others."

He was going to kill her.

Later.

Once she had spilled her guts to his brothers.

CHAPTER 29

Keras took hold of the daemon's arm as soon as Esher appeared in the mansion courtyard with her. When his brother tried to lead her away, Esher kept hold of her, stopping him.

"What are you going to do with her?" Because he needed to know where she would be held during her interrogation, and because he wanted to know where he had to go when his brother was done with her, and he could kill her and erase her filth from his home.

"You don't want to know." Keras glanced towards one of the buildings set to one side of the property beyond the bathhouse, one Esher kept locked at all times.

One that contained his cage.

Esher growled, the vision of metal bars closing in on him tearing at him, tugging the darkness back to the surface, and pulling a startled and fearful gasp from the daemon beside him.

She began struggling, trying to break free of him, and it was only when Keras touched his other arm that he realised he had closed it around her throat and had been choking the life out of her.

Tears streaked her cheeks, her eyes wild and mercury irises swirling with panic as he released her and she sucked down air.

He shoved her away from him, into Keras, and ignored his brother's glare, not caring that he had forced the daemon against him.

"Just tell me when you're done with her." Because he didn't want to see the damned cage, not until he had to see it, was left with no choice but to place himself inside it in order to protect this world.

This world.

He waited for his usual thoughts to fill his mind, images of himself lighting the fuse and watching it all burn, giving the mortals what they deserved.

They didn't come.

He scrubbed a hand down his face as he realised the reason behind that—he wanted to protect this world now.

He *almost* wanted to protect the humans.

Almost.

The only human he wanted to protect came screaming out of the house at full speed and barrelled into him, knocking the wind from his lungs as they collided, and then again as she caught him around the nape of his neck and dragged him down for a kiss that was so soft, so full of love and relief, that it stole his breath.

He swept Aiko up into his arms. His Aiko. The real Aiko. His little butterfly.

He held her as Keras and Ares escorted the daemon away, and Daimon and Cal appeared, done with their clean-up duty in the park, leaving no evidence of the battle behind.

Including the dead valkyrie.

Daimon's cold snap had been too much for her, the air inside her icy cage dropping so low that she had been asphyxiated after all. They had vowed not to mention that to Keras and the others.

Daimon nodded as he passed him, and wearily trudged after Keras and Ares. It would be a while before Daimon regained his strength after combining their powers. The first time Daimon had attempted such a trick, he had passed out and had slept for three days straight. Cal nudged Esher in the ribs, winked at him a few times, and went into the house.

Esher scowled at his back, but his anger over his brother intruding on his moment with Aiko and insinuating they were going to be up to something soon, something wicked, melted away as Cal entered the house and his voice rose in the night, loud enough for the neighbours to hear as he regaled Valen and Marek, Megan and Eva with the tale of their battle, embellishing a few things as he went.

Gods, it was good to be home.

He tucked Aiko closer to him, absorbing the warmth of her in his arms.

Literally.

"You're freezing," Aiko murmured against his chest and wriggled, and he reluctantly eased his grip on her.

"Daimon." It was all the explanation he offered, but it drew a smile from her, one that had a hint of relief about it as she glanced at his brother's back and then up into his eyes again.

"I'm glad you're all safe." Her eyes drifted back to Keras though as he walked down the corridor that led towards the bathhouse, and they darkened.

Esher smoothed his hand across her cheek, luring her back to him, out of the mire of her thoughts that coloured her eyes, and had him wanting to go after the daemon too—for her sake.

He didn't like that look in her eyes, those dark desires he could see in them, born of her pain. They made him want to hold her, to tell her that he would never let her fight, would never let her near another daemon, didn't want her to sully herself by getting blood on her hands.

He was violent enough for both of them, would carry out the revenge she needed, retribution he wanted too.

He led her to his room and changed his clothes, swapping his combat gear for a pair of blue jeans, a black t-shirt and his favourite blue-grey shirt. He focused on buttoning it, forcing his mind away from the daemon and the things he wanted to do to her, the pain he wanted to inflict on her, and the death he wanted to deliver. When he was cleaned up, he led Aiko to the main room of the mansion and made himself sit on the couch with her, holding her as he listened to the end of Cal's theatrical rendition of what had happened in the park and watched Megan healing the wounds on his brother's face and neck.

"Daimon has a wound that needs healing too," Esher said, and Megan nodded, and he did his best to focus on Aiko and those in the room with him.

But all the while, his senses were locked on the building where his cage was stored, where Keras had the daemon held captive and at his mercy.

Where he wanted to be.

Aiko brushed her palm across his cheek, shattering the hold his urges had on him, and he leaned into her touch. He tilted his head and pressed a kiss to her palm, and held her closer to him, manoeuvring her onto his lap. His eyes met hers and he held them, let her see in his that nothing bad was going to happen to her. The daemon was secure, trapped by the cage, and no daemon could penetrate the wards around the mansion.

She was safe.

He would make sure of that.

He pressed a kiss to her lips and rose spread across her cheeks when she pulled back, her eyes leaping to their company.

Cal grinned like an idiot, all I-told-you-so.

He wiped it off his brother's face with nothing more than a glare, and a small dousing of rain, just enough to wet him through again where he stood near the coffee table.

"Esher." Ares's deep voice rolled through the room and everyone stilled.

Aiko tensed.

Esher turned his head to his right, leaned back and peered past Marek to his older brother.

Ares's grim expression had a sense of foreboding trickling through Esher's blood, foreboding that turned into dark inky tendrils that snaked around him as his brother spoke again.

"You want to hurt the daemon? Keras is giving you the chance."

Aiko was quick to get off his lap, clearing the way for him. He rose to his feet and looked down at her, at that darkness in her beautiful eyes, and lingered.

"Stay here." He swept his knuckles across her cheek, holding her gaze, needing to see in it that she would do as he asked, because he didn't want her seeing what he was going to do. "I'll be right back."

She didn't nod, so he looked down at Marek, who answered his silent plea with a tilt of his head, letting him know that he would make sure Aiko didn't follow.

Esher broke away from her, taking deep breaths to steady himself as he crossed the room to Ares, and followed him to the small white building where they were holding the daemon. His heart pounded as he neared it, memories of passing days at a time shut inside it, wild with a need for violence and bloodshed, pressing down on him.

Daimon stood sentinel outside the closed wooden doors.

His brother's icy blue eyes warmed with concern as Esher approached.

He nodded to let him know that he would be fine.

Ares paused on the threshold as Daimon reached for the door. "Go and get Megan to deal with that wound I know you're trying to hide from me."

Daimon huffed and scowled at Ares, and Esher gave Daimon a look that backed up what Ares had said, asking his younger brother to see Megan about his wound, because he needed to focus and right now he was worried about Daimon and it was making it hard to keep himself level.

Daimon nodded and opened the door for him and Ares.

The female shrieked and banged against the sides of the cage, not moving it even when she put all of her strength into each attack. She gripped the thick bars and growled as she pulled on them, her desperation lacing the air. Fresh black blood rolled down her cheek from a cut across it, and splattered across her bare arms, and a rip cut from the hem of her black dress up to her hip, exposing her thigh as she fought to get free.

"Is she not being cooperative?" Esher couldn't keep the hint of sarcasm out of his voice as he approached her, because his brother should have known better than to expect a daemon to talk.

Keras shifted green eyes edged with obsidian to him and they narrowed as his black eyebrows dipped, the corners of his lips turning downwards as he stepped back from the cage.

The wooden doors slammed behind Esher, sending a ripple of fear down his back that he breathed through. He wasn't going in the cage this time.

The daemon hissed at Keras.

Screamed as shadows lashed out at her in response, slicing her legs and her arms.

As he watched, a sense of satisfaction rolling through him, Esher considered what they knew about her, searching for a way to make her speak.

One other than hurting her.

Which was a first for him.

Normally, violence was the only viable option, the only one he wanted to pursue.

But he found himself hunkering down in front of the vile wretch, pulling all of her focus to him.

She swiped at the shadows as they slithered away from her, breathing hard and fast, and then she stilled and her eyes slowly lifted to meet his.

"I want to go home," she whispered, her silvery eyes growing wilder as she edged towards him, clawing at the stone floor. "I want to go home."

Her demeanour changed, her face softening, and she held her bloodied hands out to him.

"Let me go home, Esher. Take me back to the clinic. It's too frightening here." Her eyes darkened, a vicious sneer pulling at her black lips as she looked around her and then at him.

"Your powers won't work when you're in the cage." It was what he despised most about it. At the height of his strength, when he needed to let it all flow out of him before he burst, he couldn't use a damned drop of his power.

She hissed at him and launched at the bars, her hands clearing them to reach for him. She fell just short, her hands harmlessly clawing at the air inches from his face.

"I want to go home. It's all I want," she snapped, her eyes glowing as she struggled to reach him. "If I can't have it, I'll make the world burn... you want the world to burn, don't you, my beautiful pet?"

Esher spat at her. "Pet? I'm not your fucking *pet*."

She chuckled and eased back, her lips splitting in a wide grin. "But you will be... mine... she promised."

"Who promised?" He was getting somewhere, further than Keras judging by the way his brother huffed behind him.

Her eyes grew wary and she ran her fingers down her violet hair, clawing at it and pulling knots from it as she looked around her, eyes darting everywhere, her fear flooding the room with her vile daemon stench.

"Who?" he bit out and she tensed, shrank back and then exploded forwards, her arms flying between the bars of the cage to reach for him again.

"My pet!" She swiped at him, desperation etched on her face as she struggled to reach him.

Esher smacked her hands away, so hard her left arm hit the cage and bent backwards, and she shrieked.

"I'm not your pet. I never will be. Your friends aren't coming for you." He leaned towards her and sneered. "Your only hope for survival now is to tell us everything we want to know, and then maybe I'll make you *my* pet."

Her skin paled, the colour leaching from it as she began tugging at her hair again, frantically looking at his brothers and then him, and then around her at the thick blank walls of the building.

"Would you like to be my pet?" He canted his head to his left, and her eyes landed on him, her fingers pausing in her hair.

She blinked.

Hesitated.

"Or maybe you want to die?" He raised his hand.

She flinched away, curling into a ball, clutching her head. When he didn't strike her with his power, she slowly uncurled and fixed him with terrified eyes. "She'll kill me anyway... kill me for failing... you can't protect me."

"I can. No daemon can reach you here."

Keras stepped forwards and she hissed at him, her eyes darting up to him as she backed away, towards the other side of the cage. "You know what happened to the others who faced us?"

She swallowed hard, dipped her chin just a fraction of an inch, enough to reveal she knew what had happened to her comrades.

"Your wraith friend killed Trickster," Ares put in and moved to flank Esher, folding his thick arms across his broad chest, stretching his black t-shirt tight. His eyes glowed with crackling flames as he glared down at the daemon. "You think he won't kill you too if you get out of here, away from our protection?"

She clawed at the ground again, eyes flickering between him and his brothers, and he could see she was close to talking, was afraid the wraith would kill her just as he had dealt with Amaury before they could get him to speak.

"It's why we brought you here, where you're safe... *protected*." Esher emphasised the last word, because it seemed to hit her in just the right spot, had her fear fading a little whenever she heard it. "I can protect you from the wraith."

By killing her first.

But she didn't need to know that.

"He won't hurt me." There was a certainty about her that had him feeling she was telling the truth, that she knew the wraith wouldn't hurt her. "*She* will."

"Who is she?" He edged closer, holding her focus as he felt his brothers tense.

"She promised me a kingdom in exchange for taming you, my pet." The daemon reached through the bars to him, her eyebrows furrowing as she stroked her hands down the air, as if she was caressing him.

Petting him.

He managed to stop himself from snapping and lashing out at her, and held his ground, letting her think he was fine with her wanting to touch him, calling him a fucking pet.

"A world within our old home to call our own, and I could bring you all the humans you desired. You would like that, wouldn't you?" she husked.

He leaned closer, mind filling with a vision of his fortress in the Underworld, bathed in the blood of humans, the air filled with their cries.

Keras's hand came down on his shoulder. "We should take a break."

He jerked back, baring his fangs at the bitch as he realised she had been luring him under her spell, and he had been close to answering her and claiming everything his heart desired—revenge upon the humans.

No. He didn't want revenge now. It had been all he had craved once, but no longer. Aiko had opened his eyes, had made him see the good in mortals again, and now he wanted to protect both her world and his from the machinations of his enemy.

He pushed onto his feet, schooling his features so she didn't see his anger at her for trying to play him, and his fury at himself for almost falling for it.

Keras opened the doors and stepped out into the early morning light, and Ares followed.

Esher lingered, looked back at the daemon and held her mercury gaze that promised him all the destruction, all the bloodshed, his darker side had once desired.

But now it wanted something else.

He turned away from her, closed the doors and locked them, and followed his brothers into the main house.

Aiko rose onto her feet as he entered, leaving the couch to cross the room to him. He sighed as she wrapped her arms around him, lowered his head and pressed his forehead to hers as he held her, using the feel of her nestled close to him, where she belonged, to soothe himself and ease the hold his other side still had on him.

"Has she said anything?" Valen looked over the back of the couch at Keras.

Keras sighed. "Nothing much. She confirmed we are dealing with another female, one she seems frightened of too, just as Benares and Jin were, and one who promised her a kingdom if they succeeded."

"I will hazard a guess this mysterious female desires father's throne, and gathered this group to assist her, offering them the one thing they wanted." Marek looked from Keras to Valen, and then Ares as he joined Megan, slumping onto the arm of the armchair where she sat.

"Benares and Jin wanted to rule this world." Valen leaned back into the couch as Keras rounded it, and Esher settled back on the other couch with Aiko, wedging himself between her and Marek.

"This one wants to rule a part of the Underworld." Ares slid his arm around Megan's shoulders. "Like we would let that happen."

"Any clue what the wraith wants?" Cal leaned against the wall and shoved his hands in his pockets.

"No." Keras was quick to say that, and everyone kept quiet, not mentioning his involvement in what had happened to Calindria.

When Cal's eyes grew stormy, Esher snagged his attention.

"My blade in his gut. I owe him," Esher said, tugging a grin from his youngest brother, and wary looks from the rest of his brothers.

He wanted to say it had been a poor joke, but it wasn't. The hunger to hunt down the wraith and kill him was still there, burning in his heart, blazing in his soul. Something pressed against his side, and he looked down, stared at Aiko's delicate hand where it covered the spot where his scar was beneath his blue-grey shirt.

The scar burned.

He knocked Aiko's hand away and gripped his side, a growl tearing from his lips as the wound blazed white-hot, stealing his breath.

"Fuck." He gritted his teeth.

"What's wrong?" Marek was on him in a flash, clutching his shoulders as he struggled against the pain.

He wasn't sure.

"It hurts," he bit out.

Went cold.

The wraith.

It wasn't possible.

Esher shot to his feet, head whipping towards the cage, and teleported just as internal alarm bells rang, warning him that something had broken through the wards.

Not possible. Nothing was powerful enough to break the wards. No one knew the counter-wards.

He and his brothers, Daimon and Cal, had marked the shapeshifter with counter-wards but they were on her back where she couldn't see them, and with the cage stealing her powers, there was no way she could have told the other daemons even if she did know them.

He flung the wooden doors on the white building open and stared at the cage.

At the wisps of violet smoke that hung in the air where the daemon had been.

"Fuck," Ares growled as he appeared beside him and saw what he had. "How the fuck did he get through the wards?"

"Counter-wards," Marek offered as he raced from the main house, followed by the others.

"Father created the wards. We're the only ones who know which ones he used." Cal had a point.

Their father wouldn't have told anyone about them.

Esher pressed a hand to his side as another cold wave rocked him.

His voice was distant to his ears as he stared blankly at the empty cage. "What if the wraith knew? What if... when he... his blade... it feeds him souls."

Keras sharply turned towards him. "Esher, this isn't your fault."

"If it's anyone's fault, it's mine." Valen moved in front of him, raked fingers through his violet hair and blew out his breath. "It's my fault for bringing Eva here when she was hurt. You left because of it."

Esher shook his head. The blame didn't lie with Valen. Eva had made him want to leave, that was true, because he hadn't wanted to hurt her, knowing it would hurt Valen too, but he had been the one to let the moon distract him.

He had been the one to lower his guard and allow the wraith to plunge the blade into him without him noticing.

Gods, the thought that the bastard had managed to devour a fragment of his soul before Megan had been able to reverse the damage done to him and save him sickened him, had darkness pouring through his veins and that hunger returning to consume him.

The things the shapeshifter had known, the details of his past that only he knew, made sense now. The wraith had told her everything, must have been able to show her somehow, revealing the memories locked in his soul so she could use it against him to weaken him.

To bring him over to their side.

"I'm a liability," he whispered, heart aching as he considered what he needed to do. He couldn't bring himself to look at his brothers, didn't think he could bear seeing their faces as they told him he was right, as they pushed him away to protect themselves. "The wards are useless now… they know everything I do… all of our tactics… and they know how to affect me. They know fucking everything… and that means... I have to…"

Go, he had to go. He had to leave and get as far from his brothers as he could. He needed to protect them, and it was the only thing he could do. He would never let them come to harm, would leave to keep them safe, even if it killed him.

The shapeshifter had been right and the wraith had chosen to take her rather than kill her, which meant she was important to him, and gods, maybe he could somehow use that against him. It also meant she was out there, recovering, and she would come for him again. He had to leave before that could happen.

Keras clutched his shoulder and squeezed it hard, and Esher looked at him, braced himself for a world of pain but found only love and understanding in his older brother's green eyes. "It means you have to get working on new wards."

"I'll help." Ares lightly tapped him on the arm. "I'm good with wards."

"We can each pick one, keep it to ourselves." Cal's suggestion had everyone nodding.

"Like I'd tell you my ward anyway." Valen grinned. "You'd be jealous of how amazing it was and I'd never hear the end of it."

Daimon smiled. "I've seen your wards."

That earned him a scowl from Valen and electricity arced across his fingers. "What's that meant to mean?"

"It means your wards are shitty." Ares kept a straight face. "Father always said you were the worst at them. Lacked finesse… I think those were his exact words."

Esher couldn't believe what he was hearing, stood mute as his brothers joked around him, no trace of the anger he deserved in them, no hint of distrust.

Even Keras smiled as he looked at the horizon. "It's getting light. We should get to work."

The rest of his brothers moved away, and Esher watched them go, stared after them as they broke apart and scattered, each choosing a different route around the garden, seeking something they could use to contain a new ward.

"It was not your fault, Esher." Keras remained where he was, and Esher looked at him, wanting to say again that it was, but held his tongue when his brother approached him. "This war will not be easy. It will test us, but we knew that. I worry it will test you the most though."

Because he was a liability, and he had the feeling the enemy wasn't done with him. He had resisted them this time, but the daemon had still been intent on making him belong to her, and now she was gone, returned to the mysterious female who was in charge.

Who had ordered her to turn him into her pet, into a weapon they could use to bring about the downfall of the gates and the future they wanted.

They needed to know who that female was.

"When the wraith came..." Keras started.

"I felt him," Esher finished for him and lowered his hand to his side. "I knew he was close."

Keras's slow smile said it all.

The wraith had stolen information from Esher, but in turn, he had given Esher a way of tracking him.

He watched his brother go to join the others, the hunger to hunt rising inside him again, stronger now that he knew he would be able to track the wraith once he was close enough, could use the wound he had inflicted to locate him, sure the pain would grow stronger the closer he was to the bastard.

Aiko slipped her hand into his, drawing him back to her.

He dipped his head and brushed his lips across hers, used the kiss and the way she responded, looping her arms around his neck and holding him tightly, to ground himself and push away from the urge to hunt.

There was something else he needed to do more.

He needed to make sure Aiko and his brothers were safe, and that their home was protected, ready for when the enemy made their next move, one he was sure would come sooner rather than later.

They would be ready for them.

It was agony, but he forced himself to break away from her lips and met her gaze. "Would you like to learn how to make a ward?"

"I thought only powerful beings could create them?" Her eyes darted between his, and he had the feeling his brothers had been telling her all about their world in his absence, keeping her mind occupied while he had been fighting the daemon.

He nodded and turned away from her, leading her towards the cherry tree she loved so much. "I think you'll be able to handle it."

She stopped him dead with her words.

"Because I'm like you now?"

Esher looked back at her, and he must have looked as surprised as he felt because she giggled, her brown eyes bright with her smile that warmed him, chased away the dark clouds in his heart and allowed light to shine back in.

He had meant to break it gently to her that he suspected his mother had done something to her soul, blessing it to make her immortal for him, tied to the Underworld just as he was.

But she knew.

"You broadcasted your worries a little when we were in the park tonight." She pulled him with her, and he realised that she also knew he meant for her to place a ward on the boulder beneath the cherry tree, must have read that too. "It's easier to know what you're thinking now that I'm stronger."

Clearly it was. Worryingly easy. He would have to warn his brothers to be careful around her.

"I won't go poking in their heads." She smiled over her shoulder at him, and gods, it felt so normal, hit him hard as he walked behind her, letting her lead him.

Only a few minutes ago, he had been convinced he was on the verge of losing everything he loved, was a danger to everyone and had to leave.

Rather than pushing him away to protect themselves, they had gathered around him, had shown him the depth of their love and that they were going to protect him. He only hoped he could withstand whatever trials lay ahead of him and live up to their faith in him, deserving that love.

His family.

He listened to them as they talked, as Eva asked what Valen was doing and Megan teased Ares, telling him he was messing it all up, and Keras chastised Cal for picking too simple a ward and told him to do it again.

They were his family, all of them.

Aiko included.

And he would never give up, would never give in, would keep fighting the darkness in his heart in order to protect them and their homes.

The Underworld.

And this one.

The skyline beyond the white wall enclosing the garden flickered to the otherworld, and the new-found strength beating in his heart grew stronger as he saw it looked better now, some of the damage reversed by the blow he had dealt his enemy today, removing one of their ranks and making it clear he wouldn't succumb to his darker self.

At least not easily.

"Esher?" Aiko's soft voice lured him back to her and he realised they had reached the cherry tree.

He stared at her as she smiled at him, his beautiful immortal, his little butterfly.

Her smile faded, her face falling as he drew her towards him, a flicker of heat igniting in her eyes as she looked up into his and allowed him to guide her into his arms, back where she belonged.

"What am I thinking?" he murmured, lowering his head.

Her blush answered him, but she breathlessly whispered, "Later."

He dropped his lips to hers, brushed them tenderly and shut the world out as he kissed her, giving her a taste of what was to come when his brothers were gone and they were alone. He held her close and her heat seeped into him, her soft sighs stirring fire in his veins and strengthening the resolve in his heart.

His little butterfly.

A single question rang in his mind, echoing there as he savoured her kiss and the feel of her in his arms.

What would he do for her?

For her, he would destroy his enemies and protect the humans he had once despised, ones he was learning to forgive because she had opened his eyes and his heart again. He would defend the gates and fulfil his duty, keeping their world and this one safe.

For her, he would fight the darkness and he would win. He would vanquish his other side and destroy it for good, would become the complete male he had once been.

All so he could be with her.

Forever.

The End

ABOUT THE AUTHOR

Felicity Heaton is a New York Times and USA Today best-selling author who writes passionate paranormal romance books. In her books she creates detailed worlds, twisting plots, mind-blowing action, intense emotion and heart-stopping romances with leading men that vary from dark deadly vampires to sexy shape-shifters and wicked werewolves, to sinful angels and hot demons!

If you're a fan of paranormal romance authors Lara Adrian, J R Ward, Sherrilyn Kenyon, Gena Showalter, Larissa Ione and Christine Feehan then you will enjoy her books too.

If you love your angels a little dark and wicked, her best-selling Her Angel romance series is for you. If you like strong, powerful, and dark vampires then try the Vampires Realm romance series or any of her stand alone vampire romance books. If you're looking for vampire romances that are sinful, passionate and erotic then try her Vampire Erotic Theatre romance series. Or if you like hot-blooded alpha heroes who will let nothing stand in the way of them claiming their destined woman then try her Eternal Mates series. It's packed with sexy heroes in a world populated by elves, vampires, fae, demons, shifters, and more. If sexy Greek gods with incredible powers battling to save our world and their home in the Underworld are more your thing, then be sure to step into the world of Guardians of Hades.

If you have enjoyed this story, please take a moment to contact the author at **author@felicityheaton.co.uk** or to post a review of the book online

Connect with Felicity:
Website – http://www.felicityheaton.co.uk
Blog – http://www.felicityheaton.co.uk/blog/
Twitter – http://twitter.com/felicityheaton
Facebook – http://www.facebook.com/felicityheaton
Goodreads – http://www.goodreads.com/felicityheaton
Mailing List – http://www.felicityheaton.co.uk/newsletter.php

FIND OUT MORE ABOUT HER BOOKS AT:
http://www.felicityheaton.co.uk

Printed in Great Britain
by Amazon